Where Mary Went

THEYTUS BOOKS

Library and Archives Canada Cataloguing in Publication

McLean, Lynne Sherry
Where Mary went / Lynne Sherry McLean.

ISBN 978-1-894778-96-1

I. Title.

PS8575.L4477W44 2010   C813'.6   C2010-901344-1

Printed in Canada by Gauvin Press

RECYCLED
Paper made from
recycled material
FSC® C005834

Printed on Ancient Forest Friendly 100% post consumer fibre paper.

 THEYTUS BOOKS

www.theytus.com
In Canada: Theytus Books, Green Mountain Rd., Lot 45, RR#2, Site 50, Comp. 8
Penticton, BC, V2A 6J7, Tel: 250-493-7181
In the USA: Theytus Books, P.O. Box 2890, Oroville, Washington, 98844

 Patrimoine   Canadian
canadien   Heritage

 Canada Council   Conseil des Arts
for the Arts   du Canada

 BRITISH COLUMBIA
ARTS COUNCIL
Supported by the Province of British Columbia

Theytus Books acknowledges the support of the following:
We acknowledge the financial support of the Government of Canada through the
Canada Book Fund for our publishing activities. We acknowledge the support of
the Canada Council for the Arts which last year invested $20.1 million in writing
and publishing throughout Canada. Nous remercions de son soutien le Conseil des
Arts du Canada, qui a investi 20,1 millions de dollars l'an dernier dans les lettres
et l'édition à travers le Canada. We acknowledge the support of the Province of
British Columbia through the British Columbia Arts Council.

Where Mary Went

by Lynne Sherry McLean

THEYTUS BOOKS

CONTENTS

WELL. IT'S BEEN over three years, eh," Elizabeth paused and squinted to see how far down the road she could see, and continued, "that's a long time not to see your husband!"

Mary nodded. "Enh, three years is certainly a long time."

It was a stony, hole-riddled road that Harry had said was a shortcut. They left a dirty cloud as they made their way along its broken surface, but the dust that rose up behind them still found a way in their eyes and noses. Mary felt like she was caked in it, and she imagined that it was getting all over her starched and pressed white blouse. She hoped it was just a feeling, and she hoped the billowing dirt left behind Harry's Ford would not swirl around too much before it found its way to settle back into the ground. Mary guessed the only reason she was feeling this way was because she simply wanted to look good for her Gmiwan. Three years could make a big difference.

"You nervous?" Elizabeth piped up.

"Gmiwan is going to be so happy to get home. I made all his favourites for lunch when we get back," Mary answered her sister.

"Hope the train isn't late," her brother-in-law quipped.

In the front seat, Sonny, eleven years old and susceptible to his uncle Harry's baiting, whipped around. "Oh no, Ma! What if the train is late? What if Pa's not on it? What if he missed it?" he said in a panic.

The two sisters rolled their eyes. It was Elizabeth, who could sometimes be the good big sister, who leaned forward. She reached over the front seat and placed her soft, manicured hand on Sonny's summer-darkened arm. "Now Sonny, I know you must be very excited, after all this time to see your father, but you know he will be even more thrilled to see how big his boy has gotten."

"The train may or may not be late," Mary interrupted pointedly. She looked Sonny in the eye to steady him, "But your father will be on it regardless."

The boy, soothed by his mother's words and his aunt's touch, turned forward and got back to the business of enjoying the automobile ride. First he patted his pocket full of stuff, and then a smile spread across his face as he pictured his Pa stepping off the train, suitcase in hand, and looking all around for his family. Letting the story in his head unfold, Sonny figured that when his Pa spotted him, he would put his suitcase down, stand completely still, and wait for Sonny to run into his arms. Sonny would feel his feet getting lifted off the ground as his Pa lifted him up for a powerful man hug. That's the way Sonny imagined it would be.

"And Harry, I'm sure Mary has made something wonderful for you to eat as well," Elizabeth said, winking at her sister.

Mary picked up the cue. "Oh yes. I have! I brought a jar up from the cellar, of those mustard pickles you like so much."

"And I'm sure Mary has made tea biscuits, Harry." Elizabeth winked again.

Mary carried on in a singsong voice, now in perfect step with her sister's teasing. "Of course. I have tea biscuits sitting covered up on a pan, waiting to be popped in the oven so they're hot for our lunch. That Harry, he loves my tea biscuits."

Out of the corners of their eyes, the sisters watched Harry settle back into the cushion he had placed for himself in the driver's seat, take his hat from its place on the seat beside him, put it on his head and tap it once on the top. Then, taking the steering wheel with both hands, he concentrated on the road ahead.

Both women leaned back in their seats and grinned. They let a bit more quiet go by, just to make sure Harry was well occupied again, before Elizabeth brought up the more benign subject of Hattie Blane's husband having been seen drunk and carrying on uptown again. By the time they had thoroughly explored Hattie's situation, Henderson's Drug Store changing its name to Henderson's Pharmacy, Virgil Wilson's operation, and the weather, they were almost there and Mary was grateful she didn't have to settle back into her own thoughts again.

Harry slowed the Ford almost to a stop, looked up and down a paved road, and made a left-hand turn. Everybody sat taller in their seats, as the sprawling city of Toronto gathered itself before them.

"Look Ma. It's Big Smoke. Pa said that's where we would be picking him up!"

Union Station seemed buried deep in the city, or maybe it was that Harry had to scout out a few extra streets before he found it. It seemed a lifetime to Mary before they were pulling up in front of it. Harry parked the automobile on the street, and the four of them, two starched and pressed women with netted hats and dark faces powdered light, one gangly, dark-skinned kid dressed in white, and one proper-looking businessman stepped out of the gleaming black Ford. Sonny zigzagged ahead, and the women fell in behind Harry because he had lived here with his family when they had arrived from Holland, so naturally he would know where to go.

While Elizabeth chattered, Mary listened with one ear, but at the same time she combed the crowd with darting wide eyes to catch a glimpse of Gmiwan on the odd chance he had arrived early and was wandering around thinking nobody cared enough to come and meet him. Her mind ran wild with haphazard thoughts, and her throat tightened around a clump of words, the first words that she would say to her husband. Who would speak first? She wondered. Would they embrace? More parts of her gave way to the looming reunion. Her belly jumped and quivered at the thought of being back home, of the moment after she waved goodbye to Elizabeth and Harry, of the moment she had to turn and face Gmiwan.

Something began to twitch and burn deep inside her. She quickened her pace to get away from it, until she had passed, without noticing, Harry's lead.

"Mary!" Elizabeth called to her sister.

Mary kept going.

"Maaarrry!" she called again, cupping her hands around her mouth.

Mary stopped. She turned around and crossed the distance of the great main hall.

"I was calling you, and you didn't hear me," Elizabeth said. "Harry says we have to wait here to listen for Gmiwan's train arrival to be announced." She gestured to the rows of wooden benches. "Then we can go and meet him."

Mary sighed out what remained of her resistance, gave in, chose a bench, and plunked herself down.

Sonny zigzagged his way back down the marbled station, running past his aunt, and let her lasso him with her arms.

"Arriving from Kingston. Arriving from Kingston. Train number 103 arriving on Platform Number Three," the man droned through the cone-shaped speaker over Mary's head.

"This is it!" Elizabeth grabbed Mary's arm and squeezed it. "Aren't you crazy excited? You're going to see Gmiwan! He made it! Your husband is home."

Mary stood up and her purse fell from her lap to the floor. She paid it no mind, so Elizabeth picked it up and slipped it over her arm next to her own. Mary reached for Sonny's hand, and the three proceeded like a unit through the cathedral-high hall toward the sign "Platform Number Three."

Harry had to scurry to catch up.

Through the archway, a corridor opened up to the outside again. Once there, Harry took back the lead. The four lingered at the opening where the corridor both dumped off and drew in people as if they were water and it was a pipe. It was Mary who took the first step out into the bright sunshine.

Harry looked up and down the waiting train and pronounced that they should go right to the head of the train to get ready for the doors to open and the people to get off.

Mary stood still.

Elizabeth tugged at her to come along and listen to Harry.

Mary shook her off.

Elizabeth waited a second or two, but then spun back and hurried along to catch up with her husband.

Mary stood firm and Sonny stayed with her. They held each other tightly, a pair of well-dressed Indians drawing attention from the throngs of light-skinned people passing by. Possibly Mary wanted to stay in the doorway because it was the only way out of Platform Number Three. Gmiwan, she had thought, might be on any one of those train cars. At the head of the train, they might easily miss Gmiwan getting off at the other end. Then what would happen? He'd be wandering around, thinking nobody had come to meet him, and all this before anyone figured out they were standing in the wrong spot.

The train hissed out puffs of steam, and then all the doors opened at the same time. Men dressed in blue uniforms, just like the police chief's, jumped out and dropped stepping boxes in front of each coach door. Mary, along with the rest of the waiting crowd, looked up and down the train. The panic rose in her blood.

People started spilling out of the open coaches, hugging people, and then merging with the waiting crowd.

"Pa!"

Sonny broke away. Mary looked up, and right in front of her, in the doorway of one of the coach cars, eyes fixed in a straight-ahead stare, stood her man, in uniform. Her husband; her Gmiwan. She stayed, frozen to the platform, just to let Sonny have his moment, and besides, she needed more time.

Gmiwan stepped down with assistance from the conductor, just in time for Sonny to throw himself against his father. He jumped up and down repeatedly in an effort to latch his arms around his father's neck, but Gmiwan, unaffected, just stood there looking down at him like he was somebody's poodle being a nuisance at the front door.

Sonny stopped, stayed still, and looked up beseechingly. Didn't his Pa know who he was?

Sonny, trying a new tactic, patted his jeans pocket and then dug inside. He felt around for the choicest of treasures that he kept in there. He pulled something out and held it tightly in his fist at his side for a while, just to tease his father a bit. Then, getting no response, he thrust his hand out in front to produce the prize. It was a whistle, carved from the branch of a willow tree that grew on the banks of Beaverdams Pond. It was the willow tree that Sonny had been hanging around over the past few summers and wanted to tell his father all about. But it didn't matter because Pa wasn't even looking at him anymore.

Feeling curiously invisible, Mary remained at her vantage, silently watching her son's bubbling excitement dissolve. She watched as the conductor led Gmiwan away from the door to allow a bottleneck of passengers to disembark behind him. The second person out of the train car was a uniformed woman who took a place beside Gmiwan. She hooked her arm into his and nudged him gently a few more steps away from the train.

Sonny recoiled in bewilderment. He backed away a few steps, and then turned to seek the refuge of his mother.

The woman's uniformed eyes tracked the boy. She said something to Gmiwan.

Spotting her target, the lady in uniform took Gmiwan by the arm and began to shuffle him toward Mary.

Mary gave herself a shake to break the spell, and with Sonny pasted to her side, took a few steps forward. Obviously something had happened to Gmiwan.

The woman extended her hand and said, "Hello. Mrs. Fisher?"

Mary, wide-eyed, nodded once.

"I am Lieutenant Morson. I am the nurse sent to accompany your husband into your care."

"What happened to him?' was all Mary could manage.

"Your husband has not been injured," she droned officiously. "He has fulfilled his duty and is being Honourably Discharged."

"Then what has happened to him?" Mary asked, barely audible.

"Here is his documentation, Mrs. Fisher," the woman said, ignoring the question. She urged a bland-coloured folder at her.

Mary stared down at it as nausea gathered within her.

Lieutenant Morson thrust the folder closer to Mary's stomach.

Mary's gaze left the folder, travelled up the brass and green between them, and implored the woman's face. Their eyes met. Something, maybe compassion, momentarily melted the ice blue irises that met Mary's velvet and pleading own, then disappeared back into a frozen-over pond.

Refilled with professional brusqueness, the lieutenant waited until Mary gathered herself enough to hold her trembling hand out and claim her husband's folder. No sooner had she done so, than Lieutenant Morson promptly took her leave by stepping back and away from Gmiwan. She bid them a crisp adieu, and was gone.

Throughout, Gmiwan had been standing at blank attendance to something way off in the distance. Now, when the space opened suddenly beside him, he shifted in the spot he occupied.

With fluid instinct, Mary filled the space and took her husband's arm. Sonny, still attached to her skirt, went with her in stuttering little steps. Elizabeth and Harry found them like that, coagulated, in the midst of people streaming around them.

"Oh you found him!" Elizabeth gushed.

Gmiwan, oblivious, stood stoic, as if a guard at the gate of His Royal Highness, King George's castle.

Elizabeth stepped a little closer to put herself in better range for a hug. When Gmiwan didn't move to greet her, she simply hugged him instead. But Gmiwan just stood there, wooden, like a cigar store Indian somebody had dressed up in uniform.

Elizabeth unclasped her arms and stepped back to survey her brother-in-law.

"What's wrong with you, Gmiwan Fisher?" she observed with blatant indignation. Gmiwan's brow furrowed as he broke his far-off gaze to light upon Elizabeth. She folded her arms in front of her and scolded, "What the heck? I get so old in two years that you don't recognize your own sister-in-law?"

Gmiwan blinked in slow motion and then re-attended to whatever it was off, in the distance, that fixated him.

Harry backed away. He noticed that passersby were beginning to stare at them. He didn't know what was going on, but he sure as hell didn't want anybody seeing him in the middle of it.

He stepped forward to take his wife in hand.

"Does everybody expect that I should be leaving my automobile unattended on the streets of Toronto?"

Mary, Sonny, and Elizabeth, as if on cue, stood called upon and waited.

Harry turned his back to them as a signal, and they huddled closer to him, this time grateful for his lead. Gmiwan remained vacant but seemed to respond to the empty space that had opened up around him. Absently, but obediently, he started to follow along behind them.

Elizabeth, who'd fallen into second behind Harry, turned in mid-march to crook an eyebrow at her sister.

Mary's stony look back articulated that things were definitely not okay. "Perhaps after some bannock and a nice cup of tea with Carnation Milk, Gmiwan will feel better." Mary's tone gave way to a sea of bewilderment. "If not, maybe tomorrow Harry can take us to see the doctor."

BERTHA HAD KNOWN this would be the day her third child was born, even before she had opened her eyes that morning, because sometime in that hush between the owl's call and the bird's waking song, the old familiar sting had begun. By the time the sun had reached her face, the sting had become a burning circle like the spread of a bleeding wound, and in its wake it had stolen her sleep.

"No easy day today," was about all she had to say to Jake that morning over tea and the last of the rabbit stew.

Now, as the day was drawing to a close, she had earned a rest. She cautiously lowered her weight onto the wooden chair that waited for her, as always, by the stove. She just needed a moment, one holy minute, to give way to the building pain in the lowest part of her belly. There was no need to bother looking outside; Bertha could feel the dusk. She closed her eyes for a bit, just to posture her mind for the long, drawn-out night that would come, when it was ready to do so.

She let herself drift back, deep behind shut lids. A vision of her mother's mother, Kokum, started to take form. Bertha let the watery image grow in her mind until she could clearly see, hear, and smell her grandmother's wizened face and wispy silver hair. The image blended and mingled with the hazy comfort of the ever-present smoke of the campfire pit. She allowed herself to fall deeper into the reflection until she became a part of it and could feel everything. This is where her Kokum could always be found.

Even when Misho, as Bertha called her grandfather in the old language, had other things to tend to, her Kokum preferred to keep the fire, and it came as natural as meat after skin that the old woman was also a storyteller.

She lived happily in the Western direction as a keeper of the teachings. Stories were how they were passed to her, and stories were how she passed them down.

Bertha smiled as she journeyed further into the vision. She could taste the wild ginger and maple sweetness in the steaming stew that Kokum handed her. A single drop of cool water fell upon her forearm. She looked up and recognized a cousin, about the same age as her, holding a bunch of fat leeks, glistening white and clean from just having been swished about at the water's edge. The woman-child was smiling with pride as she offered the leeks to her grandmother. Kokum accepted them with grace. She stroked the girl's hair before laying the leeks on her cutting stone.

Young Bertha set her stew aside for a moment and let the pleasant tingle of the leek's medicine fill her nostrils as she waited for the ritual to begin. Kokum would slip the knife from the sheath that was laced to her still slender waist and then she would caress its silvery edge, thanking its spirit for faithful service to her.

This knife has never killed anything. My husband made him for me as soon as we started dancing together, and this knife has faithfully helped me feed my family for many seasons.

Then, before setting to work, Kokum would lightly caress, with the tips of her knowing fingers, the smooth, flat surface of the rock, upon which she always used the knife to cut the flesh of plants and animals, as if to connect the two tools. She told the same story every time she started to cut.

Some people use a log, but I prefer this grandfather. He is mighty and can take any bad medicine out of the food that I cook for my family. I thank him every night, no matter what the weather, by bathing him at the river's edge. The river is mighty too. It can take even more bad medicine, if you honour it with respect and tobacco.

Misho and Kokum were Anishinaabe, living much farther up north than the light-skinned race cared to dwell in that time period. Half of Bertha's blood was Mohawk. When Ma took her berry picking at the summer camp, she often would tell the story about how she and Bertha's father had met. Ma always told her stories in the language of Kokum.

Our numbers had become small because we had lost quite a few to the chest sickness and alcoholic fights. We had run out of everything by Bear Moon and had nothing to dry or powder for the trip, so we stayed in the winter camp all the way to Sugar Moon so we could take a good supply of the sweet water to get us through until we got to summer camp. By this time, most of us were

Old Ones, or mothers with small children, so we knew the fishing and hunting would be bad. We were losing our good men to the alcohol and fighting, but it was our old ones who taught us what they knew about the gift of the maple tree, and it kept us from starving.

We had reached the summer camp by Sucker Moon, and the mothers would leave the children with the Old Ones to go night fishing in birch canoes made up fast by the men and boys that were still with us. We didn't even have any tobacco to offer in gratitude for the suckers that we tricked with a torch. It was a long winter, and they were suffering and hungry from the greed of the light skin as much as we were. They were only doing what they have always done by following the light of the full moon to come to the surface. That is they way they bring the still partly frozen lake to life once again. We speared enough to bring us back to health and said our prayers in hopes their spirits heard and understood.

When Bertha's Ma came to the part she loved best to tell, her voice would grow soft and singsongy.

It was a beautiful sunny day when my sisters and I were picking berries, with the kids running all over the place and, as I said, daughter, there were no healthy young men in our midst, so when a party of Bay of Quinte Mohawk brothers doing the work of Jesus came upon us, we invited them back for a meal. They stayed for all of Strawberry Moon and four of us came into the child way. My handsome big Mohawk man, that went by the Christian name of Joseph Martin, decided not to join his brothers that weren't really his brothers by blood anyway.

Gradually, as more brothers and sisters were born, and her Ma became busy and worn out, Bertha spent most of her time with her Kokum. Luckily, her father never fell to the alcohol. Through living by the old ways of the Anishinaabe, he was cured of his love of Jesus. He began to dream for the ways of his own people and their longhouses, so he started teaching his family more of the Iroquois languages. Eventually, he packed them up and took them south to live on the Six Nations of the Grand River Territory where his mother and her sisters were living. He knew that he was entitled to apply for some band money and maybe get some land. Bertha figured she must have seen about nine or ten summers before she left Misho and Kokum forever. Living among the Haudensaunee, she learned to speak in five of the six languages, plus the tongue of the light skin,

Granddaughter! Dusk is a funny time. It's that crack of time that the light must give way to the dark. Not day, not night, the body, just like Mother Earth, is not sure, and so it wonders.

If the earth broods, then the body too must reconsider itself, and this time of the day is anything's chance to take hold. It is dusk. It is the deep breath in that time takes. The earth and the body want to take enough in to heave a great sigh as they fall into sleep. This is the unguarded space that a waning storm, not willing to pass away, will use to recharge itself, and then after it has gathered more strength, rage on, keeping the things of the earth from resting. It is anything's chance. A lingering fever of the body too, will take this chance to rekindle itself at dusk, and then gradually, as the night goes on, stoke itself to a flame that goes and goes until it burns up the invading sickness, or sometimes the sorry soul who's holding it. It matters not which. A fever doesn't care because it is its own thing, and the only thing it knows is that it is supposed to kill something.

Bertha lingered on the simple, but perfectly fitted, wooden chair that Jake had made for her. She just needed to get through the highest wave of pain. While she was there, she decided she might as well have a smoke.

Pulling her weight closer to the stove, and twisting around, she reached behind her where she knew the table would be. Stretching her arm behind her, farther into the middle of the table, she found the smooth comfort of her old friend, and she let her hand rest upon it while she began using her thumb to rub its round hard belly in little circles. Suddenly, she stopped. Something had flawed its surface. Something had slighted the palm of her hand. For a moment she had to push the tiny sharpness from her mind as she gave in to the compulsion to feel her hand close around the bowl of the pipe for a brief caress, and then flutter open again. Still touching both his neck and belly with the tip of her one finger and her thumb, her other fingers expertly did the work of feeling for the yielding bag that would be beside it.

As soon as Bertha had both pipe and leather tobacco pouch on her lap, her spry fingers could tell that she had left a residue of bannock dough, still wet and pasty, stuck to the side of the pipe. She wiped it off before hastening to where she had earlier felt the flaw. Instinctively, she found the catch in the wood on the underside and plucked it off as if it were a hair that had begun to raise itself upon the skin of her husband's nose. Done with that, she loosened the leather strings on the pouch, and, pinching the edge of its opening, she exposed the rougher inside of its lip to her probing finger. Feeling around a little more, she found the spot where she had plucked the sliver, pressed her thumb against it, and began rubbing. She lifted it and spit, rubbed some more, and did not stop until the polished belly of her pipe could again nurture the palm of her one hand.

With the other, she scrounged inside her pouch. As her fingers and thumb closed around the exact amount she needed, she breathed in the scent of tobacco, sweetened and salted by the inside of the leather pouch. Keeping the pipe in one hand and the tobacco portion in the other, she made a firm but careful clamp around the pouch using the backs of her hands. Raising it up where her face was lowering to meet the pouch, she then took the leather lace that had been draped across the back of her right hand in her teeth. She pulled backward until the bag was shut tight. The bag dangled a moment before she let it fall into her lap.

Bertha pressed the tobacco snugly into its burrow, took more time to make sure it was pressed perfectly, and then bent over to feel around on the floor beside the front leg of the stool for the brittle box of matches. She picked the box up and rattled it to make sure it was full, and let it too drop into her lap. She picked up the leather pouch and put it in its place leaning against the leg of the stool in the spot where the matches had been.

She tried to save this time for when she was alone, but if there was ever anybody in the room at the time, they knew this was a ritual that deeply comforted Bertha and they tried not to disturb her.

She struck a match and drew the smoke in deeply to get her through the highest wave of the next labour pain. "Not too bad," she said aloud. She arched her back and tried to straighten it to create a line of passage through which the child might be encouraged to descend. "Be some time yet."

Elizabeth and Porter, who had been playing a game of "wet rag" in the steel tub, looked up at the sound of their mother's voice.

Elizabeth recognized that Ma was using the language of the light-skinned man from uptown, the one who sold tailor-made cigarettes. Pa would speak Mohawk when he was telling a story from the old ones, but mostly he spoke the language of the light skin. He said it was the language of doing business.

Ma could speak five of the Six Nations, all but Tuscarora. Elizabeth knew this because she heard Ma talk to the Older Ones in their own languages—Oneida, Onondaga, Seneca, Cayuga, and Mohawk—but less and less, because they were dying and their young ones came back from school speaking only the language of doing business.

When Ma spoke to Elizabeth, it was in the language of the great grandmother that she had never met.

Ma never explained much about it to Elizabeth but she would hide her and Porter whenever the Indian Agents came around looking for kids to take away, then Ma always spoke to them in the language of doing business and usually said something like, "The kids are up north helping my sister," or, "Right now, they are living with my brother Jordan. He's enfranchised y'know." Then she would give them bad directions on how to get there. She said as long as she used the word enfranchised the Indian Agent wouldn't try too hard anyway. The last time they came around there were two of them, a man and a woman, and Pa had to speak to them because Ma didn't want them to see her pregnant. He was supposed to tell them she was with the kids helping her sister with a baby up north but Pa was never very good at not telling the truth. It ended up working out anyway because the dog was trained to bark a certain way for an Indian Agent, and also to make anybody wearing a dark suit and hat feel unwelcome.

Bertha was aware her children had ceased splashing noises; She could see no more than a blending and separating of two shadows in the tub, but could feel they were looking at her. Being looked at by another person gave her the sensation of slight heaviness that started in the back of her neck, slowly warmed her shoulders, and then, sometimes, if the staring went on long enough, heated down the backs of her arms. There were times she could tell if someone was staring too long at her chest and that made her fold her arms in front of her. This sometimes gave her the appearance of being stubborn.

When she saw that her mother was only talking aloud to herself and was not really paying attention to them, Elizabeth hit Porter, whose gaze was still locked on his mother, flat in the face with the juicy wet cloth she had been hiding behind her back. The game of wet rag started again, and Bertha, knowing they were occupied with each other, began to relax again.

She let the sound of splashing fade into the distance. She raised her pipe to her lips but paused to sniff the air. The bannock did not smell ready to turn yet. There would be a better chance of them sleeping through the commotion that was bound to come later in the night after a feed of bannock, applesauce, and tea. In the morning, there would be three of them. Bertha gauged, by the coming of the next labour pain that it would be some time yet before she had to tell Jake to go get Jon.

She could tell Jake was still near at hand by the whisper of his knife on wood. She knew he was sitting on his stool out in the yard just below the window. Jake never went too far except when he had to go to Brantford to bring his axe handles to the hardware store.

They still did a lot for themselves, according to the old ways, but the money Jake's axe handles brought in made the winter easier. Jake's handles were the ones everybody wanted, because they never gave a person slivers. Jake was the only one who had the method of smoothing out the handles to a near shine. It wasn't that he kept it a secret. The old way said that if it was a good method then it should be taught to others to keep it going. But, so far, nobody had asked to learn it. Nowadays, a lot of people just made one themselves despite getting a dozen slivers or so. Others, who could afford it, went and bought one in town, just like most of those new folks who were moving into Brantford. It took strong patience to do the whole method of making an axe handle that wouldn't punish with a sliver, and that was how Jake made a little extra money for winter supplies.

Jake had that patience. He had the skill with a knife that it took to get wood down to a smooth-to-the-eye condition, but, truthfully, it was the patience to go the rest of the distance that made the difference.

Bertha took a deep drag on her pipe to let her mind wander farther back to the first time she had watched Jake make his axe handles, back to the first time that she really got to talk to Jake Stone. Bertha could see pretty good back then; her eyes were keen as a starling's. There was no hint of the opaque skin that had gradually changed their colour from black to grey. Sitting there in the gathering dusk of her kitchen, listening to the children's splattering and squirting behind her, she began to drift off to a brilliantly sunny day in the spring of her life. Back to when she saw Jake sitting on his usual rock in front of his place, where she had come upon him accidentally-on-purpose that day.

"*Sago*, Jake Stone!" chirped Bertha to him in his mother's language.

Jake watched the lithe thirteen-year-old rock from one foot to the other, all the while keeping her hands behind her back, as if any minute she was going to snap them from behind to front and spray him with a bouquet of daisies, or a frog, or something. Cutest little thing, she was.

"Whatcha doin' there?"

"Nothing now. Just finished helpin' Ma with the meat."

She squirmed in her dress like a little squirrel in your hand.

"Your Pa had a kill." Jake stated simply as he returned his eyes to his work.

"Don't know who killed it, but we got the hide this time."

Bertha didn't bother going into it much because everybody knew Jake

Stone never went with his Pa and brothers on a hunt. That was one of the reasons her family was against the apparent favour that she showed Jake Stone, that, and on account of his father was an alcoholic. Jake didn't drink even though he could if he wanted to, and he didn't hunt or compete, and he didn't hang out with the other men. Jake Stone was a soft man, so her family was suspicious that he couldn't provide.

Jake sometimes spoke Mohawk, the language of his mother, but mostly he spoke the language of the light skin. People weren't exactly sure about where his father's bones were buried. On the other hand, Bertha's family line, especially on her mother's side, could be traced back like running the fingers from the wing to the pointed tip of a well-made arrow. As well, Bertha had encouraged her children to use the language of her Kokum plus learn five of the languages of her father.

Jake's family story line was not made visible by being told and retold the way people usually did, so it had the appearance of something broken. Although people could recall that he was born on the Six Nations of the Grand River Indian Reservation, it was only because his father had wandered into town from the Tuscarora Indian Reservation. Someone nicknamed him Yankee Jim. The name stuck, and that's all anybody ever knew him by. After a while, the people thought he was a pretty easygoing guy, so a vote of nods was taken and they let him sign up to collect Band money. After that, he never left. Jake's mother was known as a hard-working Mohawk woman who kept the way of laying corn with ashes and making mats with the husks. She walked in a good way, but Yankee Jim had become bad natured over the years as he got more into the alcohol. He was a good hunter, but there wasn't much to hunt so he was more of a drinker. Yankee Jim never talked too much about where he came from and some people thought he likely had another woman and kids somewhere on the American side of the Niagara River.

"So, who are you making that for?" Bertha asked as she leaned forward and pouted her chin toward Jake's project.

"I'd make it for you Bertha, if I thought you would chop wood with it."

"I would rather learn how you make it and then sell it for a pile of wood already chopped."

Keeping his gaze at Bertha steady, Jake kept quiet and blinked slowly to signal that she should go on.

"Hmmm, chop wood, get sore, and make too much noise to hear the birds' song for half the day, or work quietly on one thing you love and still get a pile of wood. Which one would you pick, Jake Stone?"

Jake surely didn't need to reflect on her question but he took the time to consider the girl who had stopped fidgeting and stood confidently in front of him. Slender but not fragile, Bertha Martin moved like the branches of a willow tree.

"What if you never chopped wood and then there came a time that you needed to chop wood but didn't know how to? What would you do then?"

"That's when I would to learn to chop wood."

"Come sit by me," he shifted, and patted the space he made beside him.

With the fearlessness of a child, Bertha closed the space between them and slid into the exact place where she really wanted to be—beside Jake Stone.

"Watch what I do here," he said, with silken authority in his voice.

Her lips pressed together to make two thin lines of burgundy as she nodded her head and focused on the log he held up in front of them. If she wanted to learn, her Kokum always said, it was her job to position herself where she could have a clear view of what was being taught, and she had to be quiet, just in case something had to be said, not that there always had to be words spoken to teach. "One person is the person who knows how to do it," Kokum said, "and the other person is the person trying to know how to do it. The teacher doesn't get involved with the learning, and the learner doesn't get involved with the teaching, so there is not a whole lot of reason to talk. That is the way skills are passed down."

Bertha remembered that her Kokum was born before a lot of people knew about the Indian Agents, or the kids being stolen for their schools. Kokum and Misho moved around a lot so it didn't affect them as much.

Jake held the piece of oak, bark still on it, out in front of them to size it up for what he wanted. Bertha watched as he turned it up and down, and when he turned it sideways, it cast a shadow on the ground in a line that joined them together. Bertha always noticed things like that. With the wood still lying crossways in both his hands, he stood up. Bertha understood, so she too rose and held out both her hands at the exact width and height that Jake did. He let the wood roll into her cradled palms, and without letting his eyes break contact with hers, he bent to the side to reach for something just past her. He tarried there, bent over, arm reaching, eyes locked, and his chest started a fever in the place where he let it touch her bare arm. Bertha kept the wood still where he had left it with her, not flinching, while he remained stretched forward just short of leaning his weight on her. The leather laces of his shirt tickled her knee as his unseen hand felt around on the rock behind her. Then there was a scraping of metal against stone as Jake found his knife where it lay behind her. He produced the unsheathed buckhorn knife with a grin. Bertha showed him a toothy smile back.

"See how I take her in hand," he said as he released Bertha from his gaze. *Her!* Bertha let the word roll over in her mind as if it were a smooth and pleasing pebble in the palm of her hand.

Jake took back the piece of wood and then, bending down on one knee he tenderly set her on one end. Grasping her firmly with his one hand he pressed the blade of the knife on an angle against her middle to make a slit in her bark. After that, he laid his knife down beside her and began stripping her bark by hand. His sensing fingers worked poetically to find the places where the next layer of bark was most vulnerable. Without bark, the piece of oak was revealed to be pleasing in her light-skinned smoothness, and shapely, indeed, like the arch of a woman's back. Jake held her across his knee and ran his hands lightly up and down her surface.

Bertha shivered.

Jake, wood and knife in hand, came back to the rock and sat down next to Bertha. She sensed that he needed space around him so she got up and positioned herself to stand away and to the side of him. She could see very well from there and Jake gave her a quick smile before he set to work. Handling her with firmness now, he palmed and he pressed her from top to bottom. How long would she be and where would her curves and the narrows be? Bertha stood still with her arms folded in front of her.

Jake picked up his knife and set its steely edge exactly on the spot that had been warmed by his thumb, and, with his other hand now free, embraced her fullness so she was secure. Then he pressed his knife more deeply into her flesh, entering on a perfect angle that would take the blade effortlessly on its course back out. Each time the knife whispered into her body, she was left different, and she didn't resist, and she didn't flinch because he held her just tightly enough.

Bertha plopped down on a grassy spot and sat cross-legged. She figured Jake to be a man that could be trusted. That was pretty much the reason Bertha had had her eye on Jake Stone since she was nine years old.

The curtain that was drawing in front of Bertha's eyes was almost closed, and even though the sun's pure light made her head scream, in the dark, where she spent her days and nights, her memories were brilliant, and her Kokum still spoke to her constantly.

Even though after she left as a child she never again laid eyes on her Kokum, she could remember clearly a desperate winter morning, about two winters ago, that she had been bound for the third day inside because it was too cold and bright for her to venture outdoors.

A voice had come to her, *A disease of the eyes starts when a person doesn't want to see things the way they are.*

By starting to hear this voice in her heart and her head, she knew that somewhere her beloved grandmother had died. Kokum had started her Spirit Walk and now skin and land could no longer separate them. That was the day fear and loneliness began to fade from red, to pink, to nothing, like blood dropped in water. That was the day she began to receive the counsel of her Kokum again.

And her Jake, he had stuck with her all through the years of her eyes growing dim. She could trust Jake Stone not to change.

Bertha became aware that the small ones were starting to run around, probably naked, and probably because the bath water had grown too cold. Also, the bannock smelled done so she rose to tend to her duties, but the pain that gripped deep inside her, threatened to sit her back down. She thought she had better call Jake now, to let him know to go tell Jon that the baby would be coming tonight and that it wouldn't be too long now. Jon was bad for taking her time.

The evening, cloaked by her blindness and work, ebbed like the tide unseen into night. After she settled the small ones, Bertha wrapped the leftover bannock up in a cloth and set it out where Elizabeth would see it as soon as she got out of bed in the morning. If Maggie did not get there by sun-up Elizabeth would need to tend to Porter. No telling what shape Bertha was going to be in by the time the sun rose next.

She moved slowly across the floor with her feet barely leaving the wooden slats and her hand pressed against her lower back to hold the pain from getting out. No use wasting the pain when it was needed to push the baby out, and, by the feel of things, the baby wasn't going to take all night. She thought she had better have one last smoke before it got too bad, and maybe the last if things kept up at this rate. She filled her pipe, lit it, took time for a pain, and, waiting until the stab had dwindled down to a pinch, let the smoke out. No use wasting a good first puff.

After she had poured herself a tea from the blackened iron kettle on the stove she lowered herself back onto her stool and reached around again to find her smoking things.

The smoke came out of her mouth as if drawn steadily by an air current and gushed only slightly near the end as the next pain started up again all too soon. Bertha straightened her back and waited. This time, as it came on, she deeply drew in the air from the room, letting only bits of it out as she rode the rising wave. For every bit that escaped, she topped back up with keen tiny breaths until it crested. In the moment that came right after the pain had done its worst, Bertha released her breath, staying with it until it was gone, and her lungs were empty. Kokum had always said the fresh air from outside was better for it, but Bertha wasn't going to bother with that. Hardly anybody bothered with that anymore. Maybe it was only for somebody else's convenience anyway.

When the pain settled, Bertha looked all around the room as if she could actually see things. Everything was in its place. She knew everything was in its place because she had done her nightly walk-about-to-feel-every-thing-is-okay time just before she had set the bannock out. Directly in front of her was the window where she liked most to face, darkened now that the sun had long gone down. She could hear from the earnest chipping and scraping of knife against wood that Jake had returned and he was not in a peaceful state of mind. Normally he would have been inside by this time of the night, maybe still working, but not this night. Tonight Jake would not come in and place his chair by the window as he most often did. Tonight he would stay outside to watch for Jon to get there and work where he really always wanted to be anyway. He would stay there at least until the commotion was over.

Over to the right was the door; built large and tall—big enough for Jake—and never locked. The damp smell of the wood, where water from the steel tub had left its mark, reached her nostrils. In use, the tub sat in front of the door; not the best place for a bath, but it made for a straight-line walk for Bertha to cart the bath water in and out of the cabin. When the tub wasn't being used, it was pushed up against the wall, in line with the shelving and boards with hooks where almost everything Bertha had to go get was located.

Moving on in her mind's eye, she could see the sleeping area that took up the whole wall opposite the door and window. Almost everyone did it that way on purpose so that the light of the sun could easily find the eye every morning, shining with his faithful and loyal message that, every day, no matter what, there was work to be done. It was also not good to sleep right under a window or too close to the door. Wind and trouble come in that way, so it was wise to leave a little space, winter and summer.

Bertha had put up sheets of cloth to make a wall between the living and sleeping area and then another wall between the kids and where she and Jake slept. She turned around in her stool and let her eyes follow the expanse of the sleeping wall, and then follow around to the last wall, where the stove was hooked up. Late summer, whispering of fall, Bertha could cook inside all day without worrying about heating the place up too much. She used to cook outside in the summer, before the eye-skin. Some people still did, not too many though. Bertha wasn't one to get too hot very easily anyway. She liked to sit by the stove when she rested because from her stool she could reach the table and everything she needed for a smoke without getting up.

She gave herself some more time for her mind to wander back to Kokum's voice.

There was nowhere else a man could find a woman to work just like him, side by side. That's why the French men were taking up with the People's women all over Turtle Island. Their lilywhite femmes were too soft to make the journey from wherever it was that they all came from in the first place, and another terrible truth was that the French men are better lovers than the People's men. The People's men were never taught to please. Maybe we looked after them a little too good. Perhaps it was the mothers who made a mistake there. It seemed they were so worried about keeping their men good hunters and brave warriors that it ended up that was all they could be. After the light-skinned race brought their blankets, pots, guns, money, and other things to make life easier, many skills were lost. If a People are conquered, and their meat comes to them by money, what good is a warrior or a hunter? Sometimes a man was born to a Vision of medicine or clown, but most boys were raised to protect and provide for their People. The older ones say that our ways are like a lake dried up, and the hunters and the warriors with no purpose are like fish flopping around in the hot dry sun.

The men only knew two ways of being. Hunting and fighting. But the women, they have always been used to change. Women have always had to learn to swim sometimes when things were a certain way, to walk sometimes when things were another way, or to stay quiet in times when they didn't know how it was. With the men sometimes gone too much, or never coming home, the People raised their women to be able to find different ways of getting things done on their own. So with the hunting and fishing being so bad, and with so many wars being lost, women already had the skill of finding a different way of being. There is no telling for sure though which different way is the best way.

If the truth, the real terrible part, were known, the French men were more like what the People's women really needed their men to be. These men had more "go-get." So when the bold and eager Frenchman decided to go get one of the People's women, she would find that, under the blankets, it was worth getting got for. She also found that, if she played her cards right, she was fed very well. But the problem with a Frenchman is that he likes to make everything his own. If you teach them something new, they give it a name in their own language, say it is their own because they now have made it the best in all the land, like turning around and calling pimhikan, pemmican. This is how they get ahead—by having sex and changing the names of things that people give them. The lighter skinned women gave away too much of their power, and the People's women were not used to the ways of such domineering men. But still, all this together makes it hard for any woman to leave once she has made a child for a man.

So more and more, all over, the People's women started taking up with the French men. Times were getting harder. They were hungry and needed to mate with the French men so their children would be fed and maybe their sons would be more ambitious. The women followed the French men around all over the place and left their own People's men at home to drink, fight amongst themselves, and pass out around the fire.

As for the French men, they had reasons of their own. They could see that these women could not only put up with a lot more than their own women, but they worked harder, made more handsome small ones, and, most importantly, they knew quite a bit about living off the land. They needed these women to survive, but as it has already been said, once you help them, the French men have a habit of claiming for their own something they felt was useful with no mind later for the ones who gave it to them. So it seems the People's women and the French men took up together because each had a need to be something stronger. It's too bad that the People's men thought it would keep working if they acted weaker, and didn't let go of the thought that maybe their women would feel sorry for them and stay by their side. And it's too bad the women trained them that way.

The British? Well, they missed out. Those men liked the company of their *own a little too much and they liked to sit around inside and hear themselves talk. They were good fighters though, and they let the Iroquois have that land. Listen here, there is a time and place for meetings, but you can do that too much you know. Alongside of that, they didn't have a taste for the People's dark-skinned women. The People's women, for the most part, found the British to be too dry or busy with other things all the way around. The People's women weren't much on the chance that their sons might turn out to be men who spent even more time on their fancy dress then they already did. And another thing I've heard tell of is that the British never really gave much of a reason to jump under the blankets with them anyway.*

Bertha had run across a French man or two in her time and these words her Kokum spoke always came back. As far as Bertha was concerned, they were okay for some, but she found them to be too bossy. She had some friends that had shacked up with these kinds of men. She couldn't see how she could ever let a man come in and run the whole household, tell her what tongue to use, and what Spirit to pray to. Okay for some but not for her.

Bertha used both her father and her mother's tongue with the children but offered them only Kokum's teachings, even though they lived amongst the Iroquois, only because it was the way of the *kwe* to follow her grand-mother's word.

Just as Bertha was finishing her last puff, a bad pain hit. It climbed to the top with a fierceness so fast that she didn't get a chance to stay above it. It grabbed her good, and she doubled over, making it worse than it should have been. At the same time the pain hit, there came an unending tap of a wooden object on the door. Bertha knew it was Jon, that irritating daughter of Old Healing Smoke, hitting it with her walking stick. The two legs she had were too skinny to support the barrel she had let her body become, so she needed a third to keep her up for walking long distances. And to make things worse, Bertha had the unwelcome thought that Jon showing up in the middle of a strong pain like that was a bad sign. She wished Old Healing Smoke was still alive.

Jon let herself in. She knew enough not to wait to be invited. She had held back from coming long enough, in hopes that Bertha would be in bed by now. No use hanging around somewhere else when she could get Louie and the kids settled. Louie said he didn't mind her doing the "medicine woman act" but he was always saying that she had to start asking for cash and stop settling for favours and *"objets inutilisables"* from people's houses. Louie said they could use the cash to go uptown and buy the things they wanted—brand new—from the store, not these useless things. Part of Jon agreed, but then again, she would hear the words that her mother, Old Healing Smoke, and her grandmother of the same name, often spoke.

It is done because you are a holy person. Every group of people needs a holy person. Healers usually don't get married because they're a special lot. Always being in touch with the spirit world makes them more and more different than other people as they get older, and being different makes a person hard to get along with.

Jon didn't want to be alone. Times were hard. You couldn't count on people like you used to.

"*Sago.*"

"*Sago.*" Through her searing pain, Bertha strained to speak in Jon's own tongue.

"I see you're well on your way."

"Enh, ya. I think, if you will just hold on a bit, I would like to go to bed."

"Okay. I'll come over there and help you."

"*Ka.* That's okay." Sometimes Bertha fell back into Kokum's tongue when she was distressed.

Bertha straightened up in the chair and then scrounged around for something on the floor. She found what she was searching for, her tobacco pouch, but not for herself—for Jon. Jon missed smoking, and sometimes she smoked when she was out visiting a friend. Louie would give her a hell of a time when she got home with the smell of it on her mouth, but Jon was always in a better humour when she had a smoke going.

"Can I put some light in here?"

"Sure, Jon. I shoulda thought." Bertha had hauled herself up and was on the move toward her bed.

Jon busied herself looking for something with which to light the coal oil lantern. She remembered that everything was always in the same spot in Bertha's house. Had to be, or it would take Bertha too long to find it.

"That reminds me," Jon said as she struck a wooden match and held it to the open lantern. "You need some more eyebright pills?"

"I don't know if that's really working."

"I tol' ya, it doesn't really cure it. It just holds it off. My mother used to cure it completely, but it took a ceremony." They both knew that nobody was doing ceremonies anymore, unless they were hiding it—just medicines—

and more and more people were heading into town to look for a white doctor anyway.

Bertha used what might she could gather to hoist herself up on the bed. She had thrown open, and left draped on its rope, the sheet of white cotton that had been drawn across the sleeping area. With both hands on the bed, she eased her weight down on the mattress.

Jon watched Bertha. The mattress wasn't really like the one she and Louie had at home. Bertha's was actually made of furs and some Hudson Bay blankets. Old style, but somehow it looked good to Jon.

"Say, where's Jake?"

"He was waitin' for you but had to go down the road to get Maggie."

"Oh yeah, shoulda known, Maggie always comes. But then again, didn't she get married to some American?"

"Enh, ya. She did. An Italian American," Bertha winced and stopped talking to get through a pain. When it backed off, Bertha continued, "Her and the Italian got a divorce. One good thing though, Maggie never had any kids with him."

"Yeah, that's a good thing alright. That Maggie, she's always been the wild one."

"Enh, she has a good time."

Bertha, sitting full length on the bed now, leaned back against the wall. She closed her eyes and let her head fall back to be supported, all the while keeping her bulbous figure centred and braced with her two hands on the bed. Jon knew she was positioning, as her mother, who was taught by her mother, had taught her to channel the next current of pain. As far as she knew, the Haudenosaunee did it the same way.

Bertha knew that she should be resting in the precious space without pain by staying quiet, but she could feel Jon beside her, not yet content enough to sit. She knew Jon was probably wondering if she had come too early. "Tell me, what did your mother teach you about the eye-skin ceremony?"

"We don't do ceremonies anymore, Bertha. Louis says it's against the church."

"Didn't your mother teach you any ceremonies before she died?"

"She did for a while, but after that Doctor Wheeler started coming around all the time, she cut it out. He was against anything like that, said he would report it to the Indian Agent."

"Why did she listen to him?"

"They listened to each other. He wanted to know everything she knew about making medicines with plants. He only believed in medicines. Also, he was interested in knowing everything Ma told him about why people let themselves get sick, but there was one thing for sure, he was against the ceremonies. I guess, being a good Christian and all, he couldn't allow it. But even so, that doctor could tell Ma knew a lot of things he didn't know about making plants into medicines and he wanted to know everything exactly the way Ma did it so he could have more medicines. Like I said, he only cures things with medicines, so I guess he wanted to have the most medicines, then maybe make them into something a person can't just go out and pick freely.

"He gave Ma some of his strong medicines and wrote down the ones he didn't have in his cupboards, but the problem was that Ma couldn't read. Now he's always giving me medicines and telling me all the times I should be using them. I'll tell ya something, I think he is sending those plants Ma gave him to England, then making them into those pills and saying they are better. Picking is free eh, but not if it all gets picked for the pills, sent to England and never grows back. Just as well, but I kept all those papers, in case someday we can read them."

Jon had dragged a chair over from the table and sat herself down at Bertha's bedside while she was talking. "Here," Bertha said, offering the pouch. "I have some of my own tobacco I grew out back with the seeds my Kokum gave me. There are some rolling papers over there on the shelf." She gestured in the direction of the far corner. "Make yourself a good smoke."

Jon couldn't help herself. She got to her feet and crossed the room. She felt around on the shelf, which was over her head, found the small flat package, and brought them both back over to her chair. There were times she was aware that she didn't bother to act a certain way in front of Bertha, like now, not hesitating, going right for the papers, because she knew Bertha couldn't see her anyway, and it kind of made her wonder more about herself than about Bertha. Jon shook the thought off and started to tend more to the smoke she was beginning to roll in her lap, the good stuff, grown from seeds kept by the old ones.

"Do you hear that? Outside?"

Jon listened and heard it right away.

"Yeah, I do. Whatcha getting at?"

"Just listen, eh?"

Jon stopped what she was doing. She could hear something more than the bugs, and the frogs, and the trees whispering outside, and beside her, she could hear Bertha's breathing beginning to deepen, but it was even more than that. The night sounds outside were heating up—she could feel it—heating up to a rhythm that was in time with Bertha's deepening breaths, getting more fervent with each one.

There had been a stillness just before Bertha called her attention to it. Now, against the backdrop of the pulsing night, she sensed its echo. Somewhere in Jon's mind she had been listening, at least enough for it to come back to her. Gradually, she tied it together in her mind. Moments before, there had been a space of no pain that Bertha had been given, and, at the same time, the night had made itself compatible with it, resting with her.

Jon finished rolling the smoke and lit it. She couldn't help fussing with the thought a while longer. Suddenly a thought that was so clear it sounded a bit like a real voice came to her, so ordinary, while sitting there in the chair by Bertha Stone's bed, something her own mother had so long ago taught her. Something her mother's mother must have taught her. Something only Haudenosaunee told each other.

Notice the signs. Notice how Mother Earth speaks as well as listens.

Jon could swear that she heard her mother's voice for real, but in her head, speaking softly in Mohawk.

The earth and the animals and the People are connected, so they talk to each other. Jon, you have to see and smell, feel and taste, in order to hear the words, in order to really know what is going on.

Coming through the window, the song of the night had become as frenzied as Bertha's breathing. But then, the crickets' shrill chirps pitched above the throaty moan of the frogs. Their blended tunes were caught by the wind, carried by it, and became the song to which the leaves danced. A harmonic aliveness filled the night air, as if the breath of all creation whispered ancient lessons to those who could be still enough to hear.

Jon got an idea.

"Eh. I got an eel skin in the bag."

"The Mohawk way?"

"Yeah! Don't ever have no call to use it. Doctor Wheeler says it's witchcraft, but I was jus thinkin'," she whispered as if he was actually around. "It's been in Ma's bag, and I just never took it out."

By now Bertha had got on her knees, her weight still perfectly centred and her birth line straight. Jon knew by this that Bertha's opening was almost ready for the child to move through. She stubbed her cigarette out and rose to set to work.

"Maybe you would go get that eel skin."

The outline of Jon evaporated from Bertha's sight, but she heard her as she rooted around somewhere on the far side of the house.

"Here!" She held it up as if Bertha could see it. "I got it. You got some white cloth?"

"There's some cheesecloth folded up on the shelf."

Jon returned with the cloth, unravelled it, and laid it out on the bed behind where Bertha was kneeling. She laid her eel skin atop it and then carefully picked it up at both ends.

"Here now, I'm gonna tie this aroun' ya."

She stood beside Bertha's kneeling form, lifted her cotton undershirt and placed the eel skin layer inside, directly against the taut, dry, and hot surface of Bertha's own skin. She held it in place and could feel the child writhing against her palm. She reached around and grasped both ends behind Bertha's back, got up on her knees on the bed, and tied it securely before letting the oversized white cotton man's undershirt drop back down and hide it. Staying where she was, Jon placed both her hands on Bertha's shoulders and rubbed downward with her palms.

She was amazed. She had never actually done this before, or had she?

Why is it often so difficult to be born, as it can also be to die?

The night sounds were fading, or shifting somehow in her head to the voices of her grandmother talking to her mother. Was it Jon sitting by the stove eating an apple, or was it her very own hands that her Tota spoke through?

This is part of the Great Mystery.

Jon could actually feel the knots of power stuck, unwilling to push with the rest of the body's force to help Bertha's child make the birth journey.

You got to find the stones of resistance and fear, smooth them, and coax them. The bodies should let go of each other now. The travelling soul will bring their troubles and gifts. We will also have some here to share. You strive to convince them that it will turn out okay.

As if by some kind of second nature, she searched with her ears until she found the rhythm of Bertha's breathing. She sucked it in with her own breath and brought it up through her chest, then her arms, out her hands and back into Bertha's body. When Bertha pushed her breath and the pain out, Jon's palms directed the stray and clogged knots into the massive stream moving downward. They were thoughts at first, but as Jon focused upon them they became like something she could actually feel, something that passed through her palms, and then released in a steady current.

Jon was in awe of herself. "I have never done this before, Bertha. Only watched Tota and Ma, though many, many times. Now it's like I done it before."

Blood memory.

Bertha responded to the unexpected gift of Jon's skillfulness by drawing all her effort to align with it. Though Jon had been there to help with the birth of Porter and Elizabeth, she had not ever actually done this. Bertha had only seen it once when Old Healing Smoke rubbed down her own mother to get Maggie born. In the old ways, women children were not kept from childbirth, not like now, when there were so many things that were "un-Christian" and would get your young ones taken away to be put in their schools.

Bertha accepted the cramping pain as it thinned itself into a stronger beam of light, working better, more effectively, like the difference between a sharp and a dull knife. When the next urge to push came, it carried with it a force that seemed to come from the sky above, mighty and with a will of its own. Without letting any air or sound escape, Bertha opened her mouth, as a way to help open herself below.

Slowly, so she doesn't tear.

Jon, in a steady voice said to Bertha, "Go slow. So you don't tear."

At the end of the push, a small crack of no pain came, and in that hush Bertha and Jon's efforts became connected. Then everything stilled. Jon positioned herself so she could see into Bertha's eyes. Bertha could feel the telling pressure in her birth area and reached down with her hand so she could "see" if it was bulged. With the palm of her hand, she capped the greasy firm roundness that was beginning to protrude from between her legs.

Bertha looked up and said to Jon in a whisper, "It's trying to bust through now."

Jon thrust her own hand between Bertha's legs. Three of her fingers touched the wet pulsing bump, and her other finger and thumb touched Bertha's dry and strained skin. This told her that the child was not yet through, and, if it sucked back in, they would have to start farther back.

"Lay back and let me have a look!"

Jon, sharply focused and present now, took her rightful place as the one in charge, and Bertha, grateful to be relieved of making sure Jon did the right thing, was finally able to give herself completely over to her own role. Jon worked to clump up the blankets at the head of the bed. This allowed

Bertha to slowly un-crimp her legs, draw her weight back to rest on her spine and be supported by her own elbows and the blankets, all the while keeping the tip of her tailbone fixed to a spot so as to not tip or sway and discourage the child backward.

In a semi-sitting, semi-laying position, Bertha opened her mouth and her throat, allowing her head to drop back to gather more breath.

With her elbows bracing Bertha's legs farther apart, Jon placed only the first three fingertips of each hand ever so lightly upon the taught skin straining around what looked like the child's forehead. With little to no pressure, in an off-and-on way, Jon started to make little circles around the edge of the tightening skin, in a clockwise direction, first cajoling the skin in and then letting it away, just to seduce more stretch out of it.

You have to talk it into letting .

Jon thanked her mother's voice in her head and without further hesitation she pressed when the skin gave and let it off slightly when it protested, only to press quickly back down and circle round again before it shrunk back to where it thought it was more comfortable. With her fingers, Jon sweet-talked and wheedled until the skin would agree to just a tiny bit more each time.

It's like dough.

Just above her head, Jon could feel Bertha give a huge shudder, but she could not take her eyes off her work. She had to stay connected to what she was doing and what Bertha was doing.

Then it came. The big push, the one that could work if you knew how.

If you are connected, and even though some women show no sign, you can feel something push on your own insides, and then you will know it is time.

"Now?" Bertha's voice strained.

"Now!" answered Jon firmly.

Some women make a lot of noise when they are giving birth; they have to, just to let off some of the pain, but not Bertha, Jon already knew that about her. Bertha had the gumption to hold the pain with the banks of her own will and current it downward in the direction she wanted it to go.

The hole was four fingers open now, but there was no need to measure as Jon could tell by sight. Bertha's belly shifted and tightened mightily around the small body within, closing off any space or idea that it could stay any longer within its mother's protective belly. Never letting her fingers lose touch with their work, Jon felt the child's head shift, and then, finally, a fatty softness came between the firmness of the child's head and the fleshy gate that held it back. The belly above squeezed down, reaching for its flatness, and then a swell of water opened the circle from the inside out, rushing the child's head out into the world on a wave. The treaty of no violence between child and mother had been honoured.

Bertha expelled the rest of the air she had been pocketing somewhere above the pain. Taking more air deep within, she immediately sucked in for the next push. No pause for rest. They both knew the body would use the power of the last surge to circle around and thrust through to the next. Jon abided with open hands, supporting the child's head from drooping as it emerged to its neck. The child, thickly capped with glistening black hair, waited soundlessly.

At first, there was no sign from Bertha that the pain had taken hold, but then, the belly began to compress, and Bertha closed her eyes. She measured the breath she let out in exact time with the level of pain. Jon watched the belly contracting down, as if seeking its own smallness, steadily, not wildly and feverishly like a stuck deer. The child began its natural turn, and Jon applied gentle pressure for help, not direction. One shoulder peeped out and then the other. Jon made a cradle with her hands and arms for the child to slip into. There was no sudden burst forward, just a steady glide into waiting arms.

"It's a girl this time."

"Enh, ya."

"She got a veil."

The child, serene in Jon's arms for a second or two, peered through the opaque membrane, blinking and looking all around as if able to see perfectly all that surrounded her. Jon broke it open, peeled it from the small body, and set it on the bed. Then, slightly parting her mouth, the baby sucked in her first breath of air, deeply filling her belly until it thrust up the pulsing veiny cord that still connected her to somewhere inside her mother. The baby's belly bulged as if the air lingered inside, not able to find its way out, and then, opening her mouth wide, and contorting her face, squalled out her first taste of life.

"Good. She's got some fight in her. Whatcha gonna name her?"

"Mary."

"That's a good name," Jon said colourlessly while she placed the wailing Mary on the bed between Bertha's legs, exactly as she was taught to, so the child would naturally call out the rest of what still held her attached to her mother. The veil, crumpled and discarded like a washcloth, lay by her head.

Bertha, who had laid herself back down on the bed in exhaustion, suddenly bolted back upright. As her body responded to the call of the child, she bore down once more as she relinquished her final pain and expelled the fleshy disc-shaped afterbirth. Jon waited a bit longer before withdrawing her birth knife from its sheath and wiping it on the blanket. She glanced over at Bertha, who seemed to be looking right at her, as if she could actually see her, or perhaps right through her. Jon hauled her form up and made her way over to the table. She passed the blade back and forth through the candle flame several times until she felt the badness had been burnt up. By the time she got back to Bertha's bedside, the birth cord was losing its pulse and beginning to flatten, so Jon set to work. Mary continued to holler and kick as Jon grasped the cord, tied it off, and, with one hand, folded it. She placed her knife in the crease she had made and pulled it expertly through to the other side.

"I got some corn husks in my bag too," Jon said.

Bertha managed a smile through her fatigue. "I think that might be a good idea."

Jon disappeared back into the shadows and returned bearing the distinctive rustle of cornhusks. Bertha saw the flash of light as Jon struck a match. She waited for sharp odour of burning cornhusks to sting her nostrils.

"I'm smudging the child's cord for ya."

"Enh, ya. That is good."

"I could dry the veil if ya want me to?" Jon said as she passed the silver tendrils as close to the baby's heaving belly as safety would allow.

"What's the Mohawk way on that?"

Jon used her hand to gently coax the silvery tendrils to curl around the glistening umbilical. "Well I don't hafta."

"No, she's a good part Mohawk. I think ya should, if you're willing, but I just want to know what the ways on that are."

"The old ones always say that if a baby is born with the veil it is good luck to keep it and hang it on its bed. They say it gives the kid somethin' extra that makes 'em smarter and safer. To tell ya the truth, my mother said it was something extra from the spirit world, like a guardian or somethin' like that. But nowadays everybody says it's nothin' but witchcraft, and if the Indian Agent, who is a strict churchgoer, gets wind of it, he'll come around askin' questions for sure."

"You're gonna dry it for me?"

"I'll sneak it home, wash it up and bring it back tomorrow to dry on your line. When it's dry, you put it on her bed. Even though Louie'll give me a hard time if he catches me, it's not really me that has got to worry. It's you. You're the one with kids."

Jon picked the baby up and placed her in the already prepared box on the floor at the foot of Bertha's bed. She left the baby uncovered while she returned to Bertha's bedside and asked her to roll over on her side. Jon untied the cheesecloth and removed it, and wrapped the eel skin in the cover she had brought it in. She placed it back in her bag and walked over to the baby's makeshift bed. Bertha allowed herself the treat of sinking into a daze, while Jon busied herself binding the same cheesecloth that had been tied around Bertha, around the baby's belly.

"Here! I put a belly bind on 'er."

"I'll pay attention for it to fall off."

"Ya know ya gotta put that away so you will always be close, eh? I don't know if your ma's people did it that way though."

"It's a good way. I will do it."

In the box, Mary thrashed about, her small fists making patter noises against the sides. She didn't carry on too long before she settled down to a whimper and the odd wet sound as she sucked the inside of her cheeks.

Jon put the bloodied rags to soak in the steel bucket of water that Bertha always put out at the foot of the bed. "D' ya want me to bury the afterbirth?"

"Jake'll come in and get that after you leave. Put it in the other bucket."

"Ya know ya gotta bury that in the garden."

"I think he buries it in the bush somewhere."

"That's no good. For girls, ya gotta bury it in the garden, or they might wander."

"Okay, Jon." Bertha strained through her fog.

Jon set herself back down in the chair by Bertha's bed and plucked the other smoke she had made for herself from behind her ear. She thought she would have a puff or two while she waited a bit longer to make sure Bertha didn't go into a bleed.

After a while Bertha spoke, her voice sounding cloudy and distant, "Maggie'll be here in the morning to look after those rags."

"It was different this time, don't you think?"

"Ehn, ya," Bertha confirmed. "I think we did it closer to the old way this time, is what I think."

Jon paused to draw her last puff and then said as she exhaled, "I think it went better."

"You did it more like your mother this time."

"Hm, I guess, that coulda been it."

She rose up, the chair complaining against the floor as she did, and walked over to the wood stove that had long gone out. Jon lifted the latch, opened the door, and tossed the ember that was left of her smoke inside to die by itself, and then turned back around to face Bertha somewhere over in the dark.

"Louie'll be startin' to look for me."

"Okay. Jake'll settle up with you tomorrow or the next day."

"'Night, Bertha"

"Enh, ya, 'night, Jon."

Mary, soothed by the dark after the candle had been snuffed, drifted down like something heavy, seeking to go back to sleep. There she lay, suspended in a dream of something she was hungry for—searching for—denied to her. Unknown sensations battered her very being, driving her to seek the source of comfort that had been her abiding guide. Where was the thing she had followed out of the spirit world? She welcomed the absence of light as it offered some buffer between her and the un-named pulls, crushes, and burnings of things upon her. The deeper she fell into the velvetiness of no light, the denser the dream that surrounded her became. But still, there was the knowledge that it was only something she spun for herself—something to hold onto. The only thing, right now that she knew for certain was the beating of her mother's heart. Where had the real one gone? There now. All of the form she had taken for this journey began to relax within the illusion she could create for herself, for, not too far off, she could feel the faintest throbbing echo of the alluring voice that had called her to this Earth Walk.

At just about the same time as the sun, a spreading pool of light on the dusty floor began to paint the room, Mary woke from her dream to her mother's touch. With this, new ports of knowing came alive so that afterward, and indeed for the rest of her Earth Walk, everything she ever felt was relative. Lifting her and then drawing her to her breast, Bertha offered Mary the soothing softness of her breast against her cheek. Mary opened her mouth to root for the sweetness she instinctively knew was waiting for her, grasped it politely, and drew upon that which she knew she must take. It was not sweet. Though it was bitter, it was what she craved. Mary fell contentedly back to sleep at her mother's breast, this time not falling so deeply into the dark sky.

Maggie and Coyote were staying with them. Mary was nine years old and Ma had gone into another baby-sick, only this time early. That's why Maggie was there. Coyote was there only because Maggie was there. Coyote, Gramma's youngest sister was feeling her winter starting to come on, all her kids were drunks and gone off to live somewhere else, so now she was hanging around Maggie quite a bit. As for Gramma, she was getting old and couldn't come around as much as she used to.

Coyote was mean, though like most Grandmothers, she still had lots to say. She wasn't pleasant, but it didn't matter; a Grandmother has to be listened to. Every time someone complained about it, Ma always had the same thing to say, "Yes, Coyote can be a mean one, so you got to listen harder to hear the good stuff."

But Maggie was different. Everybody said she was wild, but really Maggie was only wild with her feelings. She took more chances than other people because she had a bigger heart. She was like those red raspberry bushes that grow all around the edge of the tree people, sweet and juicy to be around, and a good fight in her that would come back every year if there was a lot of sun and some freedom to wander. Maggie had a tiny waist but good muscles. There was no fat on Maggie. She brushed her long black hair shiny and sometimes kept it in braids with homemade shell clips or sometimes with fancy store-bought "barrettes" that the Italian had gifted her with. Maggie had a heart-shaped mouth and lots to say with it. Everybody said Mary took after her auntie.

Mary was anxious to sit on Maggie's lap. She fidgeted about, twirling her perfectly brushed silken black hair around her fingers and shifting from one foot to the other, but Coyote got in the way of that by sending her outside to play with Porter and Elizabeth. Mary knew there was no use rebelling. She pretended she was a baby bear and scuttled out the front doorway on all fours, wasting no time at all because she didn't want to have to take Dolly with her.

No such luck!

Dolly appeared in the doorway. "Maaawwwweeee!"

Dolly's high-pitched squeal always reminded Mary of the sound robins make when they call to each other. It could be nice to hear but too much of it was annoying.

Mary went over to her little sister, and taking her by the hand, led her to a spot where the grass was shorter, patchier. There was a pile of dirt and a pile of old cups and dishes and spoons and things. Mary pointed and told Dolly to sit.

Dolly plunked her compact little body down and watched Mary bend down, pick up an old chipped bowl, and dump out the dirt.

"I'll go get some water for you to play with. You stay here."

Mary turned around and headed toward the back of the place. The grass was up to her waist, just the way she liked it. Walking through it was like walking through lake water. She wasn't worried one bit about snakes. Ma had told her, "Make a lot of noise, and they will just squirm away from you before you get there. They don't want to get stepped on or ate. If you go quietly, like a sneaky animal, then you better move slower to give them time to not get surprised and turn around and bite you. If you have to go fast, and need to be quiet, then go fast, but step lightly. Never let your foot stay on the ground for any time at all. If you have to, run like a deer, then in your mind, make a picture that every time your front foot is just about to touch the ground, the back foot is already off the ground. It's like one foot talks to the other foot, calling each other back and forth. Always keep in your mind a picture of you running on a layer of leaves that you don't want to crush. This way you are not sinking down or up as much as you are floating forward. This is how you run swiftly and don't get caught."

The faithful steel bucket of water stood by the back door. It was Elizabeth's job to empty it at night so as to not encourage any thirsty animals to come close to the house, and she was supposed to fill it every morning so that everybody who was doing something outside could come and get a drink when they wanted to. Elizabeth was the oldest but she was also the laziest. She didn't like to work, and sure enough, the bucket was half full of leafy water from what could be a day or two ago. Ma hadn't been up and at 'em enough to notice and get after her, and Pa wouldn't bother himself with saying anything.

Mary scooped out some water with the bowl she had brought. She picked out the leaves and flicked them onto the packed down dirt. She turned to head back through the grass when a movement overhead caught her eye. It came from apple rings drying on the dancing clothesline. She thought maybe she might sneak some. Normally she wouldn't dare because even though Ma was blind, she could somehow tell everything. But Ma was out of commission, and Coyote would just eat up everything anyway, so Mary helped herself.

She was surprised that she didn't need a stump or turned-over bucket to sneak apple rings this year. She reached up with both hands and delicately tore a line in each of seven apple rings to remove them from the burlap twine, five to keep Dolly busy, and two for her to eat on the way. She tore off the sun-sweetened and slightly soft flesh in small bites as she walked back through the grass like a sneaky animal.

Dolly was using a teaspoon to scoop dirt—so dry it was more like sand—into a battered old beat-up tin cup. Mary cast a shadow in front of Dolly, causing her to look up. She produced a full cup for Mary to see.

"That's good work, Dolly. I brought you a treat."

Dolly blinked as she looked up at Mary.

Mary knelt down, closer to Dolly. "Shhhhh. Don't tell, or you will have to share with Porter and Elizabeth."

Dolly smothered a big smile and nodded in a serious and grown-up way to show she understood completely. Mary knew she could trust Dolly because her little face didn't once look away, and, besides, she knew Dolly because she spent most of her time with her. Dolly got up on her knees to get ready for the gift, but Mary shook her head and told her to sit. Dolly sat back down cross-legged and Mary placed the apple rings in her own lap while she arranged Dolly's beet-dyed dress to cover her lap. She made a bowl in the soft, thin cotton and nestled the apple rings inside.

She stood up again and put a stern look on her face. "Dolly!"

Dolly looked up.

Mary wagged her finger at Dolly. "See this line of trees all around the place?"

Dolly, wide-eyed and frowning, nodded her head.

"That is a line of trees that keeps you safe inside it. Don't go past it. I'll be right back."

Mary's eyes stayed locked on Dolly until she started to look over the nest of goodies in her lap. Satisfied her sister was safe for the time being,

Mary turned her face to the sky. She closed her eyes and started shifting
her moccasined feet until she made a perfect circle in the dirt. She turned
around and around until the sun warmed all of her face. She let herself bake
for exactly three times around and when she was back to the starting point,
she used one hand to make a roof over her eyes and opened them to see
what time it was. Past lunch she thought. The sun had already passed being
directly over top of the place.

Mary dropped her gaze to eye level and looked around in search of
what Elizabeth and Porter might be up to. She looked toward the line of
trees, paused for a bit, and then moved her attention on to the other side of
the place. She started walking through the tall grass again, only this time,
in the opposite direction than she had gone before.

Eventually she came upon her Pa, sitting on his tree stump, carving his
axe handles. She stepped out into the cleared spot under the willow tree.
"Pa, I want to stay in the house and watch Maggie cook. Coyote says I have
to stay outside."

Jake looked up from his work and considered his middle daughter for
a time. Nine years old, well muscled, Mary was a good worker. Mary was
more dependable than her older sister.

Mary waited while he did the Pa thing that he always did. He just sat
there and looked at her before answering. The playful fingers of the willow
branches teased Mary's face. She let them tickle her for a while before she
brushed them away and moved closer. She knew Pa never went against
anything Ma said, and he wasn't likely to go against Coyote either, and besides that, he never was much for an argument. Pa, who still had his knife
poised in mid-cut, looked at her a while longer and then answered, "Well,
stay outside then." He finished his cut and turned back to start a new one.

Mary turned away. She lingered a bit, and then turned to the line of
trees that surrounded them. It was like the trees were a circle fence around
them, and the blue sky above was like a bubble on the surface of the brook.
Mary suddenly felt like a water bug that was inside, thinking it was safe and
that nobody could see it, so it just stayed there, trying not to move. She had
the urge to go into the forest.

"Maaaaarrrrry!" Mary slumped at the sound of Coyote hollering for
her. She turned, and squinted until she could make out the old lady's great
figure filling the doorway of the place.

Coyote, spotting Mary fiddling around and keeping Jake from doing
his work ordered, "Git over here you! Right now!"

Mary made a big commotion with her arms and legs as she ran to the front door. When she got to the packed down dirt at the front of the place she stood silently, hoping she was going to be invited in.

"I need you to go into town and get me a pack a rolling papers. All they have 'round here is pipes, and I ran outta rolling papers. Here's some money. Don't lose it!"

Mary stepped forward with an open hand to let Coyote drop the money in. "Where's my Ma?"

"You don't concern yourself with that. She's took to her bed to get ready for her kid to be born."

"Okay," Mary sighed and turned to leave. There was nothing else she could have said.

She walked away from Coyote and straight ahead, past Dolly, to the path through the grass that went along the edge of the trees and led to the road to town. At the outer edge of the waving grass, she turned around, from habit, to see if Coyote was still in the doorway. Ma, even though she couldn't see, and even though the sun hurt her eyes, would have stayed in the doorway long enough for Mary to see her just before she called out to say goodbye. That's what people did to make other people, even company, feel like they were going to miss them while they were gone. But she saw nobody—just an empty doorway.

Mary stood at the crook in the path at the edge of the trees. It was like a snake's tongue, with one prong of the tongue more narrow and vague. This faded, less travelled sliver of a path led into the forest and was the one Pa used to search for good hard wood for his handles. Mary had been on it enough times, but only once had she gone all the way to the other end of it, and that was with Pa. Pa said it was a shortcut to town, and if Mary remembered correctly, it was faster than walking all the way around the trees on the other path.

Mary was both afraid of, and in awe of the forest. The tree people—pines, maples, oaks, birches, elms, and basswoods—watched, invited, or perhaps coaxed her in. She took the first step and breathed in deeply the green above and the brown at her feet. In the middle space, she felt small and a part of the other things of that space. All around her, the little four-leggeds made rustling noises to get away from her; dead and rotten trees gave a place for other things to live; and the odd spindly sapling poked through the thick rug of needles and leaves to try its luck by following a sunbeam. All of these goings-on were really only the first layer. There were layers and layers of other things happening that wouldn't be seen without sitting still and watching for a long time.

Way over head, in the very top of the Tree Nations, was where Spirit played the hardest. Reaching Mary's ears as hushed thunder, the Standing People swayed and competed with each other in merciless disagreement about who would survive. Remaining motionless herself, and looking up, Mary could barely feel a breath of wind on her face. The forest had a way of making her feel both unusually protected and vulnerable at the same time. Still, for some reason, she liked it in there. She decided to start moving.

As soon as she entered the forest, a path, so sharp it was as if someone had drawn a knife across the powerful hindquarter of a freshly downed buck, became defined in front of her. Following a path was easy and Pa always said Mary had a good sense of where to go next. The going seemed sprightly, a word Maggie used to describe her own path in life. After a while, however it became patchy and blurred from ferns and medicines claiming back their territories, and broken trees, branches, leaves, and other things that had fallen and landed there. None of them seemed to care that it was someone's way of going, or, she wondered, were all these things actually trying to trick her? The forest could do that. Ma said every living thing had to have a way of fighting to survive, and if a person decided to go walking around among the Standing People and then forget that they are living things, and that they too want not only to survive, but also to get bigger and stronger, then a person might have to be reminded the hard way.

Coyote said it was the Wiindeegos who were the ones that made all the trouble, and Ma had never said Coyote was wrong. The Wiindeegos, Coyote said, were greedy people, banished there for their selfishness, changed into bad spirits who craved the flesh of people, children being the sweetest catch of all. Coyote loved to take a puff of her pipe and then fix all the kids in the room with her beady little eyes and describe in detail how Wiindeegos would tear off an arm and slowly eat it in front of the person before going on to the next body part. They ate slowly because they kept hoping they would somehow be satisfied, but they never were. It is the fate of the Wiindeegos to always, and forever, be hungry.

At the end of the story Coyote would always take a deep puff and then let it out at the same time as a wicked laugh. All you could see were her biting eyes through a cloud of smoke. Maggie said to pay no mind, that it was the coyotes that she really had to watch out for. A Wiindeego was easy to spot, she said. A coyote, on the other hand, was a tricky creature. Ma said that Coyote had a hard way about her, but really, it was her way of keeping kids from wandering off.

Mary stepped lightly, picking her way along the skinny line that appeared to weave unnecessarily at times and then, suddenly, would disappear altogether. She had to stop at these overgrown spots in the path and scout out where it picked up again. Eventually she came upon another fork in the path and finally had to admit that she hadn't paid enough mind to where Pa had gone on that one and only time she had tagged along behind him to go to town. The idea crept up the back of her neck, like the cold draft in the house at wintertime, that she couldn't remember, absolutely for certain, which tong of the fork Pa had taken. She hadn't paid attention because she'd felt safe trailing along behind Pa, letting him worry about which way to go, while she searched the ground for stuff to pick up.

Well, she didn't feel very safe now. She looked right, and then left. She turned her head and looked behind her. Then it hit her! She recalled that Pa took the left-hand path because he said the other one was too muddy. Mary didn't waste a minute more. She started down the left path, even if it seemed as if it would likely take her deeper into the Standing People before dumping her back into safety on the edge of town where light was guaranteed. All she would have to do then was walk on the road until she came to the store.

Mary wasn't worried now. She just kept walking and humming and looking all around her at the things of the forest. She carried on that way for what must have been the better part of the afternoon. By the time Mary decided to check the time, the sun was now at the edge of the top of the trees. She knew this was not good. It meant that in no time at all it would slip behind the trees. The sun always seemed to fall faster into the black of night once it got itself partly hidden by the trees. The closer things got to the ground, Mary thought, the faster they seemed to fall. She knew that once the sun went into the pink, and past the ground, she would be in trouble. Very big trouble.

Mary also knew that there wasn't enough time to walk back to her place before dark. That was her second problem. So she focused on her first problem, which was at least getting to town before dark. The draft that chilled the back of her neck was now running wild all through her body like the coldest of black tea. She had no choice but to continue moving in the direction she had chosen.

When the dark came, she couldn't even see the path anymore. She didn't know whether to stand still, keep moving, or throw herself on the ground and start wailing. Finally, the forest, or the bad medicine that dwelled in it, made the choice for her.

Suddenly, some kind of giant thing rose up out of the ground in front of her. It grabbed her legs and threw her down hard. Reflexively, she stuck both her hands out in front of her to save her face, but it didn't matter because she still got scraped and scratched by sharp claws on her way down. She hit the ground hard and just laid there. She knew there was no use trying to get away. She thought maybe if she looked dead, nothing else would happen. She hoped whatever it was, it didn't eat dead things.

After what seemed an incredible, dragging long while, the years and years of pine needles that padded the forest floor started to burn where they made a cluster of lines and dents in her skin. The thing that had brought her to the ground stood stonily still, seeming to lie in wait for Mary to twitch. Finally, she opened one eye and saw that the monster that had brought her down was a rock. The cold black tea that had been filling up her stomach, her chest, and her arms and legs started coming out as tears. Mary began to wail.

She turned over to let her wail carry to the treetops where Spirit might be able to hear her better. She wailed for Spirit to use its wind voice and whisper to Pa where she was. She wailed for the Sun to come back and light everything again. All the other forest things, which made night noises, now hushed. And, after a while, having spent herself on wailing and crying for Spirit to do something to rescue her, the cracks between wails, where Mary needed to draw more breath, began to widen. It was in one of the spaces of near quiet that a whispering voice got through to her, a whisper that said all this carrying on was of no use whatsoever. Mary stopped wailing and the other creatures that had hushed themselves during Mary's orchestral keening picked the rhythm back up. Mary tightly closed her eyes again and just listened. Laying there on her back, she dug her fingers into the pine-needle rug to hold on tight until she finally got the courage to open her eyes. Slowly, at first she saw a grey hair, then a yellowing crack, and, at halfway, she realized it was light getting in her eyes. She opened her eyes all the way, and there, looking right straight back at her, was Grandmother Moon. Spirit hadn't abandoned her. Her mother's voice came to her as if she was beside her.

Spirit never leaves you alone. A person just has to learn how to find the form that Spirit is taking. Grandmother Moon is the strongest form that Spirit can take for a woman. Grandmother Moon is always there in the sky, even when she can't be seen. A person might think that it is Grandmother Moon who goes somewhere else when it is really the person who moves farther or closer. As long as there is night, there is Grandmother Moon to watch over a person, and, if Grandmother Moon cannot be seen this night, then it is because something has come between to hide her, but it does not mean she is not there. She is always there, and although she watches over everybody, she has the most understanding for women. That is why, when the day comes that we pass into being a woman, we call it getting our Moon. Grandmother Moon is a good One to bring your problems to. She is the form that Spirit takes for the special problems women have.

Full and round and yellow, beaming right down on Mary, Grandmother Moon was smiling. She had been there all the while, just waiting for Mary to notice that she wasn't alone in the dark after all.

Mary stood up and looked around. Grandmother Moon was smiling so brightly that Mary could even see a glow on the leaves of the small plants around her. She sat down on a rock, plopped her chin in her hands and her elbows on her knees. What the heck was she going to do now? Light or no light, she was still lost, and to keep moving just risked getting more lost.

Suddenly, Mary remembered the piece of the willow tree she had put in her pocket earlier, mostly because it was sticking her in the leg. She dug around in her deep pockets until her fingers found the willow stick and then she dug a little more until she also found her knife. She might as well make a flute, she thought, and if nothing else happened to get her out of this, at least she would have something to occupy her mind. It was a good thing Pa had taught her how to make a willow flute, and a good thing she kept her knife sharpened.

She loosened the lace and removed the slender knife from its deerskin pouch. She cut the willow stick at both ends, to make it the size she wanted, and then stuck the pointiest end of it into the softest part of the stick. Holding the stick firmly in one hand and turning the knife with the other, she worked at hollowing out the stick. Pale bits of the inside gathered in her lap until all the stick marrow was out and had made a tiny pile in her dress. Mary knew it wasn't really marrow but Pa had said it kind of served the same purpose to a tree as marrow did for a body.

When she felt the stick was close to hollowed, she stuck her baby finger in the end and felt around for a bit more. Then she blew in it to make sure. A few more crumbs came out and landed on the pile sitting in the fold of her dress. She added to it by making precise slices in the outside skin of the stick, and then, holding the loosened tip of bark between her thumb and the flat edge of the blade, she started peeling. Mary preferred to peel the bark off with her fingers, rather than holding the tip of it between her thumb and the knife the way Pa did. There was something endlessly satisfying about picking at the edges until a fault could be found, pinching it between her finger and thumb, and then giving just the right amount of tug to coax the bark to separate from the wood without breaking. If she could get at least one good thick strip off all in one piece, it always made the chances better of it happening again. This time, however, just to make herself feel not so lonely, she did it the way Pa had showed her. After a while, the green smell of it reached her nostrils, distinct from the other smells of the forest, making it easier for her to put all of her attention completely on what she was doing, just like a person is supposed to do when working with a knife. She caught herself sticking her tongue out.

If you keep your tongue between your teeth and someone surprises you, you won't have much more to say.

Like a snake's tail disappearing into its hole, her tongue was back in place.

And keep your tongue far up in the top of your mouth where it is safe and it has a long way to go before it says something.

Grandmother Moon had moved quite a ways overheard by the time Mary put the finishing touches on her flute. She rolled it around in the palm of her hand. Still damp with the lifeblood of the tree, it felt cool and silent in her hand as it waited to take its first breath. Mary loosened the leather strings of her medicine pouch, spread its opening just enough to allow three or four golden tobacco grains to fall into the creases of her hand and wait beside her creation. She closed her hand around both, letting the tobacco speak the language of honour and gratitude. Opening her hand and her eyes, she saw that one small grain clung while the others fell away to the earth, leaving an elusive silvery trail in their wake. Mary blinked and could not see it again, so she filled her belly with the busy air around her and blew until she had emptied it again.

The forest stopped and listened.

Mary's flute made a good sound. It made a throaty sound like the morning song of doves. She let her fingers play on the holes to change the sound and make a tune. An owl somewhere nearby answered. Mary paused respectfully and called back. Some other things began to join in, and Mary lost herself even more as she concentrated on where her part in the orchestra seemed to be most perfect.

No sooner had she forgotten herself, when the last bits of loneliness had vanished from its place inside her, than pure terror fled back in. The sharp crack of a twig breaking cut through the purple air from the trees beyond. Unmistakably, something was on foot. Mary filled her chest with the air she would need for flight, and still clutching the flute, she placed the heels of both her hands down on the rock. She held herself as tight as a drawn bow. Her feet were ready for her ears to tell her when and which way to run.

She heard a rustling noise. A growling or grunting. "A bear!" she whispered to herself.

She looked right and left until she found a tree easy enough to climb, and in a flurry of wood shavings, she leapt and scrambled up its trunk until her hands found something with which she could heave the rest of her body up to safety. Grandmother Moon, still faithful, showed her more branches by which to get herself even higher. Her flute clattered on the exposed roots as it fell below.

Once high enough, Mary found a solid perch and stopped. She sat without budging but couldn't hear anything more. The thought of the owl she had just been powwowing with came to her mind, and remaining still, she looked as far as she could one way and then the other way as she tried to pierce the darkness. People never heard of a bear being able to get an owl. That was the last thought she had before she realized the thing had found her. It was right below her. It looked right straight up at her, and, low and behold, it was not a bear. It was an old lady.

"Hey little one, you dropped this," she said in Mohawk.

Mary didn't answer.

The old lady tried the words again, this time in English, "Hey little one, you dropped this."

"Grandmother Moon?" Mary asked in English.

"Grandmother Moon is in the sky above you where she always is. Me, I am stuck down here getting a sore neck looking up at both of you," she answered in English. "Now do you want your flute back or not? You and the owl were making a pretty nice song with it."

"Who are you?" Mary asked, her fear starting to drain.

"Who are you?" the old lady shot right back.

"Mary."

"Ehn, Nekuwa."

"Holy Nekuwa?"

"I have heard that is what some call me, but, if you want, you can call me Your Majesty since you prefer to speak the King of England's tongue anyway."

Mary was excited. If her name was Holy Nekuwa, then she was the old Iroquois woman Pa often talked about. He said she had taught herself to read and write but, because she didn't like the new ways the People were living, she stayed in the forest to live by herself. Lots of people were afraid of her and said she was a witch, but Pa said he wasn't one for believing what people talked about unless he saw it for himself, and having run into her in his travels a few times, he found her to be mostly just a very wise woman.

Mary found the climb back down a little trickier than going up, but eventually her toe found the first sign of ground. Holy Nekuwa held Mary's flute out to her, but Mary put her hand up between them. It was moments exactly like this that she got her prize for being called, in the words of her mother: *The only one that listens.*

She could hear Ma again.

You do not need a lot of it because you are not going to take it out to smoke it or chew it, but I am giving you the advice to at all times be sure to keep a pinch of tobacco in your medicine bag. You never know when you are going to need it for an Elder or a prayer to the Creator.

Mary knew she was standing in front of not only an Elder, but an Elder that Pa said had a good connection with Spirit. All people, as they live longer become wiser about the things of the earth and the ways of the People, but it's usually only the rare one that lives on earth and with Spirit at the same time.

Mary undid the tight laces on her medicine pouch and shook it upside down into the palm of her hand. A few grains of tobacco the colour of burned gold landed in her hand. She then caught one of the laces in her teeth, held the bag between her one arm, pulled it tightly closed, and let it drop back down to dangle from the lace around her waist. She looked up at the woman who was patiently waiting.

"I would like to call you Holy Nekuwa. Is that good with you?"

"Ehn, it is good with me."

Mary offered her closed left hand and then opened it to reveal the precious pile of tobacco in her palm. Holy Nekuwa stared, pinch faced and one-eyed, right through Mary for a moment before she made up her mind, then, making a cup out of her own left hand, she held it out just under Mary's. Making a funnel, Mary turned her fist sideways and let the contents sift into the woman's waiting hands.

Holy Nekuwa turned one palm over into the other until the tobacco was all in one hand. Mary watched. She held it up higher as if to let Grandmother Moon have a look and then shook it around a bit. Mary took a deep breath. The woman sniffed it twice. Then, with her free hand, she produced something she retrieved from somewhere deep in her wolf skin robe. She flashed a big toothy grin, seemed to do a little dance, and held out her pipe for Mary to see. Again, with expert finger sweeps, she gathered all the tobacco up into a tighter spot and picked it all up in one pinch. She put it in her pipe, licked her thumb, and pressed it down. She put the pipe somewhere back in her clothes and produced the willow flute again.

This time Mary accepted it.

"So I take it you are lost?"

"Yes I am," Mary nodded. Her belly filled with the warm that reassured her she could trust the old woman.

"Want to come back to my place?"

"Yes, yes I do," Mary answered quickly.

"Follow me," Holy Nekuwa said as she spun around with more vigour than her stooped body belied.

Without a second thought, Mary fell in behind her, leaving only as much of the purple night air between them as was absolutely required for respectability. The woman picked along on her way making huffs and grunts as she brushed away or stepped over things in front of her. Mary thought that, indeed, the rounded shape of Holy Nekuwa did look kind of bearish as they wound through the trees for quite a ways on a path that even Grandmother Moon could not light up because it was too thickly covered in vines and trees. Mary thought it must be Holy Nekuwa's secret path to her house. Finally, the light of Grandmother Moon splashed out into a pool as they stepped into a treeless circle.

Holy Nekuwa lived in a hard teepee! It was made out of white birch bark. Not that Mary had ever actually seen one before, but she had heard relatives talk of it and had even seen a picture once. It was much larger than she had ever imagined one would be and brilliantly painted with colours of red, black, yellow, and white.

"Don't think this is where I always live! Teepees and wigwams are for those itchy moccasined Ojibwe. I'm a Mohawk—the Longhouse People, but it is only that I sometimes get tired of all the rules. Don't get me wrong; people need rules. It's just that I get tired of it, is all."

Motioning to her teepee dwelling with one hand and the sky with the other, Holy Nekuwa declared as if to nobody in particular, "We are not going to be spending the better part of this night in there. Look at that moon!"

The blanket she had been clutching at her neck fell to the ground and revealed a ravage of black and grey hair flying all over the place. Then, with both her gnarled and clawed hands, she grasped her rounded middle and began to laugh. She coddled the flesh like bannock dough, and began a chortle low in her belly, working it up through a rhythmic guffaw into a wild shriek, raised her face, and made it an offering to the sky above.

For a moment, Mary thought Holy Nekuwa seemed neither man nor woman. She could see why some people might feel afraid. Then, when the last echo had disappeared into the black, Holy Nekuwa dropped her hands to her sides, and looked here and there about her place in bewilderment. She sniffed, and then stooped to pick up her dropped blanket and put it back on, this time just over her shoulders, and not over her head. She walked over to the crackling fire just outside the teepee, eyed up the one bare spot by the fire, and settled herself on the fat log that was sitting upright.

Mary shrunk into herself as if she could actually get small enough to disappear. She thought about rabbits—they were safe until they moved.

As if reading her thoughts, Holy Nekuwa said, "You look like a rabbit standing there, like it thinks nobody can see it. Come and sit by the fire and I will give you something to eat."

If a person is glad to see you and wants you to stay awhile, they will start putting something out to eat as soon as you get there, but then again, if you don't trust them, then you should not eat. They will know it is an insult, but what can you do? If you don't want to take any of their medicine in, then you should not eat.

"I'm not hungry, thank you," Mary said respectfully. She skirted over to a flat rock in front of the fire directly across from Holy Nekuwa. She lowered herself onto it, and the rock fit perfectly. She could even sit cross-legged.

"You wanna hide?"

Mary's chin quivered as she answered, "Yes. I admit it."

Holy Nekuwa reached behind her, keeping her hands hidden for the longest time and making scratching noises like scrounging around in the dirt for something. Meanwhile the pool of black tea began to churn again within Mary.

"Aha! Here it is!"

The old woman's face glowed as she teehee'd in the firelight. And then raised something high over her head, wound herself up like a spear thrower, and chucked it right at Mary, sparks flying as the flames licked it in mid-air. Instinctively, Mary ducked just in time for it to miss her. She heard it land with a hush just behind her in the dust.

"Do you not play anything with the other children? Can you not catch? I thought you said you wanted it?"

Mary, bewildered, looked behind her at the patch of beaver hide lying like a dead thing on the ground. "Oh, a hide," she mumbled sheepishly, then gingerly picked it up and slipped it under her on the rock.

By the flickering light of the fire and through the swirling haze of smoke around Holy Nekuwa's head, Mary could see partway into the open teepee behind her. It was loaded with books and newspapers. So it was true. She could read and write. Pa had said she went into town every day and took leftover newspapers back into the bush with her. He said that she was friends with the doctor just to get books from him.

After some time had passed, with only the fire crackling, an owl started up in a tree nearby. Holy Nekuwa pulled the smoke in and kept it there while she closed her eyes. Mary looked up into the trees beyond the pulsing circle of firelight to where the hooting was coming from.

"That owl is not from these parts," said Holy Nekuwa. "That is the owl you were playing with."

Mary shrugged her shoulders. She couldn't tell one owl from another.

Holy Nekuwa eyed the child up and down. She drew a great amount of the night air into her lungs, held it there for a bit, like it was an idea. When she let the air out, her eyes flickered with firelight, and widened as if she had found forgotten money in her pocket. "That owl is not after me," she said. "And I don't feel it is after you."

Mary cocked her head to one side. "What do you mean, after us?" Her face crinkled in fear and threatened to crack open with tears. Holy Nekuwa had tricked her into coming to this secret place, this place where nobody would ever find her. Mary was afraid Holy Nekuwa would tell her she was going to die, and that was exactly what she had been afraid was going to happen to her out here.

"The owl is the animal responsible for taking people on their three-day road. It is not uncommon to see an owl in the hours before your death. The owl doesn't bring the death; he only answers a call to what is already there. It is his gift to offer himself as a guide in the dark for the People. Maybe a person should be comforted, because they know the owl knows the way on the three-day road, and will take them there, so there is no chance to get lost. Maybe by the time you are old, and most familiar with your Earth Walk, you will appreciate the owl spirit who usually just sits there quietly, patiently, looking deeply into a person to comfort them, and to let them know he is there and ready when the person is. Look, that owl has not been sitting quietly. That owl has been talking to you. That owl must have a message for you."

"But I don't understand owl hooting."

"It seemed to understand your song. You have to take the owl's song inside of you and check for a feeling."

Mary nodded, wide eyed.

"What was your song about? Is it your Medicine Song?"

"I was playing a song my mother would like, and I wanted Spirit to take it on the wind to her ears so she would find me."

Holy Nekuwa, satisfied, sunk into her form and nodded a finishing yes, as she drew on her pipe and let silence reign.

Suddenly the owl swished overhead. Mary put her hand to her cheek where she could swear the breath from the owls wings still lingered. Stillness filled the air again.

Holy Nekuwa broke into her thoughts.

"Want to hear a story?"

Mary nodded.

Holy Nekuwa, cheered by the prospect, gathered her form up, turned, and ducked inside the teepee. Mary leaned closer to get a better look. But Holy Nekuwa's big behind blocked most of the view.

"Aha!" Holy Nekuwa pronounced from inside. She emerged producing not a book but a small skull.

Again, terror clenched its fingers around Mary's heart and squeezed so tightly that she could no longer pretend even a whisper of quiet bravery.

"What is that! Is that a baby's head?"

Holy Nekuwa looked down at the little treasure in her hand and stroked it smoothly, as if it still had hair.

"No," she said as she looked back up at Mary. "It was fully grown, old as a matter of fact, and lived a good life."

"Is that what you are going to do to me?" Mary asked, her voice pitched high with panic. Cut off my head and put it on a magic stick or something?"

"What's the matter with you, child?" Holy Nekuwa's brow furled, "This is not the skull of something I killed. I found it, already dead, at a time when I needed a certain kind of container. It was happy to give me the gift of something that had served it well but was no longer useful. And, it was a raccoon, child, not a person." She paused for a while longer and then added, "I guess I can't blame you. There was that unfortunate time when the Mohawk warriors got a little too carried away." She stopped to look at Mary, a deadpan expression on her face. "Don't believe it for one minute that Mohawks eat people anymore!"

With that, Holy Nekuwa lowered her bulk on her sitting log and removed a piece of the skull that served as a lid. She put two fingers inside and stirred a bit before tipping it and letting some of the contents spill into the palm of her hand. She put the bony container down beside her, focused her attention on the contents in her hand, closed her fist around it, and, leaving some space between finger tips and palm, she raised it to her face and blew as if using her breath to tickle a feather.

She turned and offered it to the child.

Mary, doe-eyed and panting, recoiled.

"Listen to my words. Even when you are filled with fear, let bravery take you there. Check your gut. Is there really danger? Now, child, listen! Whisper Spirit a question and blow it in here." Holy Nekuwa held out her hand toward Mary.

Mary looked into the old woman's face and, with the sense of warmth at the core of her stomach, saw no trace of wicked glee. So, she closed her eyes, leaned in, and gave her breath as she had been asked.

Holy Nekuwa thrust her closed left hand up to the sky, opened it to the moonlight, and then back down toward her face. Palm open, she sniffed the powdery pile, held it still at heart level, and let the magic happen. Through wisps of smoke, her form began to flicker from old woman to something sexless, ageless, and see-through. Was it a person or an animal?

Mary watched, wide eyed with trepidation, as the shape-shifting figure before her blew the pile of powder into a flurry of sparkling emeralds over the licking flames of the fire. Utterly stunned past her own fear, Mary did nothing to prevent the old woman from putting a witch on her. Sprinkling her face, and prickling her nose, the tiny shards of magic began to sting. She shut her eyes and tried to stop breathing so they didn't go up her nose anymore. When the stinging stopped, she opened one eye and saw that Holy Nekuwa was gone.

Not only was Holy Nekuwa gone, the fire was gone. The teepee, the trees, and even the night were gone. The rock and the beaver pelt were gone, and Mary found herself sitting directly on the ground, her fingers digging deeply into a thick blanket of arid, dusty earth. Dry straws of grass scratched her face as the restless wind pestered them, and she could see nothing else but a jail of grass bending to its whim and dark scrapes of grey above them.

She looked up. The sky was dark, even though it was day. It didn't feel like the middle of summer. It felt more like the cranky end of that season when even though there was nothing else to grow, the land did not yet want to give way to the sleepy chill of winter. No snow, no rain, no warmth, no freeze—just discontent.

Mary popped up on her feet and looked around to see where she was. She scouted all four directions. She started walking through the grass with slow and measured steps, giving snakes time to get away. The wind pulled and pushed her, whipping her dress around her legs, and her hair across her face, persistently influencing where she went. She let it push her into a run and she began to lope across the tall bent grass like a deer. Without warning, the field cracked with a gravelled and curled mud ribbon. It was a secret road. She stopped short, and the dust swirled all around her like ghosts. She hurriedly searched up and then down the curled road. Neither direction gave the slightest hint of where it might lead.

Finally, as the kicked-up dust around her began to settle, Mary could see a thin, ripe, peach-coloured line on the horizon. If that was the sunrise, she thought, then that also must be the east, and if that was the east, then that was the direction to home. She paused a moment to firm up her resolve, but just as she took her first step, somebody cleared their throat. She looked to the north of her, from where the sound came, and saw a scraggly half-dressed man with pointy ears crouched atop a big rock across the road. His hair was wiry, wild, and almost white, and his face deeply lined as if he were old, yet his nearly naked frame was youthful and well muscled.

Not a large man, he looked to be a lighter skin than her relatives, maybe half-white, and his eyes—they were like the precious blue stone that Maggie always carried in her pocket. He seemed to be laughing at her.

"I wouldn't go that way," he said as he leaped off his rock and landed with both feet flat on the dusty road. He stepped out of the dirt cloud that he had made and said it again, this time with even more mirth.

"I wouldn't go that way," he said.

Mary, who had never ever talked back to an Elder, asked, "Who are you? Why should I listen to you?"

"Because you're lost. That way will not take you home. You have already gone by your home. You have to go the other way."

Mary looked closer at him. "I think I know you." But for the life of her, she couldn't remember how or where.

"Course you do!" he said, but hurried on, without explaining, "Maybe I will walk with you for a while on this road. I have been here before. It's a hard road, but if you go the way you want to go right now, it's even harder and longer."

"Why should I trust you?"

"The way I see it, you're kind of at a loss, eh?" he said, looking around. "I don't see anybody else stepping up to the plate to help you out, and not only that, you look to be a pretty good size for coyote bait. They are big around here." After that, he started leaping around, springing from side to side in one or two jumps, and then running up to perch on some rocks. He called and waved to her as if to taunt and tease her about her situation.

Mary shook her head and put her foot out to take a step in her first intended direction, but something in her stomach stopped her. She looked over at the man. He was standing sideways with one hand over his eyes, looking impatiently to the west, the opposite direction to where she wanted to go. Mary could see more clearly the two points bobbing above his head when he jumped around weren't ears, but were actually the tips of two giant feathers tied to a wad of his wild hair by a leather lace. When he stood still, they hung limp on the back of his head like the remnants of a headdress made of turkey vulture feathers.

He turned around and caught her staring at him, "Okay, fine then, I'll go with you the other way too, but I'm advising against it. It's the long way, you know, and I would rather go the shorter way."

Mary just stood there, staring at him, trying to place where she had seen him before, searching madly for something, anything that would give her a hint as to why he would bother himself with her.

"So you want me to go your way but you will go with me either way?"

"I'll be your guide," he said matter-of-factly, as if Mary should have known. "I'll try to keep you on the right track, but you have to have a little faith." And with that he got excited and started to leap around again. "Now come on, let's get going! Are you going to walk backwards or forwards? Pick a path—right *now!*"

Without wasting another moment, Mary started heading west. The little man seemed to spill over with glee at Mary's choice, and, to celebrate, he did a dance in a cloud of dust for a few moments before catching up with her. Mary noticed that where the road had previously appeared bleak and without anything more interesting than dusty rocks and brush, there was now more detail, more goings-on up ahead, and overtop of it all was the dark blue-grey gather and swirl of storm clouds. "There's going to be a storm," she called to her frolicking companion lingering just behind her.

"A thunderstorm could be scary, but it also has a way of clearing the way for things to change from the way they have been for a while," he called ahead to her.

After that, they walked mostly in silence. Mary kept a steady pace and, for the most part, ignored the light-skinned man who kept a fair distance behind her. Every once in a while she turned around to see if he was still there, and, every time, she took strange comfort to see that he was still coming along, with his hands clasped together behind his back. Sometimes he was whistling and stepping lightly, almost dancing or skipping, and other times he was looking all around him with a far-off, dreamy expression on his face, as if the brown and grey scenery were a flower garden.

Suddenly, Mary caught a flash of something other than dead trees, dried-up bushes, rocks, and endless dirt. It was a broken-down wagon, lying there, lame from losing a wheel. Its owner had at least had the sense to pull it off the road before unhitching his horse or ox and moving on. Inspecting it closer, Mary felt uneasy; its one wheel was still spinning and complaining, as if it had only just happened. The wind, probably. She moved on but had to keep resisting the urge to keep looking back at it. The little man behind her uttered not a word about the strange sight, but she could feel his eyes hotly on her back.

She continued walking with her head down for some time, thinking how her Aunt Maggie, when she caught her walking with her head down, always told her not to. She was remembering Maggie saying "Indians are always walking with their heads down because they feel bad about themselves, and then everybody they meet thinks, 'Well, if that person doesn't even like himself, then it is for sure that I won't either.'"

Suddenly, out of the corner of one eye, she saw movement. On the side of the road, two coyotes were fighting over a dead wolf cub. Too busy biting, snarling, and snapping at each other over the carcass, they didn't seem to pay Mary any mind. Knowing instinctively not to get in the fray, Mary backed off to the other side of the road, walked a little farther ahead, and then turned around. The odd little man had stopped; he was just standing there with his arms folded in front of him, quite amused with the sideshow, not the least bit afraid. Then the air cracked open with a howl so sorrowful that it made Mary's chest fill with heaviness. The two scrapping varmints stopped their yelping and scrounging, perked their ears to sharp points, and then, turning tail, ran off and disappeared into the brittle grass. On top of a large rock, stood a glorious, but vicious-looking wolf.

Mary knew in a heartbeat that there was no use running. The wolf didn't seem to see her, so Mary held herself utterly still. She checked the little man to see what he was doing. He had changed nothing about himself except that he now stood with his hands clasped in front of him. He, too, was fully enthralled by the magnificence of the wolf. Then, in one fell-swoop, the wolf leaped through the air, down from her perch atop the rock, grabbed up the lifeless and torn cub in her mouth, and evaporated into the fading rustle of the brittle grass.

In the eerie silence that followed, Mary and the funny little man across the road just looked at each other. He shrugged his shoulders, and then started walking again, so Mary did the same. She could hear him start whistling his song behind her, and, finding again an odd comfort, she purposely slowed her pace to try to keep him the tiniest bit closer.

What was that song he was whistling? It was so familiar. Mary was trying to figure out where she had heard that tune before when Maggie's voice came to her thoughts again.

Keep your head down, and you might find money. Keep your head up, and you will see how to make it.

Mary snapped her head up and sure enough, in the distance, something else was happening. When she turned to look for the little man behind her, he was gone. In his place, a coyote gave her one last look before leaping out of sight. Mary turned to look ahead again and saw that, way up in the distance, somebody was walking down the road toward her. Another traveler, she wondered, or had the spry one somehow got in front of her?

The closer she got, the more the figure took form. It appeared to be a woman. Someone she knew. Dare she, in spite of the threat of a deadening disappointment, believe it could be possible? Mary fought the thought for a second longer until she was absolutely sure. It was! It was Ma! Mary took off like a cyclone, a frenzy of running legs and waving arms, up to Bertha's bosomy embrace. They held each other for as long as it took for all traces of disbelief to leave Mary.

"Ma! Spirit answered my prayers. How did you find me here?"

Bertha just smiled.

"Ma? Doesn't the light hurt your eyes? Can you see?"

Her mother smiled and nodded her head. She took her child's hand and started peacefully walking West again. Mary had questions but she was filled with such a sense of contentment and safety that she remained content to let herself be led.

They walked for a while until they came to a building with a pointed roof, and on top, a cross like the one Maggie had started wearing around her neck after she married the Italian. Bertha gestured for her to go inside. Mary hesitated, but her mother nudged her with both hands and urged her to go ahead, her radiant smile sending peaceful assurance to Mary.

"Aren't you going to come inside with me, Ma?"

Bertha smiled and just shook her head. Mary turned to do her mother's bidding and started to walk up the flagstone path toward the huge oak carved doors, one laying open for her to go in. Midway up the path, she stopped and glanced back, continued, and then, when she reached the threshold of the building, she turned once more. Both times she stopped to look back, her mother, glowing, simply smiled and, miraculously, waved to her as if she could really see her.

Mary, doing as she was told, turned away from her mother and stepped inside the building. Then for one fleeting second, she thought she saw rows and rows of strange, long, straight-back wooden seats, but this elusive image disappeared like it was only a thought. Looking all around her in awe, she saw that the building, which had looked so stifling from the outside, actually contained a forest. From the outside, Mary could remember seeing four distinct walls but, now, on the inside, it seemed unlimited by anything made by a person. It was as if she had stepped through a gate instead of a door, as if she had stepped into a Spirit place.

Above her, where from the outside it had looked like there was a roof, was the sky, interrupted only by the silhouette of treetops. None of this made any sense, but around Mary were all manner of lush and green things. She looked down and found herself standing on a path, much like the one she had followed into the forest the day before, or whenever it was. Birds were singing, and a cool wind was playing in her hair.

Mary felt as if she could almost physically touch Spirit in this place. She raised both her hands to the sky and said the prayer of thanks that her mother had taught her. She said it in Ojibwa so Creator would understand, and she said it in the language of doing business because it seemed like a place the Light Skin used.

Gchi-miigwech Gzhe Mnidoo	Thank you very much Great Spirit
Kina Gegoo Emiizhyang	For all that you have given us
Minnwaaa Ngoding Gii-giizhgag Giizis Gii binaabid	For another day of Sunshine
Gchi-miigwech Gii-miizhyang iw sa Bemaadziwin	Thank You very much for giving us life
Wiidookwishnang	Help us
Ji namaayang Gwek Ji-bmoseyang	To pray and follow the Good Red Road
Gchi-miigwech Gzhe Mnidoo	Thank you very much Great Spirit
Gii Miizhyang Ggitsiimnaan	for giving us our parents
Miigwech ge Binoojiinmnaan	and for our children
Weweni ji-maajiigwaad	Help them to grow up to be good
Miigwech,	Thank you
Miigwech	Thank you
Miigwech	Thank you
Miigwech	Thank you
Jim Kowum Gowah	In honour of all Creation
Miigwech	Thank you
Miigwech	Thank you

* All Creation Prayer: as told by Don King, Anishinaabe Elder and Language teacher, at Ojibwa language classes in 1995 at the Niagara Regional Native Centre, in Niagara on the Lake, Ontario.

The wind caressed Mary's skin and the sky warmed her face, while the birds' songs satisfied her ears. Mary kept her eyes closed and her body open, allowing Spirit to content her turbulent mind and restless heart. With her mind emptying, her heart filling, and her body drifting toward peace, she could have remained in this silent place forever, if it weren't for someone calling her name. When she opened her eyes to see who it was, things had changed again. Night had fallen; there was only the fire in front of her, and old Holy Nekuwa enjoying her pipe.

"What was the question you asked Spirit?" the old woman asked, as if everything was completely normal and Mary hadn't disappeared from in front of her.

Mary's body started to quake and sway as if the place she sat was a log on the water. Her eyes darted from one direction to the other, and still there was no escape. The black tea filled her body again and threatened to poison her heart in her chest and make her die.

"Put your hand on your own heart and still it, child."

Mary stared back at Holy Nekuwa in wide-eyed terror.

"Do as I tell you!"

Mary's hand flew to where the pounding was.

"Press!"

Mary pressed.

"Breathe in and press," Holy Nekuwa said, her voice softer now. "Now hold the breath in and pretend your heart is a bird caught in something, and all you want to do is pick it up and help it."

Mary held her breath and listened.

"Before you can take the bird in your hand, you have to watch the flapping and wait for the exact moment that you can get a firm grip that doesn't hurt its fragile wings."

Mary nodded.

"When you have found it, press and let your breath out as you close your hand around its pulsing warmth. The bird fits perfectly in your hand, but it struggles a bit," Holy Nekuwa soothed. "If you use determined patience, finally, it accepts that it is within something stronger than itself, and it rests. You can release it when it is calm, and it will fly straight."

"What is happening to me?" Mary asked in the faintest whisper.

"You had a vision."

Mary expelled her pent-up breath, but disappointment quickly filled the space it left as the full realization came to her that, although she was unharmed, she really hadn't seen her mother, and her mother's eyes hadn't really been cured.

"You put me in that dream. You really are a witch," Mary stated flatly, more than a little drunk and dizzy from her trip back and forth.

"It is true. I put you in a dream, but a dream different than a sleeping one. It's a waking dream. It's the kind you ask for on purpose. In the old days, some people would spend time in a sweathouse, or wander off by themselves to somewhere they could be alone to fast and pray. They went because they needed direction from Creator on their life. Some got help from the Plant Nations to clear worry blocks that the mind sets out. Taking help from plants is a fast way to get help, but some get attached to it, get lost in the place between here and there and never find their way back. They suffer, and this is the consequence of being greedy or lazy. I gave you a little plant help this one time. Now you have the experience of being there and knowing what to ask for."

"I didn't know where I was."

"Never mind. It was not of this world. It is more important to remember everything you can about what happened to you. What was your question?"

"I asked Spirit how to get home safe."

"Ahhhh, good question.." Holy Nekuwa leaned back and closed her eyes with satisfaction. "Now, close your eyes. You must take some time to ponder everything that happened to you in the land of Spirit so you can figure out the answers."

When Mary opened her eyes again, a brilliant smile lit up Holy Nekuwa's face. She jumped up and disappeared into her painted teepee. After a few minutes of banging and shuffling, she popped her head back out and said, "It is a good time to feast, and then we can go to bed. I'll get things ready for you."

Holy Nekuwa's form vanished from the opening again as if she were smoke in the wind and then transformed into a dark silhouette that flitted every once in a while past the opening. From somewhere inside, the tune of clatter and muttering, and things flying about could be heard, and the night seemed to stop and listen with Mary. She pulled her knees in, and wrapping her arms around them, hugged herself into the tightest ball ever. In so many ways, the old woman had struck her as being just like anybody's grandmother, only livelier. Pa's voice came to her head.

Sure enough, just as soon as you're not looking, she does something scary and makes you think she is magic. Way ho, but it is not magic. It is medicine. Medicine power is there for everybody to have, you see, but Holy Nekuwa, she did not ever have any children, a husband, or anybody to take care of, so she had her whole life to study it. She is not greedy with it. She shares it.

Holy Nekuwa re-appeared in the doorway of her dwelling and announced, "Okay girl, I made a nice bed for you," she said, her face alight with a toothy grin. "But first—" She reached inside and produced a bowl, clearly fashioned from the slice of a pine tree because it still wore its bark on the outside, that was heaped with cranberry-speckled bannocks. "They say smoked salmon is Indian candy. Do you like it?"

Mary nodded. The mist of the lemon balm tea that boiled lazily on the fire between them touched her face and filled her nostrils, soothing her and whispering to her in the voice of the little grey-haired man. *Everything is as it should be.*

"Good then! In the morning, I will bring you home. That is, if that is what you want.

This is where we go our separate ways," Holy Nekuwa said. She was walking just ahead of Mary.

The morning was brilliant. Mary, lighthearted and well rested, scurried to catch up. Mary recognized the place where, the day before, she had chosen the path that had gotten her lost.

"Aren't you going to go the rest of the way with me?"

"I have other things I must do, girl."

Mary nodded but then remembered something.

"I won't be bringing back Coyote's rolling papers."

"What! Do you expect maybe I should take you all the way back into town?" she said, her ageless eyes sparkling with ha-ha.

Mary nudged a stray stone around on the ground with her foot and replied, "Well, no, not really, but I was thinking if you came to my place with me, you could explain what happened."

Holy Nekuwa scrounged around in the folds of her dress and produced a hawk feather. Mary stared at it. It looked like somebody had throttled and beat the poor bird just to get it. Holy Nekuwa reached out and stroked Mary's temple with it. "It was your journey. Nobody else can truly understand another person's journey. You carry everything you need within you."

Mary's heart swelled with a surge of confidence, and the old woman tickled the child under the chin with her fingers. Then she took a few steps sideways and cleared the path for Mary.

"Now git goin'," she said, and she dappled the forest with her laughter.

Mary took a few tentative steps down the skinny path before her, but soon broke into a skip, the familiarity of everything around her continuing to build her boldness now that she knew the rest of the way home. After a few more skips down the trail, Mary turned around to wave one last time but, naturally, Holy Nekuwa was gone. The rest of the way back home passed uneventfully, even quickly, and Mary was grateful. Before long, Mary could see the sunlit doorway where yesterday the path had led her to the forest's edge. Mary decided not to hurry toward the opening before her. She wanted the special peace she felt to last a little longer. She meandered, taking time to scan the treetops, tune in to the winged ones' chatter, and savour the cool passion of her living, breathing host.

When she reached the edge, she lingered in a place in-between the world she was about to leave and the one she was about to enter. It felt like a delicate, invisible skin, like that which held the yolk of an egg. Before she took one step forward, breaking the imaginary membrane and straddling the two worlds, Mary turned for one last look. Strands of sunlight, alive with dancing specks that come out from Mother Earth when it is warm, reached down from the Sky Nations, perfect and straight, as if they were a message just for her. She tarried, just to lock the strangely familiar feeling, which made her blood simmer like Ma's stew, into a place in her heart and mind that she could forever get to again, if she needed to.

As soon as she stepped out from the canopy of green and into the late morning sunshine, Mary felt odd and scruffy. She became aware that she hadn't had her nightly wash. She had a nagging sensation that she was on a new path, but every time she checked her surroundings, she was indeed where she was supposed to be. She hurried her pace into a light run.

When the friendly outline of the tiny place they called home came into sight, she called out to Elizabeth and Porter, who were outside with Dolly. It was as if it had only been an hour or so since she had left.

Dolly saw her first and called, "There's Maweee!"

All three came running toward her. Mary didn't blame them for looking so frantic; after all, she had disappeared without a trace. She was just grateful they hadn't thought she had died in the forest, or that the Wiindeegos had got her, because, if they had, they'd be running away, believing her to be a ghost.

"Oh Mary! Oh Mary!" Elizabeth threw herself into her sister, held on tight, and sobbed.

Watching over her sister's shoulder, Mary saw Porter standing, swaying like an oak tree against a strong wind. His hands dangled from drooping shoulders, and he stared straight ahead, while Dolly pulled at Mary's dress from down below.

"Oh Mary! Oh Mary!" Elizabeth cried. "Our mother died last night."

In the echo of those terrible words, Mary fell to her knees, curiously needing no other explanation, as if she had somewhere, deep within her core, known it all night.

For the rest of the morning, and a good part of the afternoon, the three summer-darkened girl children, in their white cotton dresses, stayed on the ground clinging to each other, making noises like rabbits caught in a snare trap, in the long grass, while the sun shone brilliantly, and their brother, wooden faced, kept a watchful guard.

There was lots of room in the middle of the floor for the casket. Somebody brought wooden crates to set it on, and somebody else brought a pink and white carnation-dappled tablecloth to drape over the boxes, making it look like Bertha rested upon a pedestal of flowers.

Jake had stayed up night and day making Bertha's casket out of willow because, he said, "That was the way she moved while she lived with her People. Her body may find it agreeable as it returns to Mother Earth."

All around, the place was spotted with tiny fires where candles and lanterns had been lit. People drifted in and out, whispering and moving ghostlike between the dancing flames. Mary sat cross-legged in a dark corner, and looked up every once in a while to check the goings-on around her mother's casket, then peered back into the looking glass. Ma had given her the polished and painted tortoiseshell, with a cracked mirror embedded within it, a few winters back, because she no longer had a use for it. Mary imagined her mother, at Elizabeth's age, finding a discarded mirror and making a gift of it for herself.

She held the glass further out in front of her and watched herself as she combed through the glistening length of her mane. Mary normally didn't think very much about her hair, other than to make sure she combed it one hundred times every night, and also to gather up the fallen strands, being sure to put them, just as Ma had taught her, into the wood stove. Brushing her hair a hundred strokes was a way to learn how to count. Even though Ma cut everybody's hair, just a smidge every full moon, Mary's had still grown down to the small of her back.

Mary let her hair fall back into place as she brought the looking glass closer to her face. She studied her eyes. They were good eyes, because they could see perfectly. She studied her mouth. She hoped that she didn't have fat lips because people didn't generally admire fat lips. Her mouth looked sad, so she changed it into a smile and discovered she had a perfectly heart-shaped mouth that any boy would want to kiss.

She touched her face. Was it pretty? Pretty was fairly important to getting a husband but then she heard Ma's voice in her head.

Not as important as being a good worker.

Mary looked up. Ma was still laying there, so she took to biting her fingernails off and letting them fall and be caught by the fold in her dress. After she had bitten them all off, she fluffed her dress in her lap until all the fingernails were gathered into a tiny neat pile. Later, she would take them out to the forest for the Little People. She looked up again to see if she could catch Ma's eyelashes moving.

People were passing that baby—the baby that killed Ma—all around. They said Ma had told his name before all of her blood had drained out of her. He was to be called Jake.

At the door, Elizabeth stood close by Gramma and Coyote, who were chatting with people before they entered. They paid her no mind, and they didn't even bother to introduce her, but Elizabeth never took her eyes off of them. When Dody Clark's round body darkened the door, her arms were full. Gramma and Coyote talked her up a bit, and then started their act of being all worried that she was carrying something heavy.

They were flapping their arms like hens, "Elizabeth! Come over here and take this load off Dody and find somewhere to set it."

Dody singsonged back, "Oh it's for your family. It's just some food to save you from cooking for a while."

Then after Dody, a lady came in the door, toting a squalling Dolly in hand.

Coyote scouted the room until she spotted Mary. "Mary! Git outside and watch yer sister!"

Once Mary got outside, holding her fingernail clippings tightly in one hand and Dolly in the other, she could see that Pa had taken up his usual post under the willow tree and was working on his axe handles. Mary didn't know where Porter could be, maybe up in a tree, where he liked it best of late. She unclenched her fist and viewed the delicate slivers of nail.

"Got to take these to the bush and feed them to the Little People, Dolly." She started walking, still holding a squalling Dolly, toward the bush just beyond where Pa was sitting.

"Ho, Pa," Mary said.

Pa grunted.

"Gotta go throw these fingernails in the bush."

"Give 'em here to me," he said. "I'm goin' in later."

He let Mary sprinkle the clippings into the palm of one hand, and with his other he handed Dolly a whistle.

It worked. Her sobs began to soften to a whimper until wrung out and red-faced, she finally gave in at the knees and plunked herself down. She fiddled with the whistle, sniffled, wiped her nose on her dress, and fiddled with the whistle some more.

Mary sat down at Pa's feet and let the weight of her head rest against his knee. He put down his work, and they both sat under the tree in the summer breeze, watching the comings and goings at the house. Dolly finally curled up with her head in Mary's lap, her willow whistle still clutched to her chest, and drifted into the land of dreams.

A drunk, with a bottle in his hand, strayed off the path to the house and ambled up to them. Teetering back and forth, he produced another bottle from behind his back.

"It's a present there, Jake!" he drawled.

"Won't be needing it, but I thank you anyway."

"It's a peace offerin,'" he said as he thrust it forward.

"A peace offering for what?"

"Fer d' beatin' you're gonna get from now on," he spat. "It'll likely be the only peace yer gonna git."

"I don't have a taste for that medicine there, Hank."

The man's belligerence quickly broke into a silly grin, as if it had been feigned all along, and he popped the cap, took a long drink from the bottle, and then turned his back to them. Both Mary and Pa watched quietly as he staggered back in the direction from which he came.

"Who was that, Pa?"

"He's your cousin, but he's on a bad path so we don't have him around here. He's too sick with the drink. He's been that way ever since the Indian Agent took his kids somewhere and his wife ran off." He let the space that had been disturbed by the disagreeable man be filled back up with the song of the winged ones and the locusts. Then he spoke again.

"I'm going to tell you a story, Doggie. It's a story my Pa used to tell me."

Mary loved it when Pa called her by the nickname Maggie had given her. Draping her arm across Pa's knee, Mary nestled close enough for his smell to reach her nostrils. Pa always smelled like spruce trees. Ma had smelled like cooking, but if you could catch her sitting, and she wasn't smoking her pipe, you could crawl up real close and smell the lily of the valley talcum powder Pa made sure to buy her whenever she ran out. Everybody had their own smell underneath their tobacco smoke. Coyote always smelled like pee.

Pa had the manner of speaking that would make one believe, if they shut their eyes, that he was one of the Old Ones. He rarely had much to say but when he did, a person had to listen with their whole body. It helped to stop what you were doing, let your eyes close, and pay attention to the rise and fall, the shuffle and veering, and the places where he lingered. It was like a song that you couldn't understand the words to because they seemed to all blend together, maybe another tongue, but if you listened to it like music, it made sense. Pa could cast a spell with his storytelling.

"My Pa, he used to wander around quite a bit. He was known for that. One time he had a job somewhere around Kingston, working on building a canal for the English. There was a lot of work, and in order to get the job done right, they needed men who were known to be brave. The English have always been pretty good about coming up with the ideas and pretty good about getting someone else to do the work too. My Pa didn't much like working for them, but those were the beginning of the times when a man couldn't make his way by what he knew, which for most of the People was hunting, fishing, or warfare.

"On that canal job, there were some Mohawks, some Nish, and there were also five or six Frenchmen working with him. They had a shack the English built for the men to sleep in. The Mohawks would sleep in the shacks because they are Longhouse People—they're used to that—but most of the Nish would set up their own places outside. The Nish are a travelling bunch so they have a preference for their teepees. The Frenchmen, they will sleep anywhere, but that doesn't matter anyway, they weren't around this one night because they had gone into town for drinking and women. The Mohawks and the Nish would have liked to go but they weren't accepted in town so they stayed back. They stayed in the shack playing this card game the Frenchmen taught them, and they got a hold of a bottle of whiskey, so they were drinking too.

"So the story goes on like this: It must have been maybe two or three hours after the Frenchmen left, and they were really good into their game, when a knock came to the door. Nobody got up. They knew it had to be a stranger because a Frenchman wouldn't knock, and the English wouldn't ever be out on a rainy night. There were plenty of Indians at the table so they didn't feel any concern for danger. One of the Nish hollered that if they wanted to come in that they could come in. The door swung open, and it turned out to be a big fat guy that smelled of fish, pipe tobacco, booze, and at least three months of no bath. He had boots on up to his knees and a red hat and coat that had seen a better day. He stood there looking all the Indians at the table right in the eyes. The Nish that had hollered questioned the fat guy about where the bones of his father were buried. From that night on, every Indian that was there tried to repeat word for word what it was that the fat fellow said:

"'Yo! I am the long-removed, cast-off seed of a horny sea dog that landed haphazardly in the ample loins of a Beothuk shell gatherer.'

"Nobody there knew what the fellow meant by what he said, and they figured by the way that he talked, he had likely gone crazy from the drink, so everybody looked around at each other and agreed by the eyes, that maybe they should give him a chance. The real truth of it, they were just after his money. They were hoping that he was a bad card player, so they invited the fellow to sit down and asked him to give his name.

"'Aye, I was given the name of Bastard by the shell gatherer who choked to death from the seed that blew across the ocean on the wind of change and left me as an orphan.'

"Listen to what I say little one, even though it is a common thing for stories to change, depending on who's telling it, this one is different. All who were there that night swear on their hearts that it is true, and that word for word they remember everything the stranger had to say. They considered him to be a speaker in song but they still thought there was a chance he had some money to gamble. One of the men noticed that though he had the dark skin of an Indian, his face was mostly hidden by a thick curly black beard, and a mass of hair matted into long black ropes was held down by this curious feathered hat. They questioned him again about where the bones of his father were buried.

"'The bones of my father are buried in the graveyard of God's house far across the water, and all I have of him is his gold.'

"Nobody there had ever seen gold before but knew it was as valuable as the paper money so they asked him if he had some and if they could see it.

"'Why of course you may see it.'

"He slowly reached into his pocket and lay carefully upon the table a chestnut-sized black rock.

"All who sat at the table, except the stranger, traded smirks. The Mohawk, who are sometimes known to be outspoken, asked him if that was the only money he had.

"'Why this, my dear man, is worth more than the paltry fare you will receive for even four seasons of the lousy work you do here.'

"The Mohawk knew a rock when he saw one and also knew enough to let the stranger go on talking.

"'The shell gatherer, whose affection could not be won by my father, threatened that if he forced her to leave with him she would deprive him of herself with poison.'

"At this time, everybody was starting to get more interested in the way the stranger told his story, as if he was singing a song—more interested than in a card game—so they encouraged him to go on.

"'For you see, my father was a brave and innovative leader that would never forsake his charges. Some of his men had gone missing and he knew the wily shell gatherer's relatives must have been behind it, so he said he would let his men use their guns to kill them all if they did not let him choose an equal number of their own to go with him back to England as ransom. He said that he would bring them back alive in exchange for getting his own men back alive. The shell gatherer, very likely having the knowledge that that the white men were already dead, tried to pay him with this very rock I hold in my hand to leave her one true love behind.'

"'She told my father in secrecy that it was indeed the gold that her people had been hiding from the sea travellers that had come before him. Other kings and queens from empires in the north and the south had sent their men, but they all had been tricked into passing over it because it was not the colour they thought it would be.'

"'My father laughed at her and told her to keep it, but he was a devious genius and made a plan to keep this secret and come back with more ships and take as much as he wanted. Yes, my father, he was a seasoned businessman and he knew if he brought back a scanty load to his mother country, there would be a rush of competitors upon his heels, leaving him and his queen at a severe disadvantage. So, little more than four seasons later, he returned with a fleet of ships and men, bringing with him also the sorrowful news that her true love, along with the other three young men, had succumbed to the London fog.'

"'The shell gatherer accepted the news with dignity and turned away, but already her loins had borne the fruit of my father's loins. When he saw this, he said that it was just as well that the Indian he had captured and taken across the cold sea did not come back, for now that she had borne someone a white man's son, the Indian would not have wanted her anyway. He claimed the shell gatherer and child for his own and forced himself upon her again.

"'The shell gatherer was known to be a good woman, but she must have been a cagey woman, for she pretended gratitude, and showed my father where he could easily find more than enough of the black rock to take back to his queen. Not long after that, perhaps as a result of hearing the news of her true love, she took a strange illness and passed into the Spirit World. Her People pressed my father into taking me, and, though he was known to be a daring man, he was not equipped to care for a child, so he took four shiploads of the black rocks from the earth back to his queen and left this rock as a keepsake for me. I have no memory of this but the shell gatherer's people that call themselves Beothuk gave me to a woman with another child of her own to raise and told me this story. And tonight, this is the very rock I will gamble.'

"Now Doggie, it is hard to say if the ones that were sitting around the table that night believed in his gold or not. Some of the men claimed they knew better but would pay anyways, just for a good story, while one or two of the others said the fat man had put a witch on them. It makes no difference—the end is still the same.

"They gave some whiskey to the stranger, and they drank some more themselves. They all agreed to put their money on the table, and the stranger put up his black rock. When all was said and done, each and every one of them, Mohawks and Nish alike, lost every bit of cash they had. By the end of the night, after everybody was drained, the stranger got up from the table and let out a laugh that made the men's blood flow cold through their veins. But here is the most confusing thing of all. It wasn't until the stranger pushed himself away from the table and stood up to leave that everybody noticed he had one leg missing. He had not come in with a limp and he had carried no cane. So nobody thought to look down and see that there was only one leg. It is said that when he got up and turned to walk away, it was as if the missing leg was really there—but invisible—for him to use; and after he shut the door behind him, he let out a ghostly thunderous laugh that was so deep it kicked a wind up. It is said that the wind howled and screeched as if carrying the cries of the wolves and owls whose caves and trees had been torn up when digging the canal for the money-lovers.

"Nobody in the room could say they had ever seen the chains, but they all heard the dragging of chains and the thunk, thunk of a peg leg, as he walked back into the night with all of their money.

"To this day, they still talk about that fellow. The Nish said it was Nanaboozhoo, and one of the Mohawks who had religion said it was the devil. But they all figured it might have had something to do with the fact that they were helping the English dig up the bones of their very own fathers, and also maybe because they were all drinking the whiskey. My uncle, who was there because he travelled around working with my Pa, tells exactly the same story. Everybody who tells it is supposed to tell it word for word when it comes to the Pirate's part. That's what you most often hear them call him by.

"When the Frenchmen came back from their drinking, they would not believe the story, even though all the Indians were insisting they all saw the same thing. The Indians ended up not caring if the Frenchmen believed them because they all agreed that it must have been some kind of clown spirit, or a trickster, and the reason it waited until there were only Indians around, was because the Frenchmen were even worse tricksters."

Mary, in a dreamy state of mind that she always took on whenever Pa told his stories, started to focus on a speck that had appeared between the tree line and where she, Dolly, and Pa lounged beneath the willow. Emerging in the distance, getting bigger and bigger, a long-skirted figure made her way down the path leading from the forest.

"Look Pa! It's Holy Nekuwa!"

Pa scouted in the direction Mary pointed.

"Pa, isn't it?"

"Enh."

"Is she coming to the funeral, Pa?"

"She keeps a lot of the old ways. She used to do everybody's funeral, but not anymore. A lot of people want ministers and crosses."

"I thought you said she was a witch?"

"Enh, but witch is a word that comes from being around the light skins. Holy Nekuwa is somebody who knows medicine and studies it for the good of the People. It's a powerful thing to know medicine. It can be used for good or bad. If the power is something that can be seen, like a pill, then the light skins call it medicine, but if it can't be seen, they call it magic. We have always just called it medicine, whether it's good or bad."

Just as Holy Nekuwa rounded the part of the path that passed by where they were sitting, Mary tried to spring up to go meet her, but Pa covered her shoulder with his hand. Holding her in place, he said firmly, "You may have made friends with her, but at this time she knows she has a job to do."

Gramma and Coyote made way for Holy Nekuwa. Elizabeth didn't know what was going on, but she sensed it was something important; everybody had stopped talking. When she tried to peek around Coyote's wide body, her auntie reached behind with one big arm and held her as if on a short leash. Elizabeth knew enough to hold still. She couldn't see what was going on in the doorway, but all around the room everyone stopped milling about and began squeezing closer to each other in clumps.

Holy Nekuwa darkened the doorway of Bertha Stone's place, standing momentarily in the threshold, with the sun, like glory, shining behind her. She sniffed, looked to the right, to the left, scanned the entire ceiling over her head, and then the floor right in front of where she stood. She snorted a bit and ventured a couple of steps in, her round, soft bulk rattling and jingling in the hush and swish of the steps she took. Clutching her shawl to her as if she were quite chilly, she shuffled and stopped, shuffled a few steps more, and then stopped again, as if to think. Wherever she went about the room, shuffling and pausing, people made way, like the river does for a strong current.

At one point she stopped, straightened her rounded back, looked around the room and asked loudly, "Is any woman here on her moon?"

A ripple of head shaking and whispering moved through the modest crowd, but no woman stepped forward.

After she had made her way about the entire room, Holy Nekuwa approached Bertha's coffin. Keeping one hand on the wooden edge, she completed a smaller circle around it, all the while staying focused on its interior. She paused at the foot of the casket, put one hand upon its polished flawless edge, and with the other she reached beneath her robes, revealing a tantalizing glimpse of the medicine pouch that always held such mysteries. She pulled out a half-shell and lovingly set it on the spot where her hand had been and then dug deeper into the bag. The next item she produced—a leather bound bundle tied with something red—displeased her. She sent it back.

People became restless in their spots until finally Holy Nekuwa seemed to find what she was looking for. She took out two cloth bundles, one green and the other white. Cursing and muttering, she put one back, took a pinch from the other, and deposited it in the half-shell on the casket's edge. Carrying on like this for some time, pulling things out, mumbling or cursing, pinching or putting things back, she finally came up with a man's white hanky tied with cotton twill string. She cracked a toothy grin. She pinched some of it up, re-bound it, put it back, and then took out a small box of wooden matches. Striking a match, she lit the pile of medicines in the half-shell afire, and after letting the eager flame settle into a steady, fragrant ember, she fanned it with a feather.

"This is a smudge!" she declared. "In case any of you here today may not know it anymore."

Careless of any stir she might have caused, Holy Nekuwa reverently passed her feather through rising curls of smoke, then, after she had done the same with each of her hands, she guided the silver tendrils to put grace upon her head and eyes. With both hands she held some smoke captive upon her eyes for a moment, and then took some through her nose and mouth. Conducting more of it downward, she smudged her throat, chest, and the rest of her body, lingering longest in the place where her heart was. After a cursory scan about the room, she beckoned for Maggie to come forward, motioned for her to begin a line, and motioned the others to follow.

As each person took their place in front of the smudge bowl, some with more familiarity than others, Holy Nekuwa took up a place on the other side of the casket and began to speak.

"Listen here. I have to tell you that these are the four sacred medicines we are grateful for: Sage, the medicine of women, for cleansing; Sweet Grass, the medicine of men, for healing our stormy emotions; Cedar, the medicine of women for the healing of our bodies; and Tobacco, the medicine of men, to carry our prayer. These are the medicines that the Creator gifted us to help us in each of the Four Directions as we journey around the Sacred Circle of Life. In case any of you are forgetting!"

Holy Nekuwa took the time to level a piercing stare into the eyes of each individual in the circle around her.

"Bertha!" Holy Nekuwa broke the silence that had fallen with a lusty cry, "This is your body!" she pointed. "This is the box that your husband made for your body. Look inside at the things your loved ones have placed! Do you complain about anything they have chosen?"

A great stillness answered back, until, "Where is Bertha's pipe?"
Nobody budged.

"Where is Bertha's pipe and leather pouch?" Holy Nekuwa shrieked like a hawk.

Like water shattered by a handful of pebbles, everybody in the room started to search all around them on the table, shelves, drawers, and even on the floor. Nobody came up with anything. Jake stepped forward and walked solemnly over to the spot where Bertha's humble stool had always stayed, crouched down to feel around in the dark corner and searched some more but couldn't find anything. He straightened up and turned toward Holy Nekuwa, his face imploring her that he didn't have the answer.

This time Holy Nekuwa boomed, "Who has Bertha's pipe?"

Elizabeth felt something poking hard into her chest at shoulder level. Instinctively her hand flew to where something was hurting her. She looked down at the spot between Gramma and Coyote and there, in Coyote's gnarly hand was Ma's pipe, and the pouch dangling tethered to her thumb. She knew in a flash that Coyote had been rooted out by the magic of Holy Nekuwa, and now wanted to get out of the blame. As soon as Elizabeth grabbed it, Coyote and Gramma parted and produced her to Holy Nekuwa. Elizabeth, revealed, was holding the bundle with both hands, still looking down at it. Looking up, unmindful of the onlookers, Elizabeth wasted no time in stepping forward to offer the treasure to Holy Nekuwa.

"Here, I found it!" she chirped proudly.

"Child, place that in with your mother. Then there will be no need of her to come wandering back looking for a thing that she missed."

Elizabeth did exactly as she was told and then moved back to stand in the front row of the ring of people in the room. Now, in a voice rich with the depth brought up from the gut and past the heart, Holy Nekuwa went on.

"Bertha! This is your body! You are on the last day of your Earth Walk, and we hope the Owl is nearby to guide you on the next part of your journey. Please listen to what has been said for ages. You were once a young woman with the richness of life ahead of you. You once held a sacred position as mother of the Nation. Looking after your family was a sacred duty and you were faithful.

"We are now of one mind as you start on your journey. We release you for we know it is no longer possible for you to walk together with us on earth. We lay your body here, and we lay it away. We say to you: 'Pass on to the place where the Creator dwells, let nothing happening here hinder you, do not let action while you were alive prevent your journey, let not the things which gave you pleasure slow you down, while you were here many feasts were given to you. All these things that were yours, do not let them trouble you. Do not let your relatives and friends trouble your mind. Go in peace, disregarding all things.'"

Then Holy Nekuwa dropped her gaze to the people in the room and said, "To the relatives of the deceased, to you who were related to the deceased and those who were friends of the deceased, look to the path that will be yours one day. Because of this, watch yourselves as you go from place to place. Do not be idle in your acts or with your words. Do not give way to evil behaviour. One year is the time that you must abstain from unseemly activities, but if you cannot do this for Ceremony, ten days is the length of time to regard these things for respect."

Holy Nekuwa closed her eyes and waited for her words to pass upward. The smudge bowl showed no sign of waning.

"Now where are the belongings to be removed?"

Maggie stooped and picked up a bundle and handed it to Holy Nekuwa.

"Are these the things that only Bertha can use?"

"Yes," Maggie nodded.

"Are all other things named again as another person's?"

"Yes."

"Good. Then burn them with Tobacco by the place that we bury the body."

Holy Nekuwa let silence spread throughout once again. She squinted her eyes and cocked her ears, listening for any other problems to show themselves before the end of the ceremony of bidding the spirit to leave for the journey. When she was satisfied, she motioned for Jake to bring the cover for the casket. Jake fitted the cover on, and she placed the still burning smudge bowl on top to burn out of its own accord. She set the bundle of belongings on top of the casket.

"Bring the body!" She ordered.

Holy Nekuwa, grand with authority, led the way to the sun-lit doorway, and the casket was borne out behind her.

Outside, Holy Nekuwa stood to the side of the doorway, and motioning for the casket to be loaded on to the waiting lumber cart, started to greet, with a nod, all who passed through. The late-morning warmth bathed the procession as it filed out the door, and then, using her walking stick like a gate, she cut the line of people so that four people were still left inside.

"You stay with the house to make sure the spirit does not wander back inside. Prepare some of the gifts that have been brought for the family and their guests. Cleanse the house with Sage," she ordered.

When the house had emptied, except for the four people assigned inside, the group clustered in front of Holy Nekuwa to hear her. She raised her hand and shook three strings of shells to address them.

"Listen, those of you who are here. This body is to be covered. Assemble in this place again in ten days time, for it is the law of the Creator that mourning shall end when ten days have passed. Then a feast shall be made."

She turned to Jake, who stood tall in the middle of his children huddled around him, "I shall speak for the Speaker on the opposite side of the Council Fire, for we do not have one named. Cheer your minds and rekindle your fire outside. Go inside and rekindle your hearth fire there, in peace. Put your house in order and once again be happy, for darkness has covered you. The black clouds shall leave and the bright blue sky can be seen once more. You shall be at peace in the sunshine again. I will go now with the body and see that it is properly buried." And with that she took a place beside the lumber cart and motioned for the fellow whom she knew had always been a good friend to Jake.

"Farley? Will you drive this cart?"

"Enh," Farley answered and leapt up onto cart.

The relatives and friends waited until the lumber cart was at the edge of the flattened, cleared area before wandering back into the house, a few at a time. Jake was ushered back inside by Gramma and Coyote, but Maggie and Mary stood in quiet, holding hands, while the cart bore Bertha Stone's body away forever. The sound of the wheels became fainter, and, even after the cart and Holy Nekuwa had completely disappeared behind the hill, Maggie and Mary did not stop watching. Their eyes stayed fixed upon the spot at the crest of the hill at which they knew the sad parade would reappear before making the final mile to the burial place at the top, closer to the sky. Travelling closer to the sun along the ridge of the hill, the distant silhouette of horse, cart, casket, and bent woman walking beside, could more easily be imagined as the funeral procession of some other unfortunate community member. Mary thought to herself, she could be watching lazily from the front stoop on a summer day, while eating apple rings. Something to look at, something to ponder for a moment or two, but then again like the distant roll of thunder on a windless day, her bowels growled that nothing, ever, would be the same.

Suddenly, like a strange silent catastrophe, the cart lurched forward, tipped, and stood dead at an unnatural slant against the landscape. One of its three good wheels was left spinning under the high noon sun. Just then a wind kicked up, and a group of purple clouds moved in and blocked the sun from boasting its zenith.

"Come on," Maggie said, placing a firm hand upon her shoulder, "Old Holy Nekuwa will get that driver to look after that broken cart wheel. Let's go inside. That's the end of your mother's bad luck."

They turned to walk toward the house. At their backs, the sun burned at the edges of the purple line of clouds, narrowing them into puny limbs that reached in vain for glory until it burst from behind them like white swan feathers and was regal again.

A Visit from the Good Doctor

It was not yet dark out, and everybody was just sitting around the table, looking at the woodstove, waiting for dinner, when a knock came to the door. Maggie got up to open it.

Doctor Wheeler strode bluntly in and started talking.

"How is everybody this evening?" he shouted as if they were all hard of hearing. "I am guessing tomorrow is a big day for you people."

Everybody shifted uncomfortably in their chairs.

There was an ill-fitting space where nods should have been, but Doctor Wheeler, as though ill-bred, walked over to the wall and dragged a chair across the floor and up to the table. After he had seated himself, Gramma, certain that he intended to stay, got up and removed the black frying pan of sweet onions and potatoes from the heat of the stovetop.

"So who all is going to be there?" he asked.

Jake lowered his eyes.

Elizabeth shrugged her shoulders as the doctor's eyes landed upon her.

Dolly piped up, "I'm hungry."

Mary reached over to her sister and hoisted her up on her lap. "Shhhhh," she whispered in her baby sister's ear.

Gramma coughed, and everybody took note. She picked her pipe up and struck a match. Maggie walked back over to the table and sat back in her spot. Mary jiggled Dolly on her knee.

"I'll tell you this," Gramma started. "Back when I had my last kid, Old Holy Smoke was still around. Old Holy Smoke was around the same age as me, but everybody called her that because she had an old spirit. Everybody used to call her Healing Smoke before they really knew how good she was.

"Back then, you went off to a different place to have your kid, and Old

Holy Smoke would go with you. You didn't have your kid in your bed where you sleep like they do now. That's okay. One night, sometime after supper, I got the sign of the kid coming. I didn't really want to put my night in like that. And I knew it was bad that the first pain hit just when the sun was going down and the wind was kicking up. That was a sign of trouble. That's okay. I sent my second oldest kid to go tell Old Holy Smoke to meet me and I left my oldest kid to watch the other ones. When I set off, I did not feel good about the wind being wicked, but I could see that there was a red sunset, so I took heart that the next day was going to be a good day. That's okay. The pain got bad, but I was still walking around. Old Holy Smoke never talked too much, but you could tell if she did not like something by how she acted. She told me to stand still and she started to rub down on my back. She took hold of the kid from the outside with both her hands and started to talk it into being born now. I could feel her feeling around until she had a good grip on it and then she pushed it a little, all the while talking soft to it. Maybe it was afraid of being born. We both knew that it was better if the kid got born before too long.

"That's okay, it did not work. I walked around for the rest of the night, trying to get the kid to come out until finally a bad pain hit and I had to crouch down. Holy Smoke stood back and watched me breathe the baby down. She knew I did it lots of times before so she only helped me by rubbing the baby down my back if it got stuck. That's okay. I had the kid, and Holy Smoke set to work on it, but there was a problem. I had enough kids to know there was a problem with the blood not stopping. I looked and I could see in the sky that the night was getting ready to end. It is a time you can't tell what is going to happen. If there is a war then usually one side or the other will win. Old Holy Smoke knew this so she blew some medicine powder in my face. It went in my eyes, my mouth, and in my nose. I didn't like it but I didn't complain because I knew to trust Old Holy Smoke. Then she put some of it in a pot of hot water and made a pack. It stopped the blood. She made a couple of bags out of it and told me to drink it like a tea. She told me it was Shepherd's Purse, a woman's best friend.

"After Old Holy Smoke died, people started calling her youngest sister by the name of Holy Nekuwa. Holy Smoke was old when her only kid was born, and some say the father was nothing special. They say Old Holy Smoke just wanted to try something new, but I'll say something else. Nobody ever calls her kid Holy Jon."

Gramma got up and went over to the stove again. She removed a loaf of bannock, rested it by the black frying pan she had already set aside, then brought a kettle of boiling tea over to Doctor Wheeler and set a cup in front of him.

"Doctor Wheeler. You learned quite bit in that doctor school you went to, and I see a lot of people going to see you for medicines, ehn?"

Doctor Wheeler drew his chest in and flared his nostrils as he nodded.

"Here, you have the top of the teakettle," she said as she smiled and poured him the first cup of steaming and fragrant black tea. She picked up the chipped cup of white sugar from the middle of the table, but lingered before setting it down in front of him. "Or I have maple syrup put away in the cupboard for special. Would you like that instead?"

"In tea?"

"Our people like it quite a bit."

Doctor Wheeler scooped two heaping spoonfuls of white sugar into his tea and began stirring.

Gramma offered him the can of Carnation Milk, "Cream?"

He sniffed one of the slits that had been punched into the top and widened with a knife, and then poured a dollop into his cup. Without stirring again, he sipped his sweet tea.

While he was busy looking down, Gramma's eyes narrowed into angry slits that didn't match the off-the-cuff tone of her question. "Say there Doctor Wheeler, what was that medicine Jon gave Bertha?"

"A coagulant pill."

"Oh yeah?" Gramma feigned serious consideration. "A pill eh?"

"Yes, very powerful scientific medicine." Doctor Wheeler bucked up straight with his authoritative answer.

"Did the science find out how powerful Shepherd's Purse is in stopping blood when the Healer does a prayer chant to go with it?"

"A prayer chant is not necessary with a pill."

"Where did they put the pill?"

"Why, Madam, a pill is taken by swallowing it."

"Was she bleeding in the mouth too?"

Maggie and Coyote stifled the good ha-ha.

Doctor Wheeler huffed his exasperation, "No, the pill goes to the stomach, and then the digestive system conducts it to the blood stream." He rolled his eyes and sipped his tea.

"So I take it a person has got to think about these things before she has a kid nowadays. Maybe she should guess when the baby is gonna start coming, and not eat too much, just in case someone is going to come along and make the decision to use the new way instead of the old way. After all, it's not like a person who just had a kid can get up herself and go get something she thinks might work better. Does this scientific medicine know about how fast a birthing bleed can empty a woman?"

"There are people who go to school for years and years and study nothing else but the body and medicine. Of course they know a thing or two about haemorrhaging."

"Oh yeah," Gramma turned her side to him and snorted, "That's what I figured," before she took into her tea and pipe again.

A spell of silence fell, like it was the end of the story, or like when you want to give someone else a chance to say their part, or leave if they want to.

Doctor Wheeler squirreled deeper into his chair, feeling the back of his neck.

Coyote cleared her throat.

"That reminds me of when I had my last kid. I'm gonna tell you this. After my last kid was born, my old son of a bitch started spending all 'ees time drinking in the barn or at the bar in Brantford. He was no good to us on the farm when he was like that. Truth is, he was more good when he stayed at the bar and got 'ees ass kicked there. Then he didn't come home lookin' for a fight. It didn't bother me one bit when he got 'ees self kill't in one of those brawls. He was dead inside anyway. The whiskey used up all 'ees spirit and left an empty hole that he just had to keep filling up again the next day."

Doctor Wheeler broke in, "I didn't realize your kids had a father. Was he from the reserve?"

"Enh, all of his family is from around here, has been ever since their grandfather came from up north looking for a place to sell furs," she paused, took a puff of her smoke, and made everybody wait until she let the smoke out as she said, "none of my kids go by the name of Jesus."

Laughter passed around the table like a saltshaker, the doctor tried to hide behind his twitchy smile that he didn't get the joke, and then when it settled, Maggie cleared her throat and took the interruption as a good spot for her. "Well, I'm gonna tell you this. I got rid of my alcoholic too. He wasn't even an Indian; he was a shit-tempered Italian. He was all well-to-do in his business dealings but he was a wine-drinking bastard when he got home. He used to sit at the table and go from singing "Hava Maria" to pounding his fist on the table and complaining. That bastard complained about everything from what happened to him that day to what was not to his likin' in this house. One day he got to complaining about not havin' a kid and especially no son to carry on his name. He got his self so worked up about me ignoring him that he got up and slapped me. I'll tell ya, he never expected that I was gonna turn around and plaster him back. He got a good fight out of me that night.

"But fightin' him back didn't stop him from doing it again. One time I had to bust him over the head with a kitchen chair and hold him down with a knife to his throat. I wasn't lookin' good enough and he got a hold of my arm and twisted it until it broke, and I dropped the knife. So after that I waited until he had a hangover and kicked him out, but still my problem didn't go away. He kept coming back looking for either lovin' or trouble. So I got a dog. I got him as a pup and I trained him to bite alcoholics."

Doctor Wheeler broke the spell again, "How, Madam, did you train a dog to bite alcoholics?"

"Well. I'll tell ya. Usually you keep a dog out in the yard, enh?"

"There are some types that do," he said.

"Well, I did it different. I brought this pup into the house quite a bit. I would bring him in and love him up good, and then put him in a room by himself. After that, I would soak a rag in whiskey and roll it up tight. Then I opened the door of the room he was in, and let his little nose poke through. Every time he poked his nose through I would hit him on the nose hard with the twisted-up rag. Every time he went lookin' for me through that crack in the door I would whack him on the head with the rag." Maggie grabbed a rag from nearby and twisted it up. "I hit him on the nose like this, and I hit him on the head every time he poked it through."

Then Maggie picked up a wooden spoon. "After the dog got bigger I soaked a stick in whiskey and did the same thing. I hit him on the nose and I hit him on the head, not hard enough to leave a mark, just hard enough to piss him off. As soon as he really bit it good, I would close the door up again and let him have some peace, maybe throw in some meat. Then I would let him out and love him up. After that I never had any more problems with men."

Even Doctor Wheeler contributed an amused smile to the guffaws of laughter from around the table. "Is that a true story, Maggie?"

"Enh," Maggie slapped the table, "and not only that. I got pups from that dog and I sold them to a couple of other people who had the same problem. Works good."

Doctor Wheeler put his cup to his smiling lips but he had already drunk the last drop a while ago, so he emphasized the way he set it back down. A whimper from Dolly came on the heels of the echo left by the cup and then an awkward silence reigned.

Mary stroked Dolly's hair and said in Ma's tongue, "Gramma doesn't like him so we aren't going to eat until he leaves."

Elizabeth and Porter smirked and sat back in their chairs.

"Well guess I better get back into town."

Nobody met his eyes, but Gramma was fast to take Doctor Wheeler's cup away.

Maggie stood up as soon as he stood up, to help him put his chair back, and then get the door. By the time he reached the door, she had it open for him.

After she closed the door behind Doctor Wheeler, Maggie went over to the stove to get the teakettle and poured Jake another tea. Jake thanked Maggie for his tea and he cleared his throat. Gramma was still busy and couldn't sit down for the coming story, but everybody understood that nothing bad was meant by it. Somebody had to be the one to cook. Maggie was eager to hear the story so she sat back down in her spot by Jake.

"I will tell you this," he started. "It was a good day when Spirit blew a friendly summer breath in my hair and caused me to look up from my work. I was sitting at the place where I always sat at that time of day, and doing the same work that I always do. There were days when people were nearby, and sometimes they stopped awhile and talked to me, and there were times I didn't talk to anybody all day; but on this one particular day there were a bunch of boys nearby that were about the same age as me. They were playing lacrosse. Sometimes I would rest my eyes and watch them a while, but it was Spirit's warm whisper that tempted me to leave my work and turn my face to the sun, and then my eyes to the distance. The next time I looked back, the boys had stopped playing and were huddled around in a circle. Boys in a circle can often mean they are up to no good.

"One pure white downy cloud drifted across the sky as if it had been kicked out of its camp for being lazy and aimless. I watched the cloud, and I watched the boys, back and forth like that for some time. It wasn't too long before I noticed something else. There was a girl putting time in under the big old willow tree not too far away. She was right under the cloud, which had drifted and lingered before moving on. If you didn't look hard, you would not see her because she was lying at the bottom of the tree and took on the curve of its great trunk, maybe to be agreeable with it so she could rest. The tree's long fingers danced and tickled the ground, mostly keeping her a secret. But all of a sudden she sprung up. It was then that I recognized her to be Bertha Martin.

"Her body, I noticed, was still willowy, like the tree, but had become new and womanly, and it stirred me as a young man. At first, because of the expression on her face, I thought that she was in disagreement with me looking at her, but shortly I understood that she was really busy looking at something else. It was something she did not like. She took a stubborn stance, with her hands on her hips, and then she let a holler out.

"A couple of the boys took notice of her but soon tended back to whatever they were up to, and even tightened up their ring a little more. Bertha shot out from under the tree like lightening striking, stopped short as if to make sure, and then stomped up to the tightly clustered boys. I could hear her plainly demand to know what they were doing. They paid her little mind and stayed in a solid bunch. So she seemed to change her way to something softer, and I watched as she tiptoed over to try to peek inside of their huddle. They jammed their shoulders closer together so she could not see, but suddenly the circle opened and a great commotion broke out.

"The boys were laughing and pointing, and then one of them started to chase something that was hopping and scooting on the ground. Bertha Martin broke into a good sprint and was faster than the boy. He pushed air and spit through his clenched teeth as he tried with all his might to get himself past the girl. She was a big challenge to him. He could only make it to just behind her, where he promptly tumbled over her. At the very same time that he reached her, she stooped to pick up the thing that got away. I left my work to wander somewhat closer and see what it was all about.

"It was a sparrow they were chasing. The ragged bird scuttled out from between her ankles, flapped its wings to try to get off the ground and then gave in to hopping and limping through the grass. The mud-faced boy picked himself up and dove for the sparrow. He caught up with it, grabbed it up, and dropped it again a few times. Like a herd of buffalo, the others ran to their friend and gathered around. One boy shouted for his friend to hold the bird still. They were trying to put it in a pot of some kind. They seemed to want to put the bird in the pot and pour whiskey in it. They seemed to want to know what it would be like to get the bird drunk. But the bird got out of the pot again.

"The strength the bird used to get out of the pot must have been the last it had because when it hit the ground it just laid there. They laughed and made jokes that it was so drunk it was passed out, and one of them scooped it back up.

"That was when Bertha made her move. Again, like a bolt of lightning, she was in front of that dizzy boy and snatched it out of his hand before he could really get a grip on it. Then the group got very quiet and scratched their heads, because Bertha stood there with the panting sparrow in the palm of her hand. It no longer had the strength to get away. She called them bastards before she tended back to the tiny one in her hand. She petted it and cooed at it, but it didn't budge. I approached her. She looked up and said I could have a look. I was sad to tell her that it was almost dead. She turned on her heel and walked back over to where she had been under the willow tree. She sat down cross-legged, cradled it in her lap, and there she stayed until almost dark.

"I stayed with her, in the distance, on my rock, doing my work. I knew when it died because that was when she got up. I watched as she buried it there under the tree, and I waved good-bye to her when she left. I went home, but that was the day I knew I wanted nobody else in the world other than Bertha Martin."

By this time, the air was leaden heavy again with the sizzle and smell of Gramma's cooking. Maggie got up to set the table, and Gramma brought over the black frying pan piled high with a layer of potatoes and onions and another layer of sliced bannock. Maggie put the salt and a saucer of lard on the table. Everybody dug in.

For some time nobody felt inclined to tell another story, but then Gramma coughed.

"You know," she paused to chew a bit, "I think Maggie, you should move back here. You don't have any kids there to hold you."

Maggie looked up from her dinner at her mother, but said nothing.

"Jake is going to need a hand raising these kids."

Maggie and Jake exchanged glances.

Gramma went on, "You've been here helping him out since Bertha left for her Three-Day Road." She paused to think again. "It seems to be going pretty good."

Jake nodded.

Maggie's eyes stayed locked on her mother.

Coyote perked up too, but then slumped back into her chair. She knew she was beat. If she wanted to stick with Maggie, she would have to move here too.

Gramma continued, "I think you should stay on here with Jake. If you wanna shack up, then go ahead and shack up. If it works out, maybe after thirteen moons, get married in the church."

Jake focused on what was in his plate.

Maggie cocked her head, closed her eyes to imagine it, sighed, and looked her mother right in the eye. She could see how it might work, not only for Jake and the kids, but for her too. Jake was a good man, and those were hard to come by. She nodded, "Enh, I will go get my things after the Ten-Day Feast."

The rest of the meal was pretty quiet while all the members of the family gave themselves a chance to digest, but when Mary saw that Maggie was finished eating she went over to her and crawled up on her lap. She laid her head on her Auntie's bosom and listened to her heartbeat. Mary felt her Auntie's hand stroke her hair and stop at the nape of her neck. She responded to its strength and guidance by looking up into Maggie's eyes.

"Doggie, I heard you playin' a flute the other day. Where did you get it?"

"I made it!" Mary beamed and produced it for her to see.

Maggie took it and turned it over a couple of times.

"Looks like something your Pa taught you. Can you play it at all?"

Mary nodded.

"Why don't you sit up and play us something sweet?"

Mary accepted the flute back, but stared at it as it lay in her open palm whispering something to her.

"This song is called Forest."

She put it to her lips and played what came to her heart.

Gramma took her pipe, and Coyote and Jake took their tea in both hands and leaned back in their chairs. The other kids went over and sat on the floor around Mary, Maggie, and Jake. It was a winsome lullaby, and would have been a tune to drift off to had it not been for a slight clatter that came to the window.

Everybody looked up, and everybody saw it: a wolf, looking straight back at them from the window.

Gramma got up and wrung her hands as she paced back and forth. She had a bad feeling. The wolf was the sign of unrest in the dead. Something, she thought, must be worrying Bertha. She was likely not too happy that the baby wasn't with the rest of the kids, but she should know that Jake couldn't look after a new baby. It was possible Bertha didn't know that little Jake was over at her brother Wes's place where the Indian Agent wouldn't think to look. Oh well, Maggie would be here with Jake and the kids, maybe as soon as tomorrow. She decided to send Maggie after the baby right after the Ten-Day Feast. Maybe then, Bertha would feel sure that her children were taken care of, and maybe then she would feel free to leave for her Spirit Walk. It was never a good thing for a person to linger on their Earth Walk. They could become like a ghost.

SUZY CARRIED THAT kid around with her all day. She fed it; she changed it; and she fed it again. When the hell, she thought, would it go to sleep?

"Wes!"

He jumped like she had just snapped him with a willow whip.

"Where the hell are ya goin' you sneaky bastard?"

"Jus' gonna go over to Sam's for a bit."

She took a different tactic, something softer, sweeter, like maple syrup. "Ahhhhh ,Wes. You left me here last night. We always go together."

He mustered up a firm stand. "You are a mother now Suzie, you stay home with the kid."

"Stay home to drink, Wes," she pleaded.

Wes, with his back to her, and against his own will, took on the beat dog look and let his hand drop away from the doorknob.

"Where is the booze, Wes?"

He shrugged his shoulders.

She screamed, "Where is it!"

And he hardly flinched an inch, just blinked. Her tone lowered only slightly.

"Well then, who has booze? Where were you gonna go, Wes?"

No response, not even blinking.

"It's not fair that you felt like lookin' like a hero, took your brother's kid, and now it is me who has to stay home."

He nodded. He knew that.

"I think we should give it back."

With that, Wes walked over to the chesterfield and plunked himself down. Suzie put little Jake back in the sleeping box, which they had carried him in when they brought him from Bertha and Jake's, and went over to sit down by her husband.

They stayed quiet a long time, long past the room going dark and Wes falling off into a fitful snore. But that didn't fool her. She knew damn well that if she so much as went off to the can he would be gone by the time she got her knickers back up.

Finally, Suzie got up to light the coal oil lantern, and as she did so, noticed the kid snored too. Wes stirred.

"So do you have money, Wes?"

"A bit."

"The kid is sleeping."

"Thas good."

"He cried all day, so he will likely sleep all night and not be a bother."

Wes paid as much attention as he could but seemed to be missing what Suzie was getting at.

"Wanna go into Brantford for just one or two Wes?" she asked.

"Yeah."

"No harm in us sneaking away for a coupla hours while he's sleeping."

"Okay," he shrugged. "Let's go."

THE WOLF'S COAT was the smoky colour of the tree trunks, so when she
sat very still, looking on from the edge of the forest, nobody could see her.

"Continue to listen," said Holy Nekuwa. "The ten days of mourning
have passed and your mind must now be freed of sorrow as before the loss of
your relative. The relatives have decided to make compensation to those who
have assisted at the funeral. It is an expression of thanks. This is to the one
who did the cooking while the body was lying in the house. Let her come
forward and receive this gift and be dismissed from the task."

Really, it should have been Maggie who stepped up to the place of honour in front of Holy Nekuwa, but the family had to pick somebody else
because they didn't really want her to be dismissed from the task. They would
be needing her, more than anybody else, for a very long time, so they picked
the oldest Hill girl who people felt had helped out a quite a bit.

Holy Nekuwa handed the girl a store-bought apron, checkered with
the colours of autumn corn, neatly starched, and folded into a thick square.

It was the oddest feeling. Jake looked on, and then let his gaze wander
past the old woman and the young girl to the clear blue sky that wrapped
itself all around this world up here on top of the hill where he stood at the
foot of his wife's grave. It was strange to feel the sun on the skin of his face
and his arms, yet at the same time, be so deeply cold. If only there was some
other place he could stand. He shoved his hands in his pocket to make himself take up less space and the late summer cicadas droned on.

Holy Nekuwa went on. "Continue to listen, I say. Jake. You have been a
good husband to Bertha and you thought you would walk the earth together
for the rest of your days, but no person can always know how long his journey here will be. Ten days ago, she saw you at her casket and she knew how

much you missed her, but we told her to move on to the world of Spirit. Now you too must move on with your own journey. Today you must say goodbye. You gave each other good company so you both would not have to be alone. Do not hold each other when you cannot give each other the same company. Her journey does not concern you, and your journey does not concern her. She does not expect that you will suffer loneliness and hard times for the rest of your days. You have been a good husband but you are still a father. The Wampum tells us that you abstain from marrying another woman for the period of four seasons but if you cannot, because you have practical matters to consider, you may take another wife as soon as the opportunity presents itself. Now the time is at hand for much attention to be paid to not saying the name of the deceased, lest she be called unnecessarily from her natural path. Now it is said how it is done."

Holy Nekuwa shook strings of snail shells over the gravesite and turned away. All who were present also turned away, and then Holy Nekuwa started out in front and led them to where the path took them away from the site and back to the main road. It was acceptable to start up conversation once they were out of the burial grounds.

As soon as the path opened up to the main road the group reformed from single file to a cluster. Pa, Porter, Elizabeth, Dolly attached to Mary, Gramma, Coyote, and Maggie, and Bertha's dependable friends, all following Holy Nekuwa like a dog's bushy tail. The women had dressed up in the clothes they had last used when the Minister wanted photographs taken. Mary, with Dolly in tow, caught up to Maggie and took her hand. Maggie was busy talking to Gramma so Mary just tagged along without saying anything. Mary had never seen any of her family so dressed up before, but Maggie was the prettiest.

Maggie's sun-darkened skin compared favourably to the ivory coloured full-length dress she was wearing. It was only the third time she had ever been out of her standard black pants and grey shirt. The Italian had bought her the dress to get her photograph taken. Maggie said it would also do to get married in. It had tea-stained hand-embroidered lace around the collar, waist, and hem, but the edges of the hem were grey from dragging in the dirt. The Italian had told her over and over again that ladies walked around holding their skirts up so they didn't "getta da mud on it," but Maggie had too much she had to do with her hands. The Italian dress, an arrangement of satin panels sewn together in the most perfect hand stitching, lay tapered over Maggie's curves before cascading to the ground. She gave a squeeze to the child's hand in hers and then sneaked in a quick Maggie wink.

As they rounded the base of the hill, the twittering group of women who had been Bertha's friends bade goodbye before carrying on their way further down the road. With Holy Nekuwa still out in front, it was not long before Bertha's fledgling flock broke off to a less-beaten path that led them back to their house. At the point where the path narrowed to a single line again to cut through the trees, they came upon Doctor Wheeler's horse and wagon.

Gramma snorted and took up the lead. "No fear a' the Holy Ghost wandering back to the house with that fella takin' up post," she spat.

Inside, Doctor Wheeler was munching like a rabbit on the biscuits Maggie had left on the table to cool before leaving in the morning. Now, he put the biscuit down, poked at his glasses between his eyes like he always did, and straightened up in the chair. He rubbed his fingers together and then both his hands to clear them of the crumbs before clearing his throat to speak.

"Something unfortunate has occurred, Jake. I am afraid I have some more bad news for you."

Jake wavered as he waited for the hit.

"Your son, Jake Jr. has passed away."

Jake blinked in slow motion.

"Pneumonia, Jake. They found him this morning. He must have died sometime in the night."

The family stood still where they were, stared at Doctor Wheeler, and tried to digest the news.

"There wasn't anything could be done. He will be with Bertha now," the doctor feebly offered.

Everyone looked away at the mention of their dead relative's name. Nobody uttered a word. Nobody even coughed or cleared their throat. They exchanged fleeting glances, shifting back and forth until their backs were mostly to him. It was a silent agreement they made to try to make him feel itchy to leave.

It worked. "Well, I guess I better go," he said.

Maggie moved swiftly and held the door wide for him.

In the awkward space left by the echo of Doctor Wheeler's wagon and complaining horse, the cicadas struck up their chorus again and filled it.

Gramma put her handbag down and took her place at the head of the table. She began right away, "Wes and Suzy musta let that baby die. Dody tol', me today she saw them raisin' hell last night and the kid wasn't with 'em."

"Gramma?" Mary spoke up.

"Yes?"

"I think I saw the same wolf today, the same wolf as we saw last night in the window. It was watching from the trees at the burial grounds. What do you s'pose that means?"

"I would say it means we better get Maggie moved in here." She turned to Coyote and Maggie at her right and continued, "We will go today and get Maggie's things. Coyote and I will stay there, and you can come back." She turned to Elizabeth, "You girl," she said. "You will watch over these kids and cook for your Pa until we get back tomorrow night."

With that, everybody turned to go about their business. Maggie, Gramma, and Coyote put a few things together and left within the hour. Elizabeth and Mary started cleaning up. Mary ended up doing most of the work because, as usual, Elizabeth was bigger than her and could make her. Ma always said she was a lazy one. Jake left without a word to go sit under the willow tree and work on his axe handles, and Porter wandered off into the bush somewhere. By the time supper came and went, nobody really had too much to say to each other so bedtime was pretty early.

The next day dawned grey and cranky, but it was no matter. Everyone knew Maggie would be back by the end of the day and fill the house with something good to smell.

By noon the wind was fierce, whipping up against the house, and making the Wiindeegos hiss and cackle. This west wind, the youngest and wildest of the four wind brothers, often brought trouble with him. Pa said he could feel a thousand drops of rain in his bag of tricks. Nobody could do anything outside so they closed the shutters and lit the coal oil lanterns. Pa built a fire and told Elizabeth to cook. Then he took to pacing from the one end of the place to the other, while the wind just kept blowing the day away, and along with it any hope of Maggie getting back sooner rather than later.

Just about the time the sun would normally remind people to head home, Pa had finally settled down into whittling a pair of basket-shaped earrings from an apricot pit, and the girls were making supper, the door burst open and let the wind come howling through house, just as if Nanaboozhoo was arriving. Brittle leaves and dirt blew in and swirled around the table and chairs. Pa told Porter it was a bad sign, sighed, then threw the pit into the fire, stood up, and took back to pacing.

Maybe, if someone had said "Boozhoo" out loud and offered some tobacco, nothing else would have happened. That's what Ma would have done. But no one did, and it was only a short time after dark, when the five of them were sitting down to a late bite to eat, that a rat-a-tat-tat knock came to the door. It reminded Mary of whenever Maajjii Brown sent her oldest niece over to get back something Elizabeth had borrowed. There was no way it was Maggie—she would never knock unless her arms were too full, and even then, not like that. Maggie would just get Coyote or Gramma to open the door, unless she didn't bring them, but even then, Maggie would have just hollered.

Elizabeth got up and answered it.

A man and a woman, officious and authoritative in their buttoned-to-the-neck dark blue suits, stood there. The woman had white gloves and a pill-shaped hat to match her suit. Neither one wore smiles, nor waited to be invited, before they took bold steps into the house.

Mary had a bad feeling. Pa had risen from his chair, intending to walk over and greet them, but they were swift in reaching the table and seating themselves on either side of him, one in Ma's empty chair and the other in Elizabeth's. Pa sat back down and pushed his food aside. Elizabeth began gathering the bowls of soup from the table and placing them on the shelf, away from the strangers, then she wandered over to the wood stove, exposing her open palms to the heat.

"Mr. Stone, allow me to introduce myself and my partner," the man gestured across the table. The woman half closed her eyes and cracked the leanest of smiles, as she nodded back in his direction. Then as if a mare's foot stuck in the mud, her lips sucked back into a deeply lined starburst pucker.

Mary could imagine if Gramma had been there she would have later commented that "People will always get the face they deserve."

"We are Agents from Indian Affairs," she said. "We were informed of the unfortunate event of Bertha Stone's early demise, and the subsequent death of her infant. We are inquiring as to the well-being of your children. We have conducted a search of our records and determined that neither you nor Bertha Stone have registered any of the children in this household."

She waited.

Pa stayed still, like a deer in the woods.

"This is necessary, for our records. Are they all your children, Mr. Stone?"

Pa's eyes darted to and fro, but he failed to muster up an answer.

"How many?" the lady's mouth curled and her voice stung as if she held, something pinched between her forefinger and thumb that was dirty and repugnant.

"How many?" the man boomed in a loud voice.

Pa laid his eyes, one at a time, on each of his children in the room.

"Are there anymore?" the loudmouth man demanded.

Pa shook his head.

"Where do they go to school?" The lady had taken out something to write down all of Pa's answers. "What are their ages?" she said before he could answer the first question.

"Their mother speaks five languages. She was giving them the teachings."

The lady raised her voice, while scanning all the faces around the table. It seemed she had the idea that Pa had trouble understanding.

"Do you speak English?"

Pa cast his eyes to the ground.

"Do—these—children—speak—English?" she tried again, using the same halting tone.

Pa spoke slower, "Their mother and I give them the teachings of how to feed the family and keep a good house."

She turned to her partner, "He is muttering and I can't tell what he is saying."

It was true, some people said Pa muttered, but Mary always understood him perfectly, and besides, Pa never really had much to say, unless he was telling a story. That was the only time he seemed to really come alive.

The lady stood up, and as soon she stood up, the man stood up, until both were towering over Pa. The man stared directly into Pa's face, and the woman placed both her hands on her hips.

"So!" she scolded, "These children are not in school, you do not know their ages, you have not registered them, they are not learning the King's English, and furthermore, they do not have a mother!"

Pa stood up to their height so they could hear him better. The man took it as a sign Pa was looking for a fight and grabbed Pa by the arm. He led him over to the woodstove.

"We are authorized by the Indian Affairs Act to apprehend these children and install them in an appropriate Indian Residential Institute," the lady seemed to be reciting to no particular person in the room. "For their own good," she added.

Then, just like earlier, when the wind had barged its way through the front door and whipped its room into a flurry, the worst kind of fracas broke out. Elizabeth started to scream and ran to cling to Porter. The lady and the man rushed over to them, each taking one, and began pulling and tugging to get them apart. Elizabeth wrapped her legs and arms around Porter tighter, and the lady's hat fell to the floor as she struggled with all of her might. Ghost-like, and filled with silent terror, Mary stepped out of it all, moving backwards until her shoulder touched the wall in the darkest corner of the place. While all of this was going on, Dolly walked over to stand in the middle of the floor, opened her mouth as wide as she could, and stood there squalling from the depths of her belly. Her face was knotted into a tight fist of fear and confusion as she held out both her arms to the air waiting for somebody to scoop her up and smother her nightmare in their bosom. Mary understood only one thing. These people, whoever they were, were going to take them away somewhere, and Pa was just standing there like a deer struck still before a poised bow at the moment just before its own death.

Finally, the lady, whose hair had sprouted loose from its pins, looked like a crazed woodpecker, had managed to pry Elizabeth away from Porter. Elizabeth turned and shoved. The lady landed directly on her own hat and flattened it. The man, taking things into his own hands, re-positioned himself midway between Porter and Elizabeth, where their hands and fingers clung like woody vines that had grown around each other.

He roared in a voice like thunder, "Let go!"

The man looked like a giant next to Porter. He grabbed him and yanked on the boy's skinny body until he had possession of it. The lady recovered herself and rushed to take Elizabeth roughly by the arm.

She too, shook Elizabeth about.

"You violent little heathen! Straighten out this minute!" she screeched, shoving and yanking, as if she thought she could rattle Elizabeth into submission.

Meanwhile, the man led Porter to the door, and opening it, planted his charge in its archway. The rain-laden wind rushed in past Porter, and raged through the house. Porter stood meekly in the doorway and let the rain soak his back.

"Miss Wright, bring that she-savage to the wagon, and I will stay with them both while you come back in and apprehend the infant and the other one!"

For a moment, some manner of serenity asserted itself, crystal clear, and precise in the house. The three remaining members of the family just stood there, blinking at each other.

Finally, Mary said, "Why, Pa?"

With a face that said he understood everything she meant by the question, he answered.

"They are the authorities."

PEOPLE LIKED TO tell Mary their problems. That's pretty much why nobody ever thought anything of Mayor Tom Dunsby's daily march down Main Street, Monday through Friday, at precisely 5:04 p.m. Four minutes. That was exactly how long it took him to lock up the oak door of City Hall, get down the steps, and walk three doors down to the Jackson Diner. Saturdays and Sundays, his mother cooked for him, but every weekday, except on holidays, the bell hanging from a cotton string tied to the door handle of Jackson Diner's wooden screen door, could be counted on to announce the arrival of its town mayor. Because he was the mayor, the booth located at the far end of the diner was always open. Everybody in town knew it was his favourite booth, and if a stranger happened into it, Mary would take care of it.

Buttoned up in his dark brown Thursday suit, Tom stepped inside. The freshly painted white door snapped with a wooden clap behind his back, but the cry of the bell was lost somewhere between the clank and rattle of dishes being piled on the cart and a fist-pounding debate the cook was having with two guys who were sitting at the counter. The night before, Marlene had made Fred tighten the door spring before she painted it, so the mayor was startled a bit by its new vigour. He checked to see if Mary had heard him arrive, but she had not, so he removed his hat and headed off for his booth with a scowl beginning to set on his face.

He seated himself and then scouted the room once again for Mary. There she was, back pin straight, pad in hand, perfectly white apron and shoes, so poised and complete with her rose-red smile, waiting by the Fletchers' table for their order. He wished he could see her take that crisp white cap off and let her hair unfurl like exotic blue-black silk over her shoulders. He gave himself a shake, took his jacket off, and stood up to hang it over the hooked end of the high-backed booth.

Mary finished taking the Fletchers' order, walked it over to the kitchen window, clothes-pinned it to the line, and called it out to Fred. Her uniform, pale blue like the diner curtains, but without the ruffles, was exactly her colour, coincidently just like last year's yellow was exactly her colour. But then again, to Mayor Dunsby, any colour was Mary's colour. He looked down, as the dull spot, where he had missed polishing this morning on his otherwise shiny black shoes, caught his eye.

It was obvious to everyone that the Mayor had a crush on Mary. But nobody thought anything of it because, for one thing, the Mayor was single, and the second thing was, Mary was easy to talk to. Everybody liked to tell Mary their problems. So the Mayor having a crush on Mary was perfectly understandable, maybe even to his British-born dear mother.

Mary arrived at his table with her tray and a brilliant smile. Balancing the tray expertly on her fingertips, she removed his steaming hot teapot, his cup and saucer, followed by his tea biscuit and cutlery, and placed them in front of him. She had noticed him after all.

He lifted the golden top of the biscuit off, exposing the buttery glob already melting inside, and with his knife he spread it more evenly around on top and bottom, while Mary chatted with him, "You didn't sleep well last night, Mr. Dunsby?"

She called him Mayor Dunsby when he had first come in, but when it was only the two of them, they were like old friends, so she called him Mr. Dunsby. She had a cup of tea with him most every night when she went off shift. He would wait to have his pie until she could make herself a cup of tea and sit down with him before she went home.

Mr. Dunsby, Mary believed, was a good man. She never lost memory of good things done for her, and so after he had helped her get that cute apartment over top of the post office, she had found herself becoming the only person he could talk to, and whose opinion she appreciated as being fresh and honest. It was important for the man who ran the whole city of Jackson to have a confidante that he could trust—someone who was a listener, not a gossiper.

"Yes indeed, I had a terrible night last night. You can always tell about people, Mary Stone, now can't you? "

Normally a girl would find this a good time to let the pink rise in her face and look at the floor for a good while, but Mary was not given to con-trived blushing. She laughed from her belly in the laugh that filled Jackson Diner with just that much more sunshine. She never got ashamed of things she liked about herself.

"That's right, I can tell about a person just by looking at them, if they are happy or despondent, or if they are heated up about something. People show it all over themselves but mostly in their face. And if they try to hide it in their faces, it'll come out all over 'em in how they move and where they go with themselves."

Mary's pronouncements often brought a twinkle to Mayor Dunsby's eye. Like a tiny star, it could stay hidden all day in his poker-faced dealings with all manner of folk, Monday through Friday, holidays excepted, until shortly after 5:04 p.m., when Mayor Dunsby went off duty for a bit.

"It comes out all over them, you say?"

"It comes out all over them." she repeated, only louder this time. "I'm telling you, a person will get up in the morning and pick clothes that tell how they are feeling. Then they walk around all day and carry their body to match. Like if they're fuming about something, they will be all rammy with the way they come into the room and start talking before looking around to see how things are. They can smile their faces off, and you as the person watching, have to remember that your eyes might trick you. But, if you take time, you will notice that your body will tell. If you take time to notice, you will feel your body start getting a little twitchy inside as if it might have to fight someone or something. If you are around those people all the time, you'll find they start to get on your nerves."

Mayor Dunsby always got a big kick out of the way Mary came out with things. What might take a year of university research and a twenty-page dry read, could be said by Mary Stone in one sharp sentence.

"Hmmmmm," he rubbed his chin. "I will surely have to keep that in mind. I'll have the special, please."

It was Thursday, "Hot Hamburger Open Face with Gravy Plate" night. Mary didn't bother getting into the particulars of "Gravy on the side, Sir? Fries or mashed?" because she knew exactly what he wanted to eat, and exactly how he liked it. She left him to his newspaper and tended to seating the other customers before putting the order in. Thursday was payday at the Apitipi Pulp and Paper Co. They made it that way so the wives could do their groceries on Friday before the husbands could do away with too much of the money. With groceries running out, and the husbands getting sent home from the bar at suppertime, Thursday was a pretty busy day.

As the dinner hour was drawing to a close, the Mayor, just like everybody else in the diner, reflexively craned his neck to check out whom the front door bell had just hailed in. It was Sophie, the night shift waitress. That was his cue to put his paper aside. Mary would be going off shift soon. He could never predict what kind of pie she was going to bring over. He liked it that way. And all because a couple of years ago, he had let a sixteen-year-old kid talk him into trying something different.

He let his mind wander back to the Friday night he arrived at the Jackson Diner for his usual Fish and Chips Special. Back then, he came to the diner only once a week, on Fridays, for their Fish and Chip Special. He recalled stopping short in the doorway, with his hand still poised on the brim of his hat, and noting that the diner had hired a new girl. Just a scrawny Indian kid, and not even fully grown, but, he further noted that she was the cleanest one the diner had hired yet.

"You must be the Mayor!" she shouted to him before he could even remove his hat. She seated him and was off and running.

He kept an eye on her over his newspaper. She was underfed and short but muscled like a bobcat, agile and speedy as she darted back and forth between the kitchen window, booths and tables, while also checking on the counter.

She caught his eye and gave him her 'be-one-minute sign'. He busied himself with the newspaper until she returned in a gust of lily of the valley perfume.

"Can I take your order Mayor Dunsby?" she said, arriving breathless and poised with pencil to pad.

Without bothering to look up he mumbled, "I'll have the Special please."

"Fish and Chips with Coleslaw?"

"Yes, the Special."

"What kind of pie would you like, Mayor Dunsby?"

"I don't eat dessert."

"Very good then, what would you like to drink?"

"Tea, please."

"Very good then."

Spinning on her heels, she turned and left, wiped a counter spill and clothes-pinned an order before he could turn the page of his *Toronto Star* and fold it into a firm rectangle, just the way he liked to read it. He tried to settle in, but there was so much going on that he couldn't help himself from continually looking up over his newspaper at the little bobcat in her crisply pressed yellow shift and pure white apron. He noted that she had all this niceness and neatness topped off with a matching white cap that held her blacker-than-black hair at bay underneath. He tried not to sneak peeks over his newspaper to watch her bound around on skinny brown legs and white tennis shoes from table, to counter, to window, and then back again, but it was no use. He supposed she had wandered in from that reservation near Brantford. Well, he thought, at least she wanted to work.

Before he knew it, the deep-fried sweetness of his fish and chips was wafting up from in front of him.

"Malt vinegar or white?"

"White of course."

"You should try it with malt vinegar sometime Mayor Dunsby. You'll never go back to white. Oh no, on second thought, you shouldn't try malt because then you'll just get annoyed when other restaurants don't have it." She fetchingly placed the rubber end of her pencil to temple as a third thought came to her, "White vinegar on cucumbers is better than malt."

He shook his head and snorted, lifted his fork—and using its edge, cut easily through the golden batter and into the tender flesh beneath. The salty, warm aroma reached his nostrils and made his mouth water for his food. It was kind of nice, he thought, to get his food hot for a change.

He found he had a little less trouble ignoring the chatter, comings and goings of the new waitress as he got down to enjoying his dinner, but soon enough it was over, and it became time for his tea. He shook out his newspaper as a signal.

Mary was by his side in a flash.

"For cryin' out loud, it's good to see a man with an appetite!"

She handed him some napkins. "You still look hungry."

Mayor Dunsby raised his eyebrows so he could see over the tops of his glasses and get a good look at her face—a cute little thing with too much of her mother's dark red lipstick slathered on. In spite of himself, he smiled back at her.

"Want some pie?"

He could have sworn she was teasing him.

"What goes good with Fish and Chips?" he asked.

"Big fat Coconut Cream, piled mile-high Lemon Meringue, and Steaming Wild Blueberries, cooled slightly with Vanilla Ice Cream."

He shook his head, this time with amusement. "Okay kid, dish 'er up. You talked me into it," he laughed.

Everyone in the room looked up for a second to see what could have made Mayor Dunsby laugh out loud.

After that, Mayor Dunsby started going to the Jackson Diner every Thursday as well as Friday, then Wednesday too, until it was as dependable as bees drawn to honey, that every weekday, holidays excepted, that's where Mayor Dunsby could be found, by at the latest, at 5:15 p.m. Mary chose the pie; and how long he stayed, always depended on her.

He roused himself from his memories now. He watched as Mary removed her apron and set it by her purse in the back before returning up front to select his pie. She started pouring the boiling water into a tea-for-two pot.

"Say? Can you just add a little of that to my pot while you're at it?" called out Johnny from the other side of the counter.

Even though she had her apron off, and all the regulars knew it was the sign she was off duty, nobody could ever say Mary minded a little extra work.

"How's your mother doing with that slug problem she was having?" she asked, pouring steaming hot water in a precise thin line over the limp tea bag while Johnny cradled his cup with grease-stained mechanic's hands. She looked up at him in midstream, and continued, "With her tomatoes, I mean?" Returning her attention to the tea bag buoyed in hot water, she finished, "Did she put a saucer of beer out like I told her to?"

"She sure did!" he said excitedly from behind her. "And we caught a pile of 'em the next morning."

She turned her back to him and returned the kettle to its burners, cut a wedge of Banana Cream Pie and set it on the tray with the pot of tea, two cups, and a small tin of Carnation Milk.

"Works every time, but if you really want to do what is right, you take the slug over to the creek and throw them in. They make for bigger fish."

"Sure will do that," Johnny called out as she walked away, "Fat red tomatoes in my Ma's garden and big, frisky fish for my pole all just works out dandy for me!"

Mary gave him a backwards wave, sat down opposite Mr. Dunsby and set the tray between them.

"How's fresh Banana Cream Pie sound to you tonight, Mr. Dunsby?"

"Lovely." He clasped his hands together in his lap while she placed his pie and a fork in front of him. "It's the highlight of my day to see what delightful pie you will choose for my dessert."

Mary tested the tea by letting a little into his cup, and then, satisfied that it was brown enough, poured it.

"So you didn't sleep well last night Mr. Dunsby, or did you just work too hard today?" She started stirring her own tea to coax even more of the dark ink out of the submerged bag, and continued, "I need my sleep, or I'm just no good the next day."

"You always look good."

Mary stopped stirring for a sliver of a second, as if considering what he had just said, and then proceeded with a few more circles before setting the spoon down beside her cup.

"You know, Mr. Dunsby. I get up every morning and take the trouble to look my best. I just don't feel right unless I do," she said while she poured a thin stream of Carnation Milk into her cup.

"How old are you?"

"I turned eighteen in the spring."

She plopped two heaping teaspoons of sugar into her cup.

"I think you're old enough, and I think we have been friends long enough, for you to start calling me by my first name," he said as he kept his hands still neatly folded in his lap.

She looked up from her swirling tea and right straight into his eyes for a second. He smiled back. "Well I think that is just dandy," she pronounced, "What do your other friends call you?"

"Tom." He tried to hold her gaze but she looked away.

"Well, Tom, do you know what I'm doing tonight?"

"Going roller skating at the hall?"

"Yes, that's what I'm doing, but tonight is different."

"Oh?" He unclasped his hands, put one elbow on the table, and leaned in closer. "And how so?"

"Elizabeth, you know, my sister, is coming with her boyfriend who has an automobile, to pick me up." She took a sip of her tea. "She's bringing his brother, and we are all going for burgers and roller skating."

Mayor Dunsby's shoulders sank. He re-clasped his hands in his lap. Mary went on, "It will be my second automobile ride ever, but the first one didn't count because it was a bus. Her boyfriend's name is Harry, and I can't recall his brother's name," Mary waved one hand excitedly by her head as if to coax the memory out. "It doesn't matter, they will tell me again when they get here. Elizabeth says Harry works for his father, who owns his own company, and is already well off, and his brother is an artist. In any case, it makes no difference to me. This will be the first date I have ever been on and my first real automobile ride! What do you think of that?"

Mayor Dunsby gathered himself straight and cleared his throat, "Well, I think that is very exciting for you."

"Gol' darn right!"

She sipped her tea and let herself imagine what an automobile ride would be like.

Mayor Dunsby sipped his cooling black tea and watched Mary watching the door. She was right about his not getting enough sleep, but how could she have any idea that it was her who was stealing it? At thirty-nine, he was young for a mayor, yes, but did he have license to even dream he could court a girl this young? He was already greying at the temples and he wore bifocals! Nobody could call him fat or skinny; he walked to and from work every day; ate just the right amount, but he knew things were getting a little soft underneath his suits. He had done the proper thing by waiting until she was over eighteen, but still, was it right to now interfere with the natural process of her dating a boy her own age? And if he did, how would he do it? His mind was like a monkey in a cage running back and forth from one banana to the other.

Soon enough the bell jangled, and Mary's polished and primped older sister Elizabeth made her usual grand entrance, only this time with two young men in tow. They didn't look like brothers. In fact, they weren't even the same colour. One was be-derby'd and pressed in a grey sweater and matching pants, and the other, a much darker boy, wore clean dungarees, a long-sleeved shirt, and slicked-back black hair.

Mary twitched in her seat like a sparrow on her perch as they entered, and then leapt up when they arrived at the table.

The two sisters made a big deal of each other, and then Elizabeth made the introductions.

"Of course you know my boyfriend, Harry Vanderdoody? And this is his brother, Gmiwan Fisher. Gmiwan, meet Mary, Mary meet Gmiwan." Elizabeth finished, pleased with her graceful production.

Mary took a step back to have a good look at Gmiwan and then turned,

"Mayor Dunsby, you know my sister. Well this is Harry and Gmiwan. Can you keep them company while I go change and get ready for roller skating?"

"Um," he stumbled, searching for an excuse but finding none soon enough.

Mary ushered the three into her side of the booth, turned on her heel, and sprinted off to the ladies room to change.

When Mary emerged again, she grabbed her jingling apron, emptied the tips into her purse, and noticed that Mayor Dunsby was just leaving.

"Are you going to be off now, Mayor Dunsby?" she called out.

He turned around with his hand still on the door handle and beheld her out of uniform. She wore a candy cane–striped cotton blouse cinched at her tiny waist, with matching red middy pants and her usual freshly polished white cotton tennis shoes. But his eyes were drawn most to the bright red ribbons that tamed her lustrous mane of black hair into two braids resting on her breasts. Neither plump, nor skinny, as his mother would say.

He waved good day and was gone before the echo of the bells had died away.

Mary walked over to the table and slid in next to the boy named Gmiwan.

"Gmiwan?" she said without waiting for him to answer, "Ojibwa for 'hear the rain'?"

Gmiwan nodded.

Mary looked from Harry to Gmiwan, observing that they looked nothing like brothers.

"Our mother is Mississauga from Alderville."

"Ohhhhh, where the rice grows on the water." Mary turned to Harry. "Who are your father's people?"

"Harry's father is an educated man from Holland. Isn't that glamorous?" Elizabeth answered for him. She shot Mary a look that said 'cut it out'.

Mary looked past her sister, regarded both boys, and noted that the differences between these two were clearly vaster than whose seed they sprang from. These two brothers were about as similar as the palm trees on the windows inside of the church and the pine trees on the outside

"Did you grow up in the same house?"

Harry shrugged and answered, yeah, as if he didn't understand nor care that much about what she was getting at.

Gmiwan looked away when he said, "Ma had three hundred acres of hereditary land. She gave it up to get married and go live in Louth."

"And then I came along," Harry grinned as he poked two thumbs into his chest.

Mary nodded.

"Okay, that's nice. Now we all know each other a little better but we better get going. Roller skating starts in fifteen minutes," Elizabeth said. She pushed Harry along the seat until he slid out and almost fell off the edge. Then she popped out from between the table and bench and stood next to him. She slipped her arm into his and began sashaying toward the door. When she reached it, she turned back to the table.

"Aren't you coming?"

Gmiwan and Mary looked at each other and scrambled out of their seats.

Outside, the chestnut trees of Main Street sighed with the balmy summer evening breath. It was a wonderful evening for an automobile ride. Harry's brand new CG Lebaron was parked in front of the diner, and the roof was off. Mary waited her turn to climb into the back seat after Gmiwan. Harry got it started and the sound of the engine filled her ears, travelled through the very core of her body, and tickled where she sat. They pulled away from the side of the road and started to rumble down Main Street.

Elizabeth cosied up to Harry and started chewing on his ear. Mary and Gmiwan remained at each end of the bench seat looking straight ahead, but the green sweetness of the night began to tug at Mary's hair, tingling her scalp as they picked up more speed. She could no longer resist. She pulled at each braid, untying the ribbons, and let the wind unfurl them.

"I thought maybe we might get hot dogs at the arena?" Elizabeth finally got out through her kissing and groping of Harry. "Is that okay with you?"

"Anything is okay with me tonight."

Mary gazed upward at the summer sky, splayed her fingers, and starting at her scalp, ran them up to the ends of her hair until the strands whipped and strained at her fingertips. She leaned back and, letting her head rest on the back of the seat, closed her eyes. Ahhhh, she thought, but it was good to be alive.

All too soon the automobile came to a halting stop and stole the wind away. Mary opened her eyes and took in the clear blueness of the sky, interrupted only by the pale crescent of Grandmother Moon waiting to claim the night. She lay there with her back arched and her arms overhead, heavy where they had dropped on the ledge behind her. It seemed they had come to a standstill and all because somebody, with a fair bit less of a vehicle than Harry's, was trying to get his own re-started.

"Mary?"

Called back now from dreamland, Mary sat up and looked in the direction in which Elizabeth was pointing a thumb.

"You better say hello. That Mayor friend of yours is standing right there."

Mayor Dunsby, taking his garbage to the curb, was stopped mid-stride on the walkway with mouth agape as if a surprise parade had suddenly come past his house.

"Hello Mr. Dunsby. I mean Tom!"

Tom Dunsby shuddered, as if just wakened, and then took a few steps closer to the Lebaron.

"Oh I do apologize, for staring I mean. It's just that I thought you were sick or hurt, draped over the back of the seat like that."

"Hurt?" Mary cocked her head to the side. She began to laugh at his mistake, but then stopped and put her hand to her mouth. It wouldn't do for her to make the Mayor feel foolish. "No, siree, I feel great tonight!" she said. And just then, the automobile rumbled to life and jerkily started to move forward.

"Bye Mr. Tom. Bye," she waved.

Tom Dunsby thought she looked like exotic royalty waving goodbye after a visit to his town. He sat himself on a nearby bench, lit a cigarette, which he rarely did in public, and listened until the echo of her laughter was nothing more than a throb he felt deep in his chest.

Gmiwan was turning out to be not much of a talker but that didn't trouble Mary any because she happened to be a very good conversationalist. In any case, it didn't matter because it wasn't long before they pulled up in front of the arena. With the motor still rumbling, Elizabeth leaped out of the front seat and dancing from one foot to the other, held the door open for Mary and Gmiwan.

"Harry and me are going for a little ride."

As Mary squeezed past her sister she cocked an eyebrow at her.

"We won't be long."

Mary shook her head. She need not worry about how she was going to get home because she was in the habit of walking herself to and from the arena five or six times a week, so if Elizabeth didn't come back, it made no difference to her. Long ago, she'd accepted that Elizabeth was not dependable.

The car door slammed shut, and Mary and Gmiwan were left standing in the cloud of road dirt the Lebaron had left behind.

"So?" Gmiwan said, turning to Mary. "You hungry?"

"Yes I am," she returned. "I brought a little sandwich. I usually have a bite to eat before I start skating. I brought some tea too. I can share."

"I've never been here before, but Elizabeth and Harry said we would be eating out tonight, so I brought money."

She didn't respond, so he said, "Want to eat that?"

She stopped walking and turned to look him in the eye.

"The money?"

"A little joke," he said, holding his finger and thumb up to his eye, leaving a little bit of air between like it was a key hole he was trying to look at her through. He switched back and forth winking one eye and then the other.

Mary burst out laughing and started walking again.

"I see you have a sense of ha ha, Gmiwan Fisher!"

"Thank you, Mary Stone," he called over his shoulder as he ran ahead to open the door for her.

Inside, the windowless dome and blaring music drove away any gentleness the evening had offered. Shadowy and boisterous but familiar to Mary, she grabbed Gmiwan's sleeve and began to pull him. He leaned himself into it as a tail to a kite, but when they arrived at the skate rentals, he held up his hand, and shook his head.

"Not for me. I can't skate," he shouted above the music.

"Oh," Mary crinkled her brow. "Whatcha gonna do then?"

"I'm going to get us something to eat and watch you skate."

"But I could teach you," she offered.

"Maybe so," he grinned, "but not tonight."

She shrugged and with that headed over to a wooden bench and plunked her skates down. Gmiwan followed her over and sat a courteous distance from her while she nimbly tied her skates up.

"What do you want to eat?" he asked.

"French fries and gravy."

"No hamburger?"

"No thank you," she said without turning around as she glided off and became part of the stream of other skaters.

When Gmiwan returned to the bench with two orders of French fries and gravy on the side he had no trouble finding the girl with the red middy pants on, and besides, he hadn't taken his eyes off her for very long anyway.

Gmiwan could tell this was the girl for him. She reminded him of wild strawberries growing sweet and steadfast no matter what bullied them.

After about twenty good rounds, Mary spotted him sitting on the bench, and arrived breathlessly beside him. "They smell much better than my egg salad sandwiches," she said as she dipped a fat French fry in the gravy.

"You skate like a dream."

She finished chewing. "I can dance on my skates too."

"I see there are a lot of couples skating. Do boys ever ask you to skate with them?"

"And," she popped another drippy fry in her mouth just before it could make a mess, made him wait until she was finished chewing, and then said, "I have some trophies too."

"Well, I would say so. The way you weave in and out like a little salmon bent on getting there first, it's perfectly natural that you would win any trophy you went after."

She cocked an eyebrow at him, "Little salmon, eh, Gmiwan Fisher?"

He shut his mouth tight hoping he hadn't said the wrong thing. He really had no practice with girls.

"Okay," she said. "I guess being a salmon isn't such a bad thing. Only I don't plan on kickin' the bucket when I get there."

She perked up as the first few notes of her favourite song, "Dream a Little Dream of Me," started over the loudspeaker. She stayed on the floor for three more of her favourites. By the time she got back again, he had a pencil and a pad of paper out.

"What are you doing now?" she stretched to peek. "Are you drawing a picture or making your grocery list?"

"Neither. It's a surprise."

She got up as if to leave, slowly circled back around the bench, but he hid it from her. He kept it on his lap face down until she left, and every time she came back to dip some French fries and pop them in her mouth, he hid it again. They played that game until he was finished and had put the pad of paper and pencil back in his pocket.

Finally the music ended. Mary lingered out on the floor with a few others before cruising back in for a landing, whizzing by him all the way down to the other end of the bench. She paused for moment, winded and panting a little, and then got right to the work of taking her skates off. She looked over at Gmiwan while she unlaced her skates. She sensed he was staring at her. Caught, he didn't look away.

"So, does it look like fun?"

"It does."

Tying her skates together and then sitting upright, she looked to the other side of her and said, "There's still some French fries here."

"Is there gravy?"

"There is."

"That sounds nice."

She slipped the French fry in the gravy, cupped her hand to catch any drips, and then scooted down the bench half the distance between them. He waited, startled on the bench for just a split second, and then he himself closed some more of the distance. Then, like a hawk seizes a mouse, he took the fry from her hand and poked it into his own mouth.

"Mmmmm," he closed his eyes and savoured it. "Got any more?"

Mary turned to eye up the paper carton with a small pile of fries still in it, scooted and lunged to retrieve it, and then returned to the spot in the middle of the bench. She handed it to him.

"Can you dip it in the gravy?"

She leaned over and dipped a fry in the gravy, cupped her hand under it, and tilted her body close enough that she could tell he smelled like bergamot. He waited open mouthed and eyes closed. She tried to be quick and put the fry over his mouth to catch the anticipating gravy, but it dripped on to his lip instead. He licked it off and then bit the French fry. "Another?" he asked.

She broke into laughter.

"Not until you show me what you were doing with that pencil and paper, Gmiwan Fisher."

"I was waiting for you to ask." He flipped it out of his pocket. "Do you want me to read it to you or do you want to read it yourself?"

"Ohhhh, so you weren't drawing a picture. I thought you were an artist."

"There are a lot of things that come under the heading of art, you know."

"Hmmm?" she coaxed.

"This is a poem."

"So you're a poet too."

"I wrote a poem for you to keep. It's like a picture, only with words. Do you want me to read it to you?"

"Sure."

He cleared his throat and began to recite what he had written:

Last night she woke at midnight, felt the breath of summer still
wafting through her window, beckoning her will.
Intoxicated by the wind, she felt trepidation pass
crawling through the window ran barefoot through the grass.
Fleeing for the forest the wind caressed her hair
the moonlit magic starry night urged where darkness dare.
Entering the forest safe as sacred womb
tranquil, yet so powerful this living, breathing room.
To shimmer sister lake she danced through trees like silver slip
and so unhampered by the day, took chaste uncovered dip.
Then left the cool and silver embrace to dance among the trees
the forest played a haunting song while wind her skin did tease.
Dancing in the darkness until slumber laid her down
tranquilized by the stars she slept upon the ground.
Sunlight's fingers filtered through, warming her awake
with the dawn the magic gone the dream was hers to take.

Mary felt a spell had been cast on her. She closed her eyes to make it last longer, and so it would have been if not for Elizabeth and Harry.

"Hey you two!"

Mary popped her eyes open to find her previously polished sister looking a little inside out, with her hair mussed and shirt untucked, face a bit worked up. "Come to the ladies room with me Mary please, before we go," Elizabeth said.

In the light of the ladies room, Elizabeth looked even more worked up.

"Oh," Elizabeth grasped her by the shoulders, "do you want to hear a secret?"

But Mary could see clearly past Elizabeth's glass bravado. Whatever it was, it wasn't as shiny as her sister was feigning.

"Okay," she said slowly.

"I didn't want to tell you until after I talked to Harry."

Mary stayed still and wide-eyed.

"I'm pregnant!"

Mary blinked.

"Do you hear me? I am going to be a mother. You are going to be an aunt. Aren't you going to say something?"

Picking off a chip of the thin layer her sister was painting, Mary decided to get right to the point. "You're in a lot of trouble Elizabeth. I don't see what there is to celebrate. What are you going to do?"

Elizabeth cast her eyes downward as if searching for something else to offer. "I know," she said meekly, started with a sniffle that gave way to sobbing, "I know, I know!" Her chest heaved. "Harry didn't take it too well. He says we should get married, but his father is going to kill him."

Mary let her sister fall into her arms. It seemed like for the longest time, they stayed that way, there at the end of the counter, inconveniencing the women who stared furtively and then left without drying their hands. Finally a man in a uniform came into the ladies washroom and told them to 'bury the hatchet and take their party back out to the bush.'

The arena was almost empty, and the boys were still there, Harry pacing and Gmiwan sprawled out on the bench. As they walked out together, it seemed to Mary, by Gmiwan's changed demeanour, that his brother must have told him the news too. When they got back to the automobile, Elizabeth took up her post next to Harry.

While Gmiwan and Mary didn't have much to say to each other either, they sat closer together than before, with their hands resting on the seat and their baby fingers touching.

MISS WRIGHT WRENCHED the child roughly by the arm every four or five steps. She didn't realize that Mary wasn't being stubborn, and that it was Dolly, who she was holding onto for dear life with her other hand, that wasn't able to keep up to her officious stomp down the path, and now, it was the grey stone steps that stood before the four children like a wall.

"Get up those steps!" she screeched.

Neither child had ever had occasion to mount such a coldly perfect cut stack of stones. The rock ladder seemed to lead to the dark mouth of a house that was made of precisely cut square red stones and was big enough for every person Mary had met, or probably ever would have had the chance to meet, to live in, or maybe to be kept in. She recalled the adults sometimes speaking in hushed tones of things like schools or orphanages. Mary's heart, which was already frenzied with fear, unbelievably began to gather heaviness, and sink, with what she would later recognize was pure and relentless longing.

The man in the lead held a serene Porter in one hand and a snarling Elizabeth in the other. Dolly's whimpering had grown silent again as she stared up at the mountain of dark windows. Mary told herself that she would be able to tell better what this place was in the daylight, but then inside her belly something writhed and struck like a snake at the thought that she might still be here tomorrow.

Neither the man nor Miss Wright had spoken to them during the ride in the wagon. The man had tended to the horse, and Miss Wright, having jammed herself between Porter and Elizabeth, had watched them like a hawk. All the while Elizabeth and Porter had shivered while every once in a while Dolly, who had fallen to sleep in Mary's lap, would cry out for Ma. But now they had arrived at this place.

The man shoved Porter and dragged Elizabeth behind. Porter let himself be pushed forward until he fell upon the first of the steps. The man, hauled his foot back and kicked Porter in the place that he used to sit, and Porter's head hit one of the stone steps. Then he used the momentum of Elizabeth pulling backward, as if to release her, but then pulled back and swung her around like a hitting stick, until she landed in a heap upon Porter. They both hurriedly got part way up and began scrambling up the stairs on all fours to get away from being kicked. Seeing this, Dolly wrapped her body around Mary, and Mary made the decision to do what they wanted immediately.

When Elizabeth and Porter got to the top first, Mary could tell that they were looking for a place to run, but there was no place to run. Mary stepped onto a flat stone porch of sorts that was surrounded by a railing, but they were too high up off the ground to jump. She turned around, and just beyond the man and the woman, who were climbing the steps in a two by two fashion, laughing, joking, amongst each other, Mary could see the first flickering light of a red dawn, over the road which had taken them to this place. On either side of the road there were apple trees, laden with ripe fruit, and then the road narrowed into nothing as it led back to her home where Pa must still be crying.

The man's mirth dissolved into a hard hitting glare as he stood guard over the children while Miss Wright approached the two great, dark, wooden, arched doors, reached up, and banged with the brass knocker. Even from where they stood outside, Mary could hear its thunder resonate throughout the building. Finally, they could hear footsteps and cursing. Then an outside light flicked on and chased away some of the darkness. One of the doors groaned open, and a lady's head with a white cap on top, peeked out.

The man spoke. "We have a few more students here for you."

She opened the door wider and then stepped under its archway in full view now, hands on hips, and wearing a pure white uniform.

"Well, well, well, what do we have here? A rag-tag lot, I can see. Are they all from the same family?"

She had the same accent as Doctor Wheeler.

"Yes. The mother died. We need a week to get you the paperwork."

"Do they speak English?"

"They seem to."

"Likely they shred it to pieces, but they will be speaking nothing but

His Majesty's fine dialogue in short order and unto their last breath. Welcome heathens to your emancipation!"

She dismissed the man and Miss Wright with a wave of her hand and turned to face the children. Oddly, Mary's panic spiked as she watched the man and the woman turn their backs and walk away. They were the only two people who knew the way back to their log house in the bush.

"Well fine and dandy then, come with me," the lady in white said, as she moved out of the archway, positioned herself behind all four children, and began to herd them inside. "I'm the head teacher here but I am also a registered nurse. You will refer to me as Mistress. Do you hear?"

All four of them looked at her.

"I said!" she shrieked like a witch, "Do you hear!"

As if a cat caught sniffing salt pork, Dolly leapt into the air, let go of Mary's hand and broke into a tear down the hall, bawling at the top of her lungs. Mary tore after her calling out her name.

A cornered squirrel will twitch and dart while it pains to make a decision. That's how Mistress looked when she eyeballed Elizabeth and Porter. In wordless agreement, they assumed a yielding posture, leaned against the cold cement wall. Mistress aimed her eyes at them, to bore a hole of fear into their hearts, "God help your scraggly souls if you touch one thing while I'm gone."

Elizabeth twirled her hair around her finger and scanned the surrounding walls before casting her eyes down to the moccasins Ma had made for her. Porter fixedly chewed one fingernail and kept his face veiled with his hair.

"Useless," Mistress scowled, before turning on her heel and hollering, "Sophie! Floyd!"

Mistress took off, her thick sensible-heeled shoes madly clunking on the polished floor. After only a few steps she thought she might faint but she called up the image of Father David to give her strength—Father David, the most well spoken, intelligent and handsome minister their family's Anglican Church had ever had. Under his tutelage, she had served her church as a Sunday school teacher faithfully until that monumental day in her life when he announced to the congregation that it would be none other than she who would travel to the new world of Canada to bring the word of God. Above all others, she was chosen as the worthy missionary of Father David's dream to increase God's flock by converting the savages, even above her older sister Emily, proving that a good man recognizes the beauty of brains and integrity over fair hair and blue eyes. She became determined that day never to faint, nor lose a single sheep.

She pressed on in the direction of the two that got away. It wouldn't be hard to find them since the little one was still howling like the terrifying coyotes she sometimes heard at night.

"They'll be house trained after I have them a few days," she said aloud as something warm to keep herself cool.

She dashed down one hallway, and then turned on to another, after another. She must have made a wrong turn because the yelping heathens sounded farther away. Maybe they'd fallen down and got hurt. That would teach them. Mistress stopped short, her pointed breasts surging and plunging with her breathlessness. She placed her hand on her chest to quell the burning in her lungs and bent over to try to still the dizziness. After a few gulps for air, she heard footsteps, stood up and was relieved to see that that Floyd and Sophie were dragging two little creatures down the hall. Floyd had already been there when she arrived; he was little better than the parade of long-haired, swarthy heathens who got dumped on her. Sophie, a teacher's assistant, wasn't much better. She was from the poor side of town, and the reason the church had hired her was beyond the Mistress's comprehension.

"Let's get the other two." she commanded.

"What other two?"

"Follow me!" she ordered. "And bring those two with you!"

Floyd held Dolly under one tree trunk of an arm, while Sophie dragged Mary by the hand. By the time they reached the door, it was swinging to and fro, hinges lamenting, in a wind that loomed with gathering thunder.

"Go and it is done; the bell invites me. Hear it not, Duncan; for it is a knell. That summons thee to heaven or to hell," Mistress recited the last lines of Act Two, Scene One from her beloved Macbeth, and then collapsed in a heap. "They are gone."

Sophie handed Mary over to Floyd and approached the quivering pile of white on the gleaming floor, but Mistress only caved further in on herself, gasping desperately for the air around her. Sophie had seen this before. She took two good steps backward and sure enough, like the bough of a tree held bent to the ground, Mistress sprung back up with a vicious snap.

"Floyd! Hand over those two, take the dogs, and go look for two older ones. A boy and a girl," she finally explained. "I won't get their paperwork until next week so I can't even tell you their names or where they are from. "Do you get it, you sod? Go! Now!"

Floyd let Mary's hand drop, rubbed his eyes, and sighed. Then placing his hand on Mary's back to prompt her forward, he resolutely walked over to the Mistress and handed off Dolly. Floyd let himself out, quietly latching the door behind him.

Unable to hold the slippery, squirming Dolly, who fell to the floor, Mistress grabbed her by the braid, and hauled her back up to her feet. Then taking Dolly's arm in a locking grip, she jerked her along like a dog that wouldn't heel.

"Come along, Sophie," Mistress ordered as she started down the hall with Dolly running three steps for every one of hers. "We have work to do."

Mary had lived in the bush, in one place, her whole life. Back home, there was one step, not scary at all, leading up to the wooden stoop of their place, but here, standing on a landing looking down through the railings into a pit, where an awful swampy smell was coming from, made the snake in Mary's gut uncoil and twitch. Dolly fell to her knees and started crying again. Mistress clucked her tongue in disdain and hauled the writhing child held on her side, swung her around, and thrust her out to dangle over the edge of the railing.

Mary couldn't help it. Terror-stricken, she could see only the deep iron stairwell, unsure if the see-through stairs were secure enough to hold them. Try as she might, Sophie couldn't pry Mary's fingers off the railing.

Mistress shook Dolly to get her attention. "Do you want to fall?"

Dolly, sensing the nothingness beneath her kicking feet, opened her eyes and looked about. Even a hairless baby bird knows what to do when in hopeless danger. Dolly went limp while Mary, whose eyes had rounded into full orbs of horror and cognition, let go of the railing.

"There now," Mistress sniffed, bringing Dolly back in. "Let us proceed."

After that, Mary and Dolly went peaceably, stumbling every once in a while as they learned to climb down winding metal ladderstairs for the very first time.

When they finally reached the bottom, Mistress opened a door and took them down an unpainted, grey stone corridor. At the end was a white door. Mistress took a ring of keys from one of her many pockets and unlocked it. Inside, too, everything was painted white. There was a long table made out of thick, white-painted wood, black hoses hanging on ropes, and hooks sticking out from the low spider-webbed ceiling.

Mistress plopped Dolly down so she and Mary stood side by side, motioned to the table with a wave of her hand, and ordered Sophie to go get it ready. Then positioning herself in front of the two girls, she pointed to the steel bucket on the floor beside them.

"Strip those rags off and put them in there!" Seeing the looks of panic on their faces, she let herself surge with power for a few moments before speaking again. "Is there no such thing as a shower where you people come from? You can't have it with your clothes on. If you don't take your own clothes off, I will do it for you. You are having a shower, whether you like it or not. And untie those braids while you're at it!"

Mary's eyes darted back and forth as she took in the hoses hanging with the spider webs from the ceiling.

Mistress called for Sophie. "You strip the older one, and I'll take the younger."

Sophie walked over, put her hand on Mary's shoulder, and let it rest there. It was going to happen, and Mary knew there was nothing she could do about it. She concentrated on the snake in her gut. She had to tame it before it started to whip and snap out of control. She watched Mistress scoop Dolly up, take her over to the table, and place her standing on its top. She watched her lift Dolly's dress and saw Dolly's eyes search her eyes for interpretation.

Mary used the snake on the ceiling to imagine the shape of the snake inside her and willed it to recoil and stay still. If she lost control of the snake now, Mary knew something horrible could happen. Using exaggerated gestures for Dolly's benefit, Mary started removing her own clothes and tossing them into the steel bucket.

After all of her clothes were off and all she had on was her medicine bag tied around her waist with a thin thong of doeskin, Mary stood waiting under the dangling overhead light bulb. Mistress spotted Mary standing there. She stomped over, and before Mary could possibly figure out what she was going to do, she tore off the medicine bag. She opened the bag, dug around in it, and found Mary's knife and put it in her pocket. She tossed the doeskin pouch and thong on top of the heap in the bucket.

The snake got out.

Mary was naked now, and she wailed uncontrollably.

Dolly joined the chaotic chorus.

The Mistress and Sophie had seen it all before. Sophie dragged Mary deeper into the room, and Mistress flopped the howling Dolly down on her bare bottom beside Mary. Jumping up, she wrapped her arms around Mary's waist and clung on tight.

There was a hissing noise, and the snake went wild.

The crying changed into choking and coughing as freezing cold water blasted their faces and bodies. Mistress handled her tool like a master, controlling the pressure by adjusting the nozzle with one hand, and expertly piloting its girth with the other, exerting extra pressure for the cracks and crevices of squirming bodies, especially in-between where the two children clung together. When she was satisfied they were sufficiently doused and cleansed, she twisted the nozzle, squeezed off the water until it merely dribbled at the end, and gave the nod to Sophie.

Sophie soaped them down to just a snivel, by which Mistress knew it was time to turn the hose on again. She gauged the flow to fluctuate from a spray for wide surfaces down to the occasional bull's eye sting trained in on tight spots where germs liked to hide. 'Evil,' she believed, 'liked to hide in the same places as dirt,' Father David's words visited as her ever faithful guide. 'Cleanliness is next to Godliness.'

Left to shiver in the echo of the snake's stinging attack, Mary and Dolly held each other while Mistress and Sophie busied themselves at a shelf nearby. When she strode back, Mistress brought with her a bowl and a paintbrush. She set them down in front of the girls so hard that the bowl sloshed shiny liquid over the side, making a luminescent swirl in the puddle on the dirty wet stone floor. Then she got herself a chair, sat down and dipped her brush.

Sophie stood behind the girls, one hand on each shoulder, guiding them to stand facing Mistress.

"Spread your legs!" she ordered.

Sophie separated Mary's knees with her hands, and Dolly followed her sister's compliant lead.

Mistress, without care for excess, slathered each child's genitals with what distinctly smelled like coal lantern oil. She licked the brush up in places that burned like hell. Mary knew enough not to move. Pain was an enemy she could handle, but that snake was the scariest evil magic she had ever been faced with. Mary wondered what would happen if somebody lit up a smoke around her. She pushed that thought away. Who would come near for the smell of her anyway?

It was all clear to Mary now. Mistress was a witch who practiced the very worst kind of medicine. There was no use fighting a witch. Mary raised her arms when she was told to, and Mistress's paintbrush licked her there. Then

Sophie cupped her hands dutifully while she poured some of the liquid into them. Sophie split it up between her two hands and drizzled it onto the tops of the girls' heads, first rubbing it into Mary's scalp and then Dolly's.

Next they were led back over to the long table.

"Get up there!" they were ordered.

Mary climbed up, pulled her sister after her, and then stood together side-by-side, light bulb swinging behind their heads, and trying not to tremble.

"Witches feed on fear," Mary remembered Maggie saying once. "The more fear you have for them, the stronger they get." Mary made her mind up. This woman called Mistress must really be a witch.

"Sit down!"

Mary was taught not to sit on anything bare-arsed but she was getting to know now that she had no choice, so she did as she was told. Mistress turned around, reached up to the upper shelf on the wall behind her, and pulled down a giant gleaming pair of scissors. She gathered up the full length of Dolly's black hair into a bulky ponytail and lopped it off where it ended in her closed hand. Dolly never flinched because she was too young to know about pride or beauty and how it could make you feel strong. Dolly's hair whispered its keen as it fell to the floor. Mistress let the stubby bundle of hair in her hand fall down into place, then trimmed it until she was pleased. It was exactly on level with Dolly's chin. She stood back to admire her work, and Sophie automatically stepped in and took a brush to it.

"Picture day is coming soon. Every perfect head will be counted," Mistress singsonged to herself.

Mary screamed inside when it happened to her.

After it was all done, Mistress left Sophie to finish brushing Mary's hair, turned to paint the scissors in coal oil and wiped them clean with a towel that had been folded and sitting at the end of the table. She threw the towel back on the table and gently placed the scissors back on the shelf, then proceeded over to a metal locker cabinet on the other side of the room where she pulled her keys out, unlocked it, and rustled around inside. She selected two bags that were labelled "Girl—Small," and walked back over to the table.

She waved Sophie off.

"Do clean up now," she stated expressionlessly, and then positioned herself to be heard. She shoved a bag toward each of the girls, and they, not understanding what she wanted, just blinked.

"Take it!"

Mary and Dolly did as they were told.

"Dry off with that towel beside you and open those bags," she barked. "In there are all the clothes you will need while you are here. There is a pair of pajamas, which you will put on after I am finished talking to you. There are two full sets of daytime clothes. In the morning, choose one set and put it on. Neatly fold your pajamas and place them under your pillow. Before the end of the day," she specifically targeted Mary with steely eyes, "Sophie will show you how to sew your name into every item, and then you will be solely responsible for keeping track of and always having clean clothes."

Not waiting for a nod, or a yes, or a no, as there was no real question about it, Mistress went over to lock up the cabinet and do an inspection of the premises. Sophie approached the girls and showed them which were pajamas and which were clothes. Mistress went back to lock up her cabinet and took an exceptionally long time to scrub her hands in the small porcelain sink. After thoroughly drying them, and with her back still to them, both her hands flew to her face as she exclaimed joyfully, "There's my pointer!"

She lovingly took hold of a slender stick leaning on the wall, as if it might get away again, and held it at breast level in front of her for a moment before spinning back around on her heels to face them. The Mistress's fondness for the pointing stick reminded Mary of one of Maggie's stories about the bad witch who lived on the Tuscarora's Reserve, whose mother was half Chippewa and half Tuscarora, and whose father was the son of an African slave. Maggie said the woman had bad teeth but was always dressed up in bright colours. Maggie said she kept all her magic in a stick that her African father had made for her out of the thick hollow branch of a pine tree and a mud turtle shell. She kept magic things in the shell that made it rattle. She kept it with her at all times, and if she wasn't petting it and fondling it, she was dressing it with crow feathers and painted leather. She called it her Maanaaji Stick. It could, she said, change into a snake and bite, or go into small places and find things out for her. If you got on her good side, she would do favours for you by shaking that rattle in the direction of something you wanted, but if you made her mad, it would be too late if she already knew too much about you. Maggie always said it was best to avoid people like her.

"I was sure one of those little buggers had hidden it on me!"

Her clunky steps got heavier, her chest pointier, and her head higher. A purposeful woman to begin with, her beloved stick gave her more purpose.

She charged over to the table and thrust her stick to pluck up the towel drooping over the edge and then she dangled it front of Mary's face.

Mary, who completely understood now why the adults were deathly afraid of witch magic, warily eyed the stick that was being waved at her, not knowing what manner of illness it could cast on her. She stayed completely still and avoided looking into the Mistress's witch eyes.

"Take the towel, heathen!" Mistress ordered as she twitched the stick.

No response.

Mistress dropped the towel in Mary's lap.

"Take that, and the towel I just used at the sink, and put them in the bucket over there, you dim-wit."

Mary eyed the towel on the sink and then the bucket, imagined the steps it would take to get there, where she would go after, and what might happen to her if she did, or did not.

"Are you daft?" she spat.

Mistress pretended to pick the towel up out of Mary's lap. She dramatically walked over to the sink, pretended again to pick up the towel there, and then toss both imaginary towels into the bucket.

Mary noticed the pajamas she had been given had pockets.

Mary nodded to show the black haired lady that she understood and would do as she was told.

"Good then!" she harrumphed and started to pace to and fro, alternately fondling the length of her stick and slapping it in the palm of her hand.

Mary eyed up the bucket and then the sink. It would be a triangle from here to there, she estimated, so she lowered herself off the table, and starting with a few cautious steps, she did exactly as Mistress had asked. Mistress heaved her pointy bosom in exasperation and continued to pace, stopping periodically just to give Mary the evil eye. Mary kept her own eyes as though she was looking at the sink, but they were really thrown out of focus so that she could see the bucket and her tormentor at the same time. Mary placed her hand on the towel laying over the edge of the sink, paused, and then collected the towel. She turned to find Mistress midway between the sink and the table. Mary started on the second line of her triangle toward the bucket, taking big steps and then small baby steps as she got closer to the bucket. She calculated that it would take exactly two more baby steps of her own for Mistress to reach the sink.

She could see her prize now.

Mistress reached the sink, showed her back as she did her twirl, at which time Mary took one large step, dipped down, swooped up her medicine bag, and placed the towels in the bucket. She balled the bag all up inside her fist and started walking baby steps back to the table so the evil lady would get to the sink first, and have to twirl again. This would allow Mary to shove the prize deep into her pyjama pocket. Sophie's hand flew to her mouth to press down the urge to burst out laughing. Floyd would get a kick out of this when she told him about it later.

After the trudge back upstairs to the second floor, Mistress bade a crisp good night, discharging the sanitized recruits to Sophie. It was not the dimness of the lowly lit hallways of the Indian Institute that were beginning to seep into Mary's veins, it was more the echo and the foreboding oppressiveness of a cave with an elusive white opening that grew smaller and smaller, with every step in the wrong direction. Sophie took them both by the hand to their sleeping quarters, unlocked a solid steel door with a barred window in it and led the two girls in. She bent down and put her fingers to her lips.

"Shhhhhh."

Inside there were rows upon rows of beds, some with humps and some flat. There was some stirring, and one kid sat up in one of them.

"Shhhhh," Sophie said to her too.

Mary and Dolly padded along beside Sophie, dragging their bags by the string behind them.

Sophie pointed to an empty bed and led Dolly to it, tiptoed all the way down to the end of the row and motioned for Mary to come and get in bed.

"Put your bag under the bed for now, and we will look after it in the morning," she whispered.

"Come on now, get in bed," she urged.

Mary put the covers over her legs and leaning on her elbows, lay down halfway. Sophie turned around to leave and bumped into Dolly who was standing right behind with her own bag in one hand and her other jammed into her mouth sucking her thumb.

Mary patted the sacred bundle in her pocket for courage and whispered, "Dolly has never spent one night in her life out of my bed. She will probably fuss all night."

Sophie rolled her eyes and huffed, "Fine then, if you promise not to let even a whimper out and let me go out and have a cigarette in peace, then I will let you sleep together one last time."

Mary patted the bed beside her and opened the covers to invite Dolly inside. Dolly dropped her bag and bounded into the bed. Mary closed them up with the blanket and they both squirreled deep inside together. Dolly fidgeted and squirmed long into the night, trying to get past the nose and eye-biting tang of coal oil. Finally, she found the smell of her big sister in a secret place at the back of Mary's neck where there was still hair to cover it.

IN HER NINETEENTH year, Mary took a trip. Her first one ever. She told people it was a trip, but really it was a quest. She had a question and she had to go away by herself to hear the answer. Usually all she had to do was go for a walk along the river by herself, or stay in her apartment and spend time on her tiny balcony to think things through. Not this time, however. This time she needed to make a journey: Gmiwan had proposed.

They had put the winter in easily, with Gmiwan playing his guitar and singing songs when he visited her, while Mary cooked for him and hummed along. Ever since spring's first gifts of sunshine, they had been stealing afternoons for picnics, swimming, and bike riding. Gmiwan was even learning how to roller skate. And now, with mid-summer upon them, four full seasons had passed, their friendship had caught fire.

As she sat on the bench watching for the bus to appear down the road, Mary's mind wandered back over the events of the past week. She had risen in the morning of her only day off to pouring rain, and then, just to add to the disappointment, a knock had come to her door. It was her boss, wanting to know if she could come in and work for Sophie, who was sick. Mary had pushed aside her dismay, scratched a note, and stuck it on the door for Gmiwan to let him know they would have to cancel their plans for the day.

At lunchtime, it was still raining, and the day was dragging. Mary was taking the Syms' order when Old Harold let himself in out of the rain, coughing and stamping his feet, announcing himself the way he always did. Something was different though. Along with Old Harold's proclamation of his arrival, and the knell of the bells hanging from the door handle, came a sweet melody drifting in behind him. Those closest to the door craned their necks to see what Old Harold could be doing to make such a sound. He noticed right off that he had some attention and smiled a sparsely toothed grin. He ceremoniously took his dripping hat off and let the door clap shut behind him, sealing off the haunting song.

"There's some nut out there singin' his ass off," he said, loving the attention, as he fixed his misshapen hat atop the highest perch on the coat horse in the corner, "waiting for donations or something."

Fred walked over to investigate what was going on in front of his diner, and then other people started to gather around him, pushing each other out of the way to get a better look. The Syms got up too and so Mary followed along.

Fred reached back through the shape-shifting crowd that was blocking Mary's view and took her by the hand to guide her to the front.

"You know who that is, eh?" Fred asked, smirking and nudging her.

"Isn't that your boyfriend?" Flora Fletcher sang out. "Where'd ya say he moved here from? Toronto?"

"I thought 'e had heemself a good job workin' over at the mill. Why is he beggin' with a tin cup? 'e mus be some kinda big drinker." Old Harold said as he sat himself down at the counter to wait for someone to take his order.

"Hey Old Harold, how come everybody around here only knows you as Old Harold?" Mary shot back at him

He cast his eyes to the ground and tried to rub the hat that wasn't on his head.

Befittingly slighted, he mumbled, "I didn't mean nothin' by it. I like to drink meself but I'm just sayin' ya gotta do it accordin' to yer pay."

Everyone shifted in place. They could tell Mary wasn't too happy to see her boyfriend out in the rain, singing for money.

Fred feigned a helpful tone, "D'ya want me to prop the door open so you can hear better while you get back to work?"

Mary glowered at him and returned her gaze to the spectacle of her soaking wet boyfriend kneeling on the sidewalk, arms outstretched, holding fast to his tin cup with both hands. Nobody was giving him any money. Passersby either left the sidewalk in a wide curve to get around him or crossed the street. A couple of people had left the warm summer rain, closed their umbrellas, and began to gather under the awning of Martha's Family Shoe store across the street just to watch.

"Come on, I got a business to run here, and Old Harold is waiting for his order to be taken." He grinned.

Fred hadn't had a good laugh like this in ages, and so he propped the door wide open with a chair.

Eventually, people drifted away from the window to return to their seats but adjusted themselves so they could see the show better. In fact, Gmiwan singing outside in the rain in front of Jackson Diner turned out to be good for business that day. People stayed longer, ordered more tea, more coffee, and more pieces of pie.

Gmiwan stayed and sang, and sang again, every song he had ever sung for Mary. In spite of herself, Mary couldn't help but hang on his every note. At one point, she got so distracted that she failed to stop pouring coffee into Mrs. Donnelly's cup even after it was full. Two hours after the normally busy lunch hour would have died down, the diner was still full, and Fred had risen to a state of joviality that no one had ever witnessed before.

"Hey Mary," he called out, "nobody is giving him any money and he's been singing for three hours. Maybe I should go out and give him a few bucks?"

Mary shook her head and looked out at Gmiwan, still on his knees in a puddle, with his back to the crowd that had formed under the shoe store awning. Some passersby had stopped to smoke a cigarette, or munch or sip something while they took shelter from the rain and enjoyed the show. Jackson had never seen a beggar before.

Suddenly a crash of thunder, and a flash of lightening lit up Main Street, and the crowd, some popping their umbrellas open, streamed across the street, hurrying past the singing Gmiwan who did not budge an inch. Gmiwan sang on, holding his cup high as a ferocious wind struck up and gusted in wicked harmony with the raging thunder and lightning.

About mid-afternoon, Fred couldn't take it anymore. Something like sympathy blocked out his business sense and made him stride through the archway, kicking the make-do prop out, and let the screen door slam ceremoniously behind him. He crouched as he made his way toward Gmiwan, but the wet circles the rain made on his white shirt widened and joined before he even got there. Almost everyone in the room rushed to the window again. Mary couldn't see a thing, and couldn't bear to anyway, so she plunked herself in a swivel chair by Old Harold, who by now would normally have been long gone, and closed her eyes against the image of Gmiwan finally being pelted into submission, or even struck by lightning.

Old Harold cleared his throat, and tried to put on a helpful tone. "That boyfriend 'a yers should probly try and git heeself a job to make records, or singin' in a bar where they serve up beer at least." He took a sip of his tea, "I be 'tinkin.'"

Mary turned her face away.

Fred burst back in through the front door and walked right straight up to Mary. "He wouldn't take any money. Wouldn't take no heed from me either about the lightening and all." Fred rubbed his deeply indented chin and wiped his hands dry on his dirty chef's apron, pausing to think a bit before he said, "Says he's doing a ceremony for Mary."

Like a wayward bird cornered in the kitchen, Mary's eyes switched back and forth looking for an escape from every other eye that had focused upon her.

"He says he won't stop until his cup is full of rain. He says Mary is the woman he wants to be with for the rest of his life."

A hush fell over the room.

"Thank Christ, his cup is almost full," Fred said before turning away to bellow an order into the kitchen. The last song Gmiwan sang before he brought his tin cup full of rainwater and offered it to Mary was his most recent composition, "Ma', Sweet Cherry."

Mary loved her wildly romantic Gmiwan enough to marry him, but would he be the right man for her, she wondered. She needed to walk around in the places of her childhood. She needed to put herself where she hoped she might know her heart better, and where she might find something to guide her. She did not doubt how she felt about Gmiwan; it was just that she knew feelings were only one part of a good decision.

As she set her foot down on the same ground she had walked as a child, her gut filled with the feeling of a bird trapped in a cage. Panic and anger and sadness churned in her belly, but then she became elated as the power to decide when and where she would walk washed over her. She thought of The Mohawk Institute, and all the nights she had lain on the thin mattress that smelled of moth balls, with her hand gripping the cold steel head board of the little bed, craving for the velvety comfort of being back nestled in her furs, smelling the wood smoke and hearing the breathing of people who only ever expected her to be who she really was. Mary savoured the melancholy in a way that she rarely indulged. Today was different. Today she needed to exercise her own free will to walk around where she wanted.

She didn't exactly have a plan. She only knew that to make a good decision for her future, she first needed to visit her past.

The bus pulled away, leaving its whining echo and smoky clouds to thin out and settle all around Mary. She took a few steps and stopped. She needed to get her bearings straight. The only person she knew she might still be able to contact was her old aunt. Elizabeth had said she heard that old Coyote was still living on Gramma's farm by the train tracks where Gramma and Maggie got killed.

Mary gave herself a shake and headed to the front doors of the post office/bus station.

She approached the teller at the counter and held open her hand. "I need to get to this address."

The man took the wrinkled piece of paper from Mary's hand, held it up and tilted his spectacles to focus on it.

He read aloud, "Line 3," he peered at her over the rims of his glasses, "what's the address?"

"That is the address."

"That's not an address. Do you know how long that road is and how many houses, farms, and then miles of bush are on it? You people never do anything the regular way," he snorted, "I'll call for a ride for you. Best I can do."

Mary spotted a row of chairs and went to sit down and wait. She estimated it was just past an hour when the door behind her opened and in sauntered a grown-up Farley Whitesnake. Farley used to come over to smoke cigarettes and play Snowsnake with Porter in the wintertime. The memory was spotted with spaces that had been erased by time.

"Farley Whitesnake, is it?"

He didn't recognize her, but she knew it was a Whitesnake. All of the boys had their father's juicy lips, bad-boy swagger, and a big sheepish grin when you spoke to them. "Why yes it is, but—"

"Mary Stone," she said.

He crinkled his eyes at her. "Well, I'll be. Last I heard, they stole you and put you in The Mush Hole. Ruben heard that Elizabeth got out, but we never heard what happened to the rest of you. How are you?"

"The Mush Hole, eh?! Do you mean the Mohawk Institute?"

"Everybody just calls it The Mush Hole."

Mary shook her head and cast her eyes on the ground, "Well that name fits it better," then she straightened her posture again and continued, "anyway, I took off from that place a few years ago, got a job at the Jackson

Diner and now I'm doing just fine." She levelled her gaze with his, "Say, do you happen to know how to take me to this address?" She offered up her little slip of paper.

He looked down at it.

"So what do you want me to do with that?"

She held it up in front of his face.

"Don't read real good."

"Oh, I see. Well, it says Line 3. Do you know how to get there?"

"Well, who ya goin' t' see?"

"Coyote."

"Oh," he said as his big grin came back, "Why didn't you just say so. My buggy's outside. Some people say I should buy a car," he said as he climbed in up front and started the horse moving with just a clicking sound. "But I don't understand why. The horse is still a good horse, the wagon's got a roof on it, and after a person gets in and relaxes for a while, they don't seem to mind. You know, lots of times those cab drivers won't bother themselves to come all the way out here, but we just live down the road. Ma and I got a phone put in so we could get the calls and make some extra cash if I'm around. Ma stays home and cooks all the time and everybody comes to visit us. Me, I spend a good amount of my time hunting in the bush so Ma has lots to cook with and the family's got lots to eat when they come."

"That's a happy life!" Mary declared, "Are you married?"

Mary knew it was a personal question, and she thought maybe she should explain that the only reason she brought it up was because she had marriage on her own mind. Instead she kept quiet and let him do most of the talking.

"Nope and don't know if I ever will."

"Guess you probably have to find somebody who wants to cook and take over the house some day, that is if you really want to keep your happy life, eh?"

"You put it good that way. Could be, but so far there is nobody outside of my clan."

"What is a clan?"

He turned to look at her to make sure she was joking. Nope, there it was again. The Indian Agent comes along and steals the Indian right out of the Indian. Lucky his Ma had the good sense to hide him when he was a kid.

"Say, where did they bury your Ma?"

"Up on the hill in back of our old property."

"Yeah, I was thinkin' about that when I realized it was you. After they took you, your brother and sisters, and then your Pa enfranchised, all that land, even where your place was, got sold and they built a dam. Your Ma's place and all those graves got all covered up."

Mary shook her head and looked away.

"Ma never had much luck."

"Yeah, and your Pa never saw it sold and tore up anyway. He was so broken up he just wandered off somewhere not too long after they took you. I heard he took off, married an American white woman and had some more kids. Do they bother with you?"

"Na." Mary shook her head. "Pa always just goes along with whatever the woman says."

Farley nodded. "Yeah, that's not a bad way of bein' as long as it's a good woman."

"You know, I think that sometimes people just gotta live the life they are living and not worry about the one they lost. I don't think Pa ever felt like he could do anything about it. I saw the look in his eye when they took us out the door. Ma said that Pa never raised his hand to anybody in his life, but he was the working kind, and that was what a person could depend on."

"Don't feel bad, fightin' one of those Indian Agents is like pokin' a stick in a bee hive. For every one o' those Indian Agents, there's a hundred more government workers ready to come out and finish you off with all their other rules they made up there in the big city somewhere. Can't win. Can't even hardly be strong when families have been moved around so much, nobody knows where they come from. Matter of fact, can't even get along amongst ourselves. Some people around here are still following the ways of the Hereditary Chief while others are feedin' off the money from the Band Council."

"What's a Band Council?"

"The government come in here, built some kind of an office, and put Indians that will listen to them. The reason those Indians listen to them is to get the land and money. Lots of people don't know how else to feed their family. The government wanted to get the power away from the Hereditary Chiefs and Clanmothers and it worked. There are some that are hiding the kids and sneakin' off to the bush to do ceremonies, but then there's others that are ready to go squealin' on them to the churches. Then the churches go squealin' to the government to make laws against all the old ways. The 'Prayin' Indians' get more land than the 'Bush Indians.'"

"Enh, churches," Mary nodded in agreement, but then it came to her, "do you know how to get to the Queen's Chapel, the one that The Mush Hole used?" She had decided to call it the much more befitting name from now on.

"Sure I do."

"I have changed my mind. I just realized that that is why I have come here. I need to go to the Queen's Chapel."

Farley understood that sometimes a person needed to go back to a place just to call their spirit back, and he thought about asking her if she had some medicine of her own to burn when she got there, or offering her some if she didn't, but he kept quiet instead. He liked her enough but he didn't trust outsiders, especially if there was a chance they were Prayin' Indians. He didn't need some Indian Agent comin' around.

Farley stepped up the pace of the horses and headed down Chief's Road toward the road to The Queen's Chapel. They both rode for some time in silence before Mary decided to go back to the original subject.

"Maybe someday a girl will call and ask for a horse and buggy ride."

"Hmmmm. They do call, but the ones that are leavin' can't be talked into stayin' and when they come back, they don't come back in good shape. And there'll be no skinny white girl for me. Ma said I'd have to move out, and she wouldn't be 'ceptin' no grandchildren from a light skin."

Each retreated to their own worlds, as the country-side moved past them, and they stayed that way until the wagon pulled up to the agreed upon destination.

"Well, here it is."

Mary hopped down from the wagon.

"Can you come back and get me in two hours?"

"Yeah," Farley said. He stared straight ahead, as he handed her the small bag she had been carrying beside her. The place gave Farley a bad feeling.

"See you in a couple of hours."

Farley didn't look back as he drove away; it was bad luck. Neither did Mary linger to wave.

Mary stood still for a long time facing a landscape symmetrically dotted with maple trees and gravestones. The property was framed on one side by a majestic and rushing river, and on the other side by a tangle of cedars, pines, oaks, long grass, and lost, unmarked, and unspoken of graves. She remembered that the polished and ornate stone crosses, angels, and saints that were evenly spaced amongst the maples stood not for children, but more for men and the wives of men of whom she had never heard.

Off in the distance, on the other side of the patch of unkempt trees, which she knew broke into an apple orchard, the road behind her curved and led to The Mush Hole. In front of her was a flagstone path that cut a straight line to the front doors of the Queen's Chapel. Peering at it through these trees and her memory, it seemed dwarfed.

Mary started up the path. Was it just an amazing coincidence or providence that fingers of sun reached down from the sky the moment she cast her eyes upon the arched oak doors? She placed her hand on the warm brass handle and tried the door. Inside, the cool dark air was streaked with layered colours from the majestic stained glass windows that lined the walls on either side of the church. Images of brown-skinned Indians in full regalia, kneeling and accepting all forms of plenty from British dignitaries, were cut and pieced into the glass and fell re-created across the cherry wood pews and gleaming hardwood floor. The sharp and distinct elements of goodwill passed through the air, distorted where the sun and bits of dust were, and splashed into watery caricatures on the seats and floors. Mary stepped inside the familiarity and breathed in the goodness of finally getting the chance to be here alone.

Proceeding up the aisle, she passed through the tinted air and made her way to the front of the church. She slid into a pew. Each moment was unfolding with pure presence as she began to realize one of the reasons she had journeyed here. She needed to say a prayer. Mary bowed her head and addressed God.

"Dear God: Do you remember me? I used to pray to you here in this house. You used to answer my prayers. So I have come again to drink from that lake. My journey here was to ask for your guidance in a decision I must make. A boy, whom I think I can love for the rest of my life, has asked me to marry him. I am only me, and I do not always know everything about what is good for me. I feel afraid and I feel excited. What do you think? Please show me the signs that will help me with this decision. Thank you, Amen." Mary heard her own voice echo as if she were a child again.

Mary sat back with her eyes still closed to listen for any thoughts. The more she stilled herself, the more alive the sounds around her became. The multitude of different birdsongs that filled the air outside was the church's choir. There was a window open somewhere from which a soft, warm breath found the back of her neck. Her eyes fell upon the magnificent gold cross hanging on the wall, towering over the pulpit, and her mind drifted back.

She remembered being forced to come to this place and sit in the hard wooden benches for endless hours. She was told it was where Gizhemanidoo was, but she must not call Him that. She must call Him "God." She must make of herself a lamb that He may choose to sacrifice, if He so wishes.

Who was God to Mary? For the first couple of years this place was nothing more than the other place up the road. That was until Father James was sent here. Father James was the one who came along and made a few things make sense to her and the only reason he had been sent here was because he was being punished. That's what he said himself. There never was any other person that worked at The Mush Hole that spoke so openly to the children yet not the other adults. When the adults didn't come around for Sunday service, which wasn't very often, Father James would let everybody sit any way they wanted in the wooden pews, as if they were sitting around at the kitchen table and just talking. Everybody seemed to listen to him better that way anyway. Mary recalled the first time this ever happened.

"Yep, I'm here with you little buggers all because of the shoddy work I did with the Indians up north."

He stopped for a minute and lit a cigar. Then he used the collection plate for the ashes.

"I guess I failed to turn those free-roaming Indians into Anglicans, so they sent me here where the congregation is already a captive audience. All that I have to do is stand up front and preach the word of God. I'm not a bad minister; it's just that I am recalcitrant in my belief of freewill. Yep, it's true. I'm getting old, but I'm guessing that's exactly what they are counting on!" His voice raised and he pounded on the back of the pew in front of him as if it was his pulpit. "What they didn't count on was, because I tire easier, I have been forced to become wily. You people have been dragged here from your homes because you had no religion. Y'all do so have religion!"

He had what Sophie called a southern drawl in his voice, and it seemed to pick up speed and emphasis as he went on longer. It was nice. Mary liked it. It was musical.

"Oh yea brothers and sisters, but you are all heathens who need to be folded into the flock of Jesus by His own would-be disciples. 'Let the children come,' they say as they carry out the highest act of arrogance in all of the land. In days of old, blood was shed openly in their holy crusade but now is cloaked by walls and paper. Alas there is no magical or sweeping thing I can do or say to snap my peers and superiors out of their conceited abracadabra. The last time I stood passionately to rail against the direction of these winds of change, it picked me up and plunked me here, with you, tired and sick and with not much to lose.

"Brothers and sisters, I will give you Bible teachings, but I urge you to be like Saint Thomas and doubt. Don't believe everything they 'say. I am filled with shame and remorse for them using my beloved Saviour's name, Jesus Christ, to kill the Indian in the child, and yes I am a schemer. I confess that I am scheming to atone for the sins of my fathers, one by one, child by child, I will always endeavour to undo that which has been perpetrated upon this beautiful and graceful race.

"Believe that when they call you a heathen, that what they are saying is that from the day you were born, God, the same God as their God, has been woven into your every thought and deed, and all without the bitter tonic of guilt. Your grandmothers and your grandfathers teach you that you have your natural place in this natural world. Believe still that you are part of it, not in charge of it. This is pure ancient wisdom."

Mary would never forget how he ended his first private sermon. Father James took another sip from the silver communion cup and drew from his cigar as he concluded the same way that he later often did: "Whether they call Him God, Jesus, Creator, or Great Spirit, there is only One, and He is One with all. I am a Transition Practitioner and your guide in this hailstorm of pecker-faced black robes, and neither aching loins nor tired bones will pull this ship off course."

Elizabeth said it was all cow shit, but when Mary was inside these walls she could feel Spirit. If it was Jesus, fine; if it was God, no problem; if it was Creator, no matter either. It just seemed as though whomever "He" was, he had been arrested by the soldiers of kings and queens, who dreamed they could hold "Him" captive in these walls, and what none of these Keepers of the Truth realized, was that he really goes willingly, because the hungry are who He loves.

Mary opened her eyes and took in the diminutive grandeur of the Queen's Chapel. Lush hues, silver chalices, and rich dark wood, it was strange comfort. Like the relief that is felt after a toothache subsides, one would be hard pressed to know whether it was the magic or the subsided toothache that caused this pleasure-laden moment.

After a while the cherrywood pews began to press hard on Mary's back. She stirred and shifted but could not regain comfort. She rose, squeezed herself out into the aisle, and turned toward the door she had left open. Walking back down the aisle, through the sunlit images, the skin on her arms and neck tingled as the hairs reached to touch something elusive. Shape-shifting colours danced on her, dappling her warm and cool as she passed through them and reached the gaping door.

It was good to get back outside. The air was whiter and filled with the song of bird community. Spirit was strong and present. She was thirsty. Mary looked for the red water-pump that she remembered. A steel bucket dangled from its spout, and a tin cup hung on a nail as if nothing had ever been moved. She approached it, and let her fingers light upon the handle. She knew this pump bored deeply into a cool and crystal clear underground spring and remembered that they had to sneak it. Suddenly it occurred to her that she was lucky that she had come on a day that nobody was about the property. A feeling of panic gripped her momentarily until again she was flooded with the realization that though they could come along and make her leave, she had walked here with her own two feet and nobody could make her stay.

Mary drew up on the iron lever and then pushed down with one hand while letting the water run from tepid to icy cold over her other. Releasing the lever, the water ran freely for a few moments and she cupped both her hands to catch it. She drank some from her hands and then splashed it upon her face, then she started walking, weaving her way in amongst the trees and letting her hand pass along the tops of the oversized gravestones. She did not go into the ominous thicket that was beyond the cut grass, for fear of disturbing the secrets that were kept there. This was not a day for fear. This was a day for redemption, and she was in charge of it. Finally, giving in to a luxurious fatigue, Mary sat down, and fitting herself nicely into a rounded curve in the base of the tree trunk, gathered her hair up with her hands. Perhaps, she thought, she would braid her own hair for the ride back. Perhaps she would braid her hair and prepare for Farley to come back and retrieve her. She let herself fall deeper past the mundane thoughts of time, and she began to drift off. As she was floating downward, she felt as though she were a downy feather that had fallen from the wing of a loon as it passed overhead. She meandered, in abandon to the will of a playful wind, and she drifted, until she found the dream world.

Eventually, a gentle wind moved through the orchard carrying the sweet scent of white apple blossoms to open Mary's eyes. The bird community, alive all around, darted to and fro amongst the branches overhead, and two mourning doves ventured nearby, picking through the grass, looking for something to dine upon. Mary looked up and spotted a figure walking through the trees toward her, and soon it began to take on a familiar shape. It was an old woman, cloaked in black, weaving a deliberately haphazard path around the trunks and closer to Mary.

Holy Nekuwa broke into a grin to greet her. Mary started to jump up and run toward her, but something held her down. It wasn't fear that held her down, but contentment, or peace. To cast her eyes upon Holy Nekuwa again, she surrendered to the resistance and just smiled, waiting patiently and filled with joy, for the old woman to reach her side.

Even after Holy Nekuwa had ceremoniously sat herself down in front of Mary and while she fussed to adjust, Mary waited wordlessly.

"It takes longer to get comfortable when you are old," Holy Nekuwa said to her when she was done settling in.

Mary tried to open her mouth to exclaim, 'You are still alive!' and to ask, 'How did you recognize me?' and 'How is it that you are here?'

But Holy Nekuwa had already started to speak.

"Listen and I will give you some teachings. Choosing a companion is of the utmost importance because it is the strongest of bonds in life, so it must be approached with eyes, as well as heart, wide open. Remember, heart and body will sing loudly when in the throes of being with someone you find attractive. Here, just as in the case of all other turning points in your life, you can put your trust in the good of The Medicine Wheel.

"The Wheel is in the shape of a circle because the People believe that all things exist naturally in this pattern. If you want to be in harmony with your spirit and the earth, you will always carry yourself with this in mind, and us-ing your will, journey in the direction that the sun travels around the earth, exploring Her abundant store of knowledge. The Medicine Wheel was given to us by the Creator as a mirror to things unseen within you, waiting to be developed. All of the tools you need for your journeys are contained within The Medicine Wheel. Use it with gratitude as a guide on your path through life. It is your true self and the nature of all creation that you may discover. As this is, so it is also for courtship.

"In courtship, you will find that you meet another person in one of the Four Directions of the Wheel. If it is a good pairing you will find that you have a lot of hopes and dreams in common, but sometimes we need to journey for a while with someone whose hopes and dreams challenge our own. It doesn't matter. Growth is possible in peace or in conflict. Your happiness with another human being does not depend so much on how much you are alike as much as it does on how the two of you deal with your wins and losses. It is important to remember that the first human being to take the Earth Walk was half-human and half-Spirit, and, because of this, our experience here on this Earth Walk is light and dark. That is, you must accept you will have joy and sorrow; pleasure and pain; abundance and scarcity; life and death; and so on. It is fruitless to attach oneself to any one state of being as it would be like paddling your canoe against the current. I ask you, would you not use your eyes and ears to observe the character of the river? Your bravery to attempt something unknown? Your knowledge gained from listening to your Elders as tools of survival? And your keenness to the voices of your Ancestors to hear their sacred instructions? These are tools, all there for you within the teachings of the Medicine Wheel, but you must remember that, if you take the hand of another on this journey, then the two of you must support and honour each other's journeys.

"Travelling with another can sometimes make reaching your own destination easier. Sometimes it can slow you down, or even prevent you from it. Most travelling partners find it is less complicated to divide jobs between each other in a way that is suitable to individual skill as well as fairness. In the beginning of your trip, you are both full of promise and energy, but one never can tell what kind of weather is in store. There may be times that he cannot hunt, even though it is his job, or that you cannot make clothes or cook, even though you are the one who knows how to do it. Go with each other and find a place of power to have a sacred fire. The woman shall choose the place to make a fire and the man shall light it. Both of you bring wood to the fire and feed it while you face one another. Talk of the things you hope and dream. Speak of your places in the community and what work you do. Make known to one another the things that might cause you to take separate paths. Talk of your commitment to one another. Offer tobacco to the sacred fire and ask the Creator to speak to your hearts. Ask the Creator if this pairing is well in His eyes. Ask those that have come before and those that will come after if they will whisper their thoughts. Look into each other's eyes and know each other's soul. And, if you take the hand of another, begin your walk together in a clockwise direction.

"There are teachings for the Eastern direction each day that Grandfather Sun greets us with, and also each spring that Mother Earth offers us. Your childhood is your walk in the Eastern direction. It is a time to explore your gifts in the form of play, and it is a good time to spend out of doors interacting with nature and your peers. This helps you begin to know your place in Creator's plan. If you have good relations and Elders around, you are fortunate, for it is recognized that through playful interaction with your environment you build strength that will help you move on to the next season of life. In those relationships where the two have been children and played together, their bond and their understanding of one another is deepened. This is a gift of joy to the relationship.

"The Southern direction teachings of The Medicine Wheel are offered by summer, when the sun is high in the sky. The weather can be good and the body healthy, so it is a time to build and share skills. It is a time to do the work of the People. It is also a time for you to discover the White Wolf and the Dark Wolf that resides within you and to learn how to feed the one that you wish to be strongest. Doing the work of the People and having relationships helps you with this. It is a good time to heal old injuries—this you can do for each other. It is a time of work and bounty and preparation for the next stage of life.

"You will find many rich teachings for the Western direction of The Medicine Wheel in the autumn. Watch how the four-leggeds prepare for the north wind to blow. Each time that Grandfather Sun slips behind the trees in the west, it is a lesson. It can be a pleasant time, a time to enjoy the things you have gathered for yourself, but also a time to take care of some things you might have missed or perhaps need to correct. It is a time for the two of you to gather your experiences together and build wisdom and share your bounty with your relations.

"The Northern direction of the Medicine Wheel offers the opportunity and responsibility to share the gifts of our Earth Walk. Every night, and every winter, we are challenged to use our spiritual strength to offer healing to others and joy for ourselves without the abundance of Mother Earth while She is resting. It can be filled with moments of deep joy or sometimes of great suffering. It is your hope that your walk on the Red Road will have created good things upon which you can rely. You and your travel companion may help each other face the fear of darkness and by this perhaps ease the passing into your Spirit Walk. It is favourable to keep in mind that though it is sad to see Grandmother Moon's beauty wane it is not really the end. There are many gifts to be savoured when you have journeyed together through all Four Directions, but it can be difficult to be left alone when your body is old. This is a good stage of life for you to sustain yourselves on the fruit of what you created together.

"No person can tell you how long your walk together will be. Neither of you is more important than the other. Man medicine is as much needed as woman medicine. You are both equal and must honour each other."

Mary knew that she was dreaming. And she knew by the way that Holy Nekuwa bowed her head and finished talking that she had only a short chance to say thank you. Mary mouthed the words. Holy Nekuwa smiled and closed her eyes. When Mary opened hers again, she lay staring into the oak-leaf spackled blue sky above her, satisfied that she had gotten what she came for.

The Mush Hole

Something sliced through Mary's consciousness, threatening to split her head open. Beside her, Dolly started to wail and cling. Mary opened her eyes and searched for what was making such a ruckus. In the first grainy moments of awareness, she could not remember where she was. She waited, with panic rising, for things to come into focus, then, with vicious speed, it did. She watched in wide-eyed horror as the wicked woman from the night before, the one whose name was Mistress, came marching down the aisle between the two long rows of brown steel beds, cracking that same stick of hers on the steel foot rails. The memory of being hosed down descended upon her like a flock of squawking crows. Mary reached to her neck and touched where her hair used to be.

If this were another day, Mary would have been stirring of her own accord or being gently charmed awake by the creeping sun. Dolly would have been nuzzling in deeper to persuade Mary to stay nestled in the furs and blankets for a while longer. If it were yesterday, Mary would be just waking to the needlepoint of dread that started in her chest, even before she opened her eyes, as she realized that the reason there were no wonderful smells filling her up, was because Ma was not in the kitchen. But just yesterday, hope shined all around the edges of that darkness that blocked out the sun every morning, with the thought that Maggie would be coming to live with them.

Mary's life was in three parts now: before Ma, after Ma, and after the authorities took her. In the space of one day she had been yanked out of the only place she had ever lived, dragged through the night by strangers, hosed down, and had her hair lopped off by the tallest white lady with the meanest face she had ever seen. She had spoken to Mary like she was a mangy dog that nobody wanted around, yet they wouldn't let her leave. And now it was the next day, still nobody had even offered to feed her, and dizziness was gathering in her head. Mary had heard the old ones tell stories of starving to death because somebody read the signs about the weather wrong or maybe because people didn't put enough away. Starving to death was the theme of the scariest stories told around the fire. Mary could feel the hunger threaten and push against her belly, something she had only heard tell of and never felt with Ma and Pa.

It was a bad moment. Mary couldn't be strong for her baby sister, and Dolly feeling it, began to whimper in desperation. She grabbed and pulled at Mary, begging to be held tighter and for the whispering nonsense words that her big sister might have said to her to soothe her. But Mary's body was cold, her limbs were stiff, and she trembled deep inside her core. Like a strange and violent dance, beds came alive with girls as they scrambled out from under the covers just before the woman who was like a witch reached their foot rails. Mistress blew on the gold whistle hanging on a gold chain around her neck, swept her pointer in the direction of two or three beds, and screeched out orders.

"Get moving! Get moving!" she bellowed and hissed at the top of her voice. Occasionally she would break her stride to stomp her feet, calling out, "Hop, two three four! Hop two three four," leaving in her wake two rows of hustling girls.

When the shrieking lady spotted Mary, her eyes narrowed.

"You!" she pointed. Then she blew fiercely on her whistle.

Mary stayed still like a rabbit. Dolly cowered.

"You first need to learn to make your bed. That is the very first thing you do every morning. Don't slink off to the toilet, or any other lazy trick. Make your bed! And there is a special way to make your bed. Sophie will teach you the proper way. Do you understand?" She screamed the last question.

Mary stared without responding.

"And another thing, why is that infant in bed with you?"

Mary could find no answer. Dolly had been sleeping with her ever since she was weaned from Ma.

"Children sleeping together is a gathering for the devil."

Mary looked away. Maybe it was some kind of witch-talk.

Mistress tucked her pointer stick under her arm against her body, and straightened her back.

"That infant will be leaving today anyway. We do not keep infants here, only school-age children." She looked around and then bellowed, "Sophie!"

Dolly started to scream and Mary, as she began digesting the full meaning of what was about to happen, struggled to pull out of the spiral of panic that was sucking her into blackness, though in the blackness, she knew there would be a sleepy numbness. But still, she could not afford the relief, for what would become of Dolly?

Gathering her mind back from the pull of the black, and focussing it like a yellow beam in her head on what needed to be done, Mary wrapped her arms around Dolly and whispered in her ear, "You lucky duck, you don't have to stay here."

Dolly shook her head. Mary knew she didn't buy it.

Mary whispered again, "Remember my words! Be strong!"

Dolly shook her head and her lips pouted like they always did when she was working up to start bawling.

Maybe they would be giving Dolly back to Pa, maybe they were going to give her to strangers, Mary didn't know, but she was afraid the tiny girl would exhaust their captor's patience. Mary knew only one thing for sure. She had absolutely no control over what they did with her baby sister, so she took what could be the last chance she was ever going to get. She disengaged Dolly and stood her up in front of her. She took Dolly's tear-streaked face in her two hands and brought her own face close so she could look at her eye-to-eye.

"Dolly," she said, speaking in the language of her mother's mother. "You must not let these people see your fear or they will use it to make you weak. You must keep a straight face, be nice, and always be polite."

Mistress grabbed Dolly's arm and started to yank. Dolly grabbed Mary's hand and held tightly.

"Do not speak savage here!"

The wicked woman's words were delivered at the same time as the searing hot pain of her stick came down upon Mary's arm, and the words of Ma's language dissolved into silence on her tongue, but still she did not let go. Mary's eyes locked with Dolly's.

Mistress's stick came down again, this time upon the top of Mary's hand, where the skin was the thinnest, and on the third time, when the tip of the stick also struck Dolly, Mary let her hand drop.

Still tugging on Dolly, the woman hollered for Sophie again.

Sophie arrived breathless and dotted with clusters of soapsuds.

"Take this child to the office, and I will be down shortly."

Sophie offered her hand to Dolly. Tears streamed from the corners of Dolly's swollen eyes, as she looked at Mary one last time, hoping against hope for the remotest chance that she didn't have to go.

Mary closed her eyes, breaking the contact for Dolly's ultimate good, bowed her head, and clasped her own hands behind her back. Dolly sniffled and rubbed where the stick had stung her.

Sophie came closer, bent down, then lifted Dolly up on her hip, and immediately started to walk away. Mary let herself look up again. Dolly strained and twisted to regain eye contact with Mary until they rounded the corner and disappeared.

Mistress turned her attention back on Mary, "Sophie is busy, but she will be back to teach you how to make a bed properly. Get into your clothes and come with the rest of them down for breakfast."

Mary stood motionless, waiting for the woman to leave so she could be obedient.

"Now!" she screamed as she cracked the steel bed rail with her pointer.

Mary was taught to never, not ever, disrobe in front of strangers, but the look in the woman's eye, told her that she was in danger if she didn't.

Mary reached under the bed and pulled out the bag she had been given the night before, and it worked. The woman, satisfied that her orders would be followed, turned her attention on someone else.

Mary sat on her bed and watched the other girls out of the corner of her eye. Virtually every single one of them had their dark hair in a blunt chin-length haircut. They were all dressed in the same white shirt, grey sweater, grey knee-length skirt, white ankle socks, and black hard-leather shoes. Mary watched how they put things on and copied them. She knew Mistress would be unforgiving if she got it wrong. Some of them clustered in groups, some lay back down on their beds, and some of them milled about on their own. Mary stayed put, sitting on the edge of her bed. The sweater made her scratch and the shoes squeezed and pinched her feet so tightly that she could not even move them inside.

After being marched down another set of stairs, they assembled in a cavernous hall filled with rows of long wooden tables. There was an odd quietness for so many girls in one room, and they all seemed to know where their place was. Sophie showed Mary to a seat. A bell went off, and the girls got up in single file lines with their bowls in hand. Before Mary's turn came, a great black curtain in the middle of the hall began to part. Mary had never seen anything like it. Floyd had grabbed onto the edge of it and was dragging its weight to one side all the way to the opposite wall, slowly revealing an identical other side of the room. It was filled with boys, Indian boys with shaved heads.

She was waiting in line when all the girls began chatting and twitching in their seats. The nervous anticipation rippling throughout the room prickled Mary's skin as it travelled past her. She strained her neck to see what could be happening. Suddenly, there was a collective gasp. Mary turned to see Floyd leading two ragged and sullen teenagers into the room. It was Elizabeth and Porter.

Floyd brought them purposefully to the middle of the room, and stopping them there, he threatened them with his fist before turning and walking away. Then he left the great room to its eerie whispering and gasps. That was when Mistress entered, her white heels clopping monotonously across the hall floor. Her pet pointer seemed eager as she rhythmically tapped and stroked it with her other hand. She stopped directly in front of the two ragged runaways, but instead of speaking to them, she turned and addressed the crowd.

Most of the children were already seated. Mary had reached the front of the line with her tin bowl, but the girl working at the oatmeal station had gone still, the long wooden ladle frozen in mid-air, dripping its pale goo back into the pot. Mary's heart cleaved to the wall of her chest as if it were about to leap out. She waited with bowl in hand.

"These two look like pagan savages," Mistress said as if starting a sermon. She paused to survey the room for any signs of disaccord, then continued, "their clothes are ripped and soiled, and their hair is wild and full of bugs from the fields they've run through and the tents they've lived in." Her voice thinned to a shrill point as she cried out, "they don't have any manners and they are filthy." Then she turned her pointer on her captive audience, and drawing with it in the air, she made a deliberate line around the room as if to leave none out. "In here," she hissed, "you will learn how to be functioning, law-abiding, God-fearing members of society, and outside of here, you will need this!" With the keen speed of a snake that has made the decision to bite, she brought the stick down on Elizabeth's back. She struck again and again, leaving no time for breath or defence, and the snapping sound of the stick as it met bare flesh mingled with the echo of Elizabeth's cries. Then she turned her stick on Porter.

Nobody moved.

The next sound was that of Mary's empty tin bowl clattering to the floor. She ran full speed to cross the distance between herself and her siblings, like a bird gathering wind for flight. Some who saw later whispered that Mary actually did fly. Hands outstretched, she ran until she could feel enough power beneath her to spring off the ground over the remaining distance, and, soaring through the air like a hawk after a snake, she landed on the Mistress's back. Caught with the pointer poised overhead for another thrash, the woman staggered, astonished for a moment or two under the gripping weight of a nameless attack before falling flat on her stomach, with her skirt up around her waist.

Mary emerged with her prey in hand. She broke the evil stick in two over her knee, and then threw the two pieces away in two different directions, beseeching aloud that Gizhemanidoo find a way inside here to catch them and blow them east and west forever. One piece clattered to the middle of the floor, and the other flew farther, softly planting itself in a fifteen-year-old girl's oatmeal.

Ruth looked at the arrow in her "mush" and then at the wicked Mistress spread-eagled on the floor. She touched her own missing pride of long hair, and then impulsively her hand went to a place on her arm that still stung but showed no mark. Closing her eyes, she could see again the swollen welts where the evil stick had licked her last year. When she opened her eyes, she saw Mistress, skirt still twisted and nurse's hat still cockeyed, scrambling to her feet. She passively kept watching as the woman then stomped over and snatched up one half of her broken stick from the floor and began frantically searching for the other half.

Glee tugged up at the corners of Ruth's mouth. A sweet breeze smelling of the apple orchards, which were just outside the window behind her, wandered around the nape of Ruth's neck and whispered into her ear. So with the stealth of a cat, she swiped the broken stick out of her mush and tossed it out the window.

Like a snarling rabid dog, Mistress gave up the search and turned to face Mary. The murmuring suddenly stopped, and the very air in the room seemed to cringe from what was going to happen next to the lone girl facing the Head Mistress of the Mohawk Institute. The woman narrowed her rabid eyes, crouched, and leaned over into the space between herself and Mary.

Mary, resisting the urge to back up, went still and felt around behind her with her hands. There was nothing. She felt as if she were on a cliff facing a dripping-fanged wolf with nobody but its pack looking on.

Mistress had no choice. To stay in charge, she had to dominate the heretic. She moved an inch more toward the child, but then looked at her empty hands in front of her and she wavered. Mary took that moment to change the rules. She took a straight line and charged head-on toward the very thing that menaced her. It was unmistakable. Nobody missed it. Mistress, baffled, stepped out of the way. Mary, looking up, was amazed that a path had opened up in front of her and so she headed straight for the door.

In the door, Mary ran full force into Floyd as he stepped between her and freedom. The impact with his body was like hitting a wall, and Floyd easily reached out and saved her with his big arms from a crash landing backward onto the floor. He scooped her up with the intention of holding fast until she stopped fighting. But Mary was caught, and she knew it. She stilled herself like a rabbit, and waited.

Everybody waited.

Mistress, confounded, looked around the room. She took the time to smooth down her skirt, straighten her hat, and draw in a breath. Floyd began to lower Mary down onto the floor to face her punishment just as something fell loose from her and landed first, with barely a thud.

It was the medicine bag. Mary and the Mistress locked their eyes on it as Floyd, not really sure what was going on, but feeling the twitch of the child still in hand, reflexively braced Mary by the shoulders against his body.

Mistress dove for the medicine bag. She snatched up the prize and held it up over her head like a trophy. Full of wicked satisfaction, she ripped open the top and thrust her fingers inside. She plucked out a feather and tossed it over her shoulder. It tarried a while in the air and then floated down to settle on the floor in front of Porter and Elizabeth who were rubbing the spots where the stick had bitten them.

"Carrying around stones and dirt! How primal! Get an education! Grow up! Purchase your children real toys!" She preached as if to phantom listeners as she let the amber stone and the snail shell drop at her feet. She scrounged around deeper and plucked out Mary's willow whistle. She held it up in front and turned to eyeball her prisoner.

Mary resisted screaming like a rabbit in the jaws of a coyote.

"A stick!" she snorted, "Why would anybody carry around a piece of a stick?"

Mary strained vainly against Floyd's iron grip.

"Aha, I see you like this one?" she said as her face cracked into a huge grin. She opened her pincers, let the whistle fall to the floor, and stomped on it.

The whistle that could call to Mary's mother and show her where her children were, lay crushed beneath the woman's heel.

Mary felt the power in her drain, and, in its empty place, hopelessness. Her knees buckled and she went limp in Floyd's arms.

Mistress snorted smugly and brushed herself off, then marched past Mary. Just before she walked out the door she turned, and with hands on hips ordered, "Sophie! Get the car ready. I am going to wash the vestiges of Indian dirt off and then we need to go to town and buy a new pointer. Floyd! Keep all three of them with you in the cellar until I get back and can personally tend to their training. They have not the privilege of being fed today."

That night, Mary lay in her bed, her hand warming a spot on the cold steel frame where she gripped to keep from losing herself. The abuses that had been trespassed upon her still pulsed in her body and rampaged through her head. Elizabeth, no longer sobbing, lay nine beds down, and where Porter slept, Mary did not know. Today they had learned how to wash, fold, press, and match marks on the labels to the marks on the bags. Numbers, they were called. Mary's number was seventy-seven. She whispered it, over and over again, and rubbed in a circle with her other hand, round and round, on the place where her empty belly burned, lighter and lighter, until she drifted off.

Holy Nekuwa whispered to her.

For thousands of years your people have lived, learned, gave birth, passed their lessons on, and died. They have survived the most hostile white and barren winters, shared their food so that their relations could survive, and fought the most ferocious animals and vicious enemies—all for you. You have all of your ancestral wisdom in you; you are the fruit; you are the sparkling tip of their long line. This is Blood Memory. Like those stars in the night sky, you shine back and watch each other. Never doubt; you have what it takes to survive.

MARY AND GMIWAN

TALL, WITH A gleaming steeple and a cross atop, St. John's Anglican Church was a good enough church. Mary could see it from her apartment over-top the post office and thought that if she ever got married, she should get married there. Gmiwan spoke of a Sacred Fire Ceremony but Mary had never heard of it; Harry said it was too odd; and Elizabeth told her to get with the times. Mary was curious about it, but when the Mayor told her that it wasn't recognized as a legal marriage, Gmiwan stopped talking about it. He said the time wasn't right. So on a sunny Saturday afternoon, Mary and Gmiwan got married at Jackson City Hall.

In the months leading up to the wedding, Mary went to the second-hand shop, bought a used white satin wedding gown, cut it up and redesigned it into a snappy form-fitting dress with a matching floppy hat. She removed the crinoline and re-cut the fabric so that it trumpeted from her cinched waist like a pristine lily. She dyed white, and polished to a gleam, a pair of used pumps. She could have carried a bouquet of white roses from the trellis on her terrace but instead she designed a fan of swan feathers. Ever since the day she had accepted Gmiwan's proposal she had been purposefully gathering them one by one on the banks of the Welland Canal, where she took her solitary walks on Sunday mornings. Mary noticed that when there were no ships passing through, the waters of the canal would still, and the swans would light upon its surface. Sometimes they would leave her a gift, as if they knew of her adoration.

Swans were the most elegant creations of power, disguised as beauty. Mary figured this was because they fly closer to Creator than any other living being. So Mary collected one feather for every person she wished could have been there on her wedding day but had left her life, and never spoke of their names to anyone. She assembled the fan on the eve of her wedding and dressed it in ribbons she hand-sewed from the scraps of her wedding dress. It was the only "Indian" thing she did at her wedding, and she didn't ask herself why, but she kept it a secret from everybody.

Elizabeth and Harry stood up for her, and the Mayor opened up his office and performed the ceremony as a special favour because it had to be on a Saturday; Saturday was the only day everybody could get off at the same time. When the ceremony was completed, and congratulations were in order, Mayor Dunsby held her for what seemed to her an achingly long time, but she understood. She had known for some time that he secretly loved her, but it was of no harm to her, because it was not a pushy or possessive love. It was a tender and enduring love. It was like the breeze you feel only if you stop and think about it.

Neither Mary's nor Gmiwan's bosses would give them more than the weekend off, so they spent their honeymoon moving Gmiwan's things into Mary's apartment, but it didn't matter, because nothing else was needed when there was the bliss of being naked and waking up together for the first time. They were filled with the sexy medicine of two birds building their nest in the springtime, and for weeks they secretly resented anything that sidetracked them from each other.

Now and for the past year, the name Fisher was Mary's, and she damn well liked it. Mary Fisher! Mary rubbed her round belly where the baby inside had grown, and poured more Carnation Milk into her morning tea. She took a sip of the sweet hot tea, and let her gaze soar like the morning doves over the rooftops of Jackson, and light upon the steeple of the church that she did not get married in. She smiled at the memory of some voice in her that had insisted she would never find happiness if her marriage was not sanctioned by the holy nod of the Church of England.

She had risen early just to linger in her rooftop garden before going to work. Soon the mornings would be different. The thought of her and Gmiwan having this baby warmed her to the core like the sun did on her back the start of every day. Now, she opened the creaky wooden door that took her from the patio to her kitchen and let it slam behind her just for the noise. If they stayed in her little flat above the post office, Gmiwan would have to put a good lock on the door so their child couldn't get out on the rooftop. Yes, everything was going to be different, Mary thought, but she was ready for it.

She rinsed her cup in the porcelain sink and set it on a cloth to dry. At work, she imagined the cup was waiting for her to get home. It was one of those thoughts she used to keep herself company when the shadows of loneliness lurked around the corners of her tiny apartment. Mary looked up and parted the red checkered curtains to look back out to the rooftop where her potted portulaca worshipped the sun in mounding colours. Already watered, they were reaching for fulfillment and growing in gratitude. Nearby, a plain brown cardinal hopped timidly toward the toast crumbs Mary had spread out earlier. Although she couldn't see him, Mary knew the male was somewhere, watching his mate, letting her eat first and, soon enough the red regal fellow came in for a landing. He marched the immediate perimeter first and then approached his mate and ate by her side. Mary watched him, perfect in every male cardinal way, and thought of her expressive and artistic Gmiwan and smiled. She turned away and gazed upon the wall, which had stayed starkly barren for two years but was now laden with Gmiwan's art.

Mary's shift was dragging. It was hard to keep up a cheery front with an aching back so she looked forward to the time she could sit down and have her tea with Mayor Dunsby. She had switched back to a more formal address after realizing that he burned a not-so-secret flame for her, thinking it a means of consistently communicating back to him that she did not love him the same way. There were times—although not that often anymore—when just after she'd called him Mayor Dunsby, he would nod in a way that still asked the question, "Do you love me yet?"

When he arrived, she set the tray down and carefully fitted herself in the non-negotiable space allowed between the table and bench seat of the booth. "Whew!" she patted the belly that just grazed the table's edge and proclaimed, "Just making it nowadays."

"It's a marvel how you have continued to work."

She poured the Carnation Milk in a precise stream from the can into her tea. "What else would I do, with Gmiwan gone most of the time? Might as well keep working."

He nodded, "It can get lonesome spending too much time by yourself."

This was another one of those times, Mary thought. Normally, in this type of situation, one might feel compelled to suggest to Mayor Dunsby that he take up dating. But Mary wouldn't bother because she knew the answer. She had heard him say it often enough to other people. He would respond by saying, "There's no use shopping around when you already know what you want."

So instead Mary said, "You still miss your mother, don't you?"

He poured his own tea. "I guess that must be it."

He looked closely at her now. "You do look tired. Maybe you should send for Gmiwan now and let Fred and Marlene's daughter take over for you."

She plopped two heaping sugars in her tea. "She'll get my job soon enough. I have a good plan in place. When the time comes, Sophie will use the diner's phone to call Harry and Elizabeth. Gmiwan will come straight away." Mary squeezed her tea bag until every bit of black leeched out, darkening the tea from the colour of butterscotch to coffee.

"Of course he will, but will he be going back after the baby is born?"

He adjusted the glasses on his poker-straight face. One was hard pressed to catch a glimpse of emotion on the face of Mayor Dunsby, even on election day.

"He has to," she said, savouring her first sip. "We both have to work right up to the last because Gmiwan is going to stay home with me for the ten days."

"Why ten days?"

Mary put her teacup down but kept it loosely cocooned in her hands. "The ten-day baby-sick. My mother, her mother, and many mothers before her always took a ten-day baby-sick. If you lived in a village, they built a lodge for the woman to go to, but if not, then you just stayed in bed with the baby for ten days.

"Nowadays, usually a sister or a friend comes and does your work for you. The only work the woman does is take care of the baby. It all works out just fine. The babies like it because they get to know the mothers before they have to be set down while she does her other work. They say after ten days you are really ready to get out of bed. It's not really the man's way to leave his work for ten days, but we thought, since he has to be away so much, and we don't have a grandmother, it would be better for us as a family."

Mayor Dunsby nodded, "That's interesting. Most of the time I forget you are an Indian, because you aren't like a lot of Indians, but then you go and say something like this and remind me."

"Oh?" she leaned back and pressed her hand into the small of her back, "and what are most Indians like?" She rubbed down the spreading ache.

This was one of the reasons he enjoyed Mary so much. It was completely safe for him to drop his political veneer and really discuss something.

"There is a problem with the Indians."

"Ohhhh, the Indian problem." She closed her eyes as if to visualize it.

"The problem of them being uncivilized, you mean. And then you look at me. I'm sitting here in front of you completely civilized, right?"

He nodded, "Yes, that is correct."

"But you can't go by me."

Mayor Dunsby blinked.

"I'm gonna tell you a story," Mary heard herself take on the storytelling tone of her Aunt Maggie. "When we were kids, Porter, Elizabeth, and me were playing in the bush out back of our place one day when we came across a bed of baby raccoons nestled and cozy in a hole in a tree. There didn't look to be anything wrong with them except their mother wasn't around. We made up a story in our heads that their mother must have taken off the night before for food and got killed. But the truth was, they didn't look like they were hungry or scared. They were too young to be scared of us, so we picked them up and played with them. We heard a noise and sure enough, there was the mother looking right up at us. She knew she couldn't do anything about it because we were bigger than her. We knew it too. And not only that, Elizabeth made the suggestion that now that we had handled them, the mother wouldn't like the smell of them and would probably kill them. We looked at the snarling mother raccoon and came to the conclusion that we would save their lives.

"There were three raccoons, one for each of us. So we each climbed back down the tree and took them home. We showed them to Pa straight away, and he told us we could do what we wanted but we couldn't make a pet out of a raccoon. So we put them in a box and started feeding them a milk they give babies if the mother's milk doesn't come in. Ma showed us how to, and we made it ourselves out of fish oil and nuts crushed into a powder between two stones. All of us were devoted to feeding the raccoons. It kept us occupied all summer. In the fall, Pa suggested we keep them in a cage outside because they were still too small to let go. If the truth be told, we never wanted to let them go. Pa told us again that we could do what we wanted but raccoons have a way of life that doesn't go well with ours. The raccoons started getting bigger and getting into things. They made a mess everywhere and, since we were used to living in a clean house, all of us ended up with a lot more work to do. Ma and Pa could have complained about keeping them in the house all winter but they let us learn on our own.

"The winter can be a hard time for people who don't have too much. There was enough food for us but not the raccoons. Ma and Pa said we could give them ours if we wanted to. And not only that, the raccoons started to growl and snap at us. The female became vicious. Pa said it was in their nature to become cross and they weren't animals that lived in communities such as wolves or coyotes. Porter, being the oldest, made the rule that they were big enough to put outside, and we all agreed. They had a better chance of finding food out there anyway. But we all knew in our hearts that looking at it the way we did, was really only a convenience. We were in the cold of winter, and the raccoons, with no mother to teach them, didn't know anything about getting food.

"After we put them out, they didn't seem to remember any affection they may have felt for us. They never hung around the door or came up to us when we were outside to get wood, yet they still hung around the area. All that they knew was that sometimes, if we could, we would throw scraps out for them. The end of the story is that they all got skinny and ratty looking. We found the two males dead in the spring, and we never knew what happened to the female. She could have gone off and died somewhere or she could have figured out how to survive.

"Those raccoons weren't the only baby animals that we ever brought home to try and raise. There were baby squirrels and birds, and even a baby skunk. Kids will do that, but they were the ones we kept alive the longest. With the raccoons, we finally learned that if you're born a raccoon, you have to be with raccoons to learn how to live your life like a raccoon, because in the end, you aren't anything else but a raccoon. Yes, maybe there are times that something is going to die and something else comes along and can save it but that doesn't happen too often."

"I see what you are saying, but the best survival instinct is learning how to adapt to your environment."

"Yes, but how many generations did it take the wolf to become a dog? I bet there were mistakes along the way." Mary drank the last of her tea. "And by the time it wakes up as a dog, perhaps from a nice sleep at the side of your bed because it hears a distant howl in the bush, being a wolf seems like only a dream."

"Yes, I see your point, but surely the dog is happier being a dog than a wolf because there is more food available."

"Maybe so, maybe not, but whether the dog licking your hand for a scrap is any happier than the wolf hunting all night for one mouthful of field mouse, is not my point. My point is the time it takes to get there."

Mayor Dunsby cocked his head.

"How many years and generations did it take to get to this point? How many wolves with warm fur coats were killed off before they were mostly gone? Then how many wolves died of starvation, or were killed for attacking humans because of people taking the land for farms and cities? What if you popped your mind into one life of any of those generations of learning the hard way? Would you have looked at the witless wolf laying there bleeding because you shot it for stealing chickens, shake your head in compassion and say, 'It was just on its way to becoming a dog?' Would you know that it just fathered a pup that becomes an even worse hunter or never even tries? That pup grows up and doesn't attack too much, he never gets to be leader of the pack, and so he mates with a skinny quiet female. His pups aren't too scrappy, and they can't hunt either. Eventually, either they come out of the bush or they die.

"My Pa used to say that the wolf is our brother so it must have been natural for him to take this direction when all the other ways got blocked. By this I think he was talking about all the good hunting grounds that are disappearing under farms, cities, factories, and roads. Through time, this goes on and on, until there are no more wolves left, only dogs. Then everybody says they miss the wolf."

Mayor Dunsby nodded his head, "I get your point."

Mary could tell that he didn't get her point but she knew he was the type that would never admit that.

Mary went on, "Take my Gmiwan. He was raised for most of his childhood on the Alderville Indian Reservation with his people. Then his mother picked up and moved to the city. She did it for a man. She did it because there wasn't enough to go around so her kid would need to be provided for after her first husband died; and because she did it, she lost her hereditary land. Now his mother is dead and his brother is the favourite, so Harry gets everything. Gmiwan didn't go to white school so he still believes in all of the ways his mother taught him, but the problem is that he has to make a living in the money makers' world because there is no place for him to go back to. All his mother's people turned their backs to her when she left.

"Me, I spent half my childhood with my people and the other half with strangers. I tried to go back and there was nobody to go to. So, the strangers that finished raising me made their imprint on me and I couldn't tell you if I am better off or not. I read, I write, I work, and I can put up with almost anything. I know that I am not a problem to anybody, so that part was a success, but I am still a problem to myself in ways that I cannot even begin to understand. So I look at it like this. I could have been like a baby bird and just let myself die, or I could have been like a raccoon and let myself get lazy, but I guess I was more like an orphaned wolf pup and wandered around looking for another pack. I have no idea whether that makes me happy or not. It doesn't matter. I survived.

"As for my Gmiwan? He has an artist's spirit, like his father, or so his mother told him. But Gmiwan said his mother had a warrior's spirit. She died in a fire you know. She and the youngest baby were found in the stairwell. The fire started in the middle of the night and she ran back in for the baby after she got Gmiwan and Harry to stay put with their father. Gmiwan says that both the artist and the warrior's spirit live in him but neither one are useful in the money makers' world we live in.

"Gmiwan is not so good at adapting. It's hard for him to accept that money is how we survive now. For Gmiwan, having things or being hungry doesn't matter that much, but he knows that he must learn new ways because a child is coming, so that is why he agreed to be away and help his brother from losing his last factory. But still, he is deeply depressed at not being home where he is loved and he can do what he loves. So really neither of the spirits that live within him is being fed."

"That doesn't sound very good." Mayor Dunsby cocked an eyebrow.

"Don't worry about me. I have saved for a rainy day."

"Well," he tipped his empty teapot, "I do worry about you," he said flatly. The way he said things like that, without expression on his face, made other people uneasy. His curbed ways didn't bother Mary. In her mind, a person could be the way they wanted to be.

He set both his hands on the table, the way people do when all is said and done for now, and shuffled himself out of the bench. He never had too far to slide because he always sat on the outside edge of the bench like he wasn't in the mood for company. Sometimes people would slip in on the other side and start up a conversation, and Mayor Dunsby seemed to be quite okay with it, but it was always their idea. He was a creature of habit. She watched him get up. She noticed he was getting heavier in the middle, and his skin was becoming paler and looser. He turned to lift his coat off the hook on the back of the bench where he had been sitting, and then reached for his hat. He gave the hat a feather light pat and, turning to face her, he bade good-bye with a nod of the head. The Mayor Dunsby leaving ceremony was almost complete. It was not his habit to be the first person to bid goodbye to anybody, so as he walked toward the door, he returned the goodbyes called out to him by the staff and diners. He would never turn back around as if he wished to tarry longer for more of the present company. Mayor Dunsby was a very official man.

Sophie spotted Mary, still sitting in the booth alone with her eyes pinched shut and her hands on her lap. She set the Jacobs' tray down and went to her. Placing her hand on Mary's shoulder she whispered, "What's wrong sweetie?"

"My back hurts so much that I can hardly stand it."

"Show me where it hurts, Doll."

Mary rubbed the place in her back where the pain pulled and let go, "It's starting to come through to here," she said, touching the underside of her belly, and, in that moment, as it dawned on her what could be happening, her eyes widened into liquid deep pools. She looked up. "Do you think it has started?"

"I definitely think it has started," Sophie answered. She scanned the diner for Fred and Marlene. "Just a minute! I'll be right back."

Frieda Jacobs noticed Sophie darting off to the back room with more spunk than usual. She decided not to wait for her to come back and tend to their tray of Tuesday night Liver and Onions Special, which was beginning to cool, so she rescued it herself. Something was up so she sat herself back down on the bench in a place where she could have a better view of the goings-on. She cut into her liver.

"Tender," her husband commented about his own.

Frieda nodded.

She kept one eye and ear on things as she listened to her husband talk about maybe expanding his business to car repairs while with the others she noted. Frieda Jacobs could always be counted on to know what the latest was, and right now, there was something funny about Mary Fisher.

By the time Sophie returned to Mary's side she almost had all the details worked out.

"We can call Gmiwan now because it will take some time for him to get here. Marlene is going to stay and do my shift so I can go home with you. We'll call the doctor just before we leave to arrange for him to meet us at your apartment."

Mary folded her arms on the table and laid her head on them in search of relief from the building pain in her belly. Sophie sat down across from her.

"Mary?"

Mary looked up with tears spilling out, "I'm scared, Sophie."

Sophie touched the plum-coloured petal softness of her little friend's cheek.

"Don't worry, my Sweetie! Lots of women give birth."

"Yes, but not everybody lives through it."

"I guess that's true, but mostly everybody does." Mary smiled. "There, that's what I need to see," Sophie said, "but we still have one more problem."

Mary clutched at her side and her voice strained as she asked, "What is it?"

"You don't look in any condition to walk home."

Frieda Jacobs, slicing into her liver, piped up, "Aaron and I can drive you."

Sophie set Mary out on the terrace for a bit while she went in and tended to some tea. Through the red-checkered curtains, she watched Mary sitting, still and composed, in the garden swing, her hands clasped neatly on her lap as she looked out over the town. An illusion; Sophie hadn't seen her this frightened in a very long time. She knew the wide-eyed look in Mary's eyes reflected the driving light of an approaching train rather than the miracle of childbirth on the horizon, and that Mary was likely trying to figure some way of getting out of it. Cold water, bubbling from the overfull kettle cascaded over Sophie's hand and made her shiver. She shut the tap off, poured the excess down the drain, and placed the kettle on the stove.

Sophie knew Mary's kitchen well so she prepared a tray to take outside. She chose a china saucer with hand-painted blue windmills on it and placed six sugar cookies fanned out like a flower. She took the crystal sugar bowl from its usual place on the kitchen table and the can of Carnation Milk from the icebox. Nothing matched in Mary's kitchen because every piece was purchased at the second-hand store down the street. Whether or not things matched was rarely a concern to anybody who had tea in Mary's kitchen. Each person had a personal preference as to which cup or plate was "theirs" when they visited. Sophie couldn't help it either; her favourite was the gold trimmed Country Roses teacup with the Royal Albert saucer. For Mary, she chose the cup she must have used that morning and placed rim-side down on the tea towel. She relieved the bawling kettle of its agony, flicked the burner off, and poured steaming water directly over the tea bags in the cups. Mary didn't like teapots because everybody liked their tea different, and Mary was rather serious about her tea.

"The doctor's wife said he would wait no more than an hour before setting out. She said there was never any reason to hurry with first babies."

Sophie said too cheerfully as she let herself back out on to the rooftop terrace. "Is this your regular doctor?"

"I don't know anything about him. I've never seen a doctor. I took his name and number from the phone company."

"Mary! You've never seen a doctor!"

Sophie set the tray down on the table in front of the swing and checked her friend's face for jest.

"I don't get sick," the matter-of-factness in her voice thinned out at the last syllable with the strain from the beginning of another pain.

Not that Sophie qualified as an expert, but judging from the little experience she did have, the pains did not seem long enough yet to be considered critical, so she shook off any creeping worry and started to pour milk in her tea. She was bound and bent that she would be a steady rock for her Mary.

"So this is it, my friend. You look a little scared."

Mary looked up from fixing her tea. Her eyes, instantly full, spilled the fear that had been welling up inside her. She placed her cup down and started to sob.

"I hadn't given it a single thought until the first good pain hit. I swear to God. That was when it came to me that I could die."

Though Sophie considered that any girl having a baby for the first time would have some level of fear, it was out of Mary's character to let things get to her.

That was when the light bulb came on in Sophie's head.

"Oh, is this because your mother died giving birth?"

Mary, struggling to keep her composure, nodded, "It's like the pain opened up a part of my mind that I had closed off. Elizabeth was there when Ma died. She said that Ma had the baby all right. It was a boy. They put the boy in bed with Ma and then nobody heard a peep from them. Later on, when nobody was looking, Elizabeth snuck in to get a look at the baby and started screaming. The bed was soaked in blood. Maggie was the first to get there. Elizabeth said Maggie shook Ma until her arm fell away and she had to grab the baby from falling. After that, Maggie had to hold the baby and Pa came running in. With all the commotion, nobody noticed that Elizabeth was plastered up against the wall, watching Pa shaking Ma around until her eyes fell open. Elizabeth tells this story and cries if she and Harry drink too much."

"Oh," Sophie moved to a place beside her friend on the swing and took her in her arms, "that doesn't happen all the time. As a matter of fact, it doesn't happen very much."

"But it does happen," Mary whispered into the powdery scent of Sophie's neck.

Sophie pulled away from her and took Mary's face into her hands, "Listen, you can't tell yourself these scary things! That was your mother's fifth child and those were different times. There is a doctor coming who will know what to do if things do go wrong."

Mary searched the depths of her friend's eyes seeking only something to believe in.

"You aren't even built like your mother. You told me you took after your father's side of the family," Sophie feigned sternness.

Mary sniffed and lingered in Sophie's unwavering stare before finally collapsing to her shoulder, a place she had found comfort in times before. More settled now, she let her mind drift as Sophie stroked her hair. Eventually her eyes closed, and there she remained wafting in and out of consciousness with each wave of labour.

The ticking of the wind-up clock on the windowsill tattled that over three hours had elapsed when a clatter came from somewhere inside the apartment. The good doctor had arrived, let himself in, and was apparently meeting with an obstacle or two as he made the climb up the stairs.

"I just heard a horse and buggy coming down the street," Sophie whispered to Mary. "You don't think that doctor has come here in a horse and buggy do you?"

Mary, still blinking back sleepiness, shrugged her shoulders.

He started a coughing fit, before calling out, "Hello, hello," and then took back to coughing.

Sophie called back in a singsong voice, "We're out here."

A grey-haired old man, complete with spectacles and black bag at his side, appeared in the doorway between the kitchen and the rooftop terrace. He let himself out on to the terrace.

"Which one of ya's are Mary Fisher?"

Since Sophie had the figure of a fine porcelain doll, the two girls judged it a peculiar question.

"I'm Mary Fisher. I am pleased to meet you Doctor Faulkner." Mary managed a smile and offered her hand.

He blinked and let out a snort as he realized, for the first time, the reason for his late evening trek all the way from Beamsville. He peered over top of his glasses in a way that reminded Sophie of the way her old, alcohol-stenched English professor would lock onto some fidgety student before dismissing them as unworthy of any further discussion on the matter. Next to her, Sophie could feel Mary struggle to sit up under the good doctor's scrutiny. Then, suddenly, she winced and bent forward as if someone had taken a knife to the underside of her belly.

"I think we should get her to bed, Doctor, don't you?" Sophie kept her arm protectively around Mary.

"Is she staying here with you?"

"This is Mary's apartment! I'm her friend Sophie Saunders and I'm just here to lend a hand," Sophie explained patiently while she patted Mary's leg.

"I see," he rooted around in his breast pocket and pulled out a cigar. While he searched for a match, he clamped the stogie in his mouth by keeping his lips in the high fashion of a smiling dog, exposing unsavoury decayed teeth. "You take her along inside then and get her settled. I will be along just shortly."

Sophie bore most of Mary's weight as they struggled toward the door, and she started to pray silently that Gmiwan would get home soon. Inside the bedroom, Mary eased herself down on the bed, seeming to still herself and rest in a moment between rising crests of pain. Sophie tried to console her, but Mary didn't respond. She narrowed her focus into what was happening to her. Her eyes were open, but smoky in the way of a sleepwalker as the prior wild look of fear distilled into a centredness. Then suddenly another wave took hold of her, and she drew herself up on to the bed and sat cross-legged. She placed her hands on each of her legs as if to brace her posture into a straight up-and-down position. Mary stilled herself and waited.

Sophie sensed she shouldn't dare interrupt her.

It was easy to tell when the next pain coiled to strike. Mary, sitting up full length, would pull on the narrow end of its beginning and, with her breath, coax it up and fill her chest with it. There she held it captive with tiny breaths until it seemed her chest would burst from holding its full power within. Then by compressing her chest, she redirected the very life force of the pain to where the muscles of her belly visibly surged it downward toward the opening.

Sophie watched Mary. Mary would open her mouth in the last quarter of her final exhalation, and it struck Sophie as a purposeful way to encourage the opening. Had someone taught Mary how to do this, or was it some sort of primal instinct that had long been smothered under the generational layers of Sophie's own ancestry? In any case, Sophie was in awe, and resolved with sharp detachment that she should remain rooted at the end of the bed. If Mary needed her, it would become evident.

By and by, the doctor came in through the bedroom door, bringing in with him an air of cigar smoke and whiskey. "Why are the clothes still on?" he bellowed. "Do you people expect you can have a baby with your clothes on?"

His loudness startled Sophie into a skittishness that fractured Mary's stream of focus. Sophie jumped up, and trying to follow the doctor's orders, started to fuss over Mary. She told Mary to lift her arms. Mary, although dazed, complied. Sophie pulled the frock over her head, and as she did so Mary's hair sprung loose from its clip. Then she helped Mary with her bra and panties before tucking her under the covers.

Although the doctor may have finally recognized a patient, to Sophie it seemed that there was no human being more vulnerable than a woman trapped naked in the vortex of childbirth.

Mary whispered, "Sophie, can you please take the bedspread off?"

Sophie lifted it off and began folding it.

Mary, clutching the remaining white sheets to her neck, pointed to the far corner, "Please Sophie, put it over there."

The doctor busied himself with his black bag, spreading out his tools on the nearby bureau. The polished steely appliances glinted with the moon's light, which had come to the window as if to make witness, by flickering light on Mary's face.

Sophie hated to see that the fright in Mary's eyes had returned.

She returned to her spot on the end of the bed, but the doctor shooed her away, so she found a chair up against the wall and seated herself.

When Doctor Faulkner was finished placing his tools precisely in the place he wanted them, he turned to address his patient.

"Well," he said abruptly, "How far are the pains apart?"

Mary, wide eyed, whispered, "They've stopped."

"They've stopped!" he boomed.

"They've stopped. You can go home now," she whispered.

A spreading circle of wetness on the sheets cunningly laid bare Mary's lie. The doctor and Sophie stared down at it. Mary crouched up in as tight a ball as her body would allow.

"Well, in any case, I have made the trip here tonight, and I will not be making it again any time soon," he pronounced as he rolled up his sleeves, "Lay down for me now."

Mary racked with another pain, lost a whimper as she lowered herself on the bed. She knew she was in no position to not do as she was told. The doctor was in charge. Not she, or Sophie, or the moon could do anything but watch.

The doctor drew back the sheets and exposed Mary's lower half. Her legs were still cowered up as close to her body as possible. "Here now!" he addressed Sophie from over his shoulder, "come over and hold her legs in place."

Sophie rushed over and stood by while Doctor Faulkner thrust apart Mary's legs. "Stand over there, put your hands on both her knees and stop her from closing them while I work."

Sophie stood by Mary's side and leaned carefully over her protruding belly to lay weight on Mary's legs. There was no effort required whatsoever. She knew that Mary would have no intention of causing any more trouble for herself by kicking or thrashing about, but still, for comfort, Sophie kept her touch present on her friend's legs.

Mary lay there panting when the doctor brought all his fingers and thumb together in a point and jammed his hand deep inside her. Mary clenching her mouth into a thin line, stared straight up at the ceiling, and dug her hands into the mattress as if to hold on. She held still while he groped around inside assessing her perimeters. He trespassed for the longest time, watching his patient's face, until it seemed he got what he was waiting for.

"Good," he muttered to himself, "another contraction is starting."

Mary gave nothing away. She remained braced deep within the mattress while the pain attacked and retreated.

"Not too strong," he assessed and removed his hand abruptly.

Mary lay there quietly, but beads of sweat had broken out on her face and were soaking the thin white sheet that covered only her chest now. Sophie had removed one hand from her leg to stroke Mary's brow, and had let the other slide down to pat Mary's thigh. Meanwhile, the doctor was picking up one tool at a time, holding it up in thoughtful assessment, only to put it down and choose another. After a while, he found his favoured item: a long tong-shaped instrument with rounded paddles on one end and handles on the other. Sophie shuddered and checked that Mary was still staring at the ceiling.

He inserted the device into Mary and pressed inward using both hands until he got it in the position he wanted. Then he flicked a clamp to hold it in place. Mary tolerated it as she had his first intrusion but then another pain came. Sophie could actually see the contraction gather at the top of Mary's belly and bear down in a ripple until it seemed to pull the very bulk of her abdomen deeper within her body.

Mary expelled the birthing tool.

Doctor Faulkner cursed and put his gadget aside. This time he rolled up both his sleeves. He plunged his hand deep into Mary. Sophie could not believe what her eyes told her when she saw the doctor run his other hand along the length of his arm and up inside Mary. Fresh streams of sweat, escaping in glistening rivulets down Mary's temple, were the only prelude to what was about to happen next. Mary arched her back causing the last shred of soaked sheet anchored by Sophie's weight upon it to come away. Mary braced the burden of her middle upon her elbows, lifted herself off the mattress and began tilting forward in an effort to be more upright. Pressing forward with the sheer might of her will, she gathered enough force to transfer her weight from her arms to her feet. She made of her body something like a bridge, while the doctor was still trying to get a good grip on something inside.

Their eyes met.

All other thoughts, sounds, and feeling retreated to swirl on the perimeter of that pristine space of pure intuitive knowledge that only excruciating pain can create. Mary saw in the eye of the storm that this doctor was driven by utter disrespect and drunken impatience to haul her baby out by the head, and she also saw that to him, her body was nothing more than a farm animal, and her baby, a task. Mary, throwing herself forward, gripped him by both his shoulders with her hands and pushed him out of her. He faltered backward, lost his balance, and then staggered to regain it. Mary took that instant to rock forward so that she was fully stabilized on her knees with her hands braced on her lap.

Sophie, as astonished as Doctor Faulkner, gave herself a shake and grabbed for the sheet that had dropped to the floor. Before she could scramble to Mary's side, she stopped where she stood. She couldn't help but notice the moonbeam that cast itself over Mary and held her gleaming body in a pool of light. Sophie, unable to break the spell, stayed put.

In the next moment Mary threw back her head, opened her mouth, and let out a primal scream. And then, on the tail of that same moment, she let her head drop forward, her hair soaked and dangled over her face, and through a deep throaty groan gave a mighty push. She took another deep breath, and after she had drunk in as much of the air around her as she could hold, she bore down once more. This time, as the force drew thin, tranquility seized Mary. She cradled her hands under the emerging head of her child and in two more gentle waves Mary's son was borne into her arms.

Doctor Faulkner, suddenly remembering himself, hustled over to his instruments, which lay inert on Mary's dresser-top while Sophie rushed closer to Mary's side.

Whatever passionate force of nature had overtaken Mary had vanished, and in its place, a love, like none she had ever experienced, filled her, and spilled forth as tears of absolute joy, as she and her son beheld each other for the first time.

"A son," Sophie whispered and touched her on the shoulder. "Now you must lay back and let the doctor help."

Mary's face, illuminated with the light of first love, looked at Sophie and said, "His name is Sonny."

Sophie smiled and brushed a soaked tendril off Mary's forehead, "He is handsome," she whispered.

The sight of Mary and the peaceful child touched Sophie so much that she felt she had somehow become drawn into a hallowed encounter. For Sophie this was a sweet and stinging pain.

Even Doctor Faulkner seemed struck by the scene. He stood by, tools still poised in hand, as if he too was in awe.

Suddenly the moment burst. Distress began to tingle at the tips of Mary's limbs and crept up filling her with a vibration as it went. Sophie saw it only a second later than Mary: a spreading puddle of blood on the bed beneath Mary's thighs. A cry escaped Mary's lips just before the doctor exchanged his tools for something else.

With one hand, he held the back of her head firmly in place, and with the other cupped a cloth soaked in pungent smelling ether over her mouth and nose. Mary had no time to resist; she gave consciousness over to the smothering thought of her own death.

As Mary went limp in his grasp, Doctor Faulkner directed Sophie to support the infant. After he had laid Mary down he moved to her lower extremities to position them. Sophie held fast to the child as Doctor Faulkner waved his hand, the moon glinted off his scalpel, and in one silent gesture,

he severed the cord from which the baby had taken life. He discarded the
afterbirth on the floor because nobody had thought to prepare for it.

Sonny, still with no complaint, stayed wide-eyed while Sophie wrapped
him in a towel. She laid him in the bassinette that everybody at the diner had
chipped in for and covered him again with the blanket she had crocheted.
Then, turning her attention back to Mary, inert and helpless, she covered her
friend's top half with the discarded sheet. "What do you want me to do?" she
asked Doctor Faulkner.

He pointed to the open bottle on the dresser with the rag beside it, "Soak
that rag again, and if she shows any signs of waking up again, immediately
cover her nose and mouth with it."

Sophie obeyed to the letter and stood by with rag in hand, waiting for
the slightest indication of Mary's rise to consciousness. Braving a glance at
the thrusting, searching, pushing, cutting, and sewing that was going on
down below between Mary's thighs made Sophie all the more committed
to separating her friend from this agony. There she remained, with ether-
soaked rag poised over Mary's face, until the procedure was over.

Perhaps it was the ether fumes in the room, or maybe it was the work
of a resolute mind; either way, Mary remained unconscious throughout
Doctor Faulkner's medical trussing, a remedy for the damage he'd dispas-
sionately done in the name of hurry.

Just as the peach-coloured fingers of the sun began to reach for the day
and pour through the window, Gmiwan filled the doorway of the bedroom.
Sophie, spent from the night's emotions and late hour, lay slumped in the
chair in the corner. Everything was in its place while Mary breathed rhythmically beneath clean white sheets and a flowered bedspread. The scrubbed room
glowed pink and filled Gmiwan's heart with true, deep love and he glanced at
the bassinette which he was sure would be filled with even more happiness.
Sophie stirred. She breathed a sigh of relief as she watched Gmiwan approach
his sleeping wife. She slipped out of the room, let herself out the front door,
and followed the pull home to her own sweet bed.

Gmiwan stole a peek at his child in the bassinette before lighting a
feathery kiss on his wife's cheek. Mary's eyes fluttered open and she breathed
deeply in the smell of her Gmiwan. Searing hot pain ripped at her loins as
she moved over, to invite her husband to fall asleep with her, but Mary gave
no sign of it. Just then the baby started to fuss.

"Do you hear your son?" Mary asked. Her weary voice was stained with
distress. "Can you go to him and bring him to us?"

Gmiwan lifted the child out of the bassinette and brought him close to his face. He smelled like the delicate sweetness of honey and milk. Gmiwan filled with pride. "Good Morning, my son."

The child, as if recognizing Gmiwan's voice, seemed to momentarily forget his hunger, opened his eyes and ceased his crying. Father and son drank each other in.

Once again, Mary pushed her pain down to a place just below where it pressed fiercely against the inner surface of her skin, and moved over to accommodate her family in her bed. "Bring him to us, Gmiwan."

Gmiwan placed the baby between them and crawled in under the covers.

"I named him Sonny." she whispered.

"Sonny is perfect," Gmiwan whispered back.

Sonny, again impatient with his hunger, took up his revolt. Gmiwan, swelling with wonder, watched as Mary slipped the white sheet past her shoulder and exposed her breast for Sonny. Oblivious of his mother's tender offer, Sonny's crying intensified to a wail. Mary tickled his cheek with her finger and he instinctively turned his face toward her body. He opened his rose petal mouth and Mary drew him closer so that he could take in her breast. Gmiwan and Mary drifted into the sweetest slumber while Sonny suckled.

BREAKFAST THAT NEXT morning was the first meal Mary ate at the Mohawk Institute. It was oatmeal, as it would be every single day that Mary dwelled there. Funny thing about oatmeal: at first mouthful, it tastes plain, but after waking twice empty, the stomach soon makes a gracious host as it cramps for more. No matter how unpalatable, the mushy unsweetened provision never failed to become gratifying again once she let herself refuse it a few times. Mary vowed that if she ever made oatmeal for herself she would drizzle maple syrup all over it and stir in tasty pieces of apple, then make a hole in it with her spoon to let the fat melt in the middle. Mary sat next to Elizabeth and watched the apple trees outside swaying in the gathering morning breeze and she spooned her oatmeal into her mouth.

"I wonder if they ever heard of putting apples in their oatmeal?" she whispered to Elizabeth that second day of waking up in the institute. A line shaped bruise marked her cheek.

Ruth, who sat on the other side of her, looked around to check that nobody was paying any attention and offered, "You will never taste an apple from that orchard. If they catch you sneaking one while you work, you'll get whacked good and have to work longer."

Mary and Elizabeth exchanged looks.

"Where is Dolly?" Elizabeth finally spoke.

Tears filled Mary's eyes.

"What? Tell me!"

"I don't know." Mary shook her head, and let her tears fall on the marred wood tabletop. "They took her yesterday because she was too young to be in here."

"Do you think they will just kill her?" Elizabeth asked, wide-eyed.

"I don't know," Mary shrugged her shoulders. Mary thought about Porter, somewhere on the boy's side of the great curtain. She sat up taller and faced Elizabeth. "All I know is that we are going to have to be strong in here if we're going to survive."

Elizabeth stopped chewing and let Mary's words sink in.

Mary stole a glance in the direction of the Mistress, who was busy standing guard over the oatmeal apportioning. "That woman is a bad witch."

Mary, Elizabeth, and Ruth all nodded knowingly.

Ruth lowered her voice well below the level of the bowl scraping around them and said, "If she gives you the squint eye, you're done, just don't do anything that makes her look at you."

They started scraping their own bowls for any morsels that might be clinging to the sides, and Mary thought of one more thing to say, "If ya ever run 'cross that bad 'un from the Tuscarora reserve, you just try to spot her first and stay outta her sight. Best to always avoid her," Mary quoted.

Mary's good imitation of Aunt Maggie made Elizabeth smile. She leaned forward to get a better look at Ruth.

"My name is Elizabeth. What's your name?"

"Ruth." She stayed bent over her bowl, spoon poised, and added, "I saw you and your brother get walloped yesterday for running off. Just to let you know, they give a public punishment to anybody who runs off. Just to teach everybody not to try it. I bet you thought you were going to die."

Elizabeth cast her eyes downward, unable to name the soupy feeling that filled her with a weight so heavy she felt her back bend and her shoulders hunch forward. She felt like everybody who saw her now was disgusted with her.

Ruth addressed Mary, "And you! You were as fast as an arrow yesterday. Weren't you scared?"

Mary shrugged her shoulders, "I was more scared of what they were going to do to my sister and brother."

"She never knew what hit her." Ruth indulged in a chuckle. "She got you good with the medicine bag, but you sure took her down a peg or two anyway. It's too bad about your medicine bag though," she added, reverently, "but they won't let anybody have one." She leaned even closer and whispered, "The other half of that stick you broke landed in my oatmeal yesterday."

"Oh?"

"Enh, tossed it out the window when nobody was paying attention."

Glee danced like wickedness in Ruth's eyes and at the corners of her mouth. "I had a damn good time while I was at it." Then the twinkling ebbed back into expressionless flat lines. Mary and Elizabeth grew silent as the full weight of what was happening to them settled deeper in their chests.

Ruth took a good look at the two new girls and then respectfully withdrew back into herself. She understood. Her own grandmother came to get her every summer, so she still received the Teachings. Many had been here for years without ever going back home. These ones were just going to have to learn to survive on their own. It was not her way to offer empty comfort and deprive a person of their walk. If they were ever going to make it, then the first thing they had to do was to accept the path they were on.

A relentless clanging shattered the girls' reverie. The Mistress held her pointer in one hand, and yanked back and forth on a corded bell fixed to the wall with the other. Mary looked around. The bell seemed to be a cue to everybody to take bowls and spoons in hand and rise. Ruth whispered to them to wait their turn. In a clockwise direction, each table took turns forming a line that filed past the serving table to deposit their bowls in one wooden apple crate, and their spoons in another. Mary obeyed the example set by those in line in front of her and placed her bowl on top of the previously deposited one, all the while being careful to not allow her own bowl to cause the tower to lean and topple over. She reached to nestle her spoon neatly on top of the others, when the tip of the feared pointer lighted like the tricky tickle of a big furry bee on the top of her hand.

"You!" bellowed the Mistress. She used her instrument to point to Mary's chest. "Go sit at that table." She gestured over to the last table to rise, where the kids who were last served were desperately gulping their food and scraping their bowls.

Mary complied, and Elizabeth, who ventured to tarry, was urged forward by Ruth.

No sooner had Mary reached the table of gulpers, when one of them rose. The others followed suit, until they almost seamlessly made their place at the end of the line. Instead of following the main line out the door, the lead girl of this table circled around the serving table and began to take things up and head for the door, while Mistress remained, arms folded, a new, longer pointer wagging out from under them.

Mary copying the girls at this table, moved to lift the bushel basket-sized pot that the oatmeal had been cooked in, but dropped it when Mistress blew her whistle. The pot landed mercilessly on her toes.

"You!" Mistress targeted Mary. "Pick that pot up and put the other one inside before you go to the kitchen. Never waste a trip!"

Tears stung at the corners of her eyes, as Mary rubbed her toes and wished hopelessly for her mother.

"Now!" The woman screeched.

Mistress oversaw the morning dishwashing and lunch making duties, but through all the comings and goings between clearing the hall and cleaning the kitchen, Mary got a chance to talk to some other girls. That is, the girls that would talk. A great many of them were either still not able to speak English or simply would not talk. Some of them had cavernous looks in their eyes that seemed as if the very Spirit within them had abandoned them. Perhaps it was more likely that, in shutting out suffering, they had shut in Spirit and become disconnected. They looked vacant and ill to Mary. Mary resolved not to let that happen to her.

Each day they were to sit at the next table with the same group, rotating in a clockwise direction, until it became their turn to be last served and do clean up. After cleaning up, they were to join the others in whatever work was being done. Some days it was just more kitchen work. Mary hated the job of plucking chickens the most.

The teachers were mostly light skinned, but one or two of them were actually brown skinned. Sophie called them "graduates"; Ruth called them "prayin' Indians," and Mistress always acted as though she couldn't see them.

The residents did all the work. The apples from the orchard were all sold to the canning factory in the next town. When there weren't apple orchard chores, there was plenty of grounds work and inside cleaning to do. Cleaning time usually went on for one half of the day and the second half of the day was spent in class. In the winter, they were divided into crews for sewing, ironing, cooking, cleaning, and laundry while the boys worked outside with Floyd. There was more class time in the winter. All year long, the table that was served last, stayed out of class that day to cook supper and clean. Sophie served the food to the girls and Floyd served the food to the boys, and there was never, ever the feeling of fullness in the belly.

After a while of being gone somewhere, the Mistress burst back into the kitchen with an important announcement, "We had a hoity-toity inspector in yesterday who says we have to start serving milk with at least one meal. There is a shipment of milk sitting over there in those cans," she gestured to a place just inside the door. "For supper tonight, and every night from now on, Sophie will fill each glass three quarters full with milk. It will be mandatory to drink it." Then she paused for a moment and gave her head a shake, as if she just remembered there was no one here worth talking to. She called out over her shoulder, "After lunch fill the water pitchers with the milk from the cans, and leave them just outside the door for pick up."

While the dishes were put away and the tea towels hung to dry, Mistress stood in the doorway. She led them outside to join the others in the orchard and then disappeared. Mary later learned from Ruth that Mistress hated being outside. She wouldn't even walk the children down the street to church for fear of the slightest mar on her "alabaster skin." Mary took this as good news. At least they would get a break from her the days they walked to praise Our Lord Jesus. Our Lord Jesus was rich, it was obvious, from being in his fancy house, but doing the work of Our Lord Jesus was better than doing the work of The Mohawk Institute.

Doing dishes, picking apples, and carting bushels wasn't foreign work to Mary. She was used to every family member having his or her job, but in this place the apples were not ever used to feed the people who lived here, but rather sold for the benefit of Our Lord's House. The school was huge, and Our Lord's House had grounds of rolling manicured lawns as far as the eye could see. Father Spence said the Lord maketh us green pastures to lie in so the least we could do is the same. Mistress said that one never knew when there might be an inspection. So the grounds were kept clipped and cut at their "Sunday best." Mary pitched right in at the apple orchard with a good mind because it not only gave her a chance to be outside, which was where she was more used to being, but it would also give her the odd chance to cross paths with Porter. Although they spent the better part of Sunday at church, the boys were kept strictly separated from the girls at all times. Even at the lawn lunches and afterwards, the girls went down into the basement to learn to knit, sew, and hook rugs, while the boys went out back to do groundskeeping. If it rained, they stayed in the pews to learn candle carrying and robe holding, so apple orchard time would always be their best chance to plot together.

One warm October afternoon, Mistress deposited Mary and the others into the orchard under the care and supervision of Sophie. She quickly vanished back into the dark corridors of the school. Soon after, Sophie too disappeared. At first, Mary, a basket strapped around her, hadn't noticed that Sophie was no longer walking among them picking apples up off the ground and putting them into bushels, or helping someone heave their burdens onto the waiting wagon, or holding a ladder.

Mary spotted a snake slithering past her feet. It made its way past the tree she was picking and headed for the foundation under the nearby shed. She watched it duck into a hole and heard some tinkling laughter coming from inside the shed. At first Mary figured it must be some kids who were hiding from work or found some other way to get in trouble, but when she couldn't see Sophie anywhere, she became even more suspicious.

Mary ventured closer to the shed. She sneaked around to the other side where she too could not be seen and then peered inside the window. Sure enough, there was Sophie. She was leaning with her back up against the wall, standing on one foot and smoking a cigarette. Floyd had one hand on his hip and was leaning in over her, supporting most of his weight on that piece of lumber of an arm of his, his hand placed on the wall behind, just at her ear. He leaned closer in and whispered something, Sophie gave him a puff of her cigarette, and then they both shared a laugh. Sophie was small, even for a woman. She was smaller than some of the older girls. Most of the girls thought Sophie was a beautiful woman, but Mary figured it was the song in her voice and the caring in her heart that made her pretty. Sophie told Mary once that her odd way of speaking was a British accent from the poor side of England. She said she'd come here to find her way to a fortunate marriage, but so far wasn't having much luck.

Mary looked all around. Since the Mistress was busy staying white, and Sophie was occupied with Floyd, Mary thought this would be a good chance to go find Porter.

After searching the grounds, she could only find Elizabeth.

"Porter doesn't have to pick apples," Elizabeth said.

"Where is he? I saw him earlier."

"This man in a long black dress came out and told him he needed help at the church. He told Porter to go take a bath because that is where he would be working, and he needed to be clean."

"So he's gone somewhere else?" Mary's brow crinkled as she spoke.

"Yes, to church, with this man, who is visiting Father Spence," Elizabeth answered. "It didn't seem like it was a bad thing. He treated Porter like he was a favourite or something."

"Do you think he will bring Porter back?"

Both girls just stared at each other, waiting for the answer to come, until suddenly the vehement clang of a bell split the languid cicada songs that filled the air around them. The girls looked up. Mistress's white figure disappeared from the doorway and left only the echo of the bell and the wag of its tail. In the midst of Mother Earth's all around irreverence, there was a practiced response to the aggressive toll of the bell. The other children stood up or dropped out of the trees and waited. The shed door creaked, and Sophie, blinking in the bright sun, let herself out while right behind her, Floyd came with rake in hand, feigning at successfully finding it. Floyd's sea blue eyes crinkled into a grin as he ran one hand through his dark wavy hair and leaned the feckless rake up against the shed wall. Sophie scampered over to her post at the door where her girls would line up first in groups according to their tables and Floyd sauntered over to the far end of the orchard where his boys were waiting to follow.

There were nine lines of about seven or eight girls each. Mary got in line behind Elizabeth and Ruth. When everybody had reasonably settled into their places, Sophie prepared to lead them inside but then paused as if forgetting something. She surveyed each line and then walked over to Mary.

Barely audible, she said to Mary in her English accent, "You have to get back in the work crew line," and then, averting her eyes and running her hand along the back of her neck, she continued, "Orders are that you are assigned permanently to a new table and will cycle accordingly."

Mary looked blank.

Sophie added some fibre to her tone, "Get in the other line please."

Mary shook her head.

"Now!" Sophie's voice cracked as she raised it.

Mary stayed put, and the lines hushed to attention.

Sophie slumped and sighed, "Why do you have to be like that? You must have learned by now." She tempered her tone. "What is going to happen to you when you walk through those doors and you are in the wrong line? And if you don't care about what is going to happen to you, will you please care about what is going to happen to me?"

Mary caught a few nods of agreement in her peripheral vision and dropped her gaze to the ground. Giving herself some more time to be at home with just how much she had to give in, she stepped sideways, and then trudged over to her assigned place in the other line. Sophie sighed in relief and took up her own place at the head of the first line. Mary resigned herself to being the last in the building, the last served, and the last to bed line. She would remain third from the end, beside a little girl that looked only two years older than Elizabeth, but she could not, would not, ever take up the head-down resolute shuffle that most of those around her were moving in. She would always walk with purpose, her head up, and full of Spirit.

At seven o'clock that night, Mary and the girls at her new table were still working in the kitchen. She set the two huge pots down on the floor to wait beside the sack of oatmeal that was leaning like an old drunk in the corner. She searched around for the tin cup she was to use to measure out exactly twenty-five cups in each. She spied it on the counter next to where a little girl named Ojekaada sat crouched into a ball.

Ruth said that Ojekaada had been named after sugar by her grandmother because her mother, who also had been taken and put in the institute, got pregnant by another Indian boy, but had run off with a white boy right after she had the baby. The Indian Agents, knew all about it, and took Ojekaada just as soon as she turned school age. Ruth said the grandmother tried to hide her but she was old and not as swift as the Indian Agents, and since she never learned any English, Ojekaada only spoke Mohawk. And now, Ojekaada wouldn't speak at all, probably because she got a good beating for it and didn't even exactly know why, so Mary couldn't tell what was wrong with her tonight.

Locating the tin cup, Mary grabbed it and returned to the old drunken sack sleeping in the corner. Giving way to an unbearable heaviness she let herself drop to her knees and just stay still for a bit. She let her head down, and making a rounded indent in the softness, she stabilized herself by holding on with two hands, as to not allow her weariness full reign. Some of the fatigue seeped out and she breathed into its place some newfound strength. Mary re-erected her backbone and tackled the opening of the sack. Parting the burlap with both hands, she laid it open and reached behind her where she had set her tin cup. She felt around for the cup until she found it. While keeping the burlap opening wide with one hand she scooped her tin cup in deeply and produced a heaping cache of oats that ran over and spilled back into the bag. Just as Mary was about to use her other hand to level off the tin cup contents, a searing hot pain seized it. She recoiled in terror. Still attached to her finger by its jaws was a grey rat the size of a squirrel. She slammed its body against the wall, and the rat let go. It leaped past her cheek, leaving in its wake its own bloody mark. Mary screamed hysterically, swiping and kicking at the air. Mistress spotted the rat scurrying away and surmised what had happened. She arrived at Mary's side with her hands on her hips.

"Do you have to make such a ruckus?"

Mary clamped off her screams and held up her throbbing, dripping finger.

"Go get Sophie to look after that. You're letting blood drip on the floor," she said and then saw Ojekaada. "And that one under there isn't doing any good either, so take it with you as well!" Then she turned and pointed to Ruth, "You! Escort them to the dormitory!"

Just before the three of them made it out the kitchen door, Mistress hollered again, "And you!" she aimed the pointer at Ruth. "Don't forget to come back and pick up this mess!"

Ruth led wordlessly. Mary held her arm as if in a splint, and her hand in a loose fist so that any more bleeding would be into the palm of her other hand.

Leave no trail that your enemy can find you by.

She placed her other arm around Ojekaada, who was gripping her stomach and was nearly unable to walk. At one point she stopped, bent over like broken grass, and cried out in a voice forlorn with pain. When they reached the dormitory, Ruth left with a nod and Mary urged Ojekaada forward until Sophie took notice of them. When she saw the drizzle of blood running down Mary's arm and Ojekaada in obvious distress, she put down the Bible she was reading the children, and came to them.

Sophie didn't seem surprised to see Ojekaada in pain.

"There's a few that are down with belly aches tonight. It must have been something bad in the food at dinner." She turned to Mary. "What in the world has happened to your hand, dear?" The concern in Sophie's voice filled Mary's chest with a warmth that seemed to lull the pulsing pain in her finger.

"A rat bit me."

"Oh, my word!" Sophie's eyes went wide as saucers. She placed both her hands on her cheeks and exclaimed, "Oh my goodness. You can't play with rats, my dear!" All the other girls, and even Mary, broke into laughter at Sophie's words. She turned back toward the bathroom and then forward to face the girls as if just remembering to bring them with her, before grasping them both by the hands and pulling them with her. She called over her shoulder, "Somebody keep reading."

In the bathroom, Sophie overturned a wooden box of soap flakes that had been standing by the toilet and pointed for Ojekaada to sit on it. Ojekaada, distracted from her aching belly for a moment, looked confused. She looked back and forth from Sophie to the upside down box, now with soap flakes spilling from the bottom, and blinked with incomprehension.

Sophie, taking Ojekaada's bewilderment for indolence, beseeched her, "Please Ojekaada, pretty please?" She tilted her dark curly-haired head and brought both hands together as if to pray. "Pleeeease sit down."

Ojekaada nodded, tiptoed through the spreading pile of soap flakes, to the edge of the box, turned, dropped to her knees obediently, closed her eyes, and brought her own hands together, as if to pray. Sophie was baffled for a moment, but then realized the child thought she had been ordered to start praying. She shook her head. "Oh well, that will keep you occupied for a while," she muttered and then turned to face Mary.

"Now hold out your hand and let me see. Ohhhh!" Sophie said, holding Mary's hand with both her hands like it was too hot to touch, "I have to disinfect it," she thought out loud. "But with what?"

She looked all around her and then her face lit up with an idea. She reached behind Ojekaada to lift off the lid to the back of the toilet and produced a dripping bottle of whiskey. Unconcerned about blood on her own hand, she held Mary's hand by the wrist over the toilet and poured some of the contents of the bottle over it.

Mary winced but bit her lip through the searing pain. She knew when something was for her own good.

Sophie glanced over at Ojekaada, and her face lit up with another idea. She filled the bottle lid with whiskey and nudged Ojekaada on the shoulder, "Here, drink," she made drinking motions, "Drink, drink, Ojekaada. Medicine."

Ojekaada shook her head and held her lips tight in a thin line.

"Medicine," Sophie said again, and urged it toward her.

Mary looked behind her and out the door to see who might be in hearing range and said, "*Ga noon gwats he lee yo.*"

Mary knew it was liquor, and thought about what Pa had said, but Pa wasn't going to be around anymore, and Sophie was the only adult she could trust right now.

"It means good medicine in Mohawk," Mary whispered.

"Jolly good!"

Then Ojekaada readily drank the bitter hot liquid without complaint. Sophie turned back to focus upon Mary.

"I think it would be better to wash most of the blood off first before a final coating of whiskey."

Mary remained completely still and Sophie busied herself with the new plan. In the meantime Ojekaada kept praying, and by the time Sophie was wrapping Mary's arm up in a clumsy sling, Ojekaada was sitting up straight and pretty, ankle deep in soap flakes, with a relaxed smile on her face.

Sophie, pleased with herself, led the girls back out of the bathroom. When they re-entered the bedroom, the other girls were jumping up and down on their beds, their short mop-top hairdos flying wild. The ones who were too sick were bouncing up and down where they lay as girls bounded from one bed to the other. They all spotted Sophie, but it made no difference.

Ojekaada and Mary stood in the aisle, stumped by the sight. Sophie, seeing that yet again she had lost control, composed herself into the meanest that she could be and yelled at the top of her lungs, "If you girls don't get into bed this minute, I am marching right straight down to Mistress's quarters and retrieving her!"

As the true meaning of this resonated throughout the room, one by one, each girl resolutely stopped bouncing and settled into her own bed.

"And!" Sophie still taking her stand, "if you don't stop chattering, she will hear you, and of course you *know* what will happen next!"

Mary shuffled over to find her own bed, and Ojekaada started to follow her, looking furtively back at Sophie. Sophie mouthed, "No" and with a look of determined sternness she shook her head. Ojekaada's lower lip quivered as she climbed into her own bed, which was located beside Mary's.

"Now, I will continue reading the Bible," she said with forced officiousness.

All quiet now, Sophie picked up the Bible but suddenly stopped. She wasn't sure if she had put the whiskey bottle back in its hiding spot.

She mustered up her best cold stare to hold them all in their places and rushed back to the bathroom to reassure herself. She returned just in time to see Ojekaada's tiny round face disappear under Mary's covers. She glanced over at Ojekaada's bed to find it appropriately stuffed with pillows. Sophie shook her head and picked up at the place where she had left off.

"'Psalm 126. When the Lord turned again the captivity of Zion, we were like them that dream. Then was our mouth filled with laughter, and our tongue with singing: then said they among the heathen, The Lord hath done great things for them. The Lord hath done great things for us: whereof we are glad. Turn again our captivity, O Lord, as the streams in the south. They that sow in tears shall reap in joy. He that goeth forth and weepeth, bearing precious seed, shall doubtless come again with rejoicing, bringing his sheaves with him.'"

DID THE BABY cry all night again?"

"Off and on until just before sunrise." Elizabeth hooked her arm in Mary's while holding fast to little Dottie's hand. They hurried to keep up with Mary.

Mary hurried her pace and continued, "He finally tired himself out just before sunrise." She clutched him tighter to her breast, "That's likely the only reason he sleeps now," she added, her breathlessness more evident on the crisp but sunny day.

"Poor Sonny," Elizabeth squeezed her own daughter's hand. "Do you really think your milk is too thin?"

Mary walked briskly past Jackson Diner. No lingering at the window or even looking in to see if there was anybody there to wave to. She didn't wish Marlene and Fred any more hard luck these days, but her own luck could ill afford spending time pondering someone else's plan of survival. She hoped they could hold on to their business, but she needed a plan of her own. When Elizabeth first suggested they apply for Relief, Mary was dead against it, but the luxury of pride paled from shame to humility sometime in the dark hours of the second night Sonny cried himself to sleep. Inability to soothe him with either her breast or her embrace was a merciless persuader. She knew it was the old enemy hunger that gnawed at his belly. She knew what she had to do.

They paused in front of City Hall and Elizabeth opened the door to allow Mary and the baby, then Dottie, to enter. "There's a line-up," Elizabeth observed.

"Well, let's go get in it."

Mary had never actually been in City Hall before. Never had a reason. She wondered if she would run into Mayor Dunsby. She hoped not. She waited for Elizabeth to return.

"The woman in front just told me that it's a long wait."

Mary barely allowed a sigh to escape and started to rock back and forth in one spot to keep Sonny pacified in deep sleep as long as possible.

"I am so worried about Harry," Elizabeth finally gave into her intolerance for silence.

Mary nodded to encourage her.

"Don't take me wrong. It's a comfort for him to know I can stay with you, and I too, am glad he is not there alone, but he does take after his father in so many ways."

"I don't think suicide is something you pass down." Mary gave her sister's worry a little more respectful consideration and continued, "And I don't think Harry would agree with his father that losing your business is worth killing yourself for."

"Hmmm," Elizabeth tried to reform the image of her confident Harry in her mind. "Well, I'm just glad that Gmiwan is there with him, and I just know we're going to hear any day now that they have found work in Big Smoke. Do you think we will have to move there?"

"I don't like the idea, but of course I'll go where I have to."

"With the plant gone, and his mother, and now his father, we don't have any real reason to stay here. Neither do you, I would move in a word, and I think I would really enjoy living in Big Smoke."

"Actually, Gmiwan and I decided that even if he does find work, we would try to hold on to this apartment, and maybe something else will come up around here. You know Gmiwan has the soul of an artist. There is no other work he can find that he loves as much as his art. If only he could make money at it." Mary indulged some wistfulness.

"The thirties have been dirty. There's just not enough to go around."

"This is what Gmiwan struggles with. It is hard to understand why Spirit would give him a gift he cannot use. Did you know he took some of his work to Big Smoke?"

Elizabeth was genuinely surprised. "No."

"He is going to set up on the street and try to sell it."

"Buying art is the last thing on everybody's list." She shook her head. "Not in these times."

"I know. He knows it too. But he has a drive in him that he must honour. If he doesn't sell it, he will give it. He says that Spirit did not give him a gift he cannot give."

"Harry will give him a hard time about that. Boy, you can sure tell they have two different fathers."

Mary nodded in agreement.

Then Elizabeth said, "I wonder what kind of place they found to stay in?"

Mary didn't respond.

"Mary?"

"Yes?"

"I was talking to you."

"What's the use in thinking about that? It's just another worry."

Elizabeth watched the metal clock on the wall. She endured an hour more of imposed quietness. One person at a time was called into an unseen place for an interview. When a shadow appeared in the opaque glass, the heavy wooden door would groan open, and someone would emerge, walking with a lighter step. Then the line would inch forward.

Suddenly, someone's child started to cry, breaking the dull placidity. Soon Sonny also woke and took up the lament. No amount of rocking, jostling, or sweet talk could console his hunger.

Elizabeth lifted Dottie up, straddled her on her hip, and began rocking from one foot to the other, in hopes of quelling the child's whimpering. She raised her voice to make conversation above the din, "I wish we would hear from Porter and Ruby."

Mary too, began speaking louder than the racket, "It would be nice to know if he is still working."

"That Porter, he is not afraid of hard work," then pausing before she spoke the usually unspoken, "but he drinks it all up."

"Still, I worry about brother." Mary said just below the racket, but Elizabeth heard her anyway.

"He will never talk about how it was for him in the Mush Hole but I know that is the reason he drinks." Elizabeth expressed with so much earnest that she became unaware of her present surroundings. For a moment she was back in the dark place she spent the last days of her childhood in.

"He is just like Pa, so he is not a talker. But Pa was not a drinker either. I think you're right. It was something that happened to him in that Mush Hole."

The conversation always came to a standstill at this same place. When he drove down for a visit, they let him drink, they played cards with him and his wife, and they didn't interfere when Ruby bossed him around too much. At least he didn't fight anymore.

After all morning of standing in line, their turn finally came up. Mary went in with Elizabeth, even though they knew they were supposed to go in one at a time. Mary noticed the man's silver name plate said, 'Mr. Morgan.'

"We live together," Elizabeth told the man on the other side of the desk.

Sitting posture-perfect with his hands folded officiously in front of him, Mr. Morgan scanned first one woman then the other.

"Indians are not eligible for Welfare Relief," he informed them brusquely.

Elizabeth immediately burst out crying, and the man flinched.

"My sister's baby has been crying for two nights in a row because he is starving. My daughter is losing weight, and so are my sister and I. We stood out there for three hours, just like everybody else. I clearly saw that you sent all of them away with something. My husband is away in Toronto and will probably have a job any day now."

Mr. Morgan, who had begun to sag just a little, perked up a bit.

"Who is your husband?"

"Harry Vanderdoody."

"Is he the Harry Vanderdoody that used to run the factory in Jordan?"

Winding down to a sniffle, Elizabeth answered, "Why yes, that's him."

"My father retired from that company. He put me through college while he worked there. Now I am the one who makes sure he is looked after. It's a shame losing it. Times are hard." Mr. Morgan picked up his pen and began writing the date on the top line of the form in front of him. Then he held it poised over the next line, "Your full name?"

Elizabeth anxiously answered all the man's questions and then waited for what was going to come of it.

He pulled his chair out somewhat to allow space to open a drawer almost hidden by his belly. He withdrew a brown envelope and peered inside of it. Out of the larger brown envelopes he drew out a smaller white one. He checked inside, and then made notations on the empty lines of two pieces of cardboard paper. He picked up a red pen and made a check mark on Elizabeth's form before handing Elizabeth the white envelope.

Elizabeth, in fatter times, would have acted more graciously. She would have stepped aside, and allowed Mary her turn. But these were leaner times, and Elizabeth opened the envelope and pulled out the contents. "It's bus tickets?"

"That is correct, Madam." He assumed his erect posture and folded his hands.

"What am I supposed to do with bus tickets?"

"You are to use them to go to Toronto to reunite with your husband where, if he has not yet found employment, you will be eligible for Welfare Relief."

"Why am I not eligible here?"

"Since you have a non-Indian husband, he is eligible to apply for relief, and you, as his wife will also qualify." And then he closed his eyes and shook his head from side to side, "But not here. I suggest, Madam, that you use those tickets to go to him."

"And what are these?" Elizabeth held up a small piece of paper.

"That, Madam, is a food voucher to allow you to purchase enough food for you and your daughter to make the trip. It should be enough to buy two days worth of food."

Elizabeth was struck silent in front of the man, knowing full well there was nothing she could do to change his mind.

"Next?" he called over her head.

Mary stepped up in front of him.

He surveyed just briefly to check his original assessment was correct. He took a double look at the very dark skinned baby in her arms and felt reassured.

"Next?" he waved her to the side.

"I am next," Mary offered meekly.

Sonny had become still, as if to bear witness to the exchange.

Mr. Morgan refocused his gaze upon her. "Are you married to a non-Indian?"

"No," Mary said, "But we are very much in need of food and coal for heat. My husband too is in Toronto looking for work. What can you do to help me?"

Mr. Morgan snorted, poked his glasses at the bridge, and set both his hands down in front of him, as if to support the stance he would take.

"Indians are not allowed to collect Welfare money, not in Toronto either. All I can give you is a bus ticket back to your Indian reservation."

"But I don't know anybody on the reservation anymore. I have been living here since I was sixteen. I worked at the Jackson Diner until I had my baby. I would get a job there again, but Marlene and Fred can hardly offer their own daughter a job."

"Back to the reservation is all I can do," he said.

Mary forced down the hot geyser of fearful tears that threatened from the inside. She needed to think.

"If I take the tickets back to the reserve, will I get food vouchers also?"

Mr. Morgan cast a wary eye at her. Mary sensed it, softened her features and looked away. And then, just to make sure, she added, "I could send word with my sister here for my husband to get a bus ticket in Toronto and we could be together again on the reserve."

The man released a deep sigh and brought both his hands together in front of him. He was pleased with a job well done. For a nasty minute there he thought he was going to have to send the woman away because she had no category.

"I can do that," he said as he picked up the black pen and began writing the date on a form for Mary.

Elizabeth suddenly nudged Mary and motioned her to look up.

Off in the distance Mayor Dunsby was standing at the top of the stairwell, staring at her. Mary looked away as if their eyes never met.

Struck by her veil of shame, he turned away to allow her privacy. For his part, he was not ashamed of knowing the Indian woman in the welfare line. If she would have allowed, he would have swooped in and saved her, but he knew she would never allow it. If he could have, he would have married her, would have made her his own, but he couldn't because he knew she would never have him.

When Mary got her envelope—with the words Six Nations Reserve written on it, both women, with their children in tow, hurriedly made their way back past the now-dwindling line to the front doors. Outside, the sunny day had turned to grey and rainy. Mary tossed the bus tickets to the reserve into the nearby wastebasket. Elizabeth wasn't surprised, she knew Mary had done it for the food. There was nothing on the reserve.

They walked wordlessly until they reached the General Store. They put their vouchers together and bought flour, eggs, potatoes, sugar, lard, rice, Carnation Milk, tea, and lots of walnuts and almonds for protein. Mary had used the last of the tomatoes and cucumbers from her balcony and all she had left were the dried strawberry leaves and the dandelion roots she had been making a tea out of. She still had a fair bit of onions.

At the checkout counter, Elizabeth, who had been pensively lost in thought, finally spoke, "I think I am going to use the tickets."

Mary nodded wordlessly.

"I'm going to leave all of this with you and go tomorrow."

By the time they had everything in a couple of boxes, they needed to borrow a wagon to carry it home in. Mary was silent all the way home. It wasn't until they were less than a block away from the apartment, that Elizabeth broke the silence again. "Is that okay?"

"I'll tell you what is okay, my sister. It is okay that we have some food now. And the first thing we are going to do when we get home is make a cup of tea and bake a whole bunch of bread. Then, after it's done we will have our supper, we will make you and Dottie plenty of onion sandwiches and tea for the trip, and help you pack. How's that sound?"

The steel wagon handle made a clattering echo as it met with the stone of the sidewalk that bantered back and forth between the brick and clapboard buildings on either side of the street. Dottie, like a princess, waited atop the packages while her mother and auntie held each other and cried. It happened all the time anyway, and it hardly bothered her at all anymore.

OJEKAADA GOT AWAY with sleeping in Mary's bed all the rest of the week. It made no difference what time Mistress made her rounds because Ojekaada stuffed her own bed with pillows, slid in, covered her head, and made herself another layer of Mary. Sophie didn't care one way or the other, so long as they didn't get caught. Mary felt that she and Ojekaada were gifts to each other from Spirit. Mary had slept with Dolly from the day she had stopped taking Ma's milk. Ojekaada's body felt almost the same.

But there was something wrong with Ojekaada. She was in pain all the time and had the runs. Mary and some of the others had gone through the same thing and it had passed after a few days, but not for Ojekaada. She was getting weaker and weaker.

Everybody blamed the milk, but if anyone dared to rebel against drinking it, Mistress made everyone drink it until it was all gone. It was smarter to just be quiet and look for a chance to get rid of it another way. At home, when Mary had had a bout of the runs, Ma had stopped her from eating and had given her only strawberry leaf and black walnut husk tea.

That night in the kitchen, Mary took a chance. She approached Mistress and waited exactly as they had all been taught, and then said, "Excuse me?" Mistress cast her a scathing look and turned her attention to the mess on the counter. She had noticed someone wasn't stacking the plates exactly right. Mary waited patiently for her to finish dealing with the improper dish-stacking problem. Finally, Mistress turned around and saw Mary still waiting.

"Why are you still standing there, and why are you not doing your chores?"

"I did the 'excuse me' first, and now I am waiting for you," Mary answered matter-of-factly, her hands behind her back.

Mistress huffed in exasperation. "What do you want?"

Mary began evenly. "It's about Ojekaada."

They both glanced over at the waifish six-year old huddled against the wall under the table. It was curious how she would let Ojekaada curl up in a ball, not doing her chores, but refuse to send her to bed.

"And of what concern is that to you?"

"Ojekaada has the runs, and I think it's because of the milk."

"She'll get used to it, just like the rest of you."

"She has to stop eating for a day so the badness has nothing to live on, and then she has to drink strawberry leaf and walnut husk tea to kill it and wash it out."

"What do you have in your hands?" Mistress demanded.

Mary quickly thrust both empty hands out to ease any suspicions the woman might have and promptly received a stinging whack on one from the stick. Just as quickly, Mary snatched back her hands before she could get hit on the other. One hand comforted the other sore one behind her back while hot tears pushed at the corners of her eyes. Finally a tear leaked out and started a salty stream down her cheek.

Mistress's eyes narrowed and a smile twitched at the corners of her mouth, just before she gracefully bent down at eye level with Mary and said, "The devil hides in seemingly innocuous places, but there is no mistaking his words when they are spoken." She then reached out and pinched the upper most part of Mary's ear between her fingers, letting the nail of her thumb dig deep enough to compel compliance.

Mary twisted and stood on her tippytoes as she strained to go up to where the woman was pulling her.

Mistress began to tow Mary across the room with one hand while with the other she held her Maanaaji stick at bay. Mary took scurried steps to keep up, all the way to the other side of the room, until they stopped in the corner where an iron grate allowed air from the basement to circulate. Mistress gave a shove with the underside of her forearm on the back of Mary's neck and shoulder so that she would go down on her knees. Her knees smarted where the grate met them and a warm stream trickled down the back of her ear where blood left the crescent shaped wound Mistress made, but Mary didn't look up, though she felt compelled to know if the Maanaaji stick would next come down upon her.

Mary could hear the clock ticking on the shelf over the stove.

Mistress wiped her hands on her apron, leaving a slight red smear on the corner of a letter in the pocket, and regarded Mary.

"Devil's spawn! Black Magic!" she turned and marched over to where Ojekaada was still curled in a ball, but had fallen over. She huffed in exasperation, hauled the child up, and slung her on her hip, backwards, like she had carried Dolly one time. Ojekaada stirred but then went limp again as if a sack of laundry. "Stay in the position in which the devil cannot abide," Mistress called over her shoulder to Mary before she walked out the doorway. Once out in the hallway, she hollered, "Sophie," over and over again, until out of Mary's earshot.

Mary switched her weight from side to side, each knee taking a turn being sore, while the clock on the shelf above the stove ticked for a long time. Finally Mary figured it was safe enough to turn around and sit on her bottom. She was used to the sounds and signs of this place, so when the click of hard chunky heels faded into an echo for long time, Mary thought it was likely she would have time to jump up to her knees when she heard them again.

Once in the Eden of her own room, Mistress lit her lantern. Every time she did so, she remembered a time when there was no electricity. Using her pearl-handled letter opener she slowly cut a precise line in the fold of the letter. It had been four unbearable months since she had last received a letter from her mentor, the revered, and secretly beloved, Father David. She could always find forgiveness in her heart because she knew that his work so often consumed him.

Dear Helen:

You are, by far, the church's most vigilant crusader. Your mission work is surpassed by none. This church thrives on your spirit and I know that God has already, though you are surely less than halfway through your life, prepared a place at his feet for you. This letter will be brief and it will be my last because from now on my wife, who will be my life's assistant, will be communicating with you. Anything else, as I am sure you recognize, might be seen as improper. Yes, I have been married this summer, and as far as I have been advised, you have not been apprised on this matter. Your family tells me that not even they have given you an update, as they felt they would leave it up to me. Helen, I am overjoyed to announce that I have culminated a whirlwind romance with the nuptials of myself to Emily Benson. Yes, Helen, your sister.

I know that you will share in our glee as it is surely your work that has represented your family in such good standing, whereby I have seen the wisdom and potential of joining our families in realizing the vision of the church and ultimately God's great plan.

Best regards,
Father David

The sun reached in and warmed Mary's cheek as if to wake her just before the unyielding march of Mistress could be heard, getting louder and louder. Mary hopped to her knees with nose in the corner. When Mistress entered the room, Mary stifled a flinch as Mistress approached from behind.

"Get down to the dorm and wash up."

Mary rose to her feet without a word of retort. She straightened her spine and walked out of the room, purposefully neither shuffling, nor hurrying.

When she got back to the dorm, Mary noticed Ojekaada was the only one still in bed. She gently lifted off the blanket to reveal the child curled up as if in her mother's womb, sleeping but with her eyes open.

Mary fainted.

Ojekaada died on a Friday, and at church on Sunday, Ruth showed Mary where they buried her.

"Everybody knows Ojekaada died because they found her in the morning, but sometimes they just take them out in the night, dig up a hole in this place, and put them in there."

Mary stood by the fresh mound of earth, not much bigger than the hump Ojekaada made when she was hiding under the covers in her bed. Mary wondered where Ojekaada's grandmother was and if she would ever know that she had died. Her heart lurched as she looked around her at the other heaps of dirt, all different sizes, with no names, or sacred offerings.

They let Mary stay there, not participating in the work of Our Lord for just this once, sometimes wailing, sometimes whining, and sometimes just lying there, all the rest of the afternoon. By the time it was ready for the groups to head back to the residence to prepare for supper, Ruth's shadow cast long over Ojekaada's vagabond gravesite.

"It's time," she said gently.

"I know, but she will be cold, and she will be afraid by herself tonight."

"Mary," Ruth said firmly to call her friend to reality. "You know Ojekaada is not there." She took a step back and extended one arm toward the sky.

"Look at me."

She waited for the breeze to come again. Just as a breath of the wind began to lift first Mary's, and then Ruth's shining strands of hair from their shoulders, Ruth entered its current with her outstretched hand and followed it in an arch across the sky. She closed her eyes and let her body move in a dance with the wind. Her perfect timing made the wind visible as it played together with the glinting sun in her hair.

"You know," she said, "Ojekaada is there," and she turned in a circle and arched her other arm across the sky, "and there," and breathing deeply in and then out, she spanned both hands and arched out like two full rainbows across the sky. She brought it all into her heart, crossed one foot over the other, folded at the waist, and rested there, bent in two, for three or four breaths. "And here," she said, as she stood back up and kept both hands crossed over her chest. "You know that she is with Spirit now."

"I know this."

Mary bowed her head but was unable to stop the tears.

"I know where to find her and play with her," Ruth said.

Mary looked up into Ruth's face.

"Do you want to come?"

Mary nodded.

"Then wipe your tears and come proudly with me to supper. Later tonight, I will show you."

When Mistress heard that Mary had lain around in the shade all day, she gave her the chore she reserved for those who tried to get out of work, and because she had heard that Ruth had been seen scheming with Mary, she put her on rag washing duty as well. Mistress stood watch, making sure each girl got a fair turn at taking from the pile of putrid bloodied rags that lay on the basement floor and dipping them in the scalding bleach-bucket.

Mary chose one from the reeking mound, one that had a white band around the edges where blood had not flowed. She made pinchers of her thumb and forefinger and dropped it in the steaming water. The streaks of red turned to swirling wispy currents in the steel bucket of water.

"Go on! Put more in there! It will cool down after you put a few more in there."

Mary chose the ones that had white edges to grab and filled the bucket, one by one, dropping them in until the water went from pink to red. The crimson water rose to the top of the bucket and began to run down the sides.

"There, look now! You are getting it on the floor!"

Mary knew what this meant. She straightened her shoulders, sucked in her breath, rolled up her sleeves, and stuck her hands in both at one time. She scrubbed them together, imagining that she was washing her own undershirt until it became white again. When that stopped working, she imagined she was in the kitchen, helping Ma knead bread for bannock. Finally she started to wring them out, one at a time, and hand them to Ruth to hang up on a line that was strung by the furnace. When the first batch of rags hung like patchy flags of the wounded, Mary stood with her back to Mistress and waited.

"Dump it over there!"

Mary picked the bucket up with both hands, careful not to let it slosh on her feet or clothing, and set it down by the drain in the stone basement floor. She looked at the bucket of water with things floating around in it and she looked back at the drain. Without asking, she removed the steel grate that covered the drain, set it aside, and slowly dumped the contents into it.

"Fill it! The bleach is on the floor by the sink."

Mary used the hot water tap to fill the bucket and the cup beside the bottle of bleach to measure, then carted it back to the spot where the heap of blood soaked rags waited.

Mistress lit a cigarette.

"Now switch."

Ruth's shoulder brushed Mary's shoulder and she whispered, "Remember! Tonight!"

STEALING THE NIGHT

A KNOCK CAME to the door again, and once again Mary ignored it. How many days had it been? Ignoring it was becoming much easier as she faded in and out of consciousness. Sonny was crying again, a pathetic mewl, a keen so loud in her head that it let the dreaded light, and thus the pain, flood back. She leaned her breast against him, and he was tricked again into satisfaction. Empty as her breasts were, she knew she was in better shape than him simply because she still had pain, and now he seemed to have none. The last stages of hunger have no pain.

The body mercifully lets die first the drive to eat.

She tucked him further under the covers and closer to her body. She ventured a deeper breath and wider eyes to watch him curl indifferently from her. She pretended without motion to be having a cigarette and tried to make a smoke ring with her very own breath in her very own bedroom. Alertness imposing even more now, she moved to disturb Sonny a bit just to take in some more water. Water was still something she had plenty of, but only because after she had ran out of heat, before she had run out of food, she had been clever enough to store it in cans and jars and pots. Actually, she wasn't even sure whether the pipes had or had not frozen because after the food had run out, she had listened to Ma's advice in a dream and taken to her bed.

Hunger is the People's oldest enemy. Once it has taken you down, you cannot fight it. Every scrap of energy you give to it makes it a bigger foe. You must lie still for it and keep it waiting. Sleep child. Wait for something to happen.

The wind howled and beat on her bedroom window, but still, she had to be warmer than Gmiwan.

Where was her Gmiwan? Surely he was dead by now, or this wouldn't be happening to her. She felt the struggle rise within her and wisely searched to close it off. Mary let Sonny's dry suckling lull her away and back to the place where hunger and cold were not bitter enemies but playful competitors that beckoned her. She was filled again with mischief and the joy of triumph.

Lying in the dark with their eyes wide open, they waited quietly in their beds until the familiar tinkle of Sophie's laughter could be heard from behind the bathroom door. Then, with Ruth in the lead, they tiptoed past the door that went upstairs to Mistress's quarters, past the kitchen where the rat had probably climbed back into the flour, past the dark, wooden door where the bell would give their quest away, and through the great hall. Ruth pointed to the window by which she had sat that evening for supper and she had left open just a crack, just enough so that they could get their fingers under and push it out of its painted groove.

Mary's stomach squeezed itself into a ball as tight as the fists at her side as she watched Ruth tempt the window open. She dared not look over her shoulder to see if anybody might burst from the darkness to grab them away from this night pleasure. Ruth stepped aside for Mary to crawl through the window first. She stuck half her body out the window and into the muggy cool of the dark outside and hesitated. When she felt Ruth's slap on her rear, she let the bulk of her weight pool forward. She dropped like a rock on the wet grass below and rolled out of the way for Ruth to follow, right up against the trunk of an apple tree. An apple fell and bounced off her head and hit the ground. Mary grabbed it, took a bite, and found a comfy spot on the tree trunk to lean against to enjoy the apple, and to watch Ruth drop, head first, on the ground.

Ruth searched on the ground for an apple, checked for worms, and took a bite. "It's a good night," she whispered. "Not windy. The curtains won't blow. It would be very bad if someone came along and noticed the window open."

Mary's eyes widened. She hadn't thought of that.

"Let's go further across the orchard and pick more apples," Ruth giggled, "We'll put them in a pile and get them when we come back later. We can hide them to eat at night in our beds."

The full moon glanced off every perfect apple. They made a pile of only as much as they would be able to carry back from the outer edge of the orchard, and then Ruth grabbed Mary's hand.

"Come on!"

The orchard sprawled east, west, and south, close to the Mohawk Institute property lines, then meandered north up the hill where it dwindled to a ragged edge just short of the crest. It was along this crest that the haunting silhouette of these two girls could be seen running hand in hand farther into the night. Floyd, standing in the open back door of the kitchen, couldn't make a smoke ring through his involuntary smile.

"Where are we going?" Mary managed through panting breaths.

"I told you before," Ruth teased.

"Where, where?" Mary played back.

"Ojekaada is with Spirit, right?"

The pain in the corner of Mary's heart stalked toward her like a cat upon a mouse.

"Yes," Mary answered.

"Well, we are going to play with Spirit."

They ran at top speed until they arrived breathless but full of rascal at a log fence that snaked farther away than they could see in the dark. Ruth reached it first and grasped onto it with both hands to steady herself and rest a while. Mary stood by, waiting and thirsting for air. Then Ruth heaved herself up, perched on the fence, and patted a place beside her. Mary followed suit.

"Look!" Ruth whispered as she pointed into the night.

Mary squeezed her eyes into narrow slits to focus better.

Three horses, idle and only barely alert, leaned against the fence on the far side. "Horses," she replied, "We should have brought some apples."

Ruth jumped down inside the fence.

"There's a wild apple tree just yonder," she said. "That will be their reward."

"Reward?"

"Come," Ruth motioned, "follow me."

Mary leaped down and chased after Ruth. As they neared the horses, both girls slowed to a near standstill. One of the horses, a Chestnut, turned its head to greet them. The girls waited respectfully while another, a Paint, and then an alabaster Arab stallion, also turned their heads and sniffed the air between them. The stallion snorted, and Ruth took it as a sign to approach. She patted his mighty thigh, and his muscles twitched beneath her lingering touch. She ran her hand the length of his torso, and then teased up around his neck until the liquid tendrils of his incandescent mane were entangled in her fingers. Then, tightening her fingers into a grip and springing upward, she leapt astraddle of the horse's great back. She waited while he steadied and then, leaning all the way forward, she let the weight of her chest rest upon his neck, her arms drape around it, and her cheek nestle on the tender place between his ears.

Mary wished with all her heart that she could do that too.

As if hearing that, Ruth whispered to the stallion, "Can Mary ride too?" She waited peacefully for him to feel what was in her beating heart and honest mind until the barest ripple of ascent was confidentially exchanged between the two at the spot where their loins and minds met.

Ruth reached down for Mary. Mary grasped Ruth's hand and let herself be lifted up behind Ruth on the enchanting beast. Both girls waited reverently while he steadied beneath them.

As they started to move, Mary instinctively wrapped her arms around her friend's waist firmly, but not stiffly, in an effort to become one rider. Under Ruth's invisible manoeuvre, they soon broke from their canter to a full speed, heart-pounding gallop. The night air now became the wind that pulled at their hair, tingled their scalps, and exhilarated their skin. Mary watched with pure wonder as the line of the fence approached at winged speed.

Faster and faster. Would they stop so abruptly that they would be propelled like arrows over the fence and lodged into a tree trunk? Or would they, at the very last moment, change directions? Mary resisted, clinging so tightly that Ruth might lose control of the powerful animal.

In the very second before reaching the fence, Mary felt it. Ruth bent forward and lowered her chest at the very inclination of the stallion's taking to the air. Airborne now, in the most vital moment poised over the fence, Mary was more alive than she had ever been. It was in that moment off the ground that she escaped the grip that grief had held upon her heart. She could imagine the evil spirit, too heavy with ugliness to follow her into the air, writhing in the dirt behind her. Its cries faded behind her as they lighted upon the solid ground of the other side.

They dashed toward the hypnotic edge of the forest at an unflinching pace and Ruth called over her shoulder, "Do you feel that?"

"I feel it," Mary whispered softly.

Filled with the glory of Grandmother Moon and all their ancestors gathered overhead, they both let loose a cry for Spirit in worship of the pure awesome beauty of being. Mary could feel Ojekaada and her mother keeping pace with them, and she felt no sadness, only comfort.

From that night forward, they tried to ride every full moon that they could, and any other night that the wind was right and they needed to, even in the winter.

A Small Basket of Coal

WAS IT THE next day? Or had it been two or three since the last drawn-out knock at her apartment door?

Outside Mary's locked apartment door, Tom Dunsby used the side of his fist instead of his knuckles and put a bit of his stomach into it as well.

Nothing.

Be damned, he thought, he was not leaving this time. He tried the door handle again and cursed. He was not leaving this time!

"Mary!"

He put his ear up against the wood. He thought he heard something. He did! He definitely heard a baby's cry from within.

"Mary!" He was not leaving this time. Not until he had seen the inside of that apartment.

He eyed the door up and down. He looked down the stairs behind him. The image of his standing in front of a judge trying to explain why he had burst into the apartment of his unrequited love imposed itself again. He shook it off. He focused on the exact spots that he would impact simultaneously with his shoulder and hip. He tested the move in slow motion first and found the door gave more willingly from its frame than he would have expected. He backed up as far as the brief landing at the top of the stairs would allow.

"One, two, three," he called aloud and then rushed the full weight of his body against the door.

The cowardly door complied so readily under the siege of Tom Dunsby's fully gathered resolve that it separated completely from its frame and ushered him flat onto Mary's kitchen floor.

Mary, yanked with incredible force out of her self-preserving reverie, leaped out of her bed with the agility of a startled cat, and hit the floor running. Her mind and body, unhampered with analysis, fed on adrenaline and instinct. She lighted out her bedroom door, down the hall, and into the kitchen. There lay Mayor Tom Dunsby, on his back, on her kitchen floor with the door beneath him. Still clutching the handle, he blinked at her.

Absolutely spent with her efforts, Mary began to crumple toward the floor. Tom Dunsby used his grip on the door handle to push himself off into a barrel roll that beat Mary to the floor. She slipped into his waiting arms like a baby to its cradle.

Mary didn't lose consciousness, only the power to stay standing. She stayed taut in his embrace, trying to figure out what had happened, and he couldn't resist the urge to draw her closer for comfort. The heat of his body and his radiating love for her dissolved her last shards of defence and Mary melted into his stalwart softness. He felt her curves matching the curves of his body, and decadently let it be.

"Mayor Dunsby," Mary finally spoke.

"I know," he spoke apologetically, "I have broken your door, and I will replace it. I just felt something was wrong." Awakened by his own stuffy, polite voice and the reality of the situation, he continued more emphatically, "Something is wrong here? What is going on?"

When she didn't answer, he shifted his weight so he could get a better look at her and the situation. He noticed that her face was shrunken, that she was barely conscious.

He picked her up, carried her down the hall to her room, and placed her in her bed beside her child. She smiled meekly up at him.

"Please tell me! What is happening here?"

That's when he finally noticed the frigid temperature. He noted all the water containers strewn about. He backtracked to the kitchen. Throwing open the ice box and then the cupboards, he realized that his beloved Mary and her child were starving and freezing to death.

Tom Dunsby had a temper. Though nobody, except his own deceased mother had actually witnessed it, he often felt it seething close to the underside of his skin, a leak in his armour. He slammed the last cupboard door with such force that it rattled the frosted window. He headed back toward the bedroom.

"You are allowing your child to starve to death," he accused evenly.

Mary's eyes widened at his tone and she pulled Sonny closer.

Shivering there, waif-like and sallow, she touched Tom's vulnerable spot. He walked over to the bed, pulled the blankets from the foot of the bed and covered her and the child. He nudged her over, sat down, and took her hand in his.

"I know you applied for welfare relief a couple of months ago, and I know how it turned out. When I hadn't seen you around for a while, I just assumed that you had used those tickets after all. Oh Mary," he said. He felt something sting at his eyes that he hadn't felt since he was a small boy. He closed it off in a panic and continued matter-of-factly, "Listen to me. I am going next door, and I will be no more than fifteen minutes. I'm going to get you some nourishment and then we are going to discuss this." He didn't know why, but he waited for a response from her. When she nodded her assent he leaped up and started out of the room.

"Mayor Dunsby?" she called faintly from behind him.

He turned on his heel.

"Thank you," she said.

Tom Dunsby hurried down the stairs and threw open the door to the Post Office below. He tried in vain to catch himself but was caught in a tidal wave of emotions he couldn't overpower. He barged up to the counter and waited without patience for fat Mr. Pilson to make his civil servant way up to the counter.

"Yes Mayor Dunsby. How can I help you this morning?"

It dawned on Tom that they didn't sell food at the Post Office. "I would like you to give me your lunch immediately!"

Mr. Pilson cocked an eyebrow and looked from side to side as if he stood a chance of finding the explanation for this absurd request.

"My lunch?"

Tom Dunsby brought his fist down on the counter, rattling the pen-post and stamp-licker between them. Mr. Pilson shook in his Oxfords on the other side of the window.

"Now!"

Mr. Pilson turned tail and ran straight for the lunchroom to retrieve the pail his wife had packed for him.

Mayor Dunsby snatched it out of his hand, and was about to turn and leave with it, when he had another thought. "Close this place up and after you have locked up, come upstairs and see me!"

"See you?" asked Mr. Pilson.

"Yes! See me for your orders! You will be doing some shopping for me."

Mr. Pilson, dull from years of civil service, replied, "But, sir, that is not my job."

"Do you work for the city or not?" Mayor Dunsby filed his voice down to a sharper edge and stared straight into the fat man's soul. "And am I not your employer?"

"Y-y-yes," Mr. Pilson stammered, not for one instant mistaking the threat.

"Then lock this joint down and get your lazy ass up those stairs for further orders!" he thundered, "You will do what I say because I am the *boss* of this city!"

Tom Dunsby let himself back into Mary's apartment. His heart swelled in his chest at the sight of her sitting up in her bed, hair combed, housecoat on, and ready for visitors. She smiled as he entered the room but her eyelids drooped and she leaned back into the pillow as if the mere gesture had drained her. He sat down in the chair she must have dragged over to her bed. He flipped the metal clasps and tossed open the lunch bucket. The first thing he noticed inside was a metal thermos, so he opened it, expertly, like it was his own. The welcoming smell of chicken soup reached his nostrils and without pausing he poured the contents into the lid.

"Mmmmm, who cooked that for you Mayor Dunsby?"

"Mrs. Porter."

"It smells heavenly."

He handed it to her, but her hand trembled too much to let her take it. She knew it too and let her hand fall back down to her lap. Their eyes met.

"Please, can I hold this for you?"

She nodded. She struggled to shift into a higher sitting position but sank back into herself. Tom moved his chair closer to her, and leaning in, slipped his arm behind her back to support her. It was all she needed to sit up straight. He kept his arm there while he brought the steaming cup to her mouth. Mary parted her lips and let Tom Dunsby give her nourishment. After a few sips, any resistance she may have felt was tranquilized by the fragrant chicken soup. When she had finished, she leaned back into her pillow and drifted back to unconsciousness. He determined not to leave her side, to wait until she woke again and needed nourishment. But after a few moments had passed, Sonny stirred.

Mary opened her eyes and said through a fog, "Will you lift him for me?"

Tom regretfully took his arm back and gently rested her weight back onto the pillow. He stood up, gingerly picked Sonny up, and placed the listless child in Mary's waiting arms. Tom Dunsby had never, in his entire forty years, seen at such a sight. Mary was feeding her child with her breast. He quickly adjusted his gaze to her face, but her eyes were closed and her head was beginning to fall backward.

"Please?" she said in a faraway voice as her weak arms began to give way, "Can you help me hold him?"

He hesitated for a fraction of a second and then rushed to her aid. He slipped both his hands under and cradled the baby so Mary could let her own hands drop away. He held the suckling baby while Mary let herself sleep. The sweet almond scent of Mary's breast milk mingling with the baby's breath drifted warm to his face. To him, Mary was a Goddess.

When Sonny stopped making sucking noises, Tom Dunsby lifted him up. At the place where mother and child had been joined, a drop of milk glistened as he pulled the baby away. Tom Dunsby could hardly contain the magic that he felt. He put Sonny back in his place beside Mary and then sat a while longer, watching Mary's deep, steady breathing. He would have died to do what he had always craved to do—reach over and stroke her hair. Instead he covered her and let her sleep.

Shortly after, Tom heard Mr. Pilson making his way up the stairs. Mr. Pilson stared down at the door lying inert on the kitchen floor and scratched his head. "Mrs. Fisher was in distress so the apartment had to be broken into," Mayor Dunsby offered quickly in response to Mr. Pilson's raised eyebrows. "She is resting at this moment; however, she will require some further assistance when she awakens."

He plucked his faithful pen and pad of paper from his pocket and made a list. "Here," he ordered. "I require you to purchase this list of items." He ripped off the list and thrust it into Mr. Pilson's hand. Then he handed him the pen as well. "Write this down. Get a basket of coal and supplies to feed a baby. Go to the pharmacy and ask. It doesn't have to be too much. Just enough to get through the next couple of days. Mrs. Fisher has already given me the money for it, but to make matters more simple tell the clerks to put it all on my own account for now."

Mr. Pilson waited for further orders.

"Hop to it!" Mayor Dunsby hollered, and Mr. Pilson jumped to attention and turned tail. He started back down the stairs without looking back, bent on his mission. Just as he was about to open the front door of the building and let the frigid air of Main Street hit his face, he heard Mayor Dunsby call downstairs in a softer tone, "Mr Pilson, one more thing? Can you stop by your house and see if your wife has any more of her homemade soup?"

"Yes sir!" he called back up with more enthusiasm for his job than he had felt in years. In a strange way, he liked Mayor Dunsby better too.

In his newfound vigour, Mr. Pilson slammed the front door behind him. It reverberated upstairs and woke Mary. Tom Dunsby heard her stirring and hurried back down the hall.

"Thank you so much for sharing your lunch with me."

Much to Tom's relief, it looked like some life was returning to her eyes and cheeks. He seated himself back in the chair. "Would you like some more soup?" He began to pour another cupful and handed it to her. Secretly and selfishly he had lost himself to his own desire to be her saviour. Now, he felt disappointment that she ate more steadily this time. After a while she even began to chat.

"I don't blame you for leaving your coat on. I'm sorry it's so cold in here. I think it would be a lot colder if not for the Post Office downstairs."

"I have sent an employee for a basket of coal, but my first order of business tomorrow morning is to order a new heating system in this building. In the original design this upper area was meant to be only storage. I apologize on behalf of the city."

"Are the pipes frozen?" she asked

"To be truthful, I haven't been able to give it a thought. If they are, you needn't worry an ounce, as it would be the city's responsibility to repair it." He paused before continuing. "Ummmm, that and the door." He looked away sheepishly.

Mary's laugh sounded closer to the Mary laugh that always delighted his ears.

He shared it with her and then stopped to search her face, "What's going on?"

Mary wiped away the renegade tear and said, "It's Gmiwan, Mayor Dunsby. I haven't heard from him in months. He is sure to be dead or I would have heard from him."

"You let him leave you here alone?" he asked.

"What could I do, Mayor Dunsby. There was no work to be found. I had Sonny to look after; and as you well know, Indians aren't allowed to collect relief." At this point she could no longer hold the dam back. She began to sob.

Tom Dunsby's eyes widened in disbelief, "Are you giving up?"

"Maybe," she answered.

He lifted her chin so that she had to look into his eyes.

"I cannot believe my ears!"

Mary shrugged her shoulders. By her attentiveness, she gave way to his authority.

"Listen to me," he said. "Since when do you give up?"

"Since I am sick and tired of fighting to survive," she answered flatly.

"Well that is certainly exasperating and discouraging at the same time," he huffed. "I came here to request your application for a job."

She crooked an eyebrow.

He had her in the palm of his hand, so he continued in his usual brusque manner, "There is a job opening at my residence for a housekeeper. I had thought you would be perfect for the position. That is, if you didn't mind bringing the baby about with you. Although I certainly miss my mother since her passing, it makes things even more unbearable not to have a clean house when I arrive home. I cannot endure the disarray the house has fallen into for one more day."

"I see," she responded.

Mayor Dunsby continued. "It cannot continue that way." He paused to draw a breath and check for her encouragement. "So, are you interested?" he said, looking into the face, still cradled in his hand.

She nodded.

They spent a moment looking deeply into one another's eyes understanding the conversation that was really taking place. Then Tom Dunsby, yielding to his old reliable call to sensibility, broke the spell by dropping his hand away, clapping them to together, and declaring the whole thing a fine solution.

Mary let a sigh of relief escape. There was hope peeking over the horizon.

Mayor Dunsby was about to rise from his chair when another thought occurred to him.

"And what of Gmiwan?"

She sank into herself. "I guess he is lost."

"What do you mean he is lost?" the mayor repeated as if it were ridiculous.

"I mean, something probably happened to him," she pleaded with her eyes, "or he would be here."

"He went to Toronto with your brother-in-law and was trying to get a job, right?"

"Yes."

"And where is your sister?"

"I don't know where any of them are." she said, unable to hide her utter vulnerability.

"Well," he pronounced, "that is a problem for later resolution. The most immediate issue is yours and the child's recovery and then maintenance. It is the city's fault you are in this situation, and when Mr. Pilson returns with the goods that I have asked him to purchase, we will be a shorter distance from the day that you can begin employment. And I will be all that much closer to an orderly household."

GRANDMOTHER MOON HAD spent her best glory for the night, and contracting now into a tighter sphere, she told them soon they must get back in their beds. Mary chose a smoother apple from the pile beside her and bit into its crispy tart sweetness. She let the juice run down her chin unchecked and laughed at herself. Ruth leaned back on the tree trunk, satisfied and reverent of Grandmother Moon smiling patiently back down upon them.

Mary finished chewing and then spoke up, "Thank you so much for showing this to me Ruth. You are a true friend and I am so lucky you are here."

Ruth smiled.

After a while, Mary, also satisfied, fell back on the tree trunk beside her friend and rubbed her tummy.

"Those are the best apples I have ever had," she declared.

Ruth nodded and said, "It may be because they are stolen that they are so sweet but I don't consider that they are really stolen." Mary nodded her agreement, and Ruth continued, "They say that those apples are sold to keep this place going, but I'll tell you something for sure. The money from those apples is going across the sea to England, just like the money they get to feed, clothe, and educate each one of us. My grandmother can't read and write, and she could hide me from them, but really the only way for an Indian to get an education is at the Indian schools. But as long as she stays alive, I'm going to keep my Indian ways too. My grandmother talks a lot to the other grandmothers and some people, not too many though, are starting to know that the government is just trying to get the Indian out of us. Some people are being Indian in secret, because if they find out, then the Indian Agent really starts putting the pressure on.

"Yeah," Ruth ran her fingers through her short hair, "for every kid the Indian Agent brings here to live in the school, the church gets more money, and the chance to turn an Indian into a prayin' Indian. Not me though, my grandmother says that whenever I want, I don't have to come back. She and the other grandmothers will put me in hiding."

"Have you seen my brother lately?" Mary asked.

"No."

"I searched the boys' crews at apple picking time, but I haven't been able to find him."

"Sometimes I see him leaving after the morning and the supper meal but never at lunch." Ruth glanced up at Grandmother Moon for what she was thinking.

"He could be one of the Minister's boys. If he is, you'll see him at church service in a white and black robe, helping the minister. They are learning to be altar boys. I would think he was lucky to get easy work instead of hard work, but he has a very unhappy look on his face."

"They all end up that way. All the boys that go for church learning end up with their eyes full of bad spirit," Ruth paused thoughtfully before continuing. "There will be nothing you can do about it. You have your own hard times and he has his. Just keep yourself from filling up with bad spirit."

"How?"

"By leaving no emptiness inside you. Always stay filled up with Spirit."

"How?"

"Remember your Elders' teachings and practice whenever you can." Ruth shifted beside Mary as she spoke. "They will try to take it away from you because they know it is power. They want the power." She stood up in front of Mary, a mystical woman-child silhouette to Grandmother Moon. "You don't have to show them you have something strong inside of you. Stay quiet, build, fill yourself with Spirit, and you will survive anything. Don't ever give up." Ruth let the sounds of the night blend with the echo of her words.

Mary knew the older girl was luckier than her, but it was no reason to be jealous. She knew she was lucky their paths had crossed.

"Sometimes you think you have been left with nothing and you will surely die, but you must be keen, Mary. Spirit always provides at least one thing. It is up to you to be alert enough to find it. If you spend your time crying for yourself, your eyes will be closed and blurry with tears, and your ears will be filled with your own wailing. Spirit doesn't like it when we are sad too long. It makes you like a poisonous lake. He cannot go in. You could miss the one gift Spirit left you. When you find it, thank Spirit for it; use it; but then let it go if Spirit seems to be taking it away again. Trust that Spirit will never leave you with nothing."

"Enh."

"We must get back."

Mary leapt into action beside Ruth. They gathered up as many apples as they could carry in the folds of their gowns and started back toward the residence.

Upon reaching the residence, they found their cloaked window undisturbed and waiting for them. Stealth was a trait long bred into both girls and made for an uneventful return to the dormitory, but upon arrival they found an unexpected barrier. Sophie's voice could be heard in the small hall leading to the sleeping quarters, blocking them from entering. They stayed close to the wall and crouched out of the light as they crept closer so they could hear.

"Oh Floyd, I am so afraid." In her distress, Sophie's bawling was laden heavy with her British accent. "I told you this could happen to me."

"I'm pregnant! Do you hear me?"

Floyd sighed deeply.

Sophie's voice gathered more panic, "What are we going to do?"

Floyd cleared his throat.

"Hey baby, I'm not really the father type."

Sophie's sob swelled with the full knowledge of her worst fear, "Oh my God, so you are going to leave me alone with this?"

"What do you want me to do, Doll?"

There was a long silence punctuated only by the ticking of the clock in the hall and Sophie's sniffles.

"You don't want me to marry you?" Floyd paused as if scratching his head and then finally getting it, asked, "Do you?"

Sophie sniffled.

"I'm not the marrying kind."

"But I love you."

"You love me?" he replied as if he didn't understand.

"Of course I love you. You're the first and only man I've ever been with."

"Well, I'm all muddled up," he finally pronounced. "I think I better get some shut eye."

The girls plastered themselves against the walls in the dark hallway as they heard his footsteps approaching. He emerged from the lighted doorway and paused motionless in the shadows. He scratched his head, looked back over his shoulder, and turned left to make his way to the boys' dormitory. The girls unflinchingly held their positions flat against the wall as they heard Sophie's quick steps approaching. Sophie appeared like a white ghost in her nightgown, as she too paused in the small pool of light cast into the large hallway. She looked down the hall at Floyd walking away, the outline of her perfectly feminine body visible through the gauzy fabric of her nightgown, and then ran after him. The girls slipped into the lighted doorway.

MAYOR DUNSBY PULLED up in front of the post office and parked his car in the no-parking zone because he could. He looked over at his passenger, who was looking straight ahead, probably reconciling everything that had happened with what was going to happen next. He left the engine running, and he too stared straight ahead. Of course everything was a done deal, Tom knew that; but still, just for a while longer he let himself linger in the moment before he became a hero.

It had taken him five days. His Toronto counterpart, Mayor Carpone, had helped locate Elizabeth and Harry through the welfare rolls. They were in pretty sorry shapes, too sorry to have been concerned with Mary's well-being. Drink had claimed them. Elizabeth, even through her stupor, recognized him and told him Gmiwan was "still kickin'" because she had apparently been talking to him on Yonge Street, "not too long ago but he is in a bad way." She said she asked him again to come and live with them but he wouldn't. She begged him to tell Mary that Harry might be getting some money from the sale of his Dad's property, and that they planned to use it to start another company, and then "go lookin' for Gmiwan to start workin' again."

Then things had become intolerable. Elizabeth was all over him, pawing him and crying about how she never wanted to leave her sister and how she had to follow her husband. Harry said nothing while Elizabeth cried, "I would'a called but we got no phone, and anyways, Mary's probably got no phone." Then she had looked over at Harry, who was just sitting at the kitchen table rolling a cigarette, not looking her way, not acknowledging that there was even a visitor. Elizabeth turned back to the mayor and said to him that just as soon as they got the money, they would have one more big drunk and then straighten out and try to get another business started. "Tell

Mary that, will ya please," she had pleaded. It was all that hanging off him that Tom Dunsby couldn't tolerate, but even so it had paid off, relatively speaking.

"Stay here, Gmiwan, while I go get Mary," he said and shut off the car's engine.

Gmiwan nodded. He was afraid, too.

Tom climbed the stairs and purposefully kept his mind blank. He could hear Mary singing inside just before he tapped lightly on the door. He listened for Mary's steps but, as usual, he could never quite catch them. Mary always said she was a sneaky Indian. She opened the door.

"Mayor Dunsby!" she always greeted him that way, as if he was just the person she had been waiting for to come and visit. But he knew better because whenever he was sitting having tea with her, and somebody else knocked, she greeted them exactly the same way. Mary loved visitors and people loved visiting Mary.

This time Tom resisted coming in when she stepped out of the way for him to enter.

"Come in, come in, how was your trip to your Mayor friend's in Toronto? You stayed longer than the weekend. I was getting worried. Anyway, you're back and I just put the kettle on!"

Tom took this crack of time between him knowing and Mary not, to stare deeply into her eyes. He pushed down the urge to reach and touch her hand, or brush the tendril of walnut-black hair away from her lips.

"I have found Gmiwan," He said simply.

Mary stopped breathing and waited.

"I have him downstairs in the car."

Mary's eyes darted over his shoulder and she resisted flinging herself past him.

"I must prepare you. He is in bad shape. I have no idea why, but I found him living on the streets, starving, and I think drinking. There is something wrong with him, but I don't know what it is."

She spoke, "He's down there? Right now?"

"Yes."

"And you found him and brought him here?" she whispered. Later she would need to forgive herself for not letting him relish how fine and decent of a man he really was by letting him take the time to explain how he had done it.

Tom's constricted throat severed him from words, so he just nodded and looked away. He felt Mary's hands on his face like dove wings. She stared deeply into his eyes. Then he felt her arms slip around his neck. He just stood there passively while Mary pulled herself into him, buried her face in his neck and began to cry softly. He gave himself permission to hold her while she sobbed. He felt her chest heaving against his own. He held her tighter.

"Nobody has ever loved me this much," she whispered into the hollow of his neck. If only she knew how she stirred him.

He placed his hands on her shoulders and pushed her gently away, "I may need to help you get him up the stairs."

Mary sniffled and wiped the evidence of her tears away, and then in a flash dashed down the stairs, threw open the car door, and wrapped her arms around Gmiwan.

A tear swelled from the corner of Gmiwan's eye and made its way past his rugged sun-and-acne terrain. Upon Mary's insistence, Gmiwan unfurled his lanky form from the vehicle and stood steady as an oak on the sidewalk.

Tom could see that his job was done here, but he just couldn't make up his mind whether to stop by the church to say a prayer or go home and put a dent in the Crown Royal bottle.

"See you kids, later!" he called out the open window as he drove away.

They waved and then turned to go up the stairs. Gmiwan felt his knees buckle, and he let Mary curl around and under him to begin the climb. He braced the bulk of himself with his other hand on the railing. Inside the cheery apartment, Mary listened for the sound of Sonny. Lucky silence greeted her. Mary shut the door between the kitchen and the hall that led to the bedroom. She sat Gmiwan at the kitchen table and began preparations for a tea. While the kettle boiled, she slipped away for a few moments.

Gmiwan had just gotten up and relieved the kettle of its complaining when Mary reappeared in the kitchen. She took the kettle from his shaking hand and ushered him back to the seat where she had left him.

"Today you rest, Gmiwan," she said gently.

Gmiwan watched the back of his beautiful and perfect wife as she busied herself with tea and snack making. A cheery yellow bow tied at her back secured her well-pressed apron and cinched in her tiny waist.

"Gmiwan!"

"Yes," he gave himself a shake and answered.

"Have you noticed your art hanging on the walls?"

Gmiwan let his gaze wander all around the room. He stood up and did a walk-about to survey his collection of works. Then, succumbing to the lure of his rocking chair, he sank into it, leaned back, and keeping his eyes wide open, he breathed in the sanctity of this wonderful, wonderful place.

Mary smiled and turned to spread some apple butter onto bannock.

"Pleased and content," Mary said. "Two happy companions."

She placed the tray on the table and left him to his tea and bannock while she slipped away again.

When she returned she saw that he had barely nibbled his bannock and looked lost, staring out the window at something remembered. His crinkled brow belied that it was not pleasure, but pain he revisited.

She pushed the tray aside and took his hand in hers.

"Gmiwan, come with me."

With the unquestioning faith of a child, Gmiwan rose and followed his wife.

Mary closed his hand in hers and led the way for them into the bathroom. She opened the door, revealing a bathtub filled to the brim with steaming water. The scent of bergamot encircled them and drew them in. In the flickering candlelight, bergamot oil made iridescent swirls around red rose petals. Gmiwan, utterly enchanted into passivity, closed his eyes to better feel the sensation of Mary removing his clothing.

Shadows danced across the dried blood, scratches on his neck and arms, and the protruding bones of his naked body. Like the wing of a butterfly, Mary touched the grapefruit-sized, angry, purple bruise on his side. She traced its perimeters and then pressed her cool palm against it to draw the trapped heat into her hand. She prayed to Spirit to heal her husband's wounds, inside and out, before she opened her hand to release it to the Spirit world.

Mary laced the fingers of her hands throughout Gmiwan's matted tendrils, lifted the mass gently, and let it fall back to his shoulders. Gmiwan let his head fall back from the sheer ecstasy of being touched with such precious passion. Mary moved her one hand to the small of his back and nudged him toward the steaming tub. She helped him inside and then urged him to lean back into the slant of the deep claw foot porcelain tub. Gmiwan let his nostrils fill with the forest flower smell of bergamot, and slipped into the sultry liquid until it was as high as his chin.

Mary touched his cheek and whispered, "I'll be back in a minute."

When she returned, she kneeled down beside him and whispered into his ear, "You have missed many full moons of cutting your hair and you now carry around that which should have been gone. I know your hair is your pride but it is time to start fresh."

"Do whatever you want."

She took his gnarled locks in hand and began to snip them off. As some dropped in neat masses upon the floor and in her lap, and some floated atop the oily surface of the bath water, she retrieved them and placed them in a china bowl beside her. When she was done cutting his hair, she placed her hand at the top of his head, and with a silent nod urged him to dip below the surface.

Gmiwan closed his eyes and mouth and allowed his woman to baptize him into his return to life. When he resurfaced, the candle's unsteady light and the clinging scented oil chased the last of the shadows from his ragged features. He glowed as he breathed in all the gifts this second chance offered.

Mary took up a washcloth from beside her and began to wash Gmiwan's neck. Never did she scrub; rather she coaxed and caressed the encrusted blood downward to be absorbed and dispersed by the water. Under the water's surface, she kneaded his shoulders, and stroked his chest. On his belly, she used a circular motion to soothe the last dregs of fear that might have been clinging to his insides. She let her cloth wander to his hips and found he had come to life. Gmiwan stared longingly into her eyes. Mary stopped what she was doing and withdrew her hand from the water. She began to remove her own clothing. The only sound that could be heard was the whoosh of her clothing as it landed on the wooden surface of the floor. Mary remained hidden to Gmiwan by the deep wall of the tub where she sat nude on the floral pattern hooked rug she had bought from the second-hand store.

Gmiwan reached for her hand and drew her with his eyes to stand. In the dancing firelight of the candles, the sight of her swelling darkly crested breasts, slender hips, umber skin, and glistening sex nearly drove him to heaven too soon. He pulled her insistently toward him.

Mary broke the oily surface with first one foot and then the other. She stood straddled over Gmiwan. He never took his eyes off her, his mouth waiting to take in her breast. Mary lowered herself over his hips until she felt the tip of his sex tweak her longing. She remained poised at the edge of consumption for as long as she could. Then slipping over him, she allowed him in deeper and deeper, until they were almost completely one. Feeling him begin to pulse inside of her, she leaned forward and let her breast go to his waiting mouth. Gmiwan filled his mouth with her nipple and then, in his fervour, rubbed his face between and all over her breasts until they were slathered with bergamot oil.

He could hold back no more. He slipped his hands up to grasp her by the waist and pulled her the rest of the way down. Mary and Gmiwan took up their familiar rhythm until they both cried out.

SONNY SAID THEY came by the place again yesterday."

"Who?" Tom asked as he took his first bite of coconut cream pie. Mary handed him a napkin to wipe the cream from his moustache. "The authorities."

"What do you mean, the authorities?"

"They say now that Sonny is over seven, it is the law that he attend school."

"Oh, you mean the Board of Education."

"It's not that I don't believe in schooling, and it's not like he has to live there," Mary pleaded. "It's just that last year, when we tried him in it, Sonny had a terrible time."

"I remember," he said quietly as he put his fork down. "I could speak to the principal again."

"It would have broken your heart to see what they did to that boy. I dressed him in his brand new outfit, but they called him a dirty injun, and three boys from that family that just moved here from Italy beat him up."

Tom shook his head.

"I could speak to the principal again."

"Do I have to send him? It's bad enough I was afraid they would keep him, but now this is almost as bad."

"How does Gmiwan feel about this?"

"I don't dare tell Gmiwan," she answered.

"Did he hear anything from the paper mill yet?"

"No. Nothing, and I don't understand it because there are jobs available."

"Are you sure you won't let me put in a word for him?" he offered again.

"Gmiwan says it's not right," she looked away, "but I say go ahead and do it."

"Do you want me to take Sonny to school myself?"

"How's that going to look?" she said from over her cup.

"Like I'm the mayor, and you came to me and complained about the school."

Mary kept the tea in her mouth while she considered the notion. She was back at Jackson's Diner full time, plus she was still cleaning Mayor Dunsby's on her day off. Considering that Gmiwan's only contribution to the family income was the money from the art the mayor took to Buffalo for his mayor friend to sell on the American side, it was beginning to look like she really didn't have many choices. She thought again about letting Gmiwan in on things, but shook her head at the idea of instigating anything in him that might not be so easy to manage. She swallowed her tea.

"Pride is second when it comes to your children, so fine then," she set her cup down, "I would appreciate it. I'll drop Sonny by on my way to work tomorrow morning."

"It's not so bad," Tom's hand twitched at the urge to touch Mary comfortingly on her forearm. "Sonny will toughen up." He put his hands down on either side of him on the seat. "I think it has a lot to do with his having no brothers or sisters."

"What has a lot to do with what?" Mary took on a defensive tone.

He answered it immediately, "All I'm saying is that life affords one some natural opportunities to learn some survival skills."

Mary, who had set her shoulders square to address the comment, let them sink in now, "Yes, Sonny does spend an awful lot of time on his own. His father sometimes spends the entire day locked up in his own head while Sonny wanders about the place or plays with the dog at the paint store next door. He can hang around here all day if he wants, but I don't have much time to talk to him. When it comes to conversation, Sonny talks to adults most of the time."

"How is it that you never had another child?" He was too caught up in her worries to even think about censoring his question.

Mary became still. She checked Mayor Dunsby's eyes for his intention but saw only curiosity and concern.

"Do you really want to know?"

His eyes darted left and right in a panicked effort to find a way out of hearing the answer, "No," he said, "I'm sorry, I don't know what I was thinking to ask such a question."

"I'll tell you if you really want to know."

"You must forgive me. I don't really need to know."

She waited, "Well, I'll tell you anyway." Mary drew a breath the way she always did when she was about to begin a story and then continued with the shortest story he had heard her tell so far. "It's very simple. When I woke up the next day after that doctor from Beamsville tore me up inside to deliver Sonny, I prayed to God to never, not ever, let me get pregnant again." She paused for a minute to let the thought settle. "And I say that prayer every night to keep it good."

The clang and the clatter of the Jackson Diner filled the space left by the impact of Mary's words.

"I see," said Mayor Dunsby.

"And it works," Mary paused, "that and a tea. After she had her first baby, Elizabeth remembered something Ma had showed her, so she started getting Harry to drive her up to the reservation every spring and pick a bunch of plants to make a tea with. Now we both go up. They built a dam where the house used to be, but the plant still grows. You have to pick it in the late spring, just after its flowers start turning to seeds. The plant makes something that stops a baby from coming, but if you don't pick it at the right time, it won't work. I'm always afraid we are going to go up there some year and those plants won't be there."

"Did you ever think of bringing a couple of those plants down here and planting them?"

Mary shook her head conclusively. "Wouldn't trust it. Those plants on Ma and Pa's property grew the best out of any other place there was for them to grow. Elizabeth and I both remember Ma letting other women come on to the property and pick. The flowers on them were darker, so it showed that the medicine was stronger. There's a reason for that, maybe something in the ground, I don't know, but I'm just going to keep doing what Ma taught Elizabeth. It works."

"Apparently," said the Mayor, nodding his head, "but what about the praying? How does that work?"

"God listens," Mary pointed upward. "Don't you ever kid yourself, He listens."

"To everything?" Tom ventured.

Mary, sensing that the question was more involved than it seemed, took a moment. She reached for the mayor's spoon, picked up her own, and fished her tea bag out from the last inch of tea in her cup. She placed the mayor's spoon over the tea bag cradled in her own and squeezed the last bitter drops from it into her cup. She placed the spoon with the spent bag discretely in her saucer, and the mayor's teaspoon back in its place in front of him.

"I know He hears everything. He listens, but just because He listens to everything doesn't mean He gives you everything you want. You and He have to agree on it first. Sometimes what you want might be against what someone else wants. Sometimes what you want isn't even really what is good for you. And then sometimes you have to accept that you aren't going to get what you want and so you have to figure out something else that will make you happy. That's the key to being smart—figuring out what else will make you just as happy. Maybe even happier."

"I see," said the mayor simply.

The next day was Sunday. Sunday was the day Mary cleaned mayor Dunsby's house and cooked a Sunday dinner for him. For a short while, in the beginning, she and Sonny had had every Sunday dinner with the mayor, but after Gmiwan returned, the mayor was quick to suggest that she just leave him a hot plate of dinner and take the rest home for her family to have together. It was only fair, mayor Dunsby had said because, after all, if she used her time to cook for him then she wouldn't have time to cook for her family, and he simply appreciated the home-cooked Sunday dinner. The Mayor of Jackson was a real problem-solver.

On this Sunday, Mayor Dunsby had taken to his bed, and Mary was making much better time than usual because he wasn't around to chat with. It was when she was dusting the mantle on the fireplace that she noticed the door to the one room that was always kept closed. The room she was told specifically not to clean, not ever to go in. She had never asked why. And why was that? Because it was damn well none of her business why, she told herself every time it floated to the surface of her mind like a rotten apple.

She tried to ignore it. She simply skipped cleaning that area of the house and moved on to the bathroom. She hoped Mayor Dunsby would rouse himself from bed and sit in his usual spot in the worn armchair, well within view of the room with the door half-open. She cleaned away trying to busy herself with plans for cooking the Sunday meal.

Finally, the only thing that was left to clean was the patch of floor in front of "the door." One peek in won't hurt—she turned the thought over a few times. It was probably where he kept things from his youth, or maybe it was only where he swept all his belongings that he couldn't bring himself to throw away. Whatever it was, it was secret. She felt like Eve in those bible stories at the Mush Hole church: Eve with the forbidden fruit.

She found herself on hands and knees and washcloth poised at the opening. It was dark inside. Too dark to name the square object with sharply defined lines leaning against the wall. She squinted. A picture! Perhaps a picture from his past. Maybe Mayor Dunsby had been secretly married before. Mary bumped into the door with her arm, causing it to swing further in, widening the angular crack to a gap that let the day's light leak in. It was more than a picture. There were pictures and other piles of cobwebby things that coaxed her to crawl closer, let her shoulder nudge the door, and cross the boundary that was the door's threshold. She was pretty much in the room now, so what more would it be to just stand up. She stealthily rose, granted one furtive glance over her shoulder, and walked in.

After committing to the first step inside, Mary moved without halting into the centre of the room that was actually very little more than a closet. Located in the middle of the house, windowless and tucked under the stairwell, it was more like an afterthought somebody had about what to do with leftover space. Mary felt around for the light switch, flicked it, and shut the door behind her at the same time. When the hasty little space under the stairs was illuminated, it took Mary a full second or two for her mind to absorb the meaning of its booty.

Stacked neatly in rows; piled gently in cloth-lined baskets; arranged carefully on wooden storage shelves; and hung diligently from hangers were Gmiwan's oils, sketches, painted rocks, peach pit jewellery, beaded wallets, belts, moccasins, vests, and jackets. All of Gmiwan's art that Mayor Dunsby had taken to be sold at his Mayor friend's city hall, and gave her money for, was stored right here in the dark, in this room. There had never been a hungry market for genuine Indian handicrafts in Buffalo. Mary plunked herself down in the middle of the room and let herself have a cry.

It was a strange thing that evening when Mary arrived home with steaming hot mashed potatoes, peas, roast chicken, and gravy. "Everything always happens for a reason," was Mary's favourite saying when she couldn't do anything about something. Gmiwan and Sonny were listening to the radio, but that was not the strange thing. The strange things were more so in the sequence of events. If only she had gone home, made a cup of tea, and simply sat quietly with the knowledge of where the art had been going. If only she had worked through the truth that Mayor Dunsby had been pulling Gmiwan's end of the financial weight. If only she had done both these things before blurting it out to her husband. Maybe things would have gone differently. If only she had simply taken the time to consider the impact of her newfound knowledge, and how it made her feel not only ashamed of, but also deeply sorry for Gmiwan's apparent lack of purpose. If only she had considered, like she usually did, his feelings before hers. Maybe she would have paid more attention to the radio broadcaster's report that Canada's forces were still in a poor state of shortage and there would be a vote as to whether conscription should be in place. Maybe she would have waited to share her own news until later that evening, or perhaps in a few days, or perhaps not ever. Then maybe, just maybe, Gmiwan would never have made the decision to enlist.

The late, dry, July heat picked up the dust from the road at every stop the bus made. Dirt wafted and curled in through the open windows, picked up the brilliant sunlight, and sparkled before it settled upon the solemn strangers inside. When the bus chugged forward again and built up speed, the wind burnished everything off again. Mary clung to Gmiwan, trying to absorb as much of him that she could before they got to Toronto, or "Big Smoke," as Gmiwan called it. Gmiwan, with Sonny on his lap, sat tall, and looked straight ahead at his chosen path. He knew with all that was in him that he would be coming back home someday, alive, filled with purpose, accomplishment, and that long elusive sense of pride.

In the weeks between his decision to enlist and this day of seeing him off, there had been no crying, pleading, nor gnashing of teeth. No, Mary did not believe in that. Mary believed in letting a person go where their soul is telling them they should go, but try as she might, she could not see the wisdom in it. Why would anybody freely choose to be separated from the people they loved the most? For now, in these last few moments, Mary laid her head on Gmiwan's shoulder, looked up and smiled at him when he smoothed her hair or patted her back, but after he was gone, that was when she would pull this rock of anger out of her pocket, and turn it over a few times to have a real good look at it.

Meanwhile, Sonny twitched and fidgeted on his father's lap, sometimes growing suddenly excited at something passing by on the landscape, and then others curling up in a ball and hiding in his father's chest to secretly suck his thumb. On one level he knew nothing, yet on another he felt the deep stirring and shifting of his own foundation.

The farms were patched with shorter and shorter stretches of trees, which solidified into clots of houses, fences, factories, which gave way completely to a breathing tangle of tall buildings and automobiles. Downtown Big Smoke came too soon. Mary stayed attached to Gmiwan in order for them to rise as a unit and disembark. Gmiwan carried Sonny.

There were other families and couples in the same position. Mary could see them like dotted dark spots amongst the crowd as they made their way through the grandiose halls of Union Station. All around her, they passed signs that promoted and reinforced the seeing-off of one's beloved. Some signs urged that if you couldn't go and fight, you could still feel brave, maybe even glorious, if you bought the pop or laundry detergents that pretty women in army clothes held up. Not only housewives, but even the weak, sick, or elderly could contribute to the war effort by just learning to knit socks and gloves to be sent to the soldiers. "By Golly, we can all take pride. Every man, woman, and child can do his part!"

Mary shook it off. She wouldn't be one of the ones learning to knit. And she didn't have any money to waste on sliced white bread from a company that sent a penny from every purchase toward ammunition. The minute after Gmiwan got on that train, she would be turning to face her life without him. Maybe for three months, maybe for three years, or maybe forever; Mary would be making a plan to survive, and she didn't even feel ashamed that the hardening of the heart process had already started. Living without someone you loved and needed had been a lesson she had been taught a long time ago.

By the time the pods of people saying good-bye to beloved sons, boyfriends, or husbands, gathered in a straggled line along the length of the train, it had already begun to hiss and steam. Like a an evil serpent the train was like a snake that would fill its belly insatiably with good healthy men and young boys, move on, and tomorrow, after Mary had long gone back to Jackson, would come back for more.

Mary and Gmiwan stood facing each other, Sonny between them, playing with the matchbox he had in his pocket. Some of the men started to separate themselves from their loved ones. A girl beside them cried out that she would wait forever as her boyfriend turned to wave from the carriage door, and then disappeared. He was inside and he couldn't hear her, but she wailed and sobbed into her white hanky until a mature woman took the girl's hand, but then turned and buried her own face into the chest of her husband who remained stoic; her gold band catching the artificial light from above.

Mary rested her head on Gmiwan's shoulder, and her hand on Sonny's, as she watched the path of a glistening tear slide down the face of the man who held his sobbing wife. He got rid of it with a flick of the sleeve of his jacket, and then began to lead what was left of his family away from the train. As for Mary, she disentangled herself from Gmiwan without a fuss. She stayed long enough to wave to him as he ascended the first step, and then she turned and let him go in peace.

Mary didn't bother to take the rock of anger out of her pocket on the bus ride home. Instead, she left it there to keep her grounded. She had too many things to consider, like how she was going to make a better living for herself and her son. Sonny, all dressed in white, sat obediently beside her with his empty matchbox, opening it just a crack, shutting it, and then just a crack more, and then shutting it again. Mary paid him no mind; she concentrated on turning over a few ideas she had.

Sonny, feeling his mother's gaze, looked back up and smiled sweetly, but she had already looked away. She looked like she was mad at him as she squared her shoulders and set her face determinedly. Sonny cautiously slid open the wooden match box again, this time allowing the crack just wide enough to tease what was held captive inside into a crazed dash for the sliver of light before he snapped it shut again. He caught his breath and almost started to cry when he saw that one of its little legs had made it out and twitched hysterically. Sonny thought of chickens when their heads got chopped off. Was the leg still attached or not?

A boarding house was one idea. She could keep her job at the diner and run a boarding house. All she would have to do is get up earlier to cook her boarders' breakfasts and pack their lunches. She would tend to their meals and laundry when she got off work. Of course she would stay faithful to Mayor Dunsby and keep his cleaning job on Sundays as well as cleaning the boarding house. The job at the diner was enough to sustain her and Sonny, but with two extra sources of income she would actually be able to get ahead. Mary had always been a good saver. And besides that, being busy would be the best thing for her mind.

Mary took a sturdy posture against the lurking chill of loneliness without Gmiwan. She sat up tall in her seat and set her mind to her plans. With Gmiwan gone she would have too much time anyway. Staring out the window at the farms going by, she scanned her mind for the ideas she had already come up with. Mary's place was too small for a boarding house, so she knew she would have to look at renting another place. There were a few empty places she could choose from. The old Empress Hotel was located right in the middle of town on Main Street. It was close to the diner and close to Mayor Dunsby. There were thirteen rooms, a couple with shared bathrooms. She and Sonny could live on the main floor, which used to be the bar, adapting it as their living quarters with a common sitting area for the boarders. She did a mental calculation. With thirteen boarders she could easily pay the rent and buy their food. She was used to cooking, serving, and cleaning for far more. The Empress had been empty for over seven years. Mayor Dunsby, when she had confidentially brought it up to him, thought that she should offer even less than they were asking.

Mary could hardly contain her excitement as she let the idea gel and set in her mind.

Sonny couldn't stand one more second of watching that miniature stick-leg spasm and squirm, so he pried the box wide open. Thirty-two furious bees made a furry coating on the opening for a mere second before taking flight in an angry cluster. They took to the clearest path, which was straight down the aisle of the bus. The driver, in response to the frenzy that had burst out on his bus, slammed on his brakes. Mary, who was more afraid of the fray than she was of the bees, held fast with one hand to the steel bar on the seat in front of her, and the other to her son. They stayed put while everybody else flew forward. With everybody now either piled on top of each other or tangled around a seat, the bees reformed and headed for the open windows. Mary stayed stock-still in her seat while chaos reigned. Sonny thrust the evidence back into his pocket.

"LAST NIGHT RATS were biting my eyes."

Ruth stopped, her spoon poised in mid-air between her mouth and the bowl. Her eyes squinted as she peered into Mary's.

"It must have been a dream."

"I felt them. They were trying to eat my eyes."

Ruth put the mush into her mouth, chewed, and then spoke, "I don't see any bite marks. It must have been a dream."

Mary felt her eyes.

"Maybe the rats in your dream are trying to cut out what you see." She stopped chewing and stared out the window for a bit. "Yes, that is probably what it is. There is no one to tell and nothing we can do about things around here. All we can do is survive it."

Mary cast her head downward, "I guess. I know."

"Did you know some kids cried for the milk today?"

Mary nodded, "I heard Mistress tell Sophie to figure out who wanted it and who didn't, and then for her to order the right amount."

"Why do you think she is being so nice?"

Ruth snorted, "She's not being nice. She's kissing somebody's ass, hoping nobody finds out they killed Ojekaada with that milk. And I bet she's not the only one worried. Now some kids have a taste for the stuff, so they can at least continue pawning it off."

"Tastes like shit."

"Enh."

They finished the rest of their meal, lost in their own thoughts until the witch started whacking the wall with her stick and made an announcement.

"Church is cancelled today. You will be working in the orchard instead."

Out in the brilliant sunshine, the orchard was a welcome replacement for the four dank walls of the church basement. Lately, church day, with all the sewing, embroidering, and knitting for Our Lord Jesus, was preferable only to rainy days in the orchard. Mary was even more surprised to see that Porter, along with the rest of the boys, was working among the girls.

Elizabeth met her halfway and walked with her, whispering, "Porter doesn't have to work in the church anymore."

"Is it true?" Mary asked when they reached him under the low hanging branches of the farthest apple tree.

Porter nodded wordlessly.

"I guess you're gonna miss it? Was it better work?"

Porter shook his head and cast his eyes downward.

Mary searched Elizabeth's face for interpretation.

"The minister quit and Floyd quit," she answered.

Mary recalled the conversation she and Ruth had overheard.

"Was it because Sophie wanted Floyd to marry her?"

A look of confusion flitted across Elizabeth's face. She shrugged. "Maybe, but why would the minister quit?"

They both looked to Porter. He shifted in the spot that he stood.

Elizabeth prodded him, "Why do you think the minister quit?"

"I figure," he started haltingly, "it is likely on account of the kid they found dead in bed this morning."

Mary and Elizabeth leaned in closer.

"What happened?"

"One of the older boys, Earl, he's been a church helper for a quite a while now. Well, he has been talkin' a lot about eating from a bush that's on the church property, the one with red berries. He said his grandfather taught him that it was poison if you take it a certain way. They know that's what he did, because they found some of the leaves and berries still in the bed with him this morning, along with a note."

Mary and Elizabeth covered their mouths to hold back their gasps. "Willie, who has been here the longest, and knew writing the best, read it out loud. Floyd left sometime in the night."

"Do you think Floyd killed him?" Elizabeth asked.

Porter shook his head, "Na, that kid killed himself. I don't know why Floyd is gone, but he had nothing to do with it."

"Do you think he was sick from the milk and just tried to cure himself?" Mary wondered aloud.

Porter looked away.

"Tell me. What did the note say?" Elizabeth said.

"It said nobody would be able to make him go to church anymore."

By now, Ruth had joined them. She answered the look on their faces. "I heard."

Mary asked her, "What do you think it means Ruth?"

"It means they'll dig another hole. Someday enough lost children will walk in the Spirit world that their nameless cries for their mothers and fathers will be heard. My grandmother tells me this when I go home in the summer. She teaches me how to stay out of their reach. She does not want to come here one day to pick me up and have them tell her I ran off. I told my grandmother that after this summer, I'm not coming back." She met Mary's eyes briefly and then looked away.

"I wish I had somebody to come and claim me. I often dreamed maybe Maggie would come and get me someday."

"Stop dreaming, your aunt doesn't have the power. The Indian Agents have all the power. They are going to keep you in here any way they can, and there's lots of kids in here just like you. Most of them will stay in here until every bit of the Indian is out of them. Fight that, fight that hard!"

Not much work got done that day. Looking after all the girls and the boys must have been too much for Sophie because she spent most of her time ducking behind the shed to smoke cigarettes. Mistress was nowhere to be found. Chaos reigned for almost a whole week, until by Sunday there was a new minister and a fat man with an Italian accent to replace Floyd. It turned out the old minister didn't quit. They said that he was so grief-stricken from the loss of one of his flock that he had to be taken back into the fold for a rest.

Ruth snorted, "Yeah right, grandma says there's no bigger liars than a bunch of people with their hands on the Bible."

The following Sunday, Mary noticed that all the altar boys were relieved of their duties. Porter included. The new minister was older and smiled more. He let everybody sit where they wanted to, so long as the girls stuck with the girls and the boys stuck with the boys. He said, "Personally, I wouldn't give a rat's tail for where you sit, but sometimes it's better to get to know the rules if you ever really want to figure out how to break the rules."

Mary sat with Ruth and Elizabeth, "Do you think Mistress is getting soft?" asked Mary.

Ruth turned in her seat and looked Mary in the face, "No."

"Well, she changed my seat in the eating hall, to your table, as a favour, she says. That was being nice, don't you think?"

"Mary?"

"What?"

"You know that dream you keep having?"

"Enh."

"She is the rat that is biting your eyes."

THEY WOULDN'T LET Mary and her sister spend extra time together before Elizabeth left. Mistress said that the older one would just try and talk the younger one into something corrupt. On Sunday, however, the minister didn't have a single problem with it.

"Stop giving me the dickens over this. I'm seventeen and I could have left a year ago."

"You can stay until you are eighteen," Mary argued back.

"The law says I can leave when I'm sixteen and even if I did stay until I was eighteen, that would only make you fourteen." She folded her arms defiantly. "I only stuck around so I would have Porter to go with me. We're taking the bus tomorrow and going to work in the canning factory in Vineland, and that's that."

"Take me with you too," Mary pleaded flatly.

"You gotta be sixteen to work in the canning factory."

The next day was March 21st, the day the Mohawk Institute said Porter Stone, or any other kids that had no idea what a birth date was when they got there, was the legal age of sixteen years, so he and Elizabeth packed up before breakfast, just so as they would be sure to catch the morning bus for the canning factory workers.

Ojekaada was gone; Sophie went away and never came back, then Ruth; and now Elizabeth and Porter had to turn their backs to her. These were the ones she had made family of in this place. She walked listlessly to breakfast, a straggler behind all the others today, her feet made a soft noise on the marble floors. This place, she looked around, where fathomless despair rang like hollow echoes through the cold hard hallways. She had had another family once before, but their images were faded now. They were only ghostly voices that whispered to her in her head.

Mary fell asleep that night dreaming of when she would turn sixteen.

MARY HAD NOT heard a thing from Gmiwan though he had promised to write every chance he could. He had been gone three months, and still, nothing. Every time a moment threatened to plunge her into desperate prayer that he was at the very least still living, she filled it with work. And all that work had paid off. Today, shading her eyes from the brilliant sunshine overhead, she watched from the street as city workers fastened her "Mary's Place" sign.

"Okay, Mrs. Fisher?"

Mary watched it swinging against the cloud-dotted blue sky.

"Give it a whack, Earl! See how well it stands up to bad weather!"

She shivered deep from within and pulled her coat tighter around her. Even though the sun burned off the December chill, the snow and the brittle wind would soon come to confront all that she had resolved. She slipped her arm into Mayor Dunsby's, and he melted beside her.

"You are a Godsend" she said to him.

"Thanks. I hope the rest of the constituents remember that at next election time. I'm just doing my bit to nurture small business for this town."

Mary turned to face him and cocked her head. He never let her thank him or even acknowledge how special she knew she was to him.

"Yes, I see what you mean. I guess you are going to have to start right away on a new collection of second-hand furniture so you can give it away to the next business that starts itself up in this city."

Tom Dunsby let himself linger in Mary's dancing eyes, let himself be warmed by the smile that sparkled as the frosted air left her sweet cherry-coloured lips.

"You finally cured me from being a pack rat. Mother, God bless her, was one, and I sure didn't see myself as one, but, as you witnessed for yourself, I kept an awful lot of things. I think it was more about not being able to bear throwing out the things she valued. But look now! I feel happy when I see all her treasured things being put to good use, rather than collecting dust. I guess you still don't see my own business plan."

Mary questioned him with her brow.

"Now I don't have to pay you every week to dust and clean it."

Her laughter rang in the air like the bells on the Christmas tree at the hardware store every time someone brushed past it through the narrow, packed aisles.

"I don't know about that . . ."

He interrupted her, calling out to the workman poised on the ladder overhead.

"Okay, Earl, it looks good! Come on down."

"Would you like to come in for a hot cup of tea?" she said to him.

"Why that sounds wonderful. Any pie?"

"I have freshly baked apple pie cooling on the counter as we speak sir," she responded in mock Jackson Diner waitress style. "Do come in and be seated."

Inside it was warm from the blazing fire Mary had left well stoked. The building had a furnace, but the fire made the living room so much more inviting. The cluster of her old furniture and Mayor Dunsby's, plus an old rocking chair Sonny had rescued from someone's garbage and then re-paired, came together cheerfully in front of the fire. Mary had scrubbed the flatboard floor clean and scattered it with rag rugs she had bought from the second-hand store. When the Crumms mentioned they had just purchased a brand new dining room set, complete with a china cabinet, Mary offered to buy their old table. Since the Crumms had raised ten kids, any table they had would surely be big enough to seat her potential boarders. The Crumms wouldn't take a dime for it—said it had seen far too many years of abuse. They even threw in all the mismatched chairs they had accumulated throughout their lean years, and then along with her own, Mary had a set. After that all she had to do was sew thirteen more red-and-white-checkered chair cushions to match the ones she'd brought from her apartment, along with three more curtains sets. But it was the steeped-tea dyed tablecloth that Sophie had crocheted for her that pulled the whole combination of sitting, eating, and living areas into one eclectic dynasty. "Mary's Place" was a place you could call home.

Mary left Mayor Dunsby to sit by the fire while she went into the kitchen. She returned carrying a tray laden with cups, saucers, and two slices of pie. With Mayor Dunsby, she didn't bother with sugar bowl and creamer. She knew how he liked his tea, and she brought it to him in his favourite cup with a portion and a half of warm apple pie. Lately she had even been able to talk him into letting a slice of cheddar cheese melt on top.

She set the tray down between them on the mosaic-top coffee table, a portrait of the moon's glow reflected on a purple lake. *Nightscape,* Gmiwan had christened it at the moment of its completion. Hour after arduous hour of chipping, scraping, and sanding thousands of pieces of broken cups and dishes into perfection, had brought a replication of the image inside of him to the tabletop. In some places, the grout he had mixed, pressed, and formed into place remained tinted from his bleeding fingertips. It looked like a painting, too fine and delicate to ever set your hot teacup on. But Gmiwan had glazed it, polished it, and insisted she use it like it was stone. He presented it to her for her birthday and said she could go there and discuss things with Grandmother Moon anytime she couldn't find Her in the sky.

Mary pulled her attention forward into the present.

"Well," she pronounced, "this is a fine day indeed."

Mayor Dunsby leaned back into the back of the couch with his cup of tea cradled in his lap. He thought he might leave his pie for a bit and let the cheese soften some more.

"Yes, you have accomplished a lot."

"Not without your help," she was quick to interject, "and also not without this reasonable rent!"

"I suppose the owner feels that it's better to get some kind of rent for the place rather than none." He let his gaze wander off into the snapping logs in the fireplace, "I can see his point from a business perspective, and it's just smarter to minimize deterioration of the premises by keeping it occupied. You've actually increased the value, with the changes you've made. This place will make money and be more valuable to the owner in the future. He's not a charitable guy; he's a smart guy."

"Again, thanks to you for guiding me through it. I would never have dreamed I could negotiate having the utilities included in the rent for a year."

"It's not uncommon to assist new business owners in establishing themselves. The city encourages it."

"Maybe someday I will save enough to buy it."

"Maybe someday you will," he said absently.

Seeing that he was content and drifting off, Mary removed his pie from the tray and placed it, with a napkin and his fork, closer in front of him, before she joined him somewhere in the depths of the crackling fire, comfortable in silence like old friends should be. He would tend to his cold pie when he woke up. And when he did, she would probably be gone, as she was due to be over at the diner to work the lunch hour and then get back to start the men's supper before they got home from work. From now on, this would be the flavour of all her days, even more so, now that the sign was up. Tomorrow, first thing in the morning, more interviews. She had room for seven more men, but she would not accept a single one that didn't have a full-time job; no unemployed drifters! A hard worker meant a good payer.

Mary let herself be seduced deeper into the autumn warmth of the flames as her body slowly gave into the sofa. Rest should be savoured, but when she finally gave in to unconsciousness, sweet dreams were not waiting for her. No matter how much she filled every minute of her waking day with work, at night the nightmare stole in like damp fog and claimed her. More times than not she woke drenched in the sweat of terror, or barren with a fathomless sense of loneliness. Cursed sleep.

There was nothing she could station to guard against the black of her heart. Mary knew deep within her mind and soul that her Gmiwan was not okay. It was the trickle of one hot tear making its way down the cold side of her face that woke her and caused her to leap up, desperately search through the haze for some un-named despair that she could at least pick out and extinguish. It lurked somewhere just beyond the mist watching her. She rubbed the grogginess from her eyes and went over to add a log to the fire, then headed off into the kitchen with the tray.

MARCH 21ST, 1929."
Mary repeated the words aloud seven times before she opened her eyes, one
for every year she had been here.

*Whenever you have an important thing to decide, you must always think
carefully about what will happen seven years from now.*

She lay there, keeping her eyes closed, waiting for the creak of the door
that would hail morning. She reached for the spot under her mattress and
pulled out a letter. She brought the letter to her face. It was folded four times
in a neat square.

Mistress came in hollering and slashing—a big racket day. Mary purposefully opened her eyes slowly. Gone were the days when she could be
startled by such morning tirades. Mistress was like a scrawny underfed bear,
bigger than most creatures where she lived, but the smallest of her own kind.
She prowled around looking for food to make her grow but she had dined
on the hearts of children so her appetite was unending.

You are Wiindeego and you are no good to the People.

Mary wondered how long Mistress would roam before it was her time
to be cut down, or maybe she was already dead, but like a tree struck by
lightning, just stood there for years after. Anyway, it didn't matter because
after today she no longer needed to concern herself with what kind of mood
the people that worked at the Mohawk Institute might be in. She rolled over
and began to rise in time with Mistress's procession down the aisle. By the
time she was three beds away, Mary's feet would be on the floor. Mary stood
up, and normally she would wait for Mistress to pass so she could indulge a
stretch without provoking an excuse to be yelled at, but this morning she
would need to speak to her on her way by. As she waited she noticed one of

the two empty beds at the end of the aisle was filled. Aha. The reason for the big show this morning—well soon there would be two empty beds again.

"Excuse me, Mistress?"

Mary noted the stark white that struck across the black of her hair in jagged stripes, and the deep lines that now set her face in true expression of her fierceness. She wondered if she had ever been attractive or even loved. Maybe not, maybe that was why wherever she walked, she left a wake of desperation, or maybe it really was only that she was doing the work of Our Lord. Mary blinked the thoughts away to bring herself back into focus.

Mistress twirled around, drawing and cocking her pointer stick in the direction from which she heard the voice.

"May I have a box please?"

A wave of confusion flickered across the stormy lake that was her face, then she set it right and put both her hands on her hips. The stick wagged behind her like the tail of a devil.

"And whatever for!?"

"I am leaving today."

She waited, tapping her foot.

"Today is March 21st."

"Hmph."

"May I have a box to pack my things?"

"I don't have a box."

"What will I pack my things in?"

"You ingrates pile out of here the minute the law says you can, but I will tell you that you will go nowhere! Take a look around you. This is as good as it ever will be for your kind! Here you are fed, clothed, kept clean, and baptized in the name of God! Now you are going to leave without a complete high school education?"

"Yes."

"Shows how inherently stupid you people are." She knew, from hard-won experience that there was no winning when one of them set their mind to leaving. It was the fault of the law. What kind of inane law gives rights to these people who can't even tie their own shoelaces when they come to her? She spends her life civilizing them, making them fit for society, and what for? They run out of here just as fast as they can, most of them still half savage, when she could have been getting two more years of funding. Now there was yet another bed to fill. "You'll have to sign some papers first," and with that she turned on her heels. "Recalcitrant," she muttered.

After Mistress let herself out the door, Mary reached under the mattress for the piece of paper she had hidden. She tucked it in the brassiere she had been issued. There would be no box, so she took her pajamas off, folded them neatly in the middle of the bed, and walked around to all four corners, loosening them off. Then she walked around one more time and drew each unfastened corner until they all met in the middle of the bed. Mary bent down and withdrew a cigar box, which she had plucked from Floyd's garbage years ago, from under her bed and emptied it on top of the unmade covers. She picked up the brush and gave her hair a hundred strokes. She checked her fingernails and laid the clipper beside the brush. She tucked her toothbrush neatly between the clipper and the hair brush and began folding the linens into a rectangle over her belongings. She folded them again and again until they became small enough to roll up into something she could carry. She placed her hand on where her heart beat and heard the crinkle of the letter. She took it out, sat on the edge of her bed and read it for the thirty-third time.

Dear Minister:

I sent this letter to you but it is really meant for my sister, Mary. I am afraid that if I send it to the institute they will not give it to her.

Will you please give it to her on Sunday? Thank you.

Yours sincerely,
Elizabeth

Dear Mary:

March 21st will be here in two weeks and I know that you will be leaving. I am writing to you to tell you that I have left the canning factory and have moved to a city named Jackson.

Do you remember Sophie? One day I met her at the picture show in St. Catharines, and she told me why she left. She said she lost her job because she was going to have a baby from Floyd and the institute would not allow her to work there if she was pregnant and not married. She does not have the baby.

She said she gave the baby to a well-off British couple who were visiting their only daughter in Jackson. She said that because they realized that they would only get to see their own grandchildren no more than ten times in their life, they would treat her baby like a prince. Sophie said that she gave her baby a life she would never be able to provide and she said she is forever less happy because of that, but she knows that she did the right thing. But Sophie is doing okay. She has a good job and here's the good part.

Sophie knows a lot of people because she works in a diner so she got me a job in the hardware store on the same street. I am now living with Sophie and paying half the rent. Here's the next good part. When I told Sophie that you would probably be leaving when you turn sixteen, she said that she knows of another job. Sophie said that there is an opening in the diner she works at and she would put a good word in for you. I think you should come to Jackson and apply for this job. You can stay with us until you get a pay and can move into a boarding house. There is a boarding house just down the road from the diner. Our address is 12 Main Street, Jackson. If we are not there when you get to town, come to Jackson's Diner or Sam's Hardware Store, which is just across the street.

I have some very bad news to tell you. I have left it until last because I first wanted to tell you that you have a good place to come to when you leave. Here is the bad news. Do not go looking for Dolly. After I ran into Sophie, the first thing I asked her was if she knew where they sent Dolly. Sophie said they send all the kids that are under school-age to an orphanage in Toronto. She said that the school keeps track of when they are old enough to come because the church gets more money for every kid they have in there. Sophie said that when Mistress told her to write away to the Toronto Orphanage to send for Dolly, all that Sophie got back was a letter saying the child had succumbed to dysentery. Sophie said it was ironic. I say it's cow shit and they probably just let that kid die, then got rid of her out back like they did Ojekaada.

And don't come out expecting to see our brother Porter either. He doesn't live around here anymore. At first he was on a real bad path of fighting and drinking. He had an anger in him. But then he met a woman from Florida and they took up together. She got him a job as a high steel worker in Florida and I heard they got married. So, you and me are the only ones of Ma's that are still around here and I hope that when you pack up your bag to leave, you don't do anything else, except just come to Jackson.

Yours truly,
Elizabeth

Mary tucked her letter out of sight under her rolled-up baggage and sat on the edge of her bed to wait. When she heard the creak of the door, Mistress came down the aisle and stopped at the foot of her bed. She thrust a piece of paper at Mary and then a pen.

"Sign these please. They are your release papers. Since you're sixteen on this date, you can sign yourself out," she said as if it was she who was granting the right.

Mary hurriedly scratched her signature on the empty line at the bottom of the page and then handed it back.

"And what is that you have done to your bed?"

Mary's eyes darted out of nervous habit to the roll sitting on her mattress.

"Since I did not have a box, I rolled my belongings up in my linen. I can carry it that way."

Mistress started to hit the palm of her hand with her pointer stick and cocked her head as if spying prey. She began to move toward Mary, taking deliberate steps, savouring each one until she was past and standing on the other side of Mary in front of the bundle. She patted the top of it and then grasping it, she yanked it until it unrolled and spilled its contents out upon the mattress. She snapped the linens back as if a whip and flung them over her head and behind her. They landed on the neighbour girl's bed in a heap.

"First of all, none of these are your belongings, and secondly, neither are these sheets. You may, out of the goodwill of this establishment, keep the clothes on your back and the shoes on your feet."

Mary stammered, "I guess I just thought that I would need something to sleep in when I get where I am going."

She interrupted. "So you thought you were entitled to anything you wanted?"

"No, it's just that—"

"Don't interrupt!" she screeched, "Do you think you are entitled to these things?"

Mary shook her head and cast her eyes toward the door. "That's fine. I would just like to leave."

"And what is this?" the Mistress dangled the letter by its corner.

Mary pretended with all her might that she didn't care, like a field mouse that should not twitch while an owl is perched above.

Mistress dangled it closer, and closer, then right in front of Mary's nose. That's when Mary swiped it out of her fingertips.

"You want this too?" Mary held it up between the two of them, "Will you never be satisfied until you have taken everything from me?" Mary crumpled it up in a ball and threw it in the corner. They both watched it until it came to a standstill.

Mistress raised her stick over her head but Mary just stood there, refusing to break eye contact.

"You have cut my hair, silenced my mother's language, stolen my relatives from me, and made me feel ugly, unlovable, and less than a person who is white. I don't know the real day I was born, and I don't have anybody to tell me. Maybe you, and all your people who tell you what to do, did kill the Indian in me, but I can tell you this, you did not kill me. The most important thing is, I am alive and I am leaving here, and you can't do a single thing about it anymore."

Mary's shoes made a soft noise as she walked the polished halls one last time. All the other children were in the eating hall. She would not be going down to breakfast today. She heard Mistress come out in the hall behind her, pause, and then go the other way. Mary was alone and free to leave. Once she reached the great doors that would open up to the front steps, she stopped to grab her coat off her hook. She ripped the piece of cardboard paper with number seventy-seven on it off the wall, tore it up and tossed it over her shoulder. She put her coat on and placed her hands upon the brass handles of the great doors. It was warm from the sun shining outside. She opened them wide and let the crisp sunny first day of spring bathe her with its light. She stepped outside.

Outside, on the great veranda, there was a figure huddled, a brightly coloured woven blanket wrapped around her, at the top of the steps. The small girl hugged her own knees while she watched her brother being yanked, kicking and screaming, from the car parked at the base of the Institute's steps. His long black hair flew wildly as he spit at them and yelled in a language foreign to Mary.

She passed the girl and their eyes met.

No belongings, no burdens, Mary felt light as she kept walking. When she reached the end of the long straight driveway, she was tempted to hazard a look backward.

And Sarah turned to salt as soon as she looked backward.

Mary stood, undecided for some time.

There is no word for yesterday, in the language my Kokum taught me. It is not a word of power.

She decided to do it anyway.

Mary turned and stood still and took it all in for the last time. She could feel the wind pushing at her back as it passed her, scurrying down the driveway taking with it some dry leaves from last winter, up the steps of the Mohawk Institute, and then frolic for a while in the long hair of the girl sitting there. Mary estimated that she was about the same age when she was brought to this place.

The young girl looked up, and lifting her hand slowly, she bade goodbye to Mary.

TOM DUNSBY

MARY HAD TO make sure that she was out of the house by at least 10:00 a.m. She pressed a couple more shirts and left the rest in a pile just to stay on schedule. She would stay up late that night to finish the boarders' shirts. She placed the fifth one neatly on the hanger, grabbed her purse, and dashed for the door. When she reached the door, she opened it to let some light shine on the entrance mirror and stopped to apply her cherry lipstick. A few pats on her cheeks from her compact, and she was good for the rest of the afternoon.

She walked briskly past the diner, waved to them inside, and nodded to Stan and Morris out front because that's what they liked. They hushed when she walked by, so she knew they must be gabbing about the Mayor's heart attack. They all knew where she was going. Since she never called in sick, this would be the first lunch hour she hadn't worked in, well, since she had got her job back after Sonny was born.

After a quick glance in the window of Pauline's Curtain Shoppe she patted her hat, to be sure it was in place. The lunch hour was the busiest, but they didn't mind letting her off just this once. Everybody had to do their part to help the Mayor. He had been a good mayor. Even though it was June, Mary shivered at the thought of Mayor Dunsby not being Mayor Dunsby anymore. What would he do all day? She touched her hair at the back to make sure it was still in place and thought about how unnatural it might be to call him "Tom" now. It was he who had insisted. Since he wasn't going to be Mayor, then her continuing to call him "Mayor" would be ridiculous, and "Mr. Dunsby" seemed equally so. They had settled on "Tom."

Mary thrust her hands to her sides and bustled her pace some more. Oh well, she thought, calling him by his first name befitted the seasoned friendship they now shared. She boosted her stride to a near jog. It was almost 10:15 a.m., and the hospital attendants would be bringing him at noon. She wanted to make sure he had a hot tea and lunch waiting for him when he got there. He had always been there for her, so she would damn well make sure she was there for him.

Mary had just let herself back in to the kitchen through the screened door when she heard them struggling at the front door. She checked the time, only two hours since she had arrived, and she still had more cleaning to do. She washed the smell of her cigarette from her hands, popped a mint in her mouth, and checked the simmering pot on the stove before scurrying up front to help hold the door.

Even though she had seen him several times in his hospital bed, there wasn't anything she could have done to prepare herself for the sight of his ragged and worn Teddy-bear body rising, with the assistance of two male attendants, out of the wheelchair. Even though he had lost weight in the hospital, he had a sallow, puffy look to his skin and features. He shuffled across the floor, flanked by his male nurses, and plunked his spent body into his favourite easy chair. Mary had a funny feeling that's where he meant to stay.

She gave herself a shake. Somehow, somewhere, she must have gotten the idea that although people were expected to be sick while they were in the hospital, they were supposed to look better by the time they got home. There was dullness in his eyes as if Spirit had already started to vacate. She shrugged her nagging fears off.

"Would you like some tea?" she asked the attendants.

"No thank you, ma'am," one of them stepped forward with pen and paper in hand. "If you will just sign here, Mrs. Dunsby, we will soon be on our way."

One of the attendants mouthed the pronunciation of Mary's signature as he read it. He tore off a carbon copy and handed it back to Mary.

"If there is not anything else, then we will bid you adieu, as I am sure you are anxious to have your privacy, Madame Fisher," he said in his French accent.

Out-of-towners, Mary thought to herself, let them think what they want.

Mary closed the door behind them, but not yet ready to face her friend, she turned her attention to something else. Though slumped in the chair, his eyes were alert and followed her around the room as she adjusted the curtains, straightened a few knick knacks, and then took a candy dish in the kitchen to be topped up.

When she returned, she saw he was exactly as she had left him—a man whose body drooped as if from an unseen burden that was becoming too much to carry, yet whose mind remained watchful. She pandered to one last plausible second spent in the doorway, then stepped forward with her sunshine face on, balancing a tray laden with lunch.

"Chicken Stew and Dumplings," she paused as she stumbled mentally over her ordinary inclination to call him Mayor, or Mr. Dunsby, and then finished her sentence with, "your favourite, my friend."

"Mmmmmm," he sank deeper into his thick leather easy chair, "smells heavenly."

Mary set the tray on the coffee table in front of him. She scouted around for a comfortable place to sit and chose the rocking chair, draped with a hand-knitted throw, in the far corner of the room. She walked over and tried it out. Mary had been in Mayor Dunsby's house hundreds and hundreds of times but had never sat down in the living room. Whirlwind in and whirlwind out, every Sunday, then get back to her other work.

Tom Dunsby had always imagined that Mary would have chosen precisely that rocking chair as her favourite if she had ever married him. Now, the medication made her look so blurry sitting all the way over there at the other side of the room. "Please, bring that chair closer."

Mary, with her hands folded in her lap, and ankles glued together, smiled, but the chair's tell-tale little squeak when it rocked let some of her uneasiness leak out.

"Won't you be joining me for lunch?" he asked, summoning the strength to sit up.

He fumbled for his fork and dropped it. He used the spindly French provincial coffee table to support his body as he bent forward and reached for it on the floor. His weight caused the table to scoot forward and abandon him. Like a great oak, chopped in the middle, he began to collapse forward. One last-ditch effort to seize the fickle table only sent it farther, causing everything on top to take flight and land in a scattered clatter all around him. For an aching moment he lay there, a once powerful and dignified man felled by life's span.

It was also the moment the bubble of congeniality that Mary had been diligently preserving burst. Utter compassion swelled forth from her heart.

She tarried no longer in her chair, safe on the other side of the room. She leapt to the assistance of her most faithful friend.

She removed the upturned plate from his back and picked the broken and gooey pieces of pecan pie from his suit jacket. She slipped her arm in the small space that he was trying to create between himself and the floor. She pulled on his arm but he lost power in his shoulder joint. Mary thrust her arm deeper underneath him until her hand touched his chest, and then she took hold of his other shoulder and began to tug upward. It was not enough. He groaned as he tried to push himself up with his own hands. Mary's heart was breaking for him. How could a puny thing like her be of any help?

She's a strong girl, that Mary.

She could hear her mother's voice from somewhere within. This time, she grounded her knee and foot as if they had roots that plumbed deep into the floor, drew in all the breath that she could hold, centred it in her belly, and waited to catch his effort at its zenith. Just before the point at which she sensed he might next let himself drop again, she started to haul. Tom Dunsby married his own effort with hers and in a fluid instant he was on his feet. Mary allowed him one more moment of dignity before gently guiding him back safely into his favourite chair. Tom sighed and let himself be cared for.

After she helped him take his jacket off and cleaned up the mess, she dragged the rocking chair up to a place, angular to his side in front of the coffee table. That would be her place from now on.

"My friend," she began before they started to eat, "I think we must talk about getting you a nurse or attendant."

"I don't want anybody else in here."

She knew he would say that.

"You're very weak."

She handed him his tea. The jangle of the saucer and teacup as he held it proved her point.

He put the saucer on the table and held only the hot cup within his hands and said, "I care not."

"You don't care if something happens to you?" she challenged.

He shook his head, his face washing over with Mayor Dunsby cynicism.

"I could not care less."

They sipped their tea and ate their meal in silence. Occasionally Mary would rise to take his plate from him or hand him his next course. He thanked her, with eyes of deep gratitude for each and every gesture. When she handed him his second cup of tea, this time in a thick mug without the saucer, they both leaned back in their chairs.

Tom closed his eyes for a moment, and Mary rocked, comfortable like old friends should be. Nothing was said for quite some time, until Mary got an idea. "Well," she declared, "I think I have a plan."

Tom let his eyes flutter open.

"I will decrease my hours at the diner to only the lunch hours, and Sonny will bring your supper to you every night. After I've cleaned up from the boarders, I'll come and tidy up here. Sundays, we can keep the same. It's a good plan for a couple of weeks, don't you think?"

Tom Dunsby shut his eyes again.

Mary waited.

After several minutes on the grandfather clock in the hall had ticked by, he said, "I would consider myself very fortunate to pay for such excellent service."

"Oh no, no, I mean it as a friend."

But he interrupted before she could continue, drew himself up into a stately posture, and said to her in a deeply authoritative voice, "I am only offering you a job. In my station in life, I must always be mindful and cannot allow the seeds of idle gossip to germinate."

Mary blinked in dismay.

He saw her reaction and set his hand upon her arm and he said to her softly, "Practically speaking, this is as much for your good as it is for mine. I know you are my very best friend, but let the record show that you are an extremely hard-working woman who deserves remuneration for her service. And not only that, it is selfish thinking on my part that motivates me. I do not want a stranger in here. I am a very private man. You know this. I ask you, how long could I have this premium care-taking if you were to sacrifice your income?"

Mary deferred to his good old Mayor Tom Dunsby logic. "Okay," she said, and then rose to begin cleaning.

"Say?" he asked.

"Yes?" she gathered the tray up.

"Did you see the new addition to the household?"

Mary glanced at the wooden box occupying more than its fair share of space directly in front of the fireplace. "Yep, it juts out like a sore finger," Mary said flatly.

"It will be a Godsend on long winter evenings."

"A Godsend, you say?" Mary held her hand out for his empty cup. "The boarders hounded me until I got one," she gestured to the console positioned against the wall to face him. "I bought it off of one of the customers who got themselves a smaller one."

"Those new ones don't sound as good."

"I have to agree on that. But there aren't any of them that sound as good as someone pulling out a real live fiddle!"

Tom shrugged, "Now they are talking about a box that will show electric pictures, something like going to a play, but not having to leave your house."

"Oh that should be an improvement," she said as she cocked her head and imagined it in the place where the radio stood. "That will be one of the last things I plug in at Mary's Place. I could just see how it would serve to stop even more conversations. You mark my word, it might keep you from feeling lonely, but it won't keep you from being alone."

"You never were much for keeping your opinion to yourself," Tom smiled to himself, "Would you mind turning it on for me? One of my favourite programs will be starting soon."

"I'll turn it on for you but I'm not going to sit here and listen to it with you," she puffed up and continued, "and I can tell you, my friend, I can just see you sitting in front of that thing day and night until you go rotten. You better call some friends for a good old-fashioned visit."

"Okay."

Mary turned the dial and a man's beguiling voice filled the room.

"That's it. It's already tuned to the right station."

Mary turned on her heel and headed for the kitchen. She called out to him a couple of times while she cleaned, and he answered every time, but when she went back into the living room intending to spend some time with him before she left, she found he had slid off into slumber. She flicked the lights out, drew the curtains shut, and left him there with the soft glow of the radio lighting his face.

"Sleep well, my friend," she whispered.

LETTERS FROM THE FRONT

BY THE TIME Mary got back home, she was already late to start supper for the boarders. It was lucky that she had prepared almost everything in the morning. Also, she had a new boarder interview to do before the other men got home. As she rushed around the kitchen, she noticed a package on the counter. The multitude of coloured stamps that stained the now tattered and misshapen package divulged its weary journey. It was from Gmiwan, finally, after over nine months!

Mary held the package in her hand while she lit a cigarette. She poured herself a cup of tea from the metal pot that stayed on the stove all day for the boarders. She opened the package and took out a black soft-cover book. Its frayed and defiled state laid bare a treacherous passage. She turned the book over and over in her hands. She took a sip, a puff, and opened the book to the first page. It was some kind of journal.

> By this, I grasp for the wild, untamed energy that is the quantity of the universe, suck it in, and hold it as a frenzied and whirling mass within me. By this, I persevere and toil until I have mastered the ability to release it in an undeviating burst toward my creation. And by this, I become —

Mary closed the book and held it shut between her hands, feeling its thickness near her thumping heart, knowing that the rest of the pages would make it bleed. She drew up her courage and re-opened the book to its last page.

In the darksome moments
before the night gives way to light,
the blackness will begin to pale to silver grey reflections.
This is
before the golden dawn.
This is when
my fever breaks, my insight comes,
and I am not alone.
My friend is with me.
I could not see him and so I could not feel him but my friend was there,
all night.
Holding my hand and whispering to me.
It was only when I had spent my wailing and my fevered ego
that my insight came.
This is when
I came to know what it is that I have been hiding.
There, `neath the waning moon,
my burnt out fear lay prone for me to gaze upon.
Sorry and pathetic, it lays there lifeless,
the thing I uttered in despair,

   I am afraid of what I want
   and that I will not get it.
   Better to not want it,
   better to want what you end up getting,
   even if each time grows more fiery.

Therein, somehow, has been my absurd power.
And the thing he whispered back,

   I can see what I want
   and I can have what I want
   and I can want what I have.

My friend wants for me to be happy.
So in the silver between greying night and the golden dawn
My insight comes.
And in the Golden Dawn
I see my friend in you.

                              Gmiwan

She frantically fanned through until a sketch caught her eye. It was simply entitled "Me and Hoagie." Strangely enough he depicted himself and another soldier, cavernous of eye, hunched over, and rake thin, eating out of a garbage can while the skyline behind them burst with fire and dead bodies. Mary vowed to preserve herself and never open the book again. It didn't matter, though, because later the letters would come anyway.

Someone pounding on the kitchen door, right beside where she sat with Gmiwan's book pressed into her lap, slashed through her panic and she remembered that she had an interview with a boarder applicant. She shoved the book in the kitchen drawer along with her cigarette case, and rose to answer it.

Outside, framed by the pale light of an anxious full moon hanging in a still light sky, was a man, smiling and devilish in good looks. "Mrs. Fisher?"

"Why yes, and you are Mr. Musovich?"

He offered his hand to Mary, "Please, you must call me Tony."

Mary allowed him to take her hand and lingered in his dancing eyes.

"Please call me Mary," she drew her hand away. "Everybody does." She gestured for him to seat himself at the kitchen table while she busied herself with tea biscuits.

Sitting across from him, she began the interview while he slathered the top half of his tea biscuit with butter and then strawberry jam. He popped the whole thing in his mouth and rubbed his belly while he chewed.

"Mmmmmm, is that homemade?"

"Of course, everything here is."

"I tell you, that just melts in your mouth." He closed his eyes dreamily and declared, "Just savour the flavour."

"It's good to see a man enjoy his food." Mary offered him more from the serving dish. "Ever been married?"

"Yes, ma'am, but she divorced me because I travelled around too much. But that was a long time ago. I've been travelling around with the same company for about ten years now, selling, installing, and fixing refrigerators. I've saved a little money now and I'm looking to start my own business in refrigeration, here in Jackson as a matter of fact."

"Oh yes?"

"Yes, I heard you only take working men here and I assure you that is exactly what I am."

"Did you also hear that I only take men here and I don't allow the boarders to have their girlfriends over? It keeps things clean and simple."

"I heard you run a very tight ship here and that is exactly what I'm looking for—some place serious so I can concentrate on my new business."

"Foreigners are hard workers."

"My mother was Italian and my father is Ukrainian, both hard workers."

"Ohhh," having had her question answered, Mary said aloud, before going on, "I don't think I've ever met any Ukrainians."

"They are hard-working, boring people. It's the Italians that are exciting."

"Yes, that's true, Italians are known for their passion."

That's when he winked at her. Mary rose and took the kettle with her to put back on the stove. She was suddenly so tired. With her back still to him she said, "So when would you want to move in?"

"Tomorrow would make tonight my last night at the motel down the road."

She turned back to face him and thought she caught an elusive glimpse of Grandmother Moon's full face through the window. She looked back and it was gone again. She pulled the curtains shut and sat down again because she was so tired.

"I suppose tomorrow will be fine."

My Dear Mary:

In the light of the jewel that changes from blue to cool white
my saviour shape shifts to nemesis
then
crystallizes to become my Self.
In the darkest hours of a midnight's mare
the fire my lover built for my chilled flesh was stoked to surround me.
The warriors circled
I rose up 'til I was the ashes,
fodder for growth.
Such extraordinary pain.
The wind blew through the sprawling oak
blowing as bargained the seeds far and near.
It grew and it grew, while it blew and it blew, til one day it cracked in two.
And
in its place a seedling grew
and it knew
to bend like the wind.
Such extraordinary pain.

                              Gmiwan

COVERED IN SNOW, Jackson had always been Christmas card charming, and somehow tonight, on New Year's Eve, even more so. The town stood quietly defiant of the ripples of pall cast far across the sea from a war that took so many, and would not end. Mary pulled the curtains to shut the hush of falling snow and creeping dusk out, and then turned back to making tea. She heard him cough as he made his way down the hall.

Tom appeared in the doorway of the kitchen with one hand behind his back and the other on the wall preventing his frail form from yielding to a weariness that had simply grown larger than his will to move forward. From the first time she had met him, Mary had realized that her friend had always walked around with a heavy demeanour, wearing it like an overcoat. He seemed different tonight though. Tonight he called up a silly grin for her.

"What do you have behind your back?" she said playfully.

"Guess!" he said in a cheerful voice that belied his weakness.

"Beats me," she shrugged.

He let go of the wall and thrust out from behind his back a bottle of champagne, held it up throttled by the neck with both his hands, and stumbled a bit as he did so.

"You are going to fall again," she admonished, but couldn't hide her amusement.

He put his one hand back on the heavy oak trim and neither Mary nor he missed that it faltered.

"It seems, Madam, that you may be doomed to always be scraping me off the floor."

"Back to bed!" she ordered.

"If you will take this bottle off my hands and pour us a couple of glasses, I should be just fine."

"It's not even midnight yet."

"Look who's talking? Isn't she the same one who is always telling me that I'm too damn proper?"

"Yes. But really, my friend, I do not think that you are in any condition to be drinking."

He resorted to the tone of voice he reserved for getting her to pay attention to what he was about to say. "I don't feel like waiting for midnight. Don't look at me like I'm some sort of queer bird! Aren't you always saying I'm artless and too structured?"

"I never say that!"

She stuck her hands on her hip. He held his ground and smiled.

"Well, admittedly you wouldn't exactly say it like that. However, you do say it to me in a hundred other ways."

She looked away, "I don't know what you mean."

"Will you pour us champagne instead of tea?"

"Well, if he wants champagne on New Year's Eve, he can have champagne on New Year's Eve," she mocked as if muttering to herself and turned to attend to the task of taking the tea off the tray she had been preparing.

"Go get back in bed and I will bring us a New Year's Eve party tray." She looked over at him. He was standing there still looking at her. "Only on condition that you get back in bed." She took a stern look and held it until he turned and shuffled back down the hall. "I can't be scraping you off the floor every time I turn around," she called after him.

She opened the refrigerator and scrounged around inside. "If we're going to have champagne, then we might as well have the kind of stuff that goes with it," she continued to mutter as she worked. She knew he could hear her. She found Danish blue cheese, sweet gherkin pickles, and some of her red plum preserve. She went over to Mrs. Dunsby's china cabinet and chose a crystal dish partitioned in three, then set the treats, complete with demure silver forks, on the tray in place of the pound cake. She found a tin of soda crackers and fanned them out on a blue glass dish. In the middle, she placed its matching bowl, peeled a tangerine, and filled it with the fragrant segments. Back in the china cabinet she selected two fluted glasses from an array of Bohemian crystal and set them either side of the champagne. Lastly Mary removed two white linen napkins from the drawer.

She paused. Under the linens, which must have been last pressed and starched by Mrs. Dunsby herself, as there most surely would not have been any occasion to have used them since her passing, was nestled a small black leather bound Bible. She opened the tattered cover and read the handwritten inscription on the first yellowed and tissue-thin Oxford India Paper-made page, "to Lillian Dunsby, from whose gentle hand everywhere the seeds of forgiveness and atonement are sewn." The signature was illegible, Father somebody it read. On the second page it was stamped, "The Holy Bible, containing the Old and New Testaments, translated out of the original tongues and with the former Translations diligently compared and revised, by His Majesty's special command, and appointed to be read in Churches."

Everything comes back around in a circle—everything, Mary.

Mary placed the book back in the drawer, shook her head, smiled to herself, and then she draped the linens over her arm before picking up the tray.

She found him back in bed. Although he was sitting up, his head was cocked to one side and his mouth wide open. He woke as soon as she entered.

"Mary," he started.

"Happy New Year!" Mary pushed past her worry to get into the spirit of things.

He brightened with a smile.

Mary set the tray down on his bedside table, pulled a chair closer, and grasped the champagne bottle with a little fanfare for effect. She walked over to his bedroom window and threw open the curtains. Grandmother Moon smiled from above. Mary lingered at the window with the bottle still in hand, peering at the night outside.

"Open the window a crack, for some air, would you please?"

Mary pulled the window up, letting the white, cool night air disperse some of the stale air inside. It was ominously peaceful as the snow had stopped falling and Jackson waited for midnight. She wondered if it was midnight where Gmiwan was.

"Mary?"

Mary twirled around, hair flying, as she pulled the cork on the spot with a bang, champagne bubbles spilling out over her hand into a puddle on the hardwood floor. Tom Dunsby was delighted by the resonance of her belly laugh as she dashed for the napkin she had just placed on his bedside. She grabbed it up and threw it on the floor.

"Let it soak," she said as she poured an equal amount of the sparkling liquid into each glass. "It's New Years Eve."

It didn't really matter, but still, he could tell she was trying too hard. Everybody had to try hard during these times. She handed him his glass, and their eyes met in the place where the glasses sang in the air.

Mary drank heartily from her delicate glass and then unceremoniously plunked herself in a nearby armchair. After a few more abundant sips she had her feet crossed and up on the bed.

Tom set his three-quarters-finished glass down on his bedside table and sagged into himself. Mary kept her eye on him, poured herself another glass, and set the bottle down on the floor beside her. He sighed deeply. They sat in silence and stared out the window at the noiseless snow that had begun to fall again. Grandmother Moon had disappeared somewhere.

"My mother visited me today."

Mary flinched, just barely. She drew herself in somewhat and turned to smile at him. He must be drunk, she thought. His mother had passed long ago.

"Yes, I was very pleased to see her."

He was smiling; she resolved to do nothing to steal this moment from him.

"I thought she would be very upset to see me so thin and wasted but she showed no sign of such. We drank tea and talked about the house. You know, she doesn't miss it at all. She said she is very happy and that I have nothing to worry about."

He waited for Mary to respond. Mary stayed very still. Then, in the place where only the throaty tick of the grandfather clock down the hall dwelled, a thought he was having seemed to blur the wistful smile from his face into that of dismay. Mary sat coiled for his rescue.

His brow crinkled as he spoke. "There was, however, one unpleasant aspect to the visit. We discussed the matter of my father." Mary sipped from her glass in the dangling emptiness he left.

"She said we must, because it was time to put it all to rest. You see, I always hated my father. He was a cruel man. We rarely spoke of him after he died. Did you know I hated him? Could you ever know, how heinous it is for a young boy to rise from his bed, wipe the sleep from his eyes, and in the blinding light of the room where he took his meals, witness his mother having her teeth shattered from her face? Would you be able to lie still in bed where he slammed your body so he could return to the evil deeds reigned upon your mother? Can you imagine the amount of effort it took to suppress the legacy of anger he left me with? And the guilt?"

Mary could tell he was lingering in the hellish place he spoke of, as the usual etched sternness of his face became fully set into the anger it must have been carved from. Then, in the moment that followed, sadness eclipsed. He lifted both his hands and, turning his palms upward, he looked down at them as if they held something glowing and precious. He raised them up and drew them into his chest, holding them there, where his fledgling heart struggled for every beat.

"She showed me his pain and his regret and his suffering. I felt it, and it made my heart beat stronger, strong enough to last a bit longer, my sweet Mary."

The teardrop that tarried on Mary's cheek opposed the shiver that threatened her flesh.

"It does me no good to hold anger. It does him no good. It does her no good for me to be angry. It is time for forgiveness."

He held his hand out to her, blue and cold. She hesitated.

"Come to me this one time, and sit by my side. I am going to leave you soon." His lids fluttered, and his breath stopped, as his eyes rolled back and showed only their whites. Mary shut her own eyes and let a sob escape.

Mary heard in her head, *Go to him.*

She opened her eyes and rose to let him draw her by the hand to his side. She set her glass on the bedside table, spent one more moment, and then pulled her feet up off the floor to tuck herself against him.

"I love you, Mary."

She nodded as tears streamed down her face and her heart threatened to burst from her chest. His body started to sink within itself, and Mary knew he was starting on his three-day road. A calm seized her. She reached over to gather him to her. She let his cheek fall upon her chest, and it soothed her own frenzied heart. There he rested, taking life's final breath in, holding it as long as he could, as if it was the sweetest taste ever, and then he allowed his eyes to close in synchronicity with breath and spirit exiting his body.

The resonant chime of the grandfather clock down the hall gave twelve notes to announce the arrival of the brand new year, her friend's death, and her utter aloneness once again.

At the funeral Mary was allowed to stand with the Mayor's sisters, whom he had rarely mentioned. Mary had met them once or twice when his mother was still living but never again after that. She felt animosity radiating from the women, and when it finally became too much, Mary moved away from them and stood off by herself. Later, Mary thought, she would ride with Marlene and Fred over to the diner to help with the reception. That is where her friends were. It had been three days since the clock had struck her friend's death, and three days since something had clutched in her stomach, seized what shred of peace she had been managing to feign, and left her empty. Mary would never trust New Year's Eve again.

It was a brilliantly sunny day for a funeral, crisp and tranquil under a fresh layer of snow. Mary let the priest's voice fade as she stared into the delicately white mantled branches of the treetops. She imagined if she screamed she could scatter the serene covering into millions and millions of sparkling fragments throughout the air.

Up in the branches a disturbance circled and swooped, disquieting the fragile layers into falling jewels. One of the children called out, "Look up there, Mama!"

Mary tried to focus on the winged one soaring with grace and mastery amongst the treetops above. When it lighted upon one of the lowest branches in a nearby pine tree, and the shimmering cloud around it had completely fallen away, she saw that it was a snowy white owl.

Someone else marvelled quietly, "When do you ever see an owl during the day!"

Mary smiled within herself, for just a moment she caught the fleeting sensation of peace, as if it were the glint of sunshine on the tail of a silver trout she might see swimming in a brook, but then it was gone.

The Winged Ones are the messengers from the Spirit World.

"Goodnight my friend," she whispered.

Dear Mary:

In the ocean of where I find I must dwell
there are grains of sand borne by the water
these are the ones
in the place that I matter.
My mother, my father, my sister, my brother
my friends and my children
myself
and my lover.
I am a rock
solid and dull
the ocean—the universe
the sand—my downfall.
Touching me, resting on me
lodging 'neath my soft belly
caressing and battering
'til there's nothing left of me.
The reasons I laughed
The reasons I cried
The reasons I lived
The reasons I died
Then I'm only a stone
and time is my bane
pushing me steadfastly
toward handsome to plain.
And the child walks along the beach
and the child holds me in his hand
I look at myself
and still I'm not sand.v

Gmiwan

Mary placed the letter on the pile with some other correspondence that was yet to be opened and poured herself another generous glass of wine. She had never had red wine before. This was homemade Italian-Ukrainian wine, which Tony said was made from some kind of special grapes or whatever. She lit a cigarette. It was the end of her day anyway, late by most people's standards but early by her own. All her days were shorter, although they felt longer now that Mayor Dunsby was gone. If the truth be told, she felt lost. Elizabeth was forever busy helping Harry with the business, a new kind of addiction. And Sonny went to bed early so he could be up early for school.

Just then, the kitchen door swung open and the wind rushed in behind Tony, blowing the most recent correspondence from Gmiwan, as well as the other unopened letters, off the countertop. They drifted around in the air and fell to the floor like leaves. Whether he noticed or not, he didn't make any effort to pick them up. Mary didn't bother either.

"Say! How ya doin'?" he sang out in that overgrown boy way he spoke to everyone. He had a way of making whomever he was talking to feel like they were the most important person in the room.

"No date tonight?"

"There's no good women left."

His eyes sparkled when he spotted the open wine bottle.

"I see you have finally decided to partake of my father's milk."

Mary, already somewhat uncloaked by a few sips of wine, eyed him deeply for a long moment. He stood still for it. She set her glass down on the counter, threw her hands in the air, and said, "Would you like to join me?"

Tony hastened to pour her more before filling his own. Mary silently studied him.

He made a great gesture of handing her a glass, raising his own between them. "A toast?"

She put the glass on the counter to light her cigarette. The smoke twirled and eddied between them.

"It is cute to see you smoke," he exclaimed in his strange accent. "May I also indulge, *Madame*?"

"Smoke your head off, sir." She wondered why an Italian-Ukrainian would use a French accent. She looked beyond him. The fire crackled and beckoned from the open door. All the other men had retired to their rooms, and he was in the way of where she had been headed.

Keen like a fox, he noted. "Would you like to take our drinks to the fire?"

"Yes, that is where I was headed but first I need to go out and get some more wood," she said as she set her glass on the counter and turned toward the back door.

He reached and placed his hand on her shoulder. The heat from his palm stopped her. "Please allow me to give you a well-deserved rest."

He waited. She stood erect, allowing his stinging touch to tarry.

His deep voice came from behind her, "Please Madame, it is a man's job to get wood."

She let him turn her around and she accepted the half-filled glass back that he handed her.

"Take your well-deserved cigarette, your glass of wine, and enjoy the end of your work day by the fire. Let somebody else do the work for a change."

Mary gave in. She moved past him, letting the fire draw her, and fell into the deep folds of the chesterfield. Staring into the fire, she drank of the seductive juice she held within her fingertips. Every time she raised it to her lips, it slid down her throat like comfort, each sip deepening and expanding the solace the flames gave.

He arrived back with an armful of wood and stopped short when he noted her empty wine glass set upon the mosaic table. He turned, went back to the kitchen, and set the wood carefully down.

He left the wood where it sat a moment longer and brought two fresh glasses. He set them on the hearth, and the fire seemed to be captured and contained within each. He went back to the kitchen, and returned with the wood in his arms and an uncorked bottle of wine in his hand.

Mary, through eyes lethargic from the mellowing potion, watched as he poured more of it into each of the glasses on the hearth. He thrust the largest log upon the mostly spent others, deep within the flames, and they crumbled beneath his intention. In response, the crimson liquid warming by the fire ebbed and swirled within the glasses, leaving syrupy and glistening residue upon its crystal perimeter. Tony set the bottle to warm by the fire, took the ready glasses in hand, and sat beside her.

"Madame?" he handed one to her.

Mary accepted the glass and moved to the end of the couch farther away from him and closer to the fire. She curled into a ball and sipped the ambrosia.

"Why do you have a Ukrainian name, an Italian face, and a French accent?"

He laughed aloud. He relished the bait.

"Did I never tell you I grew up in France?"

Mary shook her head, tipped her glass, teased her palate by only letting her tongue dart into it, and bring back tiny drops to savour.

He shivered without reserve and continued, his voice toned down to a gravelly whisper.

"My father was employed as a bricklayer by a French company, and my mother worked as a seamstress for a theatre. I lived there for fourteen years. My parents chose French as the language spoken in our home, and I went to French schools."

"Very romantic."

Mary could not believe her own tongue.

"And what of you?"

She noted the change in address from *Madame* and squeezed farther into the accommodating arm of the chesterfield. She cocked her head to one side.

"I mean where did you grow up?"

Mary followed the question far past the ceiling overhead and let her head rest on the back of the chesterfield.

"Madame," he said penetratingly.

She tore herself away and back into the room.

"Where did you go?" he asked.

She gave him a soft smile.

"It is too painful for you to talk about?"

Smiling still, she answered softly, "I was raised in an orphanage."

"*Ah, c'est malchance.* Your parents passed away?"

"My mother died in childbirth when I was nine. The authorities took us away from our father. He eventually remarried and started a second family. I remember that my father was a man who respected his wife's word in all matters of the home. He told my sister that he could not live without a woman. His second wife was known to be a wilful and stingy woman. She was known to have the belief that my father should not have any need of two families."

Mary stopped to light a cigarette.

"She sent me a letter two years ago to inform me that my father had died. She said he fell off a ladder."

"That is it? You did not find out any more? Did you go to where he was buried?"

"No, my sister did."

Tony drained his glass, stood up, and made his way to the fireplace. He stoked the fire, and returned to her side with the bottle that had been set on the hearth. He satiated his empty glass. Mary kept hers unseen and cocooned between her heart and her drawn-up legs. He set the bottle down on the coffee table right on top of Grandmother Moon.

"Your husband is a talented artist."

Mary looked away.

"But it does not pay the bills, eh?"

Mary locked her eyes with his and judged him genuine.

"No, it doesn't pay the bills," she said softly

"It's hard to do everything alone," he put his hand around the neck of the bottle, "and you are a hard worker, Mary Fisher."

She noted that the bottle left a red ring around Grandmother Moon and she produced her glass for him to see.

"I am empty."

He filled her glass with the last of the wine. She brought it to her lips and held it poised at the place where its redness had stained them into a swollen pout. Her dark, feathered eyes closed as she took in the aroma.

With the acuity of all he had honed in his travels, he fluidly moved into the crack he knew was there. He moved closer and took her hand in his.

Tears welled freely forth and down Mary's flushed cheeks as she let her hand sit in the strangely soothing abrasiveness of his. She quaffed back the last of her wine.

"All that I ever receive from Gmiwan is single-page letters. Well, they aren't even really letters. They are poems or pictures like notes written by some miserable castaway and vomited up from hell's depths. He doesn't even sign or date most of them," she sobbed.

Tony gathered her up and let her body rail within the confines of his arms. He closed his rugged working man hands around her wrists and bringing them down to his chest, he held her firmly against him. He smelled like hickory smoke. Mary struggled for a moment longer and then let herself fall into his harbour.

He allowed her to release the most volatile layer of her anguish into his chest before he reached for her. Letting his hand drop and move along the curve of her spine until it rested in the small place at the base, he applied pressure. Like a cat, she leaned herself into it until her neck rested in the nape of his. He nuzzled into the wetness of her tears. With his other hand, he made a shelf of his crooked finger and tilted her chin to him. Mastering the thin trace of resistance that remained, he was able to touch her mouth with his. He waited. At the moment that her lips would have parted, he made the idea his own and claimed her mouth.

Mary let herself be claimed. It had been so long. Her body dripped. His breathing became hot and ferocious as he began to devour her. She answered him with a mad ardour long caged away. The more wild she got, the stronger he held her.

"Go ahead, nobody is listening," his whisper was husky in the hollow of her throat.

So she let herself go completely, let herself be held safely restrained, let her untamed vastness be lawlessly explored. How far could she really go if somebody promised not to let go? What kind of illicit ecstasy was this? Mary screamed and she wrapped her legs around him, embracing his loins with her own and arching her back.

With one hand, he held her steady and with the other, he unbuttoned her blouse. The perfectly pressed white silk blouse slipped over her cinnamon shoulders and crumpled with a hush behind her on his lap. He moved one shoulder strap just part way down and let the breast delight in the possibility of release. He kissed her chest just above where the fire burned to be let out. He slipped the other strap just past her shoulder and stood back to behold what he would soon get to see. Dancing in perfect time, she became still for him to unhook her brassiere and let it fall away. Mary's breasts were blithe and playful in the saffron firelight and everything he had imagined. He took them one at a time in his mouth. Mary splendoured in the bitter bliss of his velvety wet insistence on her nipples, held her breath when he licked the buttery flesh under her arm, and then careened out of control when he went back to her nipples.

He placed both his hands behind her back for support and pulled her toward his end of the chesterfield. She succumbed in perfect time to his guidance. When he had slipped out from underneath her, and she was in full recline, he stopped just long enough to leave unattended the fire he had started in her breasts. Finally, he placed both his hands on her craving breasts while taking the edge of her skirt in his teeth, just letting enough cool air in to touch her skin and ask. By the way she grasped both his wrists and by her breathing, he knew he could take his hands away and use them to remove her skirt.

He eased the skirt down past her thighs and let it linger at her ankles. Mary angled her foot off the chesterfield and let it drop to the floor. She lay in the firelight with only her panties on while he bathed her in praise.

"Your hair . . . your royal brown skin . . . your delicious plum coloured nipples," he looked upward momentarily, "*Mon Dieu*, this woman is hypnotizing!"

She writhed; it called him back again.

"Oh, you are like a butterfly. So exotique as you open and close your wings!"

Finally, he bent over, his mouth touching hers.

He kissed her deeper and deeper, then grasped her flailing arms and held them down to feign for her that it was his idea, not hers. He trailed his wet kissing down her throat, between her breasts then used his tongue to trace lines on her soft belly

He let his tongue flick and tease at her groin.

She bucked, broke free of his grip, and gave in to being a hostage by clinging to the edges of the chesterfield. Holding herself down she began to keen.

He placed both his hands on the inner sides of her knees and parted her legs, again expertly past a wispy layer of resistance.

She stilled.

He let her see that he needed to look.

Moving slowly down to the far end of the chesterfield, he positioned himself just beyond her reach. While his gaze never wavered from her, he slipped his shirt over his head. She closed her eyes to take in deeper the smell of him as it surrounded her. She heard him unbuckle his pants. He bent down, his hair tickling the inside of her thighs, and he took her in his hot mouth. She had never, ever, been there before. She clasped both her hands over her mouth to stifle her own screaming. Was there nothing she could do to make this last longer? But alas, she had been away far too long, and came quickly.

When he could feel that she was coming, he gave her everything she needed to expand it, but watched anxiously for it to ebb, for this was the moment he relished most. This was the moment the juices flowed most deliciously. At the exact moment he felt her begin her retreat, he mounted her and she came again. Just after him.

They lay entwined, with him atop her for an hour or so; he spent, and Mary unable to break the spell and face what she had done. Finally, when the firelight began to wane, she pushed him off her. He let himself roll off and fall good-naturedly upon the rug, then he laughed and began gathering up his things. He gave her a peck on the cheek and turned to leave.

"Tony?"

"Yes?" he turned and flashed his impish grin.

"Be out of here before the end of the day tomorrow."

The yawning glow from the fire's bed of coals revealed his fading grin.

"What is this? I do not understand? We have only just begun—"

She interrupted his transparent attempt to recast his spell.

"I will reimburse you for three months but you are to be out of here by nightfall tomorrow."

He shook his head and rubbed the back of his neck, but then found his true wicked smile again.

"I see."

Mary turned away from him and lit a cigarette.

She sat still in the dark, smoking, drinking her wine, and letting the hot bed of coals wither. She welcomed the chill that crept into the room as the fire left guard. She got up only once, and that was just to pull out another bottle of wine from under the kitchen sink. She stared unwaveringly into the spotting of embers as if dousing them with her mind. The fire he had stoked must be left to die.

The clock on the shelf behind her, which she customarily took down to wind if company was staying too long, had stopped ticking. So, she couldn't tell for sure, but it could have been two or three hours past midnight when Jesus arrived.

She had no way of knowing, but He might have been watching her for the entire time that she had been staring into the pit where the fire had been. She recalled that she had looked away just the once, and then, it was only because she had been musing with the notion that if she took her eyes off the cold fire pit, perhaps the cold feeling in her stomach might dissipate. That was the moment He caught her eye.

He was sitting quite serenely in the armchair beside her, looking, well, just like Jesus. He had on a long flowing white gown, tied at the waist with a cord braided from something as plain as burlap. He had no crown of thorns about his head, but rather a brilliance that starburst from whichever part of him she chose to let her eyes fall upon. He did not seem distressed or stern, but rested comfortably with each of his arms draped casually upon the hand crocheted doilies she had picked up at the Salvation Army Thrift Store. He just sat there, with sandals on his feet, His legs crossed, and smiling at her. Mary blinked slowly and purposefully, but He was still there each time she opened her eyes again.

She spoke first.

"Jesus Christ, you must be really pissed with me."

It came out less a question, and more a statement. She burst out laughing at her own audacity. What did it matter, she thought, she was going to hell anyway. But He just kept gazing at her with that half-smile.

"So I guess you think I'm a sinner?" She hazarded a glance away. "And I am, but what would you know about being human? You are the way, the truth, and the life, now, aren't you? Well, that's all well and fine, but I wonder if you have any idea what it's like to be human, because that just happens to be something of which I am an expert."

Brilliant stained-glass images of friendly Indians offering bounty to regal white men wearing robes and crosses rose up all around her. It was as if, even now, she was only a skinny girl sitting on the long and hard wooden benches of the Mohawk Chapel.

She looked back at the black and white tweed easy chair that the Claytons had been going to throw out. He was still there. She looked away again.

"Some get it all in one dose, humans, I mean, and then some of us twist in the wind for a damn long time. What do you think of that?" She turned to face Him and waited for Him to answer. He didn't, so she continued, "I'll tell you what being human has been all about. It's been all about doing without, and I am not just talking about doing without things, I am talking most about doing without the people I love, and I am weary of this. I am like a ghost to the people with whom I share blood. I wonder . . . what's it all for? Didn't we appreciate what we had? Did we not fight hard enough for it, or maybe we fought amongst ourselves too much? Perhaps we trusted too much, or perhaps we were just lazy. Or, perhaps we really do need to be saved and led to the Kingdom of Heaven where the Son of God makes a place for us to dwell. I notice we aren't the same colour . . . does that matter? I have an idea. What if it was us who are the missed opportunity . . . more or less . . . like what happened to you. Do you think we have any teachings for your religious law makers?"

She lifted her glass of wine, "I don't know, but I think they might have used you, my friend. I think they used you to put us down . . ."

He interrupted her. "It's about love and forgiveness, nothing else, only love and forgiveness."

"He said that. He did," she said to herself just before she fell into his eyes, which seemed the stillest lakes ever.

He reached over, touched her cheek, and whispered, "You were forgiven before you did anything you think is wrong, but you cannot feel this until you forgive yourself, nor until then, can you offer it to anybody else."

Mary dropped her wine glass with a soft thud and it bled over the braided rug at her feet. He leaned forward and, using the crook of his finger, stopped the tear on her cheek. "Love is all there is," He said.

Mary nodded, closed her eyes, and when she opened them again, He was gone.

She sat unwaveringly for a quite a while to let it all absorb. She didn't dare move. It seemed at least an hour passed, when the clock behind her started to tick again, seemingly all by itself. She thought of the wine. She picked the bottle up by its neck, carried it to the kitchen, and promptly dumped its remaining contents down the sink. But still, she believed. Then, after she noticed the letters that had been strewn across the kitchen floor, she believed even more, and this was because one of the letters was from a lawyer's office and one of the letters was from Gmiwan. Earlier, when she had put aside her unopened correspondence, she hadn't noted either.

She opened the lawyer's letter first. Apparently she was sole benefactor of Tom Dunsby's estate, and apparently he was the real landlord of this building she called Mary's Place.

The other letter was actually not a letter, but a telegram from Gmiwan; neither was it a poem, nor a picture this time, but rather simply, a two-lined type-written communication:

> Dear Mary: Will be home on August 20th train at Union Station at 19:00. Please send someone. Will send notification if date changes.
> Gmiwan Fisher,
> June 6, 1945

To the end of her days, Mary believed she had spoken to Jesus in her living room, so she never would drink red wine again.

MARY WOULD ALWAYS consider that it was more than simple luck that the man who rented the room that Tony vacated turned out to be half Indian. Wayne, gnarly and wild haired, had a body that was wiry, spry, and quick like lightening, no different from his wit.

"*Gi do ji bwem?*" was the first thing he had said to her when she opened the door to him one windy afternoon.

"What did you say there, fella?" She couldn't help but warm to the sparkle in his eye.

When he spoke again, she thought he said something like, "Way na boo shoo."

"Do you know any English?" Mary spoke slower and louder as if he was hard of hearing.

"I am speaking English!" His laughter rang out, "I say my name is Wayne Boozhoo."

"Oh," Mary answered sheepishly, but then added, with a tinge of defiance, "But what did you say to begin with?"

"I asked you 'do you speak Ojibwe'?"

Mary just nodded as if to say 'Oh I see,' said nothing, but regarded him with more interest.

"Well, do you?" he repeated.

"Not anymore."

"Well then, don't you think you should?"

"And why should I?"

"If for the only reason that you have some '*Nish* blood coursing through your veins, perhaps?"

"What makes you say that?"

"Takes one to know one."

"I admit it, but really I would say there was a fair bit more Mohawk."

"So?"

"So what?"

"Would you like to speak Ojibwe? I would teach you Mohawk, but that's not my specialty. And it doesn't matter anyway, so long as you keep one of the old languages alive."

Mary rubbed the place on her hands where she would be stung for speaking her mother's language.

"When I say '*Gi do ji bwem*?' you repeat this, '*ban gi e ta go*'.

He waited.

"Well, say it."

Using an old trick she learned to feel better, she travelled further past Mistress's half-smile and raised stick, and in her mind's eye Mary forced herself to dwell in the fragrant kitchen of her mother's house while the aunties talked and sipped tea.

Able to catch his playfulness now, she volleyed back, "I suppose it wouldn't hurt."

He waited.

"*Ban gi e ta go*," she repeated perfectly. "Now what did I say?"

"You said, 'Only just a little.'"

Amusement spread across Mary's face as she repeated it once again for good measure, "Ban gi e ta go. It has a nice ring to it. It's kind of like Bingo, you want to go?"

His laughter rang out as a crow could be seen taking flight from its perch on the "Mary's Place" sign overhead.

"I knew I liked you from first sight!

"That's good, but what brings you to my front door? Are you looking for a room?"

"I'm looking for work and a room. Do you have any?"

"I just happen to have a vacancy that recently opened," she started, but before she could even tell him the price, he interrupted.

"I'll take it. Can I have it now?"

"You pay by the week here, and I'll need two in advance."

"Let me in and I'll give you cash down on the barrel head. It's not cold out here but I hate to do business out on the street."

Mary gave a start and stepped aside for him to enter. She had been so caught in his spell that she had abandoned her own business protocol. She skipped the tour and took him right to the chesterfield in front of the fire-place where money and a list of rules could be exchanged.

After Wayne had lived there a month, Mary could tell he was a person she could trust, so she hired him. After all, it wasn't like she was desperate for money anymore, but she was always desperate for a man's handy ways around the house. And besides, it was good to have someone around with a good sense of ha-ha.

It was over one of their smokes on the back porch at the end of the day that Wayne suggested Mary take a Sweat.

"That's something I only ever heard tell of," Mary said thoughtfully as she let the smoke curl lazily of its own will from her lungs. My mother used to speak of it, but we had nothing going on like that on the reserve. I heard that it was against the law and they would take your kids away if they caught you. How do you know about stuff like that?"

"Around here, the old ways have been lost, but I know of some Old Ones who still practice in secret." He went silent.

Wayne always spaced his sentences with a long silence.

Mary knew enough to not fill them with her own words.

"It's the Old Ones that keep the ways," he continued, "but they went away, at first because the young ones didn't ask them, or seem to care about them. It's not their fault, because so many of them have been rounded up and carted off to those schools, and besides that, it has been two or three generations now since practicing the old ways was legal. So there are some old ones who have hidden them to keep them safe. There are not very many of them left, and they have a hard time trusting anybody."

They smoked the last half of their cigarettes in quiet repose.

"So, where would I have to go to have a Sweat?"

"I know a place, but remember! It's a secret. You can't tell anybody about it." Mary waited. "Not too far from here. About five hours by bus."

"Have you ever done a Sweat yourself Wayne?"

"More times 'an I could shake a stick at."

"You think I should do this?"

"I don't think it will do you any harm. It's good for what ails ya. Think of it as cleaning out your attic."

"How long do you think I would have to be away? Gmiwan's coming home in a month."

"As long as it takes."

Mary nodded. She had known the answer anyway.

"You sure you can handle this place without me?"

Old Wayne just nodded without either of them bothering to look at each other.

"You know, I was entertaining the idea of maybe shutting this place down before Gmiwan comes home."

" I don't think that's a bad idea. I don't think it's a bad idea at all."

"You don't?"

"Nope."

"Maybe I'll give them all notice before I go."

"That would be okay."

"You sure?"

He lit another cigarette and nodded at Grandmother Moon.

"I don't mean for you to leave. You will stay, won't you?"

"Maybe I will. Maybe I won't."

Even though it wasn't really okay with Mary, she knew it didn't matter what she thought.

There was no bus station, just a wooden post on the side of the road that was once painted red, and a white woman.

"Mary Fisher?" she said, extending her hand in greeting.

Mary, suddenly timid, was slow to respond.

"Hello, my name is Erica; you are surprised that I am not an Indian?"

"It's just that when Wayne said—" Mary let her voice trail off, as what more could she say that wouldn't be impolite.

"I'm a member of the 'Gone-Indian' Tribe," her eyes danced with mischief.

The pleasant-faced blonde woman smiled and in spite of herself, Mary returned the smile. Mary guessed Erica to be only ten years older than herself. Not exactly an "Old One." An almost palpable release of tension descended upon Mary. There was no denying the calming affect that radiated from the woman. Mary sighed, offered one of the small bundles of tobacco Wayne had made for her to give to her hosts. 'First thing, offer tobacco and tell them thank you. Maybe even in the old language, *miigwetch*,' she could hear him say.

"*Miigwetch*," she uttered and then extended her own hand.

"Come," Erica accepted the bundle and took Mary's bag from her. "Let's get you there. The Grandfathers are almost ready. Have you fasted?"

"Yes."

"Have you had any booze?"

Mary shook her head.

"Good then. Just gotta ask. Hop in."

Erica tossed Mary's bag in her red Chevy pick-up, sprinted around the front end, and jumped into the driver's side.

"Whatcha waitin' for kid? Nothing is happening here. We gotta go!"

Erica started the engine.

Mary took one last look at the smoking tail-end of the bus as it pulled away, shook her head, shrugged her shoulders, and then ran to catch up as Erica threw the clutch into first gear.

Mary was rarely comfortable with long periods of silence between people, which is why she was known to others as having the gift of gab, but there was something about Erica that put Mary at ease, at least enough to allow Mary to give herself up to the experience. Really there wasn't that much choice at this point anyway.

"So, how's my good friend Wayne?" They gathered speed in the opposite direction to where the bus had headed, seemingly back-tracking her daylong journey.

"Still full of haha, I can say."

"Crap!" Erica wrestled with the gearshift and wrenched it until the truck groaned and began moving backward.

Mary kept her hands on the dash and twisted around, but it was a solid metal wall, heavily pocked, she noted, from many other clashes no doubt.

"There it is!" Erica cranked the steering wheel around and around until the truck bore sharply and purposefully off the road and into the thick treeline. Though Mary's mind was a frenzy of gathering and sorting, she did notice that there was a red ribbon tied to a branch hanging over the most obscure and narrow opening through which the truck ploughed. Erica jammed the vehicle into park, leaped out, and ran back to grab the ribbon.

"Ha. Love that part!"

Back on the move, the truck heaved and lurched on its hinges as it rammed its way through the trees and over the vague and overgrown rutted pathway. Mary remained solidly braced and silent.

If you are not sure of what to do next, stay still.

"My husband's the Fire-keeper," Erica yelled over top of the clatter of the logs crashing against the wooden truck bed rails in the back, "I'm not sweating today. I'm prepping the feast."

Branches swatted Mary's arm.

"Close the window!" Erica hollered, "Oh never mind. Here we are!"

She let off the gas and the truck dipped downward as they followed a sluggish corkscrew where the path grew more travelled. Eventually it opened to a clearing on the floor of a shallow valley. People, a few women draped in blankets with coloured skirts peeking out, but mostly skinny, half-naked, grey-haired men were standing around a robust fire.

Erica bounded out of the truck and went to speak to the longhaired old man who kept the fire, touching his arm or his cheek now and then. Mary stepped out of the truck and, turning in a circle, realized that they were surrounded and hidden by ancient cool green cedars and that dusk was falling, bringing with it a dense cover of grey mist.

Erica returned to her side.

"You look a little shaken up. Didn't Wayne tell you about how we have to hide this place?"

Mary nodded, "He may have left out a few details."

Erica's face lit up again as she grabbed Mary's hand. "Come on, let's go. The women have already gathered the cedar boughs, and the Grandfathers are ready. You're fine with what you have on. Just take your shoes, stockings, and earrings off. All we have to do is smudge you!"

Mary kicked her shoes off, shoved her earrings and stockings in her skirt pockets and let herself be led to the fireside. The small crowd parted to allow her into the semi-circle. A fire crackled in deep tones, its heat not squandered by tall flames but rather focused intently in a thick bed of coals that incubated throbbing orbs of glowing red rocks. A woman, old like most of them, maybe older, stepped forward, but nobody else let their gazes meet Mary's. Later Mary would recall that she never did get to know her name.

The Old Woman stood in front of Mary holding a large bowl-shaped shell and a long, beaded white feather and then spoke as if to everyone, "The four sacred medicines are Tobacco, Sweet Grass, Sage, and Cedar. Now I will tell you of Cedar. Cedar is generally considered to be most beneficial to women, but men have used it as well. I have seen it used to purify physical ailments or as a drink to maintain strength.

If you ever have a cold, pick some fresh cedar from the lowest boughs . . . not too much from one tree . . . show gratitude by not leaving the tree weak . . . boil it . . . drink it as a tea and breathe it in deeply.

"Sage is used to purify the air or any bad medicine that may be clinging or lurking. It too is considered by most to be a feminine plant."

If you are having trouble with your moon . . . take a tea made of sage leaves. . . it is good too if you want to delay grey hair.

"I have seen Sweet Grass burned to soothe strong emotions and take prayers to the Creator."

Sometimes people do not get along so well . . . if you want to sweeten your relationships . . . burn sweet grass and ask that your prayers be answered.

"Tobacco is the most sacred medicine because it is the medicine of the Elders. It is most commonly thought that Tobacco is offered in exchange for wisdom, whether from other creations, such as a tree or a lake, or from an Elder, an Ancestor, or from the Creator. It is also used as an expression of gratitude."

. . . always have some Tobacco in your medicine pouch.

"These are the things I know of Tobacco, Sweet Grass, Sage, and Cedar today. There are many other people who know many more things."

Deep within Mary's belly, something was beginning to stir and spread throughout, something warm like molasses, filling in a cold space. She placed both her hands on the lowest part of her belly, and she could swear the Old Woman said what she said next because she had noticed.

"Blood Memory! Much of what you know, and can do, is from your Ancestors. Their voices speak in your veins. It is you who chooses to listen, or not."

Your Ancestors are always whispering to you. You must walk the Red Road to hear them.

Mary remembered the other tobacco bundle she had in her pocket, reached in, and offered it. The Old Woman accepted it and then handed Mary the shell. It was hot but Mary dared not let go of it even though the sweet acrid scent of what burned inside filled her nostrils. The Old Woman fanned the embers to a bolder glow with her feather.

"This is a swan feather, a gift to me from the one who taught me while on his Earth Walk and whom now guides me while on his Spirit Walk. He told me that the swan flies closer to the Creator than any other winged one."

She passed her left hand through the silvery grey tendrils of smoke and then the other. She used her left hand to usher the smoke up to her face, letting it linger at her eyes, nose and mouth, before directing it downward to her throat, heart, loins, and legs.

She took the shell back and waited until Mary followed suit.

"We are here not only for ourselves, but also for the Seventh Generation." She gestured to the fire. The logs had begun to burn down and revealed molten hot rocks. She continued, "The Grandfathers are fully present and ready to release their wisdom."

In the years to come, Mary would replay in her mind the events that followed over and over again, and never would she be able to explain why she lost track of the others who were present. How many of them were there? Were they walking behind her? How far away from the fire had she really walked? From then on, she could only ever see and hear herself, the Old Woman, and the Fire-keeper.

They began to move away from the fire, the Old Woman in the lead, and go deeper into the shadows that had been pitching and reeling against the looming cedars that guarded the place. Mary could feel that the fire-warmed ring of dry and caked earth changed beneath her feet to a mossy and damp loam. The farther they crept, the more the crackle of the fire blended with the swish and babble of water cascading somewhere nearby. As they passed a pile of rocks, the Old Woman shone her lantern high and gestured, "These are many of the Grandfathers from past Sweats. Others have been put to rest back in the fields."

The Old Woman turned around to face Mary and grasping her with keen eye contact she directed, "Walk up to the path of cedar boughs. This is symbolic of the birth cord. It will lead into the lodge, which is symbolic of a mother's womb, and then follow until you enter. When you enter, crawl in backwards and move inside clockwise along the outer edge of the lodge, all the way to the other side of the door. Be mindful of the pit that is in the middle. Wait for me there at the far side of the eastern door."

Tension began to pool in the pit of Mary's stomach until it overflowed in her chest and coursed through her veins as dread. She could not make her one foot go in front of the other.

"Are you afraid?"

Mary flashed her eyes, wide with foreboding, at the Old Woman.

The Old Woman's light touch on Mary's shoulder did some to ease her but it was really the soothing tone of her voice that gave Mary the splinter of courage to nudge past the line of distress that had drawn itself between her and the cedar-bough birth cord. Mary set one foot forward while the Old Woman's touch pressed lightly to encourage.

Once both feet were actually on the path, it was much easier to just follow. Mary crouched at the entrance and drew the canvas cover aside.

"Die a good death," she thought she heard the Old Woman say.

Half inside, Mary twisted around and saw that it was sheer black. She resisted. With her mind and her heart already in, it seemed to her as if the entire power of the lighted universe let go and the utter darkness inside took over, pulling her. She crawled backward the rest of the way in.

Mary was left to sit for only an instant after the flap of canvas had chopped off the reaching fingers of light and then the Old Woman raised it again for her own entrance, left it that way for some time and then almost without perception slipped in and let the flap fall closed again.

With the flap closed, the Old Woman seemed to take some time to herself, which made the inside seem full of light and shuffling sounds, though there really was no light, and there really was no movement. Mary waited, trepidation building. Finally, the Old Woman began to speak to her.

"You may feel some anxiety. This is natural. If you need to cleanse in any way, such as crying, vomiting, spitting, please do so in the pit. You may take your clothes off if you like. It is dark, and you may be yourself."

Without warning the Old Woman called out.

"Fire-keeper!"

After some scraping and scuffling sounds, the darkness cracked open and the flap was parted again.

"For the ones who keep the traditions," came the faceless voice of the Fire-keeper as he dispensed using buck deer antlers, into the pit, a well-rounded hefty Grandfather. The Grandfather pulsed with radiance.

"*Boozhoo Misho*," the Old Woman said.

Then there was a sprinkling of light all around the Grandfather, as if fireflies had been released, flashing once, and then flying off into the night.

"Please accept our gift of tobacco as thanks for your wisdom."

The glowing stone was placed deftly in the pit by the unseen Fire-keeper, then three more, two more, and then the last one, each time, dedicated aloud by the Fire-keeper to some form of life, and to whatever might be the endeavour of that life form. Then the flap was closed and it was dark again, except for the throbbing light of the Grandfathers clustered together in the lowest crevice of the pit.

"Thanks is offered to the east for all the gifts of renewal and light that help our people. Thank you for every spring that comes into our life," came the formless voice of the Old Woman as she poured water seasoned with cedar into the pit. The Grandfathers spoke in husky tones as the drink and prayer were given, making the air heavy with the steam that rose and gathered within the confines of the lodge, clinging to the skin, and choking the breath. It seemed forever to Mary who struggled mightily within herself to stay crouched below the line of panic, but then, in spite of her drive, the panic took on its own life. It would not stay in the place she put it. Descending now upon her head like a wet blanket that she could not breathe through, it fit itself around her, casting her a coward. She shivered in its icy hot grip and felt herself begin to dissolve. She searched in the dark for the door but realized that her eyes had been closed and the terror had seeped through her skin and into her core. Wrapping her arms around herself, to feel if she was still there, she gasped for air to cool the fire inside. It was as if her throat had closed.

I'm going to die, she thought. These people will toss me in the river and nobody around here will have any clue who I am! she screamed inside herself.

. . . breathe out . . .

She realized that she had been holding her breath. She let her breath out, and a cool vacuum opened inside her, sucking in the air around her. Mary focused upon every breath she took in and let out until the burning in her veins receded, and the shrieking in her head abated. Mary watched as the beast of fear shrivelled and settled in the pit of her stomach.

An ease started to wash over her like warm rain, gently filling in the jagged places where fear had been gouging. It was so hot, and Mary was sweltering, so she unbuttoned the clinging cloth that bound her and let it slip somewhere behind her. She remained in her kneeling position, aware that her senses were gathering keenness where anxiety gave way.

Four more Grandfathers were placed in the Lodge. "Thanks are offered to the South for all the gifts of summer, fullness, of youth, of passion, of sensitivity, of physical and emotional strength. Thank you for the summer."

Sometimes she was not listening to the words that the Old Woman was saying, but rather she was getting more and more fully into the sensations her body was receiving from all around her. She was aware that a fine spray of sweat glazed her skin and made it more alive. She explored the sensation beneath her knees. Though abrasive, if grasped with too much vigour, or rubbed between the fingers and thumb, the cedar became pliant. She held one within her hand, bending and caressing it until she could perceive its hidden soft nature. Releasing it, exactly as she had found it, she delved her fingers deeper into the bed and came up with a handful. She raised them to her face, breathing in deeply, filling herself with their cool green and spicy essence. She let them go, and they tickled as though butterflies upon her lap. Mary became aware of an ache in her knees, so she let herself relax into a cross-legged sitting position.

Nestling deeper into the bed of cedar boughs she watched passively as the fourteenth Grandfather was set in.

"For the ones who lie in unmarked graves," announced the Fire-keeper.

Light, strange and brilliant, suddenly streamed in, heralding the entrance of four more Grandfathers.

"Thanks is given to the West, where our gifts of dreams, of prayer, and of meditation, come to us. In the autumn of our lives, we pass on our knowledge, keep the ways, and learn perseverance."

A pain started in her left arm. Numbness crept to her fingertips. 'A heart,' she heard in her head. She felt the monster inside rise and rear its ugly head. No! She would not leave, she said to herself. She could not leave. She would die before she would leave.

Whenever you see a bear . . . you can be sure you are meeting fear . . . you say hello M'kwa.

The roaring in her ears began to die down to something like a distant echo, and time passed, but how much, she could not tell. Something drizzled past her brow and into her mouth. Salty and slightly bitter, she tasted the fluid from her own body, and waited, in bliss, as the light again cut the darkness. More time passed.

Six more Grandfathers. "Thanks are given to the North, where we receive the gift of true wisdom. The white snows of winter and the white hair of our Elders remind us of the time that we must train our mind to overcome our body."

Some place on a road lined with broken things, as though left to fade away in the elements, she was walking under a threatening sky. She kept her eyes sharp for something that might trip her or grab her, but every time she looked up, there was this wiry, wild-haired guy watching and nimbly following her along as she journeyed. He was old, but then again he wasn't. She didn't know who he was, but then again, she did. It seemed every time she saw him there was thunder and lightning in the sky. A dash of cold droplets hit Mary in the face and yanked her off the dusty, grey road. That must have been how she got so drenched.

She counted twenty-four Grandfathers to get herself grounded.

There was a rattling that burst beside her, and the Grandfathers expanded to touch it. Fear's gnarly hand clutched down Mary's throat, tearing and searching for her gut and her heart to grasp, pull out, and cast into the pit. Mary's body writhed to escape. Wispy things like spider webs tickled—no, tormented—her skin. She screamed and threw herself flat to get away from them.

"There is nothing to be afraid of; they are only your Ancestors," she heard the Old Woman say in a voice as soft as Mother Earth.

Mary drew closer to the voice she trusted although her body remained still. Eventually, somewhere in the quiet, the tickling touches on her skin became graceful gifts that thrilled her.

Content now, to lie staring up at the dark, all of her senses began to fade. It occurred to her that she might be dying, and a subtle convulsion moved through her body as she made one last attempt to rebel against where she was sinking. Something started to resonate in her ear. A drumming, at first low and faint, was rhythmically getting more and more present, until it completely surrounded her. She was in the drumbeat. She let herself completely go.

Her senses began to rise, only now more brilliant, less dulled, by physical limitation. She could see, hear, and say anything she wanted to. All around her, or somehow completely within her, a dark, fluid sliver began to expand, dispelling the haze around her, like the yolk that grows within the white in which it is suspended. The dark sliver formed and fattened into a laughing old soul.

Mary smiled at her old mentor, Holy Nekuwa. No words left Mary's lips, yet there was communication. Holy Nekuwa asked Mary a question, but Mary didn't know the answer. No, she asked Mary what her question was, but Mary couldn't find it. She told Mary to let the harmony of the drumbeat lead her to her heart where all things are. Mary let herself enter the cyclical beating stream and be carried with it. Along the way, she watched, without passion, her mother's casket being borne up the hill; her father crying; the suffering of people and children she did not recognize yet she loved; the empty space left by people she missed; and the wispy figure of her husband, who was hardly there at all.

One by one, they became more and more distant as the current of the drumbeat bore her through a place of growing silence. There she became like a curled-up fern, nubile and without defence, yet aware that unfurling would lay bare the space for each experience to make its mark. Mary felt Holy Nekuwa urge her to stay furled for a while longer, and she felt like she was drifting off to sleep, maybe forever.

Suddenly the resounding beat of the drum grew louder, calling Mary to become alert. Then a sparkling urge to dance filled her with joy, and a light more brilliant than the sun warmed her from the inside out. Mary wanted to stay in this place forever.

This is your Spirit that you have hidden from the pain. Your Spirit is one with the Spirits of those that have gone before you and those that will come after.

Mary understood.

Follow the beat of your heart back and take your Spirit with you.

Within the same moment, Mary was back, lying in her bed of cedar, which had allowed everything dark and vile that had seeped from her pores to pass through and into the earth.

Mother Earth will digest it.

Mary could not be sure how long she had lain there before enough clarity gathered for her to become aware of tepid drops lighting softly upon her face, some pooling in her closed eyes, some slipping silently down the crease from her nose to her mouth. She reached for some of the acrid drops with the tip of her tongue. Her hair, soaked as if dipped in a pail of water, ran through her fingers like the strings of a mop.

The Old Woman, as if sensing Mary's heightening consciousness, touched her on the shoulder with the warmed metal of the water container.

"Do you have any more prayers?"

The cedar boughs rustled as Mary shook her head.

"Fire-keeper, open the door!" the Old Woman called out.

With more definition rallying in her senses, Mary became aware of the muted snap of the fire outside. At the same time, she heard the scuffling gait of the Fire-keeper's approaching footsteps. Mary waited passively for the blast of moonlight. When it came, the Old Woman urged Mary to ready herself to creep out front-ways in a clockwise direction toward the block of star-speckled sky.

As the bus pulled into the barren parking lot, save for one vehicle, Mary smiled at the sight of Wayne. Leaning up against a black convertible, with his arms folded across his chest and his face upward taking in the late afternoon sun, he looked just like home to Mary. She wondered who he had talked into letting him borrow this smart looking car. Even though she had only met him a month or so earlier, her "Blood Memory," as the Old Woman would say, told her they had travelled together before.

As she stepped off the bus, she knew him well enough to know that he wouldn't be rushing over to greet her. He would, as usual, keep his distance. But he had that impish grin of his, which signalled that he was amused with her, to greet her. He walked the long way around the convertible, tried the passenger door, and opened the trunk. "Or, do you just want to throw your bag in the back seat?" he asked as if they had already been talking.

"Could do," Mary answered.

He closed the trunk with a gentle click and hopped over the door into the car seat.

After they got going, he lit a cigarette and offered her one.

Mary shook her head. "Not going to smoke anymore."

"Good kid."

"So how'd it go while I was gone?"

"Bill, George, Carl, Angus, and the other Bill will be gone by next week."

"Six more to go, eh Wayne, but not including you?"

"Seven, kid."

Mary nodded and stared straight ahead.

When they got home Wayne showed her a letter on the kitchen counter. It was from Gmiwan. Mary picked it up and noted that it was tattooed with world stamps, several more than usual. This letter had definitely taken the long way. After she opened it, her eyes were immediately drawn to the date, and sure enough, it was dated for earlier than the curt telegram that he had sent to notify her of his return:

Dear Mary:

I have been shattered
Fragments of me scattered array
First the strike
Then the blow
How will I ever find my way home?

In the beginning I was barely there
Must have happened once before
Still you held me
I held you
How will I ever find my way home?

I must have laughed and cried too loud
Fractured the cosmos, broke open the sky
Pieces of me
Pieces of you
How will I ever find my way home?

A beating heart is a lighthouse
Lost vessels bring back the knowledge
I want it all
To bring back the truth
How will I ever find my way home?

Gmiwan

She glanced over at her friend, contentedly smoking his cigarette and smiling back at her. She imagined him gone, just for practice. A bottomless cavern of loneliness yawned open inside her, threatening to swallow her, not because they had been friends for all that long, but more because she was sick of goodbyes. Sick and tired. She would have liked to go to bed or light a cigarette and maybe pour a glass of wine, but instead she removed the precisely folded lace-edged white handkerchief that was peeking out of the pocket of her crisply pressed yellow cotton blouse and laid it out on the table top.

She placed the letter in the handkerchief. She noticed how the letter was mud streaked and torn, one of its corners hanging by a vestige of Canadian Armed Forces issued paper. Mary let herself float above the site where Gmiwan might have been crouching to write it, lingered too long to stop a tear, but then called herself back, her knees on the verge of giving way.

Wayne cleared his throat and Mary looked across the room at him. He had one eyebrow crooked almost as if amused, but she knew he wasn't teasing her, for as he rested his head in one of his hands, with the other, he wagged an abundant braid of tobacco leaves. Mary wiped away a single tear with the back of her hand, walked over to him, and took the medicine he offered. Then he stood and placed his hand on the pouch that he always kept on his belt and patted it.

His ever-present smile vanished but only for a second or two as he said to her, "You're gonna need one of these."

Mary waited.

"A medicine bag. Make yourself a medicine bag."

Her mind, her heart, and her soul, fused by time and desperation, stood crystal clear in this vintage moment.

The wily mirth returned to Wayne as windlessly as it had left. He began to untie the leather laces on the flap of his own pouch that threaded between two circular openings where once the eyes of a coyote had peered. With ethereal traces of reverence, he lifted the tawny fur of the coyote head flap and held it open while he reached knowingly inside. Mary looked away.

It is impolite to ask of or look inside someone else's medicine bag.

Wayne nudged her shoulder, and she looked up, first into those dancing blue eyes, and then at the bundle he offered her.

"Take this too."

The bundle was wrapped in something that looked as if it had unceremoniously been torn from the sleeve of an old plaid flannel work shirt of his. She held out her hand and accepted it.

"It's a starter kit. You're gonna need it."

Mary nodded.

"It's got the other medicines in it. Learn about them kid. And make yourself a bag."

"What do I make the bag out of?" her voice faraway and weary.

"You'll find something."

Mary nodded again and walked back over to where she had left Gmiwan's letter on the tabletop. She broke off a piece of the tobacco and sprinkled it on the letter, folded it up into the precise two lines it had arrived in, ever so careful so as not to detach the corner hanging by a shred, then added two more folds to seal the medicine inside. She wrapped the letter deftly in the laced cloth and put it in her left breast pocket.

Sweetly, sharply a trill broke the silence.

Wayne and Mary looked for it. On the branch just outside the window, a crimson cardinal was perched so close they could see his small chest heaving an exquisite and courageous song.

"Messengers of Creator, that's what birds are. The Creator is always talking to us. It is us who are not always listening. Remember that. Remember this too. Before boat loads of new people came across the big water and named that winged one on the windowsill after some of their holy men, he already had a name. He was named by the human beings with whom he had been sharing the bounty of this land since the creation of life. The human beings knew him by how they saw him: Redbird. Then it seemed like the new people thought they could go around and give everything a new name as a way to claim it all as their own, as if the human beings that were already living here never existed. We have those human beings' blood dancing in our veins, we are those human beings, and we are still here."

Mary listened as she watched the Redbird on her windowsill and an image came to her. She thought of Gmiwan's courage and devotion as he sang in the rain, though it thundered, and lightning threatened, and how he would not stop until his cup was filled with rain. He said his mother's mother had told him when he was a small boy to do this if he wanted to show a woman what kind of mate he would be.

Mary walked over, picked up the telephone and dialled her sister's number. Maybe Elizabeth and Harry wouldn't mind driving her and Sonny to pick up Gmiwan at the train station in Big Smoke.

There now. My grandmother told me these stories.
I have done what she asked, and now they are written.